The *Glory* slowed as the *War Pig* surged forward

Ryan grimaced and waited for the smoke to clear. He caught sight of his target as smoke shredded around her forward progress.

The Deathlands survivor fired, and his bullet tore a hole in the deck a foot from his target. He worked his bolt, then fired again. The bullet sparked off the iron of the *War Pig's* starboard chaser.

Ryan could see one of the officers shouting as he realized the enemy was shooting for the powder kegs. The officer grabbed the cask of gunpowder by the port chaser, pressed it over his head and with effort charged the taffrail and threw the powder into the sea.

Ryan swung his scope to starboard. A huge man in red and black seized the starboard chaser powder cask and raised it over his head with ease. Ryan pulled the Longbow's trigger. The .338 Lapua Magnum bullet hit the cask of black powder at over 3,000 feet per second.

The bow of the *War Pig* disappeared in a thunderous black-and-orange pulse.

Other titles in the Deathlands saga:

JAMES AXLER

DEATHLANDS®

BLOOD RED TIDE

A GOLD EAGLE BOOK FROM

WORLDWIDE®

TORONTO • NEW YORK • LONDON
AMSTERDAM • PARIS • SYDNEY • HAMBURG
STOCKHOLM • ATHENS • TOKYO • MILAN
MADRID • WARSAW • BUDAPEST • AUCKLAND

Recycling programs
for this product may
not exist in your area.

First edition September 2014

ISBN-13: 978-0-373-62628-1

Special thanks and acknowledgment to
Charles Rogers for his contribution to this work.

BLOOD RED TIDE

Printed in U.S.A.

O Captain! My Captain! Our fearful trip is done,
the ship has weathered every rock,
the prize we sought is won, the port is near,
the bells I hear, the people all exulting.
—Walt Whitman

THE DEATHLANDS SAGA

This world is their legacy, a world born in the violent nuclear spasm of 2001 that was the bitter outcome of a struggle for global dominance.

There is no real escape from this shockscape where life always hangs in the balance, vulnerable to newly demonic nature, barbarism, lawlessness.

But they are the warrior survivalists, and they endure—in the way of the lion, the hawk and the tiger, true to nature's heart despite its ruination.

Ryan Cawdor: The privileged son of an East Coast baron. Acquainted with betrayal from a tender age, he is a master of the hard realities.

Krysty Wroth: Harmony ville's own Titian-haired beauty, a woman with the strength of tempered steel. Her premonitions and Gaia powers have been fostered by her Mother Sonja.

J. B. Dix, the Armorer: Weapons master and Ryan's close ally, he, too, honed his skills traversing the Deathlands with the legendary Trader.

Doctor Theophilus Tanner: Torn from his family and a gentler life in 1896, Doc has been thrown into a future he couldn't have imagined.

Dr. Mildred Wyeth: Her father was killed by the Ku Klux Klan, but her fate is not much lighter. Restored from pre-dark cryogenic suspension, she brings twentieth-century healing skills to a nightmare.

Jak Lauren: A true child of the wastelands, reared on adversity, loss and danger, the albino teenager is a fierce fighter and loyal friend.

Dean Cawdor: Ryan's young son by Sharona accepts the only world he knows, and yet he is the seedling bearing the promise of tomorrow.

In a world where all was lost, they are humanity's last hope....

Chapter One

"I smell the sea," Doc Tanner reported.

Ryan Cawdor, leader of a group of seven companions who traveled the Deathlands, still mostly smelled and tasted his own bile from the jump. He stepped out from the shadows of the yawning redoubt blast doors. Someone back in the day had constructed a warehouse-sized building around the entrance to the redoubt. It was a blockhouse, and Ryan suspected it probably served as camouflage too. At some point the ruse had failed. Holes in the walls that a man could step through and twisted iron rebar indicated the structure had taken artillery fire.

The wind moaned through the holes and emptiness. Ryan sniffed the air. Doc was right. They were close to the sea. The air also smelled like rain was coming. Depending on what hemisphere their jump had taken them, a golden sunrise or sunset spilled through the blasted out front door. Ryan looked at the thick layer of undisturbed dust and bird shit coating the floor.

No one had been here in a very long time.

Ryan took point and his companions spread out behind him.

"It smells tropical," Doc opined.

A corner of Ryan's mouth turned up slightly. Doc was definitely damaged goods, but there was nothing wrong with the man's nose. Ryan jerked his head toward the blackened holes on both sides of the building "Jak, Ricky, check our flanks."

Jak Lauren and Ricky Morales, the two youngest members of the group, moved out. Ricky raised his silenced DeLisle carbine and peered out one of the smaller blast holes in the wall. "Nothing but rocks, Ryan. Nothing's moving!"

Jak held his Cold Python and peered to one side. "Jungle. Quiet."

"Hold positions. J.B., you and me, cross fire on the entrance." The two men took oblique angles on the shattered blockhouse entrance. J.B. Dix, also known as the Armorer, squatted behind a pile of rubble. Ryan stood behind solid wall. He shouldered his Steyr Scout rifle and risked a glance outside.

Ryan stared.

J.B. cradled his scattergun and peered at Ryan quizzically. "What?"

Ryan gazed on something he had seen only a few times in his life.

Krysty Wroth, Ryan's lover, held her blaster in both hands and tilted her chin at him. "What is it?"

"Yo, Ryan!" Mildred Wyeth called. "You're starting to freak me out! What do you see?"

The one-eyed man waved his friends forward. The redoubt and the blockhouse concealing it were on a steep hillside. A raddled predark road zigzagged down through the forest to a lagoon painted in pink and gold with the setting sun. All eyes stared at the lagoon and what lay anchored there.

"A full rigged ship!" Doc declared. "How delightful."

"What does that mean, Doc?" Ryan asked.

"In my time a full-rigged ship meant a ship with three masts, all square rigged."

Ryan snapped out his Navy longeyes.

He gazed on the vessel, knowing that such a ship was a rare thing. The few villes that could build boats of their own from scratch produced ketches or small fishing boats.

Ricky had been born in a port ville in old Puerto Rico, and he gasped at the sight of something so magnificent. "She's beautiful!"

Ryan agreed. The ship below was perfect. Her lines were utterly clean. She was a design from some far better time, built to sail the world's oceans using the power of the wind alone. Ryan took in her masts and yards.

"Have you ever seen a ship as nice as that, Doc?"

"In my time, dear friend, and I had never expected to see the like again. Indeed I had the pleasure of touring my country's good sailing ship *USS Constitution* in my youth, upon an idyll in New York City. She was a frigate, and an antique even then."

"Jesus." Mildred shook her head. "I took a tour of the *USS Constitution* when I was in college, and that was in my time."

"Big boat," Jak commented.

Doc sighed happily. "This vessel is rather smaller than the *Constitution*. If pressed, I would name her a sloop-of-war."

"Why?" Ryan asked.

"Well," Doc replied, "she is a wooden ship, Ryan. Given skilled carpenters and blacksmiths, every single piece of her can be replaced. Indeed, except perhaps the keel, I would dare to wager that not one plank or spar upon that boat is original. Like an organism slowly replacing its cells as they wear out, the structure never changes, but new wood, new iron, new crews and new life have invigorated her throughout the centuries and—"

Mildred interrupted him, pointing a finger at the mast.

It flew a blue flag with a white skeleton hand embroidered on it. "Yeah, and they're flying the goddamn Jolly Roger!"

"Hmmm." Doc frowned. "Traditionally the pirate Jolly Roger was black, symbolizing death, or occasionally red for blood. A sea blue ensign should represent the sea and would denote a more commercial enterprise."

Mildred rolled her eyes. "Um, and the skeleton hand?"

"What that denotes I cannot fathom," Doc admitted.

"It's been in a fight," J.B. stated.

Ryan nodded. The Armorer was right. The ship's sides were torn and scored. The sails were currently reefed, but Ryan could see blackening and damage. Men worked in the riggings and hung from the ropes along the sides, effecting repairs on holes that were clearly cannon shot. They moved with clear purpose. Ryan stepped out of the blockhouse. His friends followed him, blasters trained on their flanks. He crossed a weed-choked wag parking circle and took point at a shattered guard gate that had once stood sentinel on the road. He waved his companions forward. Ryan pointed his longeyes down the hill. Men on the beach were tending cook fires. Others loaded barrels onto a pair of small boats, and Ryan suspected they were barrels of fresh water. He eagerly scanned the sailing ship again from stem to stern.

"I'm getting a real strong idea we're probably on an island," Ryan surmised. "And we're probably going to need a way off. Maybe we'll need a parley."

"No need for a parley!" an opera-quality voice said, then laughed. "Your ship awaits!"

Ryan spun and snapped his longblaster toward the roof of the blockhouse. A bronze-skinned man looked down at him from the eaves. He stood barefoot and wore striped pantaloons and no shirt. Platinum-blond ringlets curled around his skull. Doc would describe his features as "cruel and sensuous." He was muscled like a gladiator, and his every muscle, tendon and sinew stood out in high relief. Veins snaked down his arms in road maps of strength. Nonetheless he stood languorously relaxed. Ryan put his crosshairs between the man's golden brown eyes. It was bad enough that he stood there, unafraid. Even worse that he stood there unafraid and unarmed. "Who are you?"

"Your superior, and I command you to drop your blasters."

"I could chill you," Ryan stated.

"You could," the titan responded. "Worst mistake you'll ever make. All your mates will die."

Ryan considered the fact that in his experience only a handful of people knew about the mat-trans units and what they did. Any jump without a specific code was random. The fact that there was an ambush here, waiting for them, minutes after a random jump was thought provoking.

Ryan fired. The man above twisted with incredible alacrity even as the Scout kicked against his shoulder in recoil. He realized that the man had dodged his shot and flicked the bolt for a follow-up shot, but the man had already dropped out of sight. The man's voice boomed from the roof. "Now, Mr. Hardstone!"

The ground shifted beneath Ryan and his companions' feet. The earth opened up and swallowed them. The one-eyed man had only moments to register that a pit trap large enough to hold seven people and constructed thick enough up top to escape detection had been built outside the redoubt. Ryan hit the layer of underbrush that had been laid there to cushion the fall. Dirt had been piled three feet high above the trapdoors to conceal them, and the dirt cascaded all over the companions. Ryan landed on his feet and he spit dirt as the jolt ran up his legs.

"Cast your nets, boys!" the man of bronze called. Heavy

deep-sea netting fell across Ryan's head and shoulders and entangled the Scout. He dropped his longblaster and went for his panga and SIG Sauer handblaster. A second net and a third weighted with iron fell across him as he struggled to draw steel. Men leaped into the pit. As they landed on the netting, it encumbered the companions and pinned them down more. Ryan shoved his SIG free of the heavy strands. The bronze man suddenly stood next to him. The man stomped on netting, and it yanked the rope over Ryan's blaster arm down. The shot busted cuttings on the pit floor.

Ryan's vision went white as a belaying pin rammed into his back just above his right kidney. He heard J.B.'s Uzi snarl off a burst and their captors shouting. "Watch him! Watch him! Watch him!"

A man screamed. "He cut me! Little white runt cut me! Oh, rads and fall out," the kidnapper moaned. "He cut me bad…"

Jak was still in the fight.

A huge hand closed around Ryan's wrist and squeezed. The one-eyed man's blaster hand popped open against his will and the SIG fell. "You're fast," the man admitted. "Fastest I've—"

Ryan struck quick as a snake strike with his blade. He thrust straight for the right eye. The strong man snapped his head aside, but the edge still whispered a hair-thin cut across his cheek and nicked his ear in passing. Ryan found his wrist plucked out of the air like a bird before he could retract it. The bronze hand squeezed with sickening strength. "So fast," the titan mused. He jerked his head at the man behind Ryan. "Onetongue!"

A thick arm snaked around Ryan's neck and Onetongue slapped a wet mass of folded rags across Ryan's mouth and throat and held it there with great strength. The sop reeked.

Ryan's vision spun, his limbs loosened and his gorge rose even as he tried to hold his breath against it. His knees buckled beneath him. The titan held his wrists effortlessly.

"The knife!" a man bellowed from somewhere. "Someone get the fish-white son of a gaudy slut's knife!"

"I got his knife!"

"Well, he has another— Fuck! That's twice! Together! One three! One…three!"

Ryan heard a net-snared Jak snarling as his opponents piled on and the meaty sound of blows landed like rain. Ryan struggled as well, and consciousness drained out of him like a barrel with the bung knocked out. He couldn't hear any of his other companions as darkness claimed him.

Chapter Two

"Wake up, ya rad-blasted lubbers!" A cascade of cold seawater drenched Ryan and wrenched him out the blackness the drug had taken him to. His skull split from the sedative hangover. The shouter shouted on. "And your sluts, too! Wake up!"

Seawater flew by the bucket, and Ryan's friends gasped and jerked awake. Rough hands yanked Ryan up and kept him from falling as the shackles binding his legs tried to trip him. His hands were manacled before him. The one-eyed man blinked in the dimness and confusion and fought to collect his wits as he was hustled forward. His jacket, boots and all weapons and equipment had been stripped from him. As his head slammed into a low beam, he saw stars and buckled. Rough laughter greeted his discomfort. He could hear his comrades' moans and groans as they were manhandled behind him. Ryan was half carried, half dragged up two companionways between decks.

"Make way! Make way! Seven fresh fish for the captain!" Male and female voices hooted and catcalled. Ryan was bum-rushed into the blinding light of the sun and a broadside of jeers.

Despite the hangover from the drug, Ryan instantly knew he and his friends were at sea. He also knew he had been deliberately thrown facing into the sun. He got a knee beneath him and rose. He perceived the bronze gladiator figure from his capture whipping forward. Ryan raised his manacled hands, but the huge fist shot beneath and buried itself into his guts. Ryan dropped to boos and derision. It took a supreme act of will to keep from vomiting.

Ryan forced his limbs to obey him and rose again.

A voice from the side spoke low. "Strong bold bastard, I'll give him that."

The one-eyed man shook his head and tried to blink his vision straight. The voice belonged to a red-haired, bullet-headed man built like an aged, sun-ravaged gorilla. He gave Ryan a look of grudging sympathy and lifted his chin in warning. "Best look to starboard, mate."

Ryan blinked and caught the next blow coming out of his right peripheral vision. He was too drug addled to do anything about it. The fist took him in the side of the neck and dropped him with white fire racing down his right arm.

The bronze gladiator loomed over him. He wore a bandage over the knick Ryan had given his cheek and another on his ear. "Captain will speak to you now."

Ryan squeezed his manacled hands into fists, pushed off the deck and stood again. Mixed mutters of admiration and speculation greeted his effort. He reeled. The deck spun and he could still barely see. Ryan spit. "And just who's the captain of this bastard tub?"

The bronze fist hit Ryan in the guts again, and he doubled over. An uppercut ripped him erect, and a right cross crushed him to the deck, vomiting. The blond, bronze enforcer squatted over Ryan and leered as he cocked his fist. "Oh, you…"

A voice like a rasp on slate spoke. "Mr. Manrape."

All chatter and cheering ceased. Ryan's abuser shot to his feet. "Captain!"

"Every man on this ship has the right to ask who the captain is exactly twice," the voice continued. "Once, when he is first brought aboard and doesn't know, and the second, the day he kills me and stands before crew."

The assembled men on the deck chanted in unison. "We know the code! We keep the creed!"

Ryan rose for the third and he thought possibly the last time. The only good news was that throwing up seemed to have cleared his head a little. He took in the crowd. He estimated about a hundred were on the deck and in the rigging. That told him the ship probably kept four watches. Most were on deck now effecting repairs from the previous battle and watching the spectacle the new prisoners presented. The worst part was that Ryan couldn't see land on the horizon. The crew was different than any Ryan had encountered before. Despite the relaxed discipline of the moment, the symmetrical arrangement of the crowd told Ryan each man or woman was standing at their station.

The crew did not exactly wear a uniform, but nearly all wore loose white pants of identical cloth and red or white striped shirts. The uniformity of the clothing told Ryan they bought or traded for cloth in bulk and shared it among themselves. He reined in his drug hangover and found himself startled again. Hardly any of the crew was armed. The pirates and sea raiders Ryan had encountered were usually festooned with blasters and blades. Every crewmember he surveyed carried a knife or a marlinspike or both, but those were working tools.

Ryan looked up and saw sailors up in the tops on lookout with longblasters, and several were pointed his way. There was that, and a ring of men surrounding him tapped belaying pins into their palms with practiced familiarity. Ryan heard his companions being hurled to the deck behind him. Krysty drew a lusty chorus of catcalls. Doc drew jeers and noises of disgust. The rest of the companions fell somewhere in between. They took Ryan's lead and rose behind him. Ricky and Mildred had to hold Doc up. He wasn't doing well. Ryan squinted up at the quarterdeck and beheld the captain.

He was something to see.

The man was black, his skin a lot darker than Mildred's. His black, wavy hair was shot through with gray and pulled into a short pigtail. The man's eyes were black from pupil to iris with almost no white showing. It gave him a gaze that disturbingly resembled a shark's.

The captain was a mutant.

He was not tall, but his shoulders were impossibly broad. The captain wore a black broadcloth shirt cut to fit his frame and black trousers. A sash that had to have weighed five pounds with all the spun gold gleaming through it girded his waist. His shirt was open to his solar plexus against the heat. Twisted and raised white lines girded his throat like a choker of thorns. Ryan instinctively knew it was a hanging scar. The captain's right hand was twice the size as was usual, locked in a curled rictus and covered with orange fur. The nails were silver, long and sharpened like claws. Ryan could tell the hand was not the captain's own but something that had been affixed.

The mutant grated through his damaged voice box. "I am Oracle, captain of the good ship *Hand of Glory.*"

A tall man with a short beard, mustache and spectacles stood beside the captain. He was dressed nearly the same except that his blouse and trousers were blue and white, and undoubtedly he was an officer. *"Glory!"* the man shouted.

"Glory!" the crew roared in response. *"Glory! Glory! Glory!"*

Oracle's flat black eyes stared eerily at the prisoner before him as the cheers died down. "What is your name?"

"Ryan Cawdor."

"You have been on the waters?"

Ryan knew he and his friends' lives hung in the balance. Lies or subterfuge would not serve them shackled and out of sight of land. "A few times. Never for long."

"Are you able? Can you hand, reef and steer?"

"No," Ryan said, shaking his head. "But I've pulled on a rope, hurled a harpoon and fought in boarding actions. Steered a bit."

"You stand like a man accustomed to command," Oracle observed.

Manrape leered. "I can break him of that habit, my captain."

"Never commanded a ship." Ryan kept his eyes on Oracle. "Don't claim the ability."

Oracle's eyes narrowed and his gaze went opaque. "With time and tides, Mr. Ryan. Perhaps."

Ryan tried to marshal his thoughts. "Captain, I—"

The blue-clad officer beside the captain bellowed with the unmistakable timbre of long command. "You don't address the captain directly, fish!"

Manrape lunged in. His fist rammed into Ryan's right thigh in a charley horse from hell. Ryan's leg spasmed, and he dropped to one knee against his will.

Oracle stared at Ryan like a cipher. "I do not ordinarily press men, Mr. Ryan. I prefer volunteers, but we live in extraordinary times." Oracle turned away and walked back toward his cabin. "I leave it to you, Commander Miles."

The officer eyed J.B. "That fish had some very fancy blasters."

J.B. looked at Ryan, who grimaced against his pain. "He's J.B., armorer."

"Mr. Forgiven!" Miles shouted.

A fat man with lank black hair hanging like the curtain of a jellyfish from his bald pate waddled forward. He wore blue like Miles and bore a great brown leather book and a predark pen. "Aye, Commander!"

"Rate Mr. J.B. temporary Gunner's Mate until proved otherwise or signed to the book. Have Smithy ease his irons six inches apiece so he can work. If he's useful, strike his chains tomorrow."

Miles gave J.B. a deadly look. "You try to sneak a blaster, a blade or a thimbleful of powder, and by the nukecaust breaking of the world you will kiss the blaster's daughter while the whip pounds your cock and balls to paste."

J.B. nodded. "I'll—"

"Shut your filthy piehole, scum!" Miles roared.

J.B. tensed but fell silent.

Miles pointed at Mildred. "This one had med supplies."

"Mildred can sew a man," Ryan answered. He and the companions were very careful who they let on that Mildred was a genuine physician. "She's a healer, hoping to learn more."

Commander Miles seemed pleased. "Wake up old Bonesaw and tell him he has a new temporary saw mate until proved otherwise or signed."

Forgiven wrote in the ship's book. "Aye."

Miles gave Mildred the evil eye. "And listen to me, bitch. You steal meds or let a man deliberately die on the table, you'll kiss the blaster's daughter while every man aboard takes you."

A woman with hair as red as Krysty's, but six inches taller and two hundred pounds heavier, held up a huge callused hand and made a fist. "And woman!"

The crew cheered. Miles rolled his eyes. "Sweet Marie to have firsts."

Forgiven entered Mildred's name and made a check by it.

Miles nodded in approval at Jak and Ricky. Ryan started to speak. "They're—"

"They're young, light and tight, and this ship is short of top men." Miles nodded at a mutie who looked like a six-foot, shaved gibbon with bright pink skin and golden eyes. "Mr. Movies, I want Whitey and Softboy here able in the rigging ASAP."

Movies put a pink knuckle to his brow and spoke in a soft voice that sounded like it was unused to human speech. "Aye, Commander Miles."

Manrape looked at Ricky with open lust. "What is your name?"

Ryan gave Ricky credit for scowling at Manrape as if he were shit he had scraped off his shoe. "Ricky."

Manrape closed his eyes. "Ricky Softboy, young, light and tight…"

Ricky made a Puerto Rican hand gesture that had been ancient in Doc's time. *"Mama bicho!"*

The crew laughed at Ricky's bravado. Manrape smiled beatifically. "Oh, my soft Rickito."

"Manrape wants a new wife!" someone called from the rigging. The catcalls resumed.

"Ship's business!" Miles thundered. The increasingly horrible suggestions and bets died down. The commander ran an appreciative eye over Krysty. "And her, Mr. Ryan?"

"She's mine," Ryan stated.

Sweet Marie called out lustily. "We'll see how long that lasts, Cyclops!"

The crew whooped.

"Write Red into the log and rate her lubber, powder monkey, gopher and the like, until proved otherwise or signed."

Forgiven scratched in the log. "Aye."

The commander weighed and measured Doc and found him wanting. The knockout drug, the beating and the rude awakening had left the time-trawled man staring at his shoes. "And this?"

"Doc is—"

"Doc?" Miles perked up. "He's a whitecoat?"

Ryan sought for anything that could save his friend. "No, but he's educated. He's—"

A thatch-headed young man shouted happily, "He's just a fucking old stick!"

"Shut up, Wipe!" Miles snapped. Wipe flinched and stood at attention. Miles sighed at Forgiven. "Old Stick, rate him lubber, let him pull a rope until he proves himself ordinary seaman or breaks." Doc seemed completely oblivious to his sentencing.

Forgiven made a derisive noise and a note. "Aye."

The commander gave Ryan a smile that held not an ounce of warmth. "And you, Mr. Ryan, word is you can pull a rope, heave harpoon and lance and fight a boarding action."

Ryan knew what was coming. He was the leader of a group of the shanghaied aboard a ship in dire straits. He was mostly likely to be worked until broken or made an example of. "I can."

"Rate One-Eye lubber, until proved otherwise or signed."

"Aye."

"Mr. Manrape! I don't want any of the new fish together in number on deck until proved otherwise or signed. Let them mess together but separate their hammocks. Clap Red, Whitey and Softboy in irons until the next watch. Put Ryan to work now."

Manrape sneered openly at Doc. "And this one?"

Commander Miles laughed. "Put Old Stick to work immediately. Let Mr. Ryan have him as a comfort."

RYAN WORKED LIKE a slave. The knockout drug and the beating did him no favors as he hauled on ropes to bring fresh spars and sails aloft. Small boats brought casks of water, and by the crew's grumbling, far too little bush meat from the forest. Ryan staggered beneath their weight to bring them down into the dark depths of the hold.

Their complaints and worry about the food situation were nearly constant. Ryan was treated like a pariah, a pressed man and probably rebellious if given any chance. No one talked to him except to scream about how he was doing his every task wrong. Crewmen laughed when he threw up or fell, but some gave him grunts or nods as he rose again and again and returned to his tasks. If there was any solace in the situation, it was that every other member of the crew was working just as hard as he was. The ship had been in a battle and barely escaped. The urgency among officers and crew to get the vessel seaworthy and under sails again was palpable.

Doc was not doing as well.

The knockout drug had addled him. He had been put to work picking apart torn rope and rigging for caulking material. Doc was spending more time talking to the rope scraps than picking them. Manrape stalked the decks with a knotted rope end of his own and it fell upon Doc again and again. The old man whimpered and looked to be spiraling into a genuine episode. Ryan tottered beneath two wooden kegs roped to his shoulders. The ships bell clanged the hour and the commander called out, "Miss Loral!"

A lanky, grinning, raven-haired beauty in officer's blue produced a pewter whistle on a chain from her ample cleavage and piped the change of watch. The crew put away its equipment and gear and began filing down the hatch. Miss Loral looked at Miles, who shook his head.

Miss Loral shook her head at Ryan. "Not you, Ryan! Watch on watch! And you, Old Stick!"

Ryan had already worked straight through two four-hour watches, and now it would be twelve hours without rest. He was handed hard bread at intervals, and he was given as much water as the rest of the crew, but Ryan could see his sentence written on the wall. They were going to break him and destroy Doc. The new watch filed up. Ryan hadn't seen J.B. or Mildred, but he saw Krysty, Jak and Ricky with each change of watch and they shot him increasingly concerned looks. Jak and Ricky filed by. Jak hesitated, but Miss Loral's voice cracked like a whip. "Into the tops, Whitey!"

Jak was without his Colt Python and his smorgasbord of knives. He knew he would only get Ryan and himself punished if he tried anything. He frowned and moved toward the port rigging. Ricky shot Ryan a grin and tossed a piece of salted mystery meat the size of a deck of cards between two buckets by Ryan's feet.

Ricky shot Ryan a wink.

Manrape appeared out of nowhere behind Ricky. He grabbed the youth by the back of the neck and lifted him off the deck with one hand, caressing his buttocks with the other. "Aiding and succoring a man sentenced to watch on watch, Ricky Softboy?"

Ricky cursed and flailed in the titan's grip.

Ryan stepped forward despite the kegs strapped to his back.

Doc's voice thundered across the deck. "Cursed pederast!" The entire deck stared as Doc rounded on Manrape. The old man drew himself up to his full height and his eyes flashed with imminent violence. "Should you wish to compulse young Ricardo into the role of catamite, then you shall be forced to come through me!"

Manrape dropped Ricky and turned.

"Doc!" Ryan shouted. "No!"

Doc produced a marlinspike with the same oil-on-glass

speed he could draw his sword from his cane when properly motivated. The crew barely had time to gasp as Doc
lunged for Manrape's heart. Manrape slapped the mar-
linespike out of Doc's hand as if he was swatting a fly,
and his backhand tossed Doc to the deck. For a moment,
silence reigned.

Commander Miles's familiar roar broke the silence.
"What in the last megaton that boiled the seas is going on?"

Manrape sighed happily. "Old Stick, unsigned, attempted murder of the bos'n with a marlinspike."

Miles glared down at Doc in terrible judgment. All
fight had gone out of the old man, and he twitched and
mewled on the deck. The marlinspike lay damningly beside his hand. Miles's eyes filled with rage. "Witnessed?"

More than a dozen men chorused. "Aye!"

"Clap Old Stick in irons! Take him to the captain for
judgment!" Miles shook his head. He already knew the
sentence. "String a rope, and prepare to pipe all hands
on deck to witness the mighty hand of the *Glory's* creed
and code."

"Can't you see he's damaged!" Ryan shouted. "The drug
you gave him stuped him!"

Shocked silence fell across the deck. Ryan expected
a second rope to be rigged beside Doc's. It was Manrape
who spoke. "Perhaps One-Eye is right, Commander. Why
bother the captain? We have a cure for those who are drunk
or addled on duty."

"We know the creed. We hold the code," Miles intoned. "Mr. Manrape does not press his injury and begs
mercy." Miles jerked his head toward the starboard rigging. "Ship's punishment, then! Seize Old Stick into the
shrouds. See if that clears his head. Failing that, let the
gulls have him as an example to those who might be like-
wise tempted."

Crewmen seized Doc and carried him over their heads
to the starboard rail, laughing. Ryan took a step forward.
A huge, raw, red hand slammed onto his shoulder. "Best
case, you hang right up there next to him in the shrouds.
Worst case, you hang alone from the yardarm."

Ryan tensed with frustrated rage as the crewmen lashed
Doc spread-eagled in the shrouds ten feet above the deck
and facing inward. "Mr. Hardstone!" Miles called.

The big red-headed man removed his hand from Ryan's
shoulder and snapped to attention. "Aye, Commander!"

"You have empty seats at your table. One-Eye will mess
with you and your mates."

"Aye, sir!"

"The captain says until he is proved otherwise or signed,
One-Eye is your responsibility."

Ryan was starting to have a very bad feeling about being
proved otherwise.

Hardstone gave Ryan a none-too-pleased look. "Aye, sir."

"Mr. Manrape!"

"Aye!"

"Let Mr. Ryan stand another watch for his insolence."

"Aye."

Miles turned on his heel and returned to the quarterdeck.

Manrape stroked his chin. "Mr. Forgiven!"

The purser looked up from counting a pallet of green
bananas. "Aye, bos'n?"

"Would you gaze on the ship's dictionary for me when
you have a moment?"

"Aye. And what would you know?"

Manrape looked up at Doc. "The meaning of the words
pederast and catamite."

Chapter Three

Krysty staggered into the fo'c'sle. The hammocks had been stowed and tables hung from the ceiling above as the watch got ready to mess. They were at anchor so lanterns were lit. Commander Miles had considered Krysty unfit for most duties aboard ship, and she was half convinced he was right.

That had not stopped Krysty from being assigned to run up into the rigging to bring the top men water several dozen times; running messages between decks; scrubbing the decks and heads; taking nails, rope, twine and supplies to the repair crews; being speeded along with a rope end when it was perceived she wasn't moving fast enough; and enduring more sexual innuendo and gropings in passing than she had been subjected to her entire life in the Deathlands.

Sweet Marie called out from her mess table. "Over here, girlie!" Krysty looked that way. Sweet Marie sat with J.B., Jak, Mildred and Ricky. Two crewmen sat with them, the pink mutie, Mr. Movies, who seemed to rule the rigging, and a huge sagging, bull of a man. "You mess with us!"

Krysty sat down to the sound of whistles and hoots "Flame on flame!" someone called.

"I'd pay hard jack to see that!" a crewman replied.

Krysty stared the big woman in the face amid the jeering. "I'll chill you."

Sweet Marie threw back her head and laughed. "Oh,

I'm not one to force myself on anyone, but when your man is corruption down in the Old Place and you're all alone, you'll remember your Sweet Marie when every shark comes circling."

Krysty reserved comment.

A small, pretty, dark-haired and olive-skinned woman made her way over to the table. Krysty saw that her eyes were milk-white without pupils. She made soft clicking sounds as she unerringly wove through the crowd and clutter. Crewmen called out to her. "Gypsyfair! When you gonna mess with us?"

The woman called back in bemused disgust. "Shut up! I'm walking belowdecks!"

Gypsyfair sat down and turned her milk-white gaze on Krysty. "Nice to meet you, Red. Too many norms and not enough muties on this ship if you ask me."

Krysty tried to hide her surprise. The blind mutant grinned. "Your hair don't move normal, girl."

Sweet Marie's mass visibly sagged. "Red's mutie?"

"Yeah?" Krysty bristled. "So?"

Gypsyfair laughed. "Now I've seen Sweet Marie eat things that would choke a stickie and ask for seconds, but eat a mutie girl? She just won't do it."

Despite all her innuendo Sweet Marie turned beet red.

Krysty blinked at the giantess. "But, I thought you were…"

"I ain't mutie!" Sweet Marie snarled. "I'm just big-boned!"

Krysty thought of several retorts but kept them to herself. She nodded at the mutant top-man acrobat. "Mr. Movies."

He nodded. His voice was a soft chirp. "Hello."

Sweet Marie nodded at the man mountain beside her.

"This is Gallondrunk." Krysty noted the puckered scar just above his left temple.

Gallondrunk stared at Krysty for long seconds. "Pretty."

Sweet Marie sighed. "He's never been the same since he took that bullet to the brain off Scoshia."

Movies suddenly became agitated. "Bastard bluenoses!"

Sweet Marie shrugged. "Bonesaw got the bullet out, but Gallondrunk'll never reef, hand or steer again. Still, he's the strongest man on the ship, and he's a chilling machine with that walrus lance he cherishes." She patted the giant on the shoulder tenderly. "Even worse chiller than he was before. Got the gift of emptiness, don't you, darling?"

Gallondrunk spent long moments processing the question. "I like to help. I like to give 'em the iron."

He turned his gaze on Krysty again. She realized the giant was staring more at her hair than her. "Pretty."

Another crewman came over bearing a steaming bucket. He was one of the handsomest men Krysty had ever seen. He had long black hair, a luxurious black mustache and hazel eyes. He put the heavy bucket onto the table and twirled his mustache. He had some sort of very thick accent. "And you must be Miss Krysty."

Sweet Marie made a disgusted noise. "Speaking of circling sharks, this is Goulash."

Goulash rolled his eyes. "Gulyas."

"Whatever, he may be the worst sailor aboard other than you, girlie, but he's a dead shot with a blaster and our best hunter and scout ashore."

Goulash ladled beans and three lumps of bushmeat onto Krysty's wooden platter. She stared hard at the mystery meat. "What is it?"

Goulash blew a lock of black hair off his brow and pointed his ladle in turn. "That is monkey. That is sloth."

He pointed last at a small mass of twisted bones and gristle. "That is mutie…something."

Krysty decided to go from worst to best. She picked up the mutie mess and began stripping meager meat and tendon and spitting bones.

Krysty looked at her friends. "How's it going. Mildred?"

"Bonesaw is a drunk, and when he isn't drunk he's sampling whatever meds he has. Strangely enough he seems to care about his patients. He likes the way I sew."

"J.B.?"

J.B. shoveled down beans. "I wasn't allowed in the armory or near the cannons. I cleaned blasters. Mostly single shooters. Homemade. I think they're desperate short of—"

Sweet Marie spoke low and dangerous. "You best keep that talk between you and Gunny till you get your short ass signed, Specs."

Krysty changed the subject. "Jak?"

"Big boat."

Sweet Marie, Movies, Gallondrunk and Goulash spoke in harsh unison. "She's a ship!"

"Ship," Jak amended. "Big ship."

"You all right?"

Jak almost smiled. Krysty had seen Jak up in the rigging and knew that despite their circumstances Jak was enjoying hanging from the rigging and being in the tops. He was already as agile as a monkey, and he was learning a new skill set. It didn't mean he wasn't planning on how to murder the entire crew, but part of him was enjoying the work.

"Ricky?" Krysty asked.

Ricky's fists clenched. "If one more person pinches my ass…"

"You and me both. Has anyone seen Ryan?"

Sweet Marie sucked the meat off a monkey bone. "Captain's working your man watch-on-watch. Can't imagine he'll last much longer without falling asleep on duty or collapsin'. Then it's ship's punishment."

Krysty bit her lip. "Like Doc?"

Sweet Marie looked at Krysty with genuine sympathy. "Best you forget about Old Stick, girl. He's done. Eat. Sleep. If you gotta worry, worry about your man."

THE SHIP'S BELL RANG. First Mate Loral piped the change of watch as the sun set. Ryan had been going twenty-four hours straight. "One-Eye! Take supper with your mates!" Ryan managed not to collapse to the deck. Loral called to the purser. "Mr. Forgiven! Rate Mr. Ryan waister!"

Crewmen made approving noises of Ryan's elevation from One-Eye to his name and from lubber to waister. His bravery, work ethic and sheer toughness had not gone unnoticed.

Mr. Forgiven came forward bearing the book. "Come along, Wipe!" The thatch-headed sailor who had named Doc "Old Stick" bore a large bundle. Forgiven opened his book and flipped to a page. "Mr. Ryan, neither proved otherwise, nor signed."

"Mr. Forgiven."

"One hammock, mattress and blanket." Wipe dropped them at Ryan's feet. Forgiven held out his pen. "Sign or make your mark for your issuables."

Ryan signed the indicated space in the book.

"You have been promoted from lubber to waister, until proved otherwise or signed." Wipe set down a leather belt sheath with two implements on Ryan's bedding. Forgiven nodded. "Ship's knife number 12, Marlinspike number 42 and sheath. Mr. Ryan, these belong to the ship and are your responsibility until you're chilled in action, leave ship's service or should you buy implements of your own preference in port that meet ship standard and then these seen returned to stores. You understand?"

Ryan understood all too well. The beating at Manrape's hands had been one test. Working him watch-on-watch had been another. Now he was being issued the tools that could be the keys toward mutiny or escape. He was being tested again. "I understand."

"Sign."

Ryan signed.

Forgiven nodded and walked away. "Very good."

Ryan drew the marlinspike. It was twelve inches of tapered iron coming to point like a sharp, flathead screwdriver with a hitch loop at the top. It was made for splicing, knotting and hitching rope and line. Ryan slid the spike back into its side pocket and drew the knife. It was simple, with well-weathered wood grips and a full riveted tang. The blade was five inches long, discolored and pitted from salt and sea. It was a working man's knife. The spine was thick for strength and the edge was thin as a razor and shaving sharp. The knife had been sharpened so many times the blade was starting to lose its original line. Ryan hefted it in his hand.

"Don't even think about it," Hardstone muttered.

Manrape pulled his trick of appearing behind Ryan out of nowhere. For a big man he moved very quietly. He whispered like a lover. "Think about it, Ryan."

It took all of Ryan's will not to turn and slash. Manrape laughed and resumed his walk along the gangway. "Think about sticking me, while I think about sticking little Ricky." He looked up as he walked beneath Doc moaning in the shrouds and laughed.

Ryan slammed his new knife back in its sheath and gathered up his bedding. Hardstone jerked his head toward the hatch as the second watch came up and the ceaseless work continued. "Follow me. You mess with us. Word is the last hunting party brought back a barrel or two of bush meat. Enjoy it. We lost a lot of stores in the battle when the hull was pierced. Boiler and Skillet are both in the med. We'll be on hard rations and badly cooked at that when we sail." Hardstone limped for the hatch. Ryan stopped beneath Doc. Earlier Doc had been mumbling to his wife and children hundreds of years gone. Now Doc moaned, pleading to a baron only he could see.

Ryan flinched. Doc was spiraling down into the cellar of the horrors he had experienced. "Doc, you have to listen to me. You're going to die up in those ropes unless you get it together."

Some rational section of Doc's unraveling mind sobbed in response. "Oh to be so blessed…"

Ryan could sense the nearby crew listening in. Doc's utter loyalty to his friends often shored up his sanity. "Doc, we're in a hard place and it's getting harder. I need you. We all need you." Ryan grasped at Doc's words and his talents. "You said it yourself. This is a square-rigged ship. A thing from your time. You know about these things. Find something. Anything! Anything that could make you useful and get you cut down so we can get you to Mildred."

"Mildred…"

"Doc." Ryan put the iron of command in his voice. "You and I are friends. Now we're watch mates. You die on my watch, and Krysty will never forgive me."

"Krysty…"

"Loves you," Ryan snarled. "Now you got to get yourself together, get yourself down out of those shrouds and make yourself useful! Tell me you hear me!"

A barely sane whisper responded. "Ryan…"

"Doc, you heard me. I know you heard me. Tell me

you…" Ryan's shoulders sagged in defeat as Doc's chin had dropped to his chest and the evening breeze stirred the rivulet of drool hanging from his chin.

Manrape cooed. "Mr. Ryan, are you talking to a man under ship's punishment?"

Ryan spun. Manrape lunged. Ryan was three steps too slow from exhaustion and still holding his bedding. He started to drop the bundle and go for the knife and marlinspike, but Manrape's rope end slammed into his chest. Ryan fell back onto the deck. The tactical part of his mind noted that one end of Manrape's double-ended rope was loaded. He gasped like a fish and tried to breathe.

Manrape knelt and put a knee on Ryan's chest. The blond titan held his rope end between his legs and dangled the knot over Ryan's face in horrible metaphor. "You haven't been proved otherwise, so I can't kill you. But know this. You are unsigned. You do not know the creed. You are not protected by the code. You're lucky because we need every hand able or otherwise and for the good of the ship, so I'll not put you in the med. This time. Now go mess with your mates."

Manrape rose and walked away whistling. Chilling rage boiled behind Ryan's eye and the red mist clouded his vision as he reeled to his feet. Hardstone stepped between them and gathered up Ryan's meager belongings. A sailor Ryan had heard called Atlast hurried to his side. Atlast was the ship's master of sails and spars. He was a head shorter than Ryan and Hardstone, but his shoulders were just as broad, his legs bowed like a horseman and what could only be described as a whiteman's Afro was pulled back and barely restrained by a short pigtail.

"Listen, Ryan. We need the likes of you aboard this ship, then, don't we? Best you go easy like around the bos'n."

"Go easy." Despite his rage, he knew Hardstone and Atlast were looking out for him. "Around Manrape?"

"Don't rock the bloody boat, then. You've felt the thunderbolt."

"The rope," Ryan muttered.

"Yeah, well, Manrape's rope end has two ends, doesn't it? One's a regular rope end knot, the other's a monkey's paw he's woven in, and that paw holds four good grams of lead shot. One end's for fighting, one end's for fun."

Hardstone handed Ryan his bedding. "Go down and string your hammock. Wipe should be below and will show you where. I'll save you a bowl of meat and beans."

Ryan knew it was the best offer he was going to get.

Chapter Four

"Heave away, boys!" Manrape called. "Heave away!"

The *Hand of Glory* cast off. The captain had deemed the ship ready for sail. The watch hours had been changed. Six hours of dreamless sleep and a bowl of leftover beans with biscuit broken into it had done Ryan a world of good. He wore stiff canvas pants and a blue-striped jersey someone had sewn to his proportions. He was still sore all over. His hands were well callused from life in the Deathlands, but working a wooden ship watch-on-watch had ripped his hands to shreds. Twenty-four hours barefoot on a wooden deck and rope riggings had left him limping and leaving bloody footprints that got him roared at wherever he went.

Ryan heaved against the horrible weight of the capstan bar next to Onetongue. Despite his fatboy body, Onetongue's muscles rippled beneath his flesh, and unlike every other sailor aboard he never seemed happier than when confronted with back-breaking work. Hardstone and Wipe heaved on the bar ahead and groaned like everyone else as they slowly moved clockwise and the capstan shaft wound anchor cable. Four more pairs heaved on bars behind them.

Ryan risked a glance back at Doc. The old man hung limp from the shrouds in the morning sun. Blood ran down his cheek and chin and spattered his shirt. Ryan had been belowdecks eating, but he had heard the roars and catcalls above and heard the story. Just before the watch had changed, a gull had gone for Doc's left eye. Doc had jerked awake with a scream and frightened the bird off, but the gulls circled in wait above the tops. They sensed the bound man's weakness. They sensed no one was going to defend him. Ryan knew without a shadow of a doubt that Doc was going to die hanging from those shrouds this day, and there was nothing he could do about it.

Ryan snarled as the rope end thudded into his back with all of Manrape's strength behind it. "You look back at Old Stick one more time, Ryan! One more time, and I will seize you to the shrouds beside him!" The rope end slammed between Ryan's shoulder blades a second and third time. "Now heave!"

Ryan gritted his teeth against the "fun end" of Manrape's starter. More than the knotted rope tenderizing his flesh, Ryan felt Captain Oracle's eyes on him from the quarterdeck. Oracle always seemed to be watching him. Ryan heaved. The capstan turned. Ratchets and palls clacked with monotonous rhythm as the crewmen threw their muscle against the bars and hauled the dragging anchor off the rocky bottom.

Doc's voice rose out of nowhere in song.

"A is the anchor that holds a bold ship."

The crew glanced up at the insane, shroud-seized man.

"B is the bowsprit which often does dip..."

First Mate Loral laughed. "Sing more!" The capstan men grunted as the song met the rhythm of their heaving and the clank of the pall and ratchet.

"C is the capstan upon which friend Ryan does wind..."

Onetongue shot Ryan a smirk as they heaved together.

"And D is the davits, on which the jolly boat hangs."

"What's a jolly boat?" Wipe gasped.

"Shut up, Wipe," Hardstone snarled. "I wanna hear."

Doc's voice rose. In his less broken moments he was

a powerful orator. Ryan only seldom heard it, but Doc's singing voice was a clear, beautiful tenor. It sang out now.

"E is the ensign, the white Hand of Glory on Blue, F is the foc'sle that holds the dear Glory's crew."

Noises of amusement and approval traveled through the crew from stem to stern.

"G is the gangway, on which Mr. Manrape makes his stand. H is the hawser, which seldom does strand."

Manrape's rope end hung limp in his hand as he stared up at Doc.

"I is the irons where the stuns'll boom sits. J is the jib-boom, which Mr. Atlast will tell you does dip."

Atlast roared from his precarious perch at the prow. "Ha!"

"K are the keesons of which you have been told, and L are the lanyards that always will hold. M is the main mast, so stout and so strong. N is the North Star that never points wrong. O are the orders of which we all must beware, and P are the pumps that cause sailors to swear..."

The crew laughed and the men on the capstan heaved in time with Doc's song.

"Q is the quadrant, the sun for to take. R is the rigging that always does shake. S is the starboard of our old bold ship, and T is for the topmasts that often do split. U is for the ugliest, one-handed old captain of all..."

Every head snapped a look at Oracle. The captain stood like a statue of ebony, staring at Doc.

Doc continued without missing a beat. *"V are the vapors that come with the squall. W is the windlass upon which we all wind, and X, Y and Z? I confess, I cannot put in a rhyme!"*

The crew laughed and cheered. Men with two free hands clapped and those who didn't whooped and pounded wood with their fist or stomped their feet. Commander

Miles put his fists on his hips. "Sing another, Old Stick! That anchor is only halfway up, much less catted!"

Doc licked his cracked lips and stared at the birds circling him with intent. "I know a song about seagulls…"

Men laughed. Hardstone made a grudging noise. "He's a bold, old scarecrow, I'll give him that."

Wipe did his slow mental math. "But…"

"But what, Wipe?"

"You were laughing at him just yesterday."

"Well, he deserved laughing at yesterday!"

Manrape stared at Doc with a strange light in his eyes. "Sing me a song about seagulls, Old Stick, and I will cut you down from the shrouds."

Captain Oracle's hanged-man's rasp cut all chatter like a knife across a throat. "Mr. Manrape, have Old Stick cut down."

"Aye, Captain! Mr. BeGood! Mr. Born! Seize that man down from the shrouds!"

"Take him to Bonesaw." Oracle watched as the twins cut Doc down. "I am without a servant since our last battle. When this man is fit, send him to my cabin. He will never make sailor, but perhaps he can pour wine and amuse us."

Manrape nodded. "Make it so!"

Doc seemed to barely have a bone in his body as he collapsed to the deck. Sweet Marie pushed through and pressed a dipper of water to his lips. Doc drank and raised his head.

"My captain?"

Oracle's eyes narrowed.

"I crave a boon."

The deck went silent. Oracle stared at Doc like a cipher. Ryan wasn't quite sure whether Oracle was considering in what manner to have Doc killed for his impertinence or whether the captain didn't know what the word boon meant.

"What?"

"If I am to serve, may I have my cane to lean upon? It is my only comfort."

Oracle turned to the ship's purser. "Mr. Forgiven, fetch Old Stick's cane from stores and bring it to my cabin."

"Aye, Captain."

"And strike Old Stick's name from the ship's book." Oracle turned and resumed his pacing of the quarterdeck. "Enter 'Doc' into the log, serving in the captain's quarters until proved otherwise or signed."

The crew cheered.

Onetongue and Wipe pounded Ryan's shoulders. Ryan and Doc exchanged a look. There were few secrets aboard a sailing ship. The crew knew that Ryan and Doc were friends, and all knew of Ryan's whispers to Doc to save himself. The old man had cheated death and been elevated. It was a lucky thing, and the crew would take luck wherever and in whatever form they could find it. Sweet Marie scooped Doc up in her arms like a child and took him belowdecks to the med. A secret was now aboard the *Glory*. One only Ryan and his companions knew. Once Doc had his cane, and if Ryan gave the signal, Doc would draw his concealed sword and drive it through Captain Oracle's heart.

"AGAIN!" THE MEN IN the mess shouted and clapped. "Again!"

Doc held up a hand. "Dear shipmates, I beg of you, let an old man break his fast."

"Let him eat!" Hardstone bellowed. "He's sung it seven times already!"

Ryan smiled wearily. Doc had indeed sung it seven times already. Doc was dealing with a crew that was mostly illiterate, but most of his watch mates could now sing his abridged version of *The Sailor's Alphabet* by heart. Onetongue shoved a wooden stoop of small beer into Doc's hand. Doc sighed happily. "Bless your heart, Mr. Onetongue."

Onetongue drooled happily. "Welcome!"

Ryan regarded his messmate. The man was bald, bat-eared and blubbery. However, Ryan recalled the terrible strength of Onetongue's arms as he'd simultaneous drugged him and choked him unconscious. "Onetongue."

The sailor regarded Ryan warily. "Yup?"

"That's an interesting handle."

"Oh! I u'thed to have two tongue'th! But the previouth cap'n couldn't stand my thlobbering and thtuttering so he cut one out! Now I th'peak real good! Thep't for the lith'p."

Doc sipped his small beer and lime with relish. "In my circles, and in several languages, a lisp was considered a sign of refinement."

Onetongue beamed happily and pointed an accusing finger at Wipe. "Th'ee!"

Ryan had no desire whatsoever to discover the origin of Mr. Wipe's appellation. Doc took a seat across from Ryan between the twins. They were young and wiry topmen with skin burned brown and hair bleached blond. These same young men who had gleefully seized Doc into the shrouds had, like most of the crew, done a complete one-eighty and now doted on him.

Doc had been entered in the log as Captain's Manservant until signed or proved otherwise. He still messed and slept with the crew. Doc stared sadly at the stew Wipe ladled him from the kid. Ryan nodded in agreement as he mechanically shoveled the food down. It was chipped dried meat, dried peas and dried plantains boiled into a viscous mass. The job of cook had fallen by default to Mr. Forgiven, and forgiven he was most certainly not. Suggestions of how Forgiven might be tortured and murdered for his culinary crimes grew in imagination and severity with every meal. His unofficial name aboard ship was now Unforgiven, and he hardly dared to show his face belowdecks.

Doc reached into his frock coat. His kerchief was wrapped like a parcel, and he unwrapped it to reveal a decidedly runny, fist-sized wheel of cheese.

Onetongue sighed. "Chee'th!" Atlast looked at it lovingly. "Oh, a tidbit from the captain's table! You're the lucky monkey, Doc, aren't you, then?"

"Our good captain declared it past its prime." Doc pushed it toward Atlast. "Dear shipmate, would you take your knife and cut each man among us a portion? A good sailing man must share with his messmates."

"Oh indeed, and thankee!" Atlast drew his knife and began dividing the dilapidated cheese into eighths with geometric precision.

Doc spoke low. "Ryan, I fear for our young friend Ricky."

Ryan kept his face neutral. "Manrape."

"The same."

"What've you heard, Doc?"

"As you may have surmised, Manrape is not our esteemed bosun's given name. Like many aboard this ship, his moniker was earned."

"Got that feeling the moment I met him."

"Well, the word about ship is he plans to press the matter of his affections upon young Ricky once the boy is rated able up in the rigging and next time ashore. Ricky is no acrobat upon the yards like dear Jak, but he has taken serving this ship well to heart. He is young and quick and learns his new trade well. Sad to say his speedy grasp of hand and reef only sends him ever more swiftly into Mr. Manrape's most untender—" Doc made a face "—embraces."

"You've got the captain's ear. There's nothing you can do?"

Doc flinched. "I did broach the subject."

"And?"

Doc stopped short of going pale. "The good captain told me sailors settle these matters among themselves, and just from his demeanor I received the strongest impression not to broach that or any other ship's subject with him without being asked first ever again."

"The commander?" Ryan suggested. "I saw you talking with him."

"He seemed to find the subject quite distasteful, but when I pressed him he said that 'a buggered boy can do his duty as well as any other man.'" Doc shook his head and ate a spoon of stew. "The first mate is another man not to be pressed lightly."

Atlast handed out slices of cheese. "Too right."

"Ryan, I have read this ship's creed and code. No sailor may lay his hand upon a shipmate aboard ship in anger without provocation. Should he, the lashing is to equal the damage inflicted. Should a sailor murder his shipmate aboard ship, it is death, the nature of execution to depend on the circumstances of the crime and the local availability of materials. Ryan, I tell you, some of the proscribed methods stop nothing short of the Roman Circus."

Ryan didn't know what the Roman Circus was, but he got the gist. He grasped at straws.

"Manrape seems sweet on you, Doc. Not like Ricky, but you've got no influence?"

"I have considered it, and Mr. Manrape's entire demeanor toward me has changed since I sang from the shrouds. Indeed, he has become genuinely solicitous of my welfare.

Yet, were I to demand he leave our Ricky alone, I fear he would insist that I make him." Doc stared deeply into his stew. "Shall I make him?"

Throughout the mess men drank their small beer, swore about their stew between mouthfuls, laughed, joked, smoked and took the few pleasures sailors had in their free time. Ryan's mess table went silent. None of Ryan's and Doc's messmates had seen Doc in battle with blaster or sword. None knew how dangerous the man from the past was once he set himself upon the path of violence. All they saw was an old man who had gone from a figure of fun and torture turned into an exotic and lucky ship's mascot. Hardstone spoke low and slow as he smeared his cheese across a piece of bread with his knife. "Ryan, tell Doc to stand down."

"What if I kill him?" Ryan asked. "On shore."

Doc was aghast. "Dear Ryan, I beg of you, as a friend, do not even think of it!"

Hardstone grunted around his food. "Listen to your friend, Ryan."

"Mr. Manrape, whatever his proclivities, has risen to the rank of bosun," Doc continued. "In my day a bosun was an able sailor and responsible for overseeing nearly every part of the day-to-day running of the ship. We had a saying that it was sergeants who made an army run. Bosuns run a ship. Good ones are invaluable, and the *Glory* is short-handed. The crew will hate you for it. As bosun, Manrape also has many allies and associates aboard. They would surely seek your demise, and many of our dear companions would suffer by association."

"Listen to your friend," Hardstone repeated.

"Manrape is the worst of us, and the best," Atlast said as he savored his cheese. "Knows the ship from stem to stern, he does."

Onetongue slobbered around his mutated and shorn soft palate. "Taught me all I know about th'ips! Th'aved my life more than one'th!"

Wipe sighed. "Beautiful speaking voice."

Hardstone contemplated his small beer. "Ryan?"

"Yeah?"

"We're messmates, and I like you."

"Glad to hear it."

"I was a sec man before I was a sailor, a Deathlands man, like you."

Ryan nodded. "It shows."

Hardstone nodded his thanks. "Some then, well as now, thought me a hard man, but save for the Captain himself, there is no better fighter aboard the *Glory* than Manrape. You've seen my gimp. We'd recently lost a bos'n. Many thought I should be given the post. Manrape was up and coming and challenged me for it. We both had our fair share of supporters. So, Manrape and I rowed the dinghy ashore one soft, fine morning and decided it between us."

"Hard way to decide rank on a ship." Ryan frowned. "The captain allowed that?"

Hardstone sighed bitterly. "There wasn't too much to choose between us as able sailors. Bos'n is the first man in a boarding action and stands at the captain's side if boarded. It had to be settled." Hardstone stared into his warm, weak beer. "And he's bos'n now, and I'll never go into the tops again. And I'll tell you what else, Ryan. Manrape's dark night itself in a fight. Even with all your Deathlands steel in hand, I'd bet no bounty upon you."

"I appreciate your honesty." Ryan read the writing on the wall. "Ricky's going to have to stand for himself."

"That is the way of it," Hardstone agreed.

Atlast tucked back into his stew. "Aye."

Chapter Five

Ryan stood deck watch. A moderate attempt had been made to work him to death the previous day, and he had been given light duty to recover. He had not been sent to the med, but he'd been issued a small jar of foul-smelling liniment. A tiny scrap of paper with Mildred's handwriting said, "Use it!" He'd been reissued his own Navy long-eyes and had spent his watch walking the rails surveying the sea and occasionally reporting to Miss Loral that there was nothing to report while his shipmates muttered envious insults about Deathlanders and their land-lubbing, weakling ways and needs.

Ryan snapped the optic shut as dusk began to fall. The ship's bell rang the hour. He took a deep breath as the evening breeze ruffled his hair. He was still stiff and sore from the beatings and hard labor. He was sunburned and smelled like a rottie, his hands and feet were raw meat and he was eating food barely fit for man or mutie.

But Ryan felt surprisingly good.

He looked down at the rad counter pinned to the open neck of his jersey. The air here on the outer edge of the Caribbean barely registered a rad. Ryan took the dipper from the water barrel and drank. One of the twins shot down a shroud so fast Ryan couldn't fathom how he didn't burn his palms off. He plunked down on the rail with perfect alacrity.

"Hard work, Ryan? Walking the deck like a baron in his ville? Feeling a bit parched?"

Ryan sighed, drank water and waited for it.

"You know, Ryan, Purser Forgiven is kinda fond of me."

"And?"

The topsman grinned. "And I could requisition you a nice silk pillow from the captain's cabin. You could rest your gaudy soft little Deathlands hands on it. Mebbe have Wipe hold your cock for you when you step to the siphon."

Nearby crewmen laughed.

Ryan held out the dipper. "If I cared, Born. If I even cared at all."

"Yeah, you'd chill me. Whatever." The twin grinned and drank. "By the way, if you want to chill Born, which I recommend highly, he's over there."

Ryan turned to see the other twin grinning and waving from the opposite rail. The one-eyed man waved back. "Naw. If I wanted to chill Mr. Born, I'd chill the bastard right in front of me."

The correctly identified twin started backward and grabbed for a shroud as he nearly fell overboard. "Nuke-storm it! For a man with only one eye, you don't miss much!"

The twin called out to his brother. "BeGood! Ryan wants to chill you with his soft, Deathlands..." Born trailed off. His brother was gone. He shot his gaze back up into the rigging.

"Ahoy! Topmen!" Born called. "Anyone seen my triple stupe brother—"

"Man overboard!" Ryan roared. He vaulted barrels, coils of rope and an open hatch as he ripped off his shirt.

Crewmen shouted in alarm. "Who? Where away?"

"My brother, BeGood!" Born bawled. "Off the starboard rail!"

Miss Loral stepped in Ryan's path. "Belay that, Ryan!" He skid to a halt with a snarl and restrained himself from throwing the woman in after BeGood. Miss Loral sensed the danger she was in. "Last swim you'll ever take, Mr. Ryan! Don't do it!"

"Barrel and a line!" Commander Miles bellowed. Onetongue and Atlast secured a line around an empty cask and sent it over the side. The barrel landed in the purple water with a splash and bobbed forlornly in the *Glory's* bow wake, paying out line and swiftly disappearing into the gloom. The crew shouted into the gathering dark, "BeGood! BeGood!"

Gypsyfair screamed out of all relation to her size. "Shut up!"

The crew shut up while the little mutant cupped her hands behind her ears and turned her head slowly, clicking like the second hand on a chron. Her shoulders sagged. "Nothing above water, nothing within my range."

The waters didn't stir. Oracle rasped from the quarterdeck, "I admire your sense of duty toward your messmate, Mr. Ryan. I know not what the waters are like where you come from, but no one swims here without a spear in hand, a bright sun above, clear water below and many mates fool enough to muster to him." The crew scanned the murk and muttered in loss and agreement. Born fell to his knees, howling and pulling his hair.

Oracle continued. "Dusk has fallen. The night feeders rise from the depths. Mr. BeGood has fallen down among them."

"No one heard him yell," Ryan countered. "No one heard a splash."

The entire crew on deck and above looked at Ryan in shock at his challenge to the captain.

"Ryan's right," Gypsyfair agreed. "I didn't hear nothing until Ryan and Born shouted, and I hear everything."

Born ceased his howling. "My brother is a first-rate

top man! He don't fall from no rad-blasted rail in calm water! Much less without a sound! If he did, he'd have been laughing!"

Ryan put his hand on the rail where BeGood had sat grinning at him moments before. It was dripping wet, as if BeGood had already been soaked before he had fallen. "Captain, BeGood didn't fall. Something rose up to the rail and took him."

Oracle's voice rose from his breaking slate rasp to a landslide. "Beat to quarters! All hands on deck! Prepare to repel boarders!" The drum beat to quarters. Shouts and footfalls echoed below. "Sharpshooters, top men! Look alive! Watch below, report to the armory! I want every lantern lit and—"

Screaming broke out on the blaster deck below Ryan's feet.

The one-eyed man didn't wait for orders. "Watch the starboard rail!" Ryan drew his knife and his marlinspike and ran portside. In the pale glow of the ship's lanterns, Ryan saw man-sized, gray octopods climbing up the side of the hull. Crewmen boiled on deck armed with swords, war clubs, axes and butchering implements of every description. Far too few had blasters. Ryan had heard the crew had expended far too much of their ammo in the last battle with no hope of replacement soon, and they were saving their black powder for their cannons. The one-eyed warrior vainly yearned for his Scout, his SIG and his panga, but no one was hustling him his weapons. Ryan hefted his knife and spike in each hand and waited for the creatures suckering their way toward him. He counted more than two dozen. "Sharpshooters! The sides!"

Blasterfire crackled and popped from the tops, but it was far too slow and sporadic. Two of the eight-armed muties burst as high-powered longblasters exploded their

soft heads, but Ryan knew the shooters in the tops of the
three masts were trying to cover port and starboard as well
as bow and stern. Goulash shoved in shoulder to shoulder with Ryan, brandishing a beautiful, filigreed hunting
sword and a double-barreled scattergun sawn down into
a handblaster. He leaned out over the rail and pulled one
trigger and then another. Two octopods smeared off the
hull in riddled ruins. The Hungarian waved the swiftly
creeping creatures upward. "Ha! Come then!"

"Goulash, get the hell back from the rail! Reload!"

An octopod launched out of the water like a rocket.
It shot up level with the rail, and Goulash screamed and
thrust his sword. His attack was instantly entangled as two
arms wrapped around his wrist and elbow. His sword clattered to the deck as an arm cinched around his neck and
squeezed. Ryan lunged, but the creature simply fell away
before his attack and let its weight pull Goulash over the
rail. The Hungarian fell gasping and struggling into the
dark sea below wrapped in the octopod's embrace.

Ryan knew in an instant that the good ship *Glory* was
not being boarded and taken. Her crew was being harvested. The silent night creep ended. Octopods shot up out
of the water like an artillery barrage and hit the rails in
full assault. There were scores of them, not counting the
ones that had attacked through the blaster hatches below.
Gypsyfair screamed and brandished her knife as an octopod pulled itself over the rail and rose. Ryan had seen
squids and octopuses before. Out of the water their bone-
less bodies had no buoyancy or leverage and were reduced
to creeping and pulling themselves along by muscular con-
traction. This octopod suddenly stood up straight, using
its eight arms like legs. It shot out an arm and snatched
the blind mutant's knife out of her hands.

Ryan wound up and threw.

A marlinspike was a poor throwing weapon at best, but the half pound of iron revolved twice and slammed into the octopod's head-body and rippled its gray flesh. Light strobed across its body in bizarre flashes, and it turned on its attacker.

Ryan had seen battle with man and mutie in every corner of the Deathlands as well as in some of the farthest flung corners of the nukecausted world. He didn't flinch as the octopod ran toward him across the deck, seven feet tall on its eight arms with horrible shuffling speed. Ryan held his knife low and charged. He collided with the mutant octopus and hurled his left shoulder into the creature. It rocked back beneath the force of meeting its adversary's frame, but its suckers gripped the deck and arms instantly snaked around Ryan's limbs. Toothed suckers bit through his pants and directly into his bare flesh.

Ryan slashed, but it was like stabbing a stickie. His blade barely cut the thick, rubbery flesh, and in an instant a suckered arm constricted around his biceps while three others wound around him. The creature was using four arms to stand on and four to control Ryan. The contractile power of the octopod's arms was sickening. Ryan stared into its golden, alien, rectangular eyes and knew he going to board the last train west. The webbing between the mutie's forward arms flopped up and its head tilted back. It opened the underside of its body like a flower and a dark parrot beak twice the size of a human fist prolapsed out and opened. The arm around his biceps twisted and turned his blade away. The other three arms pulled him in.

Doc appeared out of nowhere.

He stalked across *Glory*'s deck like an avenging scarecrow with his sword unsheathed. The creature holding Ryan paused and one of its eyes bulged and watched Doc lunge and lance an oncoming octopod between its alien optical organs. Doc's opponent shuddered, released black ink like a chilled man releasing his bowels and instantly went limp.

"Between the eyes!" Doc's voice rose to operatic heights. "Shipmates, slash not! A swift thrust or a sharp blow, but between the eyes or not at all! That is where you shall find their brain!"

Ryan managed to twist in the cold, horrid, sucking grip. He felt the horrible beak scrape against his stomach, but its curved slick surface slid snapping across the plates of his stomach muscle. His blade was out of position to stab, so he desperately slammed the knife's handle down between the octopod's eyes. It was a weak blow, nearly all forearm, but the octopod's protruding eyes squeezed shut and re-tracted into its head. The grip of every arm encumbering Ryan weakened, and the creature sagged. Ryan felt the mainmast against his back, and he put a foot against it and reared up. He put all of his weight behind it as he snapped his head forward and butted the octopus between the eyes.

Every suction cup released at once and the octopod slimed off of Ryan to flop shuddering to the deck. Ryan scooped up Goulash's fallen sword. It was short, heavy, curved and not particularly well balanced. The thick blade had been designed for sliding around bones and penetrat-ing deep to finish off downed big game. It would do for octopod between-the-eyes butchery.

Atlast screamed and screamed. He lay on the deck hold-ing an octopod aloft with both arms and legs. The octo-pod had all eight arms suctioned against the deck and it inexorably contracted down, beak snapping to crush his skull. Its golden eyes snapped up just in time to see Ryan round on it.

The one-eyed man turned his wrist as he lunged the blade between the octopod's eyes up to the hilt. Atlast screamed as the creature belched a bucket of ink on him, went limp between his limbs and collapsed on top of him. Ryan ripped his sword free. Three octopods charged him, scuttling on the tips of their suckered arms. He heard the pop of Mildred's target revolver, and one of the aquatic mutants dropped, dripping ichor between its optical organs. A silver pinwheel of steel revolved over Ryan's shoulder and Jak's ship's knife sank into cephalopod ganglia and dropped it. The remaining octopod took a look at Ryan as he charged and turned toward the rail.

It met Captain Oracle.

Oracle rammed his orange-furred prosthesis between its eyes up to the wrist. He twisted and yanked the paw free with hooked brains, guts and multiple hearts trailing between the silver claws. Manrape knelt above another, driving his fist between its eyes like a piston. Doc skewered one, and octopods convulsed and fell from stem to the stern as the crew counterattacked with a vengeance and scores of armed crewmen boiled out of the hatches like angry ants. The skin of the remaining octopods rippled and flashed like strobes.

Ryan's teeth flashed in the dark as he heard J.B.'s Uzi blasting tight bursts belowdecks. The octopods with crewmen prey released them, and they all began hurling themselves over the rails. Ryan heard splashes as others belowdecks ejected from the blasterports. Ryan lowered his sword. The octo-muties had come to feed, and the food had fought back with far too much vigor for their taste. Wounded crewmen lay in lakes of blood and ink, twisting and screaming from tentacle tearings and beak bites.

Doc shook blood and ink from his blade. "Captain! All known species of octopus are poisonous! Like spiders, many are not dangerous to man, but this species is unlike any I have ever seen."

"Wounded to the med!" Mildred shouted like she was in surgery. "Tell Bonesaw to administer any antivenin we have!"

Crewmen gathered up their blood- and ink-stained companions. The dead octopods and their ink were already starting to smell like a rottie attack. "Miss Loral," Oracle grated. "I want a death and damage report ASAP! Commander, I want any sail set that can catch a wind!"

"Aye, Captain!" Miles wiped ink from a Japanese *wakizashi* short sword. "What course?"

"Due east, Commander! I want good, deep Lantic beneath us, without a spec of land, rock or reef on the horizon within the hour."

"Aye, Captain!"

"Mr. Manrape, have the waisters get this filth off my deck."

"You heard the captain, Hardstone!" Manrape shouted. "Get this squid filth overboard! I don't want to see a spec of blood or a drop of ink on this deck come the light of dawn!"

Crewmen ran to the jobs and stations.

"Ryan!" Gypsyfair screamed and clicked and pointed at the deck. "There! There! There!"

Ryan stared at a pile of cordage in the glow of the ship's lantern. The cordage had not been there before and was just a few feet away from where he had dropped his first octopod opponent with a head butt. "Watch the decks for anything out of place!" Ryan shouted. "The rad-blasted things can camo!" Ryan rounded on the pile of cordage with his sword before him. The pile of cordage rippled and changed color. The octopod tried to rise but seemed strong enough to only get three arms beneath it. It reeled like a drunk before Ryan in retreat. The one-eyed man raised his sword for the killing thrust. The octopod's siphon suddenly contracted and Ryan recoiled as a liter of stinking black ink hit him under high pressure. "Fireblast..."

Crewmen charged in from all directions, brandishing blades, and cut off the creature from Ryan and the rail. Its camouflage flashed off, and the octopod returned to its normal slick-gray color. The golden eyes bulged outward in two directions as the seamen advanced. The octopod flopped headfirst into the water barrel and crossed its eight arms above it in defense. Half a dozen of the crew closed in for the kill.

"Gypsyfair!" Oracle called. "Sweep the decks, stem to stern! Boarding pike and blaster men to her!" Gypsyfair began echolocating the deck surrounded by a phalanx of blasters and sharpened steel.

"Lover!" Ryan turned as Krysty flung herself into his arms. She kissed him for long moments and then leaned back. She surveyed his sucker-torn, ink-stained face and torso. "You look like you just got thumped by stickies, and you smell like they pushed you down a pest-hole privy."

Ryan's teeth flashed through the ink covering his face. "I love the way you sweet talk me after we've been separated."

Fresh shouting broke out. "Kill the thing!" "You kill it!" "I'm not getting within reach of it!"

Ryan hefted his sword. Krysty took his six with her blaster as they approached the armed crowd surrounding the water barrel. The octopod's head was at the bottom, and its arms roiled like a snake mating ball at the surface. No one wanted to get close to it.

"Get Gallondrunk!" Sweet Marie shouted. "He'll pin that squid in the barrel stem to stern with that walrus lance of his! Then we chop it up proper!"

This suggestion was met with great enthusiasm.

"Belay that!" Oracle ordered. The crew parted before

him. "Mr. Manrape, I want a section of grating lashed to the top of that barrel. Put a guard on it. And get Boiler and Skillet out of the med and into the galley. They've been nursing their wounds long enough."

Manrape looked quizzical for the first time in Ryan's experience. "Aye, Captain."

"That beast is a hundred kilos if it's an ounce, and our stores are spoiling. We need meat if we are going to make it across the 'Quator."

The crew seemed pleased with the idea, and men and women began whispering about calamari and the delights of Brazil.

Oracle turned back for the quarterdeck. "And Mr. Forgiven could use some fresh ink. Speaking of which, Purser, rate Mr. Ryan ordinary seaman."

Chapter Six

J.B. worked. The good ship *Glory* was short on blasters. The majority of the weapons in the armory were typical, home-rolled, break-open, single-shot longblasters and pistols. The *Glory* had standardized on .45 caliber, and they had molds and enough lead to make thousands of bullets, and they could fire black powder or smokeless with equal facility. They punched primers out of predark coins that could be found anywhere.

Cases were the main problem. They had no machinery on board to extrude scavenged brass or aluminum. Smithy had to do it by hand. They were saving and reloading old cases, and by the buckets of split cases at J.B.'s feet some had been reused far too many times than was safe. The sharpshooters in the tops had assiduously cared for predark hunting longblasters of .308 and 30-06 caliber. Reloading them was even more problematic. A number of the crew had personally acquired arms taken as booty or acquired otherwise, which were stored in the blaster room, but most of those had but a handful of shells left to them after the last battle.

What they also had was several crates of blasters in various states of disrepair that were beyond Gunny's knowledge or ability to fix. They kept those to sell for their parts in ports of call. J.B. liked Gunny, and Gunny liked him. They were men of similar minds. Unfortunately, what Gunny most understood was black powder and muzzle-loading cannons. Between him and Smithy, they could produce the simple springs, hinges and screws to keep the primitive blasters serviceable. The gas systems, trigger groups and bolt assemblies of predark semi-automatic blasters and assault weapons were beyond their skill.

They were not beyond J.B.'s.

The Armorer had disassembled every last waste weapon, made a list of things he felt Smithy could handle, requisitioned his tool kit and gone to work. If J.B. hadn't liked Gunny already as a brother armorer, the fact that Gunny didn't pull rank but instead watched with awe, asked intelligent questions and eagerly helped in whatever capacity he could won J.B.'s admiration. J.B. finally rose from the worktable and nearly hit his head on the low deck beam above. He sat back down and checked his chron. They had been at it for eleven hours straight. He and Gunny had cannibalized ten broken and corroded AKs and produced two that might function through another battle or two, though they only had enough ammo for slightly less than a mag each. Six M-16s had produced one working longblaster. Strangely enough they had nearly a case of 5.56 mm ammo but only one serviceable magazine. Several scatterguns and a few handblasters were now also in temporary working order.

Gunny shook his head in delight at the bonanza of working blasters. "Oh, that shines, J.B.!"

The Armorer stretched. He sighed as he felt familiar strong hands start to knead his shoulders. Mildred spoke low from behind him. "Hey."

He looked up and smiled at her. "Hey."

"How's it going?"

"Did some good work today."

Mildred smiled indulgently at the gleaming weapons. "I can see that."

"How's it in the med?" J.B. asked. He'd heard the screaming all through the night.

Mildred's face went tight. "Doc was right. The octopods were poisonous. Whatever Bonesaw's using for antivenin might work on snakes, but no one bit last night lived. We lost fifteen. The sucker wounds were ugly and prolific. Ryan's covered with them, but none are deep and none are going septic."

"How you and Bonesaw getting along?"

"Well, first off, the ship's healer is named Bonesaw. That tells you something right there."

"Bad?"

Mildred made a grudging noise. "He can plug a bullet hole. His sewing isn't bad, and he's actually pretty good at setting bones. Those octopus arms snapped a few. He's got some interesting herbals going on, but…"

J.B. knew Mildred well. "But that's not what's bothering you."

"Bonesaw knows I'm more than just a healer."

Gunny smirked. "Everyone does."

J.B. knew everyone knew too. One of the problems the companions had was that just about any group they met who learned of Mildred's talents were reluctant to let her go, some violently so. "You got a little bossy about the wounded up top."

"Yeah, well there's this Hippocratic Oath thing of mine, J.B. Just isn't made for this brave new world of yours."

"How's Jak, Ricky?"

Mildred made a face. "Jak's fine."

J.B. let out a long breath. "Ricky?"

Mildred's face twisted into an expression the Armorer was genuinely afraid of. "Bad enough the ship's healer's name is Bonesaw! But the bosun's name is Manrape. J.B., the kid's ass is on the line and you better do something!"

J.B. looked Gunny in the eye. He hated asking for favors, but he asked now. "Ricky's an armorer, not as good as me but better than you, and he's an accomplished machinist. This ship needs him."

"And he's becoming an able top man," Gunny replied. "He can do all three wearing a dress."

J.B. stopped just short of reaching for the closest loaded blaster. "I can steal ten blasters while you're cleaning your monocle. I'll cut Manrape to shreds."

"And you can't imagine what will be done to you, but you can imagine Mildred weeping while she watches."

"YOU'D LET THAT HAPPEN?"

"You've seen Manrape. Have you known anyone so fast? Anyone so strong? He is a demigod among us and a demon in battle."

J.B. had met several demigods and demons, self-professed and otherwise. Manrape was admittedly something of a juggernaut

"This ship is in trouble, matey. When the final battle comes, we'll need him more than you and all your lot put together." Gunny looked away. "Sacrifices have to be made, mebbe."

Mildred pleaded. "J.B.!"

"The officers, do they keep their weapons separate?"

Gunny nodded. "Aye, they do."

"Tell the captain I want to strip, clean, polish and tune every one of them, and tell him I need to requisition Ricky for it while you and I go over the cannons."

"Aye." Gunny chewed at his mustache. "I can do that. It will just prolong things, but it will give Ricky a few days' respite. Can't imagine the cap'n saying no."

"Thanks."

Mildred looked close to tears. "Thanks, J.B."

"I should've thought of it earlier."

"A few days' respite, then what?"

J.B. rose and set his fedora on his head. He almost took Mildred's hand but looked at the grease and grime covering his. Mildred smiled and took his hand anyway. "There's some soap in the med. Why don't I wash those for you before you start touching me?"

J.B. liked the idea of Mildred washing his hands very much, and touching her more, but his mind was still fixed on the problem at hand, and that was keeping Ricky's rear contact point water tight. He nodded to himself.

"I'll talk to Doc tomorrow. Talk to him about this creed and code."

Doc took his morning walk around the ship. He felt mostly recovered from his fit and being seized to the shrouds. Crewmen hailed him from the rigging. Those busy at their labors nodded and smiled. Those with a free hand patted him solicitously like he was a beloved child. Doc smiled, tipped his swordstick or exchanged a few pleasant words with his shipmates as he passed.

He took the gangway down to blaster deck and walked forward. He stopped by the galley. Boiler and Skillet stood at the octopus barrel and the cookfire, respectively, engaged in hot debate. Boiler was a big, florid man with a huge gut that bespoke he liked sampling his own wares early and often. He wore a bandage around his head from the wound and concussion he'd suffered in the ship's previous battle. Skillet was a lanky black man whose wildly beaded hair would give Mildred a run for her money. His left arm was in a sling. The cooks were very grumpy about being ousted from the med.

"Well, how would you cook it?" Skillet snarled.

Doc peered into the barrel from a prudent distance.

The octopod's great, gray head pressed against the section of iron grate nailed to the top of the barrel. Doc noted the barrel had been bolted to the deck. He also noted the creature's rectangular, horizontal pupils flicking back and forth between the two cooks.

Boiler stared into the barrel and pointed his butcher knife at the cephalopod. His postapocalyptic English accent was even thicker than Atlast's. "Well, I've cooked flying squids right proper, then! Haven't I?"

"Flying squids is small! This one's huge!" Skillet waved his cleaver in protest. "You cut that thing into calamari rings and fry it? All you'll have is two hundred pounds of rad-blasted rubber! It'll be mutiny after what Forgiven's been servin'!"

"Peels it, pounds it, and simmers it soft. That's what the Greek always said about fish with arms! I say we peel that gray skin off and simmer it succulent!"

Doc watched with great interest as the octopod's pupils slammed open like a cat's eyes in the dark at the announcement. Skillet scratched his assiduously cultivated beard at the thought. "Might work. Might use some slush from the morning salt pork to give it some flavor."

Boiler spread his arms to the deck above happily. "And now he's cooking, then!"

The octopus shuddered.

"And pepper," Skillet decreed. "Lots of pepper."

"Excuse me," Doc said.

The octopod flicked a glance at Doc and then went back to devoting one eye each to the cooks. The octopus's arms contracted around the bars confining it. To Doc's eyes it seemed much like a man going white-knuckled at his sentencing. Doc loosened the hilt of his swordstick and leaned perilously close to the barrel. "Forgive me."

"Nothing to forgive, Doc." Skillet waved his cleaver in

warning. "But I wouldn't get too close. Rad-blasted squid tried to walk off last night with its arms through the grate. Nearly took the barrel with it."

Boiler nodded. "Which is why we nailed it down, then, isn't it?"

Doc peered at the alien eyes regarding Boiler and Skillet simultaneously. "Forgive me, good Skillet, but when I first said forgive me, I was speaking to your captive." The cooks gave each other looks. Doc's peculiar behavior was already a high source of humor and discussion aboard. The fact that Doc wanted to talk to dinner would earn both men wide-eyed attention at mess. The octopod eyes snapped to center to regard Doc in binocular vision.

Doc bowed slightly. "I say again, forgive me, for I am an icthyologist by training rather than a teuthologist, but am I correct in my assumption that you understand human speech?"

The creature in the barrel pressed the top of its huge head against the grate. It ejected water from its siphon and sucked in air, and then the tube vibrated and let forth a sibilant hiss. "Yes."

Boiler screamed. Skillet flailed backward and nearly sat in the cook fire. Nearby crewmen shouted in alarm. The two cooks brandished butcher knives and cleavers. Doc could not contain himself. "By my stars and garters!"

Ryan appeared at Doc's side with his knife in hand. He kept a wary eye on his erstwhile, eight-armed opponent. "Doc, take a step or two back."

Doc was utterly focused on the octopus. "How, pray tell?"

The octopod's speech sounded like a snake gargling, but it was oddly very clear. "We learned."

"From whom?"

"From humans."

Doc pondered this fascinating development as crewmen gathered around brandishing marlinspikes, knives and tools. Other crewmen ran bawling for the officers and the captain. "Why would humans teach you speech?" Doc asked.

"They modified us. They wished to use us as weapons."

"What happened?"

"The war happened," the octopus replied.

"What happened to the humans who taught you?"

"We ate them."

The crowd erupted.

"Sky fire!"

"Kill the fucking thing!"

"Captain!"

The octopus shuddered under the verbal barrage but kept its alien gaze locked on Doc. "That was many generations ago." The alien voice seemed almost plaintive. "I have not eaten a human in months."

"Fry the squid in crumbs!"

"I haven't had calamari in months!"

"Captain on deck!" Commander Miles bawled. The crew parted like water as the captain strode through them. Oracle took in the scene of Doc and the two cooks. "What goes on here?"

"Oh, Captain!" Boiler was genuinely upset. "I ain't cooking nuffing that talks! Am I, then? Much less eating it!"

Skillet pointed his cleaver at the barrel. "Squid can talk, Cap'n."

Oracle's face went blank.

Ryan nodded. "Doc's interrogating it."

The crew on the blaster deck held its breath. Oracle nodded curtly. "Carry on."

"Thank you, Captain."

Doc continued. "So you and your species continue to teach yourselves human language generation to generation?"

"Yes," the octopod stated.

"Why?"

"It is useful."

"For what?"

"Survival."

As a man who had studied ichthyology, the prospect of a sea creature he could converse with humans intelligently was almost more than Doc's soul could bear. "If I implore the captain to spare you, would you promise not to do harm to any member of this ship?"

The crew erupted in anger.

"Quiet in the captain's presence!" Miles bawled.

"Yes," the octopus replied.

Oracle addressed his prisoner. "You and your brethren attacked us."

"We were hungry."

"My crew is hungry," Oracle countered. The octopod recoiled.

Oracle continued. "How are you to be trusted?"

The creature spent long moments staring. "To my knowledge no cephalopod has ever told a lie."

Doc straightened. "I believe him."

For all his mass, Boiler's voice rose to a childlike shriek. "It will crunch our skulls like snails, won't it? Eating our poor brains and then be slinking over the rail in the night, then!"

The octopod kept its golden, rectangular gaze on Oracle. "I am without my brethren. I am far from home. I am a coastal animal. I could not swim from the open ocean to the littoral waters without being eaten. I could not swim all the way back to the Caribbean without exhausting myself and dying before the breeding season. I will not desert this ship until it returns to the Caribbean, and only then if given permission." The eyes of the crew on deck snapped back and forth between their captain and the octopod in the barrel. "I give you my word I will not eat any member of the crew under any circumstances."

"Other than serving as a source of intellectual intrigue for Doc—" Oracle's sharklike eyes met the inhuman gaze of the cephalopod "—how would you serve this ship and your fellow crew members?"

The genetically engineered cephalopod spoke by rote. "Coastal infiltration and observation. Underwater demolition. Clandestine shipboard and port facility kidnapping and assassination." The octopod's eyes flicked about the crowd. "Any task requiring an anthropoid crewman to go into the water, or beneath the hull, I can perform with greater alacrity or be of great assistance. You have a significant mass of seaweed clinging to the bottom of your hull. I can begin removing it immediately and subsist on the barnacles infesting the bottom for at least a week."

The crew stared in shock and awe at their potential non-humanoid shipmate.

"Mr. Forgiven!" Oracle rasped.

The purser waddled forward. "Yes, Captain!"

"Sign Mr. Squid into the book and remove the grating. Unbolt the barrel and take it up top someplace out of the way and bolt it down again. Let that be his bunk, and see that it is filled with fresh seawater every other watch."

Dumbfounded mutters rippled through the crew. Forgiven's fat jowls worked in shock as he opened the book and his pen hovered over an empty line. "And rate him…?"

Oracle turned his flat black stare upon Doc. "How should Mr. Squid be rated?"

Doc spoke without hesitation. "Specialist, subaqueous."

Forgiven's pen drooped. "Sub, aquee...?"

"Ship's dictionary," Oracle advised.

The captain's voice dropped. "Doc, you are responsible."

"Aye, Captain!" Doc enthused.

Forgiven jumped as a seven-foot suckered arm snaked out of the barrel, took the pen from his hand and signed Mr. Squid on the line. The purser shook as he took the proffered pen back and the arm retreated back into the barrel. "Very good, Captain. Mr. Squid, sub-aqueest, specialist...signed."

Chapter Seven

The Caribbean

Captain Emmanuel "Black" Sabbath stood on the incredibly high stern of his ocean-going junk *Ironman* and watched the island ville burn. Despite the Caribbean summer heat he wore a black frock coat, black knee breeches and hose, along with a wide-brimmed black cockle hat with a silver buckle. At his hip he carried a hooked cane knife. He drummed long fingers on the worn rosewood hilt in meditation. "Oracle's not here."

Blue snarled and tapped the little island on her chart. She didn't like being wrong. "He'd have to have come here! This is the only ville with a ropewalk within range. Much less manioc fields, a sawmill and a pig farm. He has to resupply."

Sabbath glanced at his daughter. Blue was pretty, black haired, and would have been beautiful like her mother except that visible blue capillaries formed a delicate, spider-web tracery beneath every visible inch of her skin. She wore black as was the custom of many ship's captains in this age, but her blouse and breeches were deliberately cut to hug her slender curves. Her logic was flawless. The burning ville would have been the last chance to take on cordage, lumber and salted meat and fish while allowing a window of escape. The smoke rising into the sky and the recently cleaned blade at Sabbath's hip had determined the *Glory* had not come into port. "And yet he is not here, nor has he been."

"And we know why." Sabbath's son, Dorian, lolled against the taff rail. His giant, brass and ivory-handled butterfly knife made lazy, flashing figure eights in the morning sunlight. Open, the weapon was thirty inches long and was a short two-handed sword. Closed, the double handles served as his baton of office. He was tall and rangy like his father and had his mother's good looks in masculine form without the mutations. Dorian tossed his black, unbound hair contemptuously. "Oracle's gone all doomie again."

If Blue were a cat, she would have arched her back and hissed. She was a pure sailor, one of the best, and believed in little besides winds, tides, a well-oiled blaster and sharp steel. Despite being a mutant herself she had no use for prophecy or mutie visions.

Sabbath knew better.

He turned to his astrologer. "Oracle's not here."

Ae Sook was beautiful, Korean, and when Sabbath had taken the junk years ago she had come with it. Her manicured, gaudy-red nails tapped the intricate brass astrolabe in her lap. Skydark had broken the world and compasses were often unreliable given the rampant electromagnetic anomalies, much less the irritating habit of the poles themselves to wander. Nevertheless, despite the poor, broken and battered Earth's condition, the stars still looked down on her from their fixed positions and they could be used as tools for navigation. Ae Sook was not a doomie, but she observed the movements of the stars and planets as her mother and her mother before her and divined horoscopes. She spoke with a thick accent.

"Captain Dorian is correct. Oracle is moved by his visions. It makes him difficult to predict. Captain Blue is also correct—in the end, the needs of Oracle's ship must dictate his actions. If he avoided this last chance here, then we must look for the desperate and the unlikely."

Sabbath gazed on his available fleet. He had two ships besides the *Ironman* beneath his feet.

His son's red painted ship the *War Pig* was aptly named. She had two screws that had been converted to coal and that gave her the power to maneuver any way she liked and push against bad weather. But she ate that coal like a pig, and in the intervening century her steel masts and spars had been replaced by wood and she had never sailed efficiently since. Still, she carried a devastating weight of shot with her cannons, she had a very large crew of very dangerous men and muties and few could match her in a stand-up fight. Sabbath had been recently tempted to move his ensign to her and make her the flagship of his fleet, but the ship was best suited to his son's middling sailing ability.

Sabbath sighed as he looked on his daughter's ship, *Lady Evil*. The *Lady* was a schooner, her flush deck, deep vee hull and two steeply raked masts were a delight; she was painted sky blue and it was just possible she was the fastest sailing ship left in the broken world. The *Lady* was the terror of the Caribbean and the Gulf coasts of the Deathlands, but she was small in the scheme of things. There was only one ship Sabbath knew of that could freely sail the great oceans with the weight of shot and yards of sail to ask by your leave from no pirate or baron, and that was the *Hand of Glory*. She had once been his. She had been his flagship. Sabbath's fist clenched around the hilt of his butcher blade.

Oracle had taken her from him.

Under Sabbath's captaincy she had been the *Hand of Doom,* and he had ruled her with an iron hand.

Oracle had returned her to glory and to the volunteer ship she had been for more than a century. Sabbath stared up into his junk's rigging. The sails of his three masts were fully battened, and the bamboo slats spreading through the black, lateen rigged sails looked like the fins of a great fish. Sabbath had exaggerated the effect by painting the battens sheaths white like bones. She was a beautiful ship, and big, but she could not match the *Glory*'s sailing ability. *Ironman* carried a respectable weight of shot, but her dramatically upswept hull and compartmentalized chambers were not ideal for blaster decks. As far as Sabbath knew, the *Glory* was the only perfect ship still afloat, and skydark might fall again before the hand of man could ever make another like her. "He's heading south."

Dorian snapped his massive balisong shut and rose. "The Brazils! A hungry and thirsty journey in his condition but plenty of villes! He's fast enough to make sail for it, get resupplied and…" Dorian trailed off. "Then what? He can't make Africa or Europe from there. What is left but to come back into our teeth?"

"He's heading south," Sabbath repeated.

Blue was shocked as she saw it. "He's going to round the horn."

"In the southern winter?" Dorian was appalled. "Radmadness! Triple-stupe bastard!"

Blue admired the gall of it. "If there is one ship that could do it…"

"There are two I know of," Sabbath said.

"Aye, Father," Blue agreed. "I can—"

"The *War Pig* can chase him around the horn." Sabbath corrected.

Blue bit her lip. Dorian stopped short of strutting like a rooster across the stern. "Aye, Father! I can!"

"And chase him you will, but you'll not catch him, nor try to."

Dorian tapped his double hilts in his palm. "No?"

"No, you'll push him. Give him no rest or respite. Stay under sail down the south. He will outpace you, but when you hit the Horn? While he is tearing sails and snapping spars in the storms, you drop sail and go to your coal. Again, don't try to catch him. Push him. Push him to breaking with his skeleton crew watch on watch, breaking with the scurvy, hunger and despair, and then push him to me."

Dorian smiled like a child pulling the wings off a fly. "You and sister Blue will take the Northwest Passage."

"It's summer, sweet winds up the Deathlands east and no better sailing across the Great White North. With luck we beat the chem storms and have even better winds down the Deathlands west into the Cific. Oracle has never sailed outside the South Cific before. He'll be sailing by dead reckoning and rumor. Once he rounds the Horn he'll have to hug the western coasts, and we'll have him."

Blue flipped through her chart book. Many of the maps were more than a hundred years old. The apocalypse had reshaped entire coastlines, dropped entire island chains beneath the sea and generated new ones. The Caribbean Sea was better charted than most, but beyond it, most modern charts were little more than forlorn suggestions. The fact was, like the first age of ships, vast stretches of ocean were once more uncharted. Where a modern chart read 'Here there be monsters' it had been written in deadly earnest. Blue collected and collated every chart she could buy, steal, copy or take in plunder. Her library took up a good portion of the captain's cabin on the *Lady*. A sheet of vellum stretched from floor to ceiling on her starboard wall, and on that she laboriously pieced together her masterwork, her chart of the world. Blue sighed.

By her estimate it was ninety percent incomplete.

She had never sailed farther south than the night-glowing ruins of Recife; however, her initial jealousy toward her brother's southern run around the Horn was tempered by the idea of taking the Northwest Passage in convoy with her father and sailing the Cific. "What course?"

Sabbath turned his eye to the operations on shore. The surviving ville people howled in mourning and loss. Pigs squealed as they were slaughtered. Meat roasted in huge pits for the ships' dinner while pork side, belly and fat back were cut into bricks and salted away. Crewmen loaded the small boats with plundered lumber and cordage and fresh fruits and vegetables and topped off water casks. The choicer of the ville's young men and women were argued over and divided up for entertainment purposes.

"Set me a straight course, north for the Rock. It will be hard sail, across open ocean, but I don't want anything to do with any Deathlanders. We'll be running short on supplies by then so when we get there we'll relieve a few Newfie villes of their women and salt cod before we round into the Labrador Sea and take the Passage."

Blue was already flipping through her charts. "Aye, Father."

Sabbath opened his own chart book. "Dorian, you're going to do just about opposite. Head south until you hit the southern continent and follow the coast down. I've never heard of anything big enough down there to match you, but that doesn't mean they won't try. Don't get night creeped by a horde of war canoes or let a bunch of motorboats take a run at you. Stay out of sight of the coast as much as possible. Stop only for water and supplies." Sabbath gave his son a stern look. "And no prizes. Stick to the mission. You don't fight anyone unless they attack you first."

Dorian quirked his lips in disappointment but nodded. "Aye, Father."

"And you don't attack Oracle, not unless he turns to fight you, or you come on him at anchor in a bay and he can't maneuver. If it all goes glowing night shit and Oracle sinks or somehow escapes us, we'll meet up here in August." Sabbath tapped a point on South America's west coast. "There's a ville called Coquimbo, about two hundred miles north of the Valparaiso Crater. The baron there's name is Zarro. When I first traveled the western coast I stopped there for supplies. Zarro and I came to an agreement and I helped him and his sons take a rival ville by loaning them some cannons and men to man them. You sail in to port and say your name is Sabbath, you'll be feasted well until we arrive."

"Aye, Father."

"If you take Oracle before rounding the horn, head back for home with *Glory* in tow and we'll see you next year."

"Aye, Father."

"Very good." Sabbath snapped his book shut and turned back to the rail. He watched as a short, chubby teenaged girl was torn from her family and her homespun shift ripped from her onshore. "Mr. Kang!"

Sabbath's seven-foot Korean second mate stepped forward. He had come with the junk as well, and after an initial period of disgruntlement, he found piracy in the Caribbean suited him quite well. He carried a cat of nine tails in a shoulder bag at all times, and every man in Sabbath's fleet lived in horror at the prospect of feeling the lash propelled by the giant's right arm. "Aye, Captain."

Sabbath pointed his book at the weeping girl. "That one.

Bathe her and bring her to my cabin as a belly warmer, now."

"Aye, Captain."

Sabbath licked his thin lips. "Ae Sook, you will assist me."

"In all things, my captain."

Black Sabbath strode to his cabin with his loins stirring. "We sail with the morning tide."

RICKY CLEANED THE captain's blasters. Compared to the barons and warlords the youth had encountered since leaving Puerto Rico, Oracle's personal arsenal was sparse in the extreme. Then again, Oracle's preferred combat method seemed to be disemboweling his opponents with a mutant orangutan paw prosthesis. He had a beauty of a single-shot Thompson/Center Contender that, according to rumor, he was quite proficient with and could reload with his paw. It was chambered for .45-70. Ricky was a confirmed blaster lover, and he knew the round was ancient, pre-Deathlands American and usually used to take bison. He couldn't imagine firing it from a fourteen-inch blaster. He aimed the oiled, tuned and gleaming blaster and yearned to shoot it. Ricky lowered the weapon as the lurking fear closed in.

He might as well stick the weapon in his mouth. The question was whether to try and shoot Manrape first.

Ricky's weapons, and those of his companion's, were locked away. They had been allowed to bear arms during the octopod attack, but they had been relieved of their weapons afterward. The companions would not be allowed to touch them again until they were signed to the book. Ricky had heard rumors that there were some other special weapons in the captain's cabin that were off limits to him and to J.B. The young man jerked up as a tall shadow fell across the door. He had no bullets for any of the weapons he was cleaning, and he clawed for his ship's knife.

Ricky sighed with relief as Doc's rangy frame filled the doorway. The old man held a wooden case. "Doc! Don't sneak up on someone like that!"

"Young Ricky," Doc said gravely,. "you have a conundrum."

Ricky stared at the weapons on his workbench and saw nothing that made sense. Doc often didn't. "What's a conundrum?"

"You have a problem."

"Yeah, Doc. If getting butt-chilled by a bronze statue is a problem, I've got a problem."

The subject matter was clearly to Doc's distaste. Yet Doc seemed to be in a rare clear, cold mood. "Fight him."

"Fight him?" Ricky began gesticulating. "Fight him how?"

"Challenge him."

"Challenge him?" Ricky repeated. "Challenge him how? No one's going to give me my blaster! With blades? I can't beat him! *Madre de dios,* Doc! Bare hands? I haven't been rated ordinary seamen yet, much less able. What do I challenge him for? The right to be bosun?"

"For the personal rights to your rectum."

Ricky was shocked speechless to hear such a thing come out of Doc's mouth.

Doc struggled to keep his voice steady. "When I was hurled into your time, I was captured by unethical men."

Ricky had heard the stories. "Doc—"

"I was made sport of and abused. Cruelly."

Ricky couldn't meet Doc's eyes. "Doc, you don't have to—"

"Look at me!" Doc demanded. Ricky looked. He stared at the time-trawled man, ripped from his family and torn from his time. Ricky gazed on Doc's chron-damaged visage and knew that in reality he was almost as old as Ryan. He had seen Doc's skill with blaster and blade and knew that in his time Doc had been a learned scholar who had married a beautiful woman. Now he was old, broken in body and sometimes in his mind. Doc regained his composure.

"Ricky, my young friend. Fight. Rage."

The youth did not know what to say. "Doc?"

Doc's eyes grew clear. His voice filled with the terrible gravitas of his message. "You must fight."

Tears stung Ricky's eyes for Doc and himself and the future that awaited him in the darkness belowdecks. "But how, Doc?"

Doc set the case he carried on the workbench. "With these."

Ricky opened the ornate box. It contained two of the most beautiful handblasters he had ever seen. Their grips were lustrously polished fruitwood. Clouds of golds, blues and purples swept through the steel of the barrel and lock work in gorgeous swirls of case hardening. The triggers and bead front sights were gold plated. The weapons were perfectly identical. Separate slots held individual bullet molds and intricately tooled silver powder horns for each blaster. Ricky took out one of the weapons. It was heavy and well over .50 caliber. He turned the weapon about for several moments and found writing along the bottom of the barrel.

"Fabbricato in Italia?" Ricky shrugged. "What's Italia?"

"Italy."

"What's Italy?"

"It is where they once made Berettas. Perhaps they still do."

Ricky perked up. "Oh!"

"Those are working replicas of weapons before my time but made in Mildred's. Do you know what they are for?"

Ricky nodded at the weapons soberly. "For dueling."

"Yes, for dueling. J.B. sought me out, and we discussed your situation at length. I have spent the day pouring through the creed and code and then the logs of this ship. It has been a long time, but within living memory of some of the crew, the pistols before you have been used to settle affairs of honor aboard this ship. The precedent is there. You are not signed, but you are well liked, your cause one of great sympathy, and none aboard, not even Mr. Manrape, I dare say, would gainsay you the right to defend yourself."

Ricky lowered the most beautiful thing he had ever held. "But, Doc. If I'm challenging, doesn't Manrape choose the weapons?"

"I am no lawyer, my young friend, and the times have changed, but I have gone out, as we said in my time. Our Mr. Manrape has made very clear, and publicly, his intention to violate you. I believe the gauntlet has already been thrown and the next move is yours."

Ricky considered this new and horrible option. "If I challenge Manrape, I think he'll throw me down and take me right there."

"Possibly, but this is not exactly a challenge, it is a response and exactly why you send one of your seconds. A duty I would be honored to accept."

"Seconds?"

"Trusted friends, willing to assist in all manners of protocol and engage by your side should the rules of the duel be broken."

Ricky was a young man from postapocalyptic Puerto Rico. Duels there were mostly informal and consisted of two men going into the forest with machetes and only one coming back. However, some were occasionally public spectacles and friends got involved. "Then I'd have no other second than you, Doc."

Doc bowed low. "Then I shall be honored to deliver your response to the bosun publicly. Should he refuse, or accept and then attack you before the appointed time, his loss of prestige on this ship would be incalculable, and your seconds would be well within their rights to seek his life. By the by, from what I have read in the ships logs, two seconds are customary."

"Then I choose J.B."

"An excellent choice."

Ricky once again considered his immediate mortal or moral destruction. "What happens?"

"Assuming I am correct in my assumptions, the captain shall order the ship to make the first immediate landfall. You, Mr. Manrape, and your seconds, as well as a handful of neutral witnesses, shall row ashore. There, in the sight of all, I shall load and prime both pistols, and Mr. Manrape shall have first choice. You and he shall stand back to back, take the agreed number of paces, turn and fire."

"And?"

"And lead shall fly, my young friend."

Ricky gulped. "And?"

"And one or both of you may fall. Of course, those pistols are smooth bore and it is quite possible one or both may miss. However, should both of you survive the first volley, then the judge, whom shall most likely be Commander Miles or First Mate Loral, shall ask if honor is satisfied. It is very likely that Mr. Manrape shall say no, and, given that you had first choice of weapons, he can ask for a second round of fire or else to continue with weapons of his choosing including bare hands. I fear a second round in any form will go very badly for you. I suggest in the strongest terms possible that you make your first shot count."

Ricky felt the walls of the room closing in on him.

"Ricardo," Doc asked, "shall I present myself to the bosun on your behalf?"

Ricky hefted the huge, primitive, beautifully crafted blaster. He took up the other in his left hand. There was something comforting and final in their cold, heavy weight. Ricky nodded. "Do it."

"I shall, and pray allow me to give you one more piece of counsel before I do…"

Chapter Eight

"C'mon lover!" Krysty encouraged. "Stick it deep!" Ryan thrust his half pike. The brass ring jangled against his pike head but bounced off and spun flashing away. Atlast cackled above him in the shrouds. The Englishman dangled the ring tauntingly on a length of ship's twine. "By the 99 bloody red balloons that went up, Ryan! If you handle your cock like you handle a pike, Red's not going to be yours on this ship for long! And what she sees in a half-blind Deathlander like you is beyond me!"

Sweet Marie leaned on her half pike and laughed. She had skewered the ring with sewing machine precision, but Atlast hadn't been dancing it. "Mebbe he can lick his eyebrows. It's all I can think of!" Idling observers laughed. Sweet Marie rolled her eyes. "Course she's a mutie. Who knows what they prefer."

Krysty bristled. Mr. Movies hung effortlessly by one hand from the yardarm like a six-foot pink simian and answered with utmost seriousness. "I prefer blondes."

Sweet Marie laughed. "Who doesn't?"

Ryan stood stripped to the waist and sweating on the deck. He had fought with spears, lances, javelins, harpoons and more than a few crudely pointed sticks and prevailed, but none had ever been his weapon of choice. The half pike he held was eight feet long with a thick shaft. The spearhead was a foot long and far narrower than the wood. It made the weapon look odd. Usually a spearhead flared out with sharp, leaf-shaped or diamond edges and sometimes lugs for blocking or hooks for snaring. The half pike's blade was a simple quadrangle spike. The weapon was made for battle aboard ship. It might have to be thrust through rigging, siege netting or open portholes and was designed to slide along, around or through any obstruction as ships clashed. As Atlast had pontificated at the start of the lesson, "Boarding pikes is made to tickle a man."

Accuracy was everything.

As Atlast had explained it, modern ship fighting was mostly "a broadside, a blaster volley, and then in through the smoke!" Sometimes an opponent had predark auto cannons, rocket launchers or mortars and then the battle was a lopsided horror, but on the seas of the broken world more often than not weight of shot and weight of crew with sharp steel told the tale.

And when it turned into an open brawl between anything from scores to hundreds of men on heaving decks, a disciplined cadre of men with half pikes, in formation, could plug a gap or drive an ill-disciplined mob before them into the sea. On the *Glory* the pike team was called the Phalanx. They were chosen men and women. Two eight-man teams, one from each watch, that could come together to form a solid wall of steel or break into flying half or quarter teams and run to trouble spots. Ryan had heard it muttered the Phalanx had saved the *Glory* in her last terrible battle, and he'd heard they had taken losses. Atlast was pike captain.

Ryan had applied for the Phalanx.

He had excelled at the morning drill, but Sweet Marie, Onetongue and the other five members of the pike squad, including Wipe, wore a brass ring on a bit of cord around their necks. Ryan had to earn his. He let out a slow breath.

Atlast cajoled him. "C'mon, Ryan!" The Englishman danced the glittering ring in the air. "You can—"

Ryan struck like a snake. The ring rasped around his spear point and stuck. Atlast yanked the cord and pulled the ring free. "You think you can do that again and—"

Ryan lunged and lanced the ring again. "Again!" Atlast shouted. "Again!" Ryan lunged and lunged and lunged at the glittering target as he went into his battle zone. On his sixtieth thrust the twine holding the ring parted. Ryan stepped back, chest heaving with the brass ring halfway down his spearhead. Atlast stared at the string in his hand and shook his head. "Sixty thrusts, fifty-five scores."

Ryan wiped sweat from his brow. "Fifty-six."

Onetongue was giddy. "That really thine'th, Ryan!"

Wipe was happy beyond words. "Eee!" Strangely enough, pike technique was one of the few things that Wipe actually excelled at.

Ryan shrugged at the praise. He lowered his pike and removed the severely battered ring. Onetongue happily handed Ryan a bit of leather cord to hang it on. "You're a Phalanx'th man now!"

Ryan tied the bit of leather around the ring, walked over to Krysty and put it around her neck. She gave a rare blush and her hair stirred around Ryan's fingers.

ORACLE CALLED OUT from the quarterdeck. "Mr. Forgiven!"

"Aye, Captain?" the purser replied.

"A tot of something for the Phalanx."

"Aye, Captain."

"Let Miss Red have a taste with her man."

"Aye, Captain."

"You heard the captain!" Atlast bawled. "Phalanx! Rack pikes! Then report to the rum barrel at your ease!"

The Phalanx racks were around the main mast. Most

of them stopped just short of running to get in line at the barrel. Crewmen watched Ryan in envy of his drink and his drinking companion. Skillet appeared and assisted the purser. A tot of something appeared to be a stoop of a small beer, a shot of cane liquor, the squeezings of half a lime and a dusting of spices Ryan couldn't name. He took his stoop and Krysty's hand. They walked to the forecastle to take the breeze off the prow and enjoy the rare bit of rest. Ryan sipped the concoction. "Not bad."

Krysty drank. "I like it!"

Ryan knew his woman well. "You're sad."

Krysty reached under her bulky jersey and pulled her battered boots from under her belt. The long-serving blue leather cowboy boots with the falcon design were in poor condition. The soles, which had been repaired countless times, were holed in two places each.

She heaved a sigh. "Ryan?"

The one-eyed man stared at the sad, faded blue leather. "They served you long and hard."

"I asked Gypsyfair to fix them."

"And?"

"She asked how I'd pay."

Ryan considered the image and raised an involuntary eyebrow. Krysty rammed an elbow into his ribs hard enough to make him wince. "They aren't ship's issue or ship compliant. Manrape said if he saw them scraping his decks, he'd take it out on you."

Ryan took a long breath. "Take the silver off them before you throw them overboard."

"I already did." Krysty gave the boots one last look, then flung them into the sea. She felt as if she was abandoning a trusted old friend.

"What do you hear about the duel?" Ryan asked to distract her.

"Ships all rad buzzed about it."

Ryan's drink turned bitter on his lips. He scowled into the ocean's vastness. It heaved a beautiful, dark green as the *Glory* sliced through it. "And if that wasn't Doc's most stupe idea yet, I don't know what is."

Krysty lifted her head. "You're just jealous."

"Of what?"

"You want a piece of Manrape. You'd rather it was you rowing to the beach and seeing who comes back. I can see it in your eye. So can the crew. So can Manrape."

Ryan considered what he owed the bosun. "I won't deny it."

"Lover, if you lay a hand on him, or kill him outside the creed and code, it's not just you who's going to suffer."

"I know. The duel's on. The question is, what's the fall-out? If Ricky loses, it's going to be bastard bad."

"I know."

Krysty looked down into the sea. Her boots were gone. Ryan put a hand on her nape and slowly massaged. Krysty sighed and bowed her head beneath his caresses. Her titian tresses responded and moved silkily around his caressing hand. They were on opposite watches, and nearly all the time they'd spent together since being shanghaied had been stolen moments they could count on the fingers of one hand. Ryan changed the subject.

"How are you holding up?"

Krysty sighed. "I'm about as useful as bird shit on a pump handle aboard this ship. All the women on board have specialties. Gyspyfair can find things in that special way of hers. Sweet Marie is twice as strong as most men aboard. Miss Loral came to the *Glory* a stone-cold chiller who already knew everything there was to know about sailing. All of the women aboard can do something."

Ryan began kneading Krysty's neck and shoulders. She

stopped just short of sagging against the rail beneath his fingers. Ryan spoke low. "I'm going to get you off this ship."

"We're in the South Lantic, heading south. Where're we hopping off?"

Ryan knew what Krysty was getting at. They just didn't have a lot of choices at the moment, and strangely enough, this ship was one of the safer places they had been in a while. The air was clean, and what few stretches had spiked his rad counter at all they swiftly left in their wake. Food for the moment was three squares and had markedly improved in taste since Boiler and Skillet had been ousted from the med. Truth was, the companions had been in far worse situations and had served as sec for far worse folk. Worse still, these folk, for the moment, were their shipmates. Ryan had sweated like a slave beside them and this day had joined the Phalanx. He genuinely liked some of his shipmates and respected most of them. Night creeping them to escape sat wrong with Ryan.

"I've spoken with Doc, and he's spoken with J.B. and Jak. If Ricky's duel goes wrong tomorrow, and fireblast , I can't see it going right, we have a plan. It isn't a good one."

"What if it goes right?"

Ryan shrugged. "Then we serve the ship until we figure a way off it."

"Then I need to find a niche to fill, and fast."

Ryan leaned forward and smiled into Krysty's hair. "I know a niche I want to fill, and I want to take my time."

Krysty grinned up at Ryan. "Well, rumor is when there's humping to be done on this ship, you sneak down into the orlop and do it among the cable tiers."

"Orlop and cable tiers." Ryan quirked an eyebrow. "And who's been telling you about that?"

"I'm ship's gofer. I had to learn the ship fast, and I get a lot of invitations." Krysty gave him a sidelong glance. "You might try learning too."

Ryan stared down at his naked torso and the fading whorls of bruising that fists, starter ropes and tootched suckers had pounded into his flesh. "Baby, I've been learning the hard way."

"It's three days until Sunday."

"And?"

"Sunday's the day when there's class. Training men to be officers and specialists. This ship has lost plenty."

"Officer? Ryan snorted.

"You already know how to read and write. You can read a map and use a sextant and the tech and blasters on this ship are kid's stuff to you. You whaled. You can learn. Lover, you're liked aboard this ship. Half the crew will bend over backward to help you."

"If it goes bad with Ricky, they'll never trust me."

"Then learn everything you can anyway. It'll be useful when we take the ship."

"When we take the ship?"

"When we take the *Glory* or blow her up and take the whaleboat. That's your plan isn't it?"

"Pretty much," Ryan admitted.

"Then you make me a promise."

"What?"

"You leave Manrape alone."

Ryan's fists clenched.

Krysty put her hands on his chest and locked her emerald gaze with his chilling blue. "When the time comes, give me the signal. I'll call on the Earth Mother, and Gaia willing, I'll rip that bastard limb from limb. Then I'll go straight for Oracle. You leave the super muties to me. You need to deal with the blastermen in the tops, the crew, blowing the powder room and getting the whaleboat in the water. Oh, and then getting me in the whaleboat. I won't be in too good a shape."

Ryan wasn't sure if Manrape was mutie or simply peak human, but he was pretty sure the bosun wasn't ready for Krysty with a bad Gaia rising. Oracle, however, had survived being hanged. The crew spoke in awe of his battle prowess. The captain had harvested Mr. Squid's brethren like he was picking fruit, and Ryan didn't want that silver-clawed, orange-furred horror Oracle had for a right hand anywhere near Krysty's flesh.

"I'll leave Manrape alone for now. I'll let you know if I change my mind. If there's time."

Krysty ignored the caveat. "And you'll apply to Commander Miles for training?"

Ryan grunted in the affirmative. He knew his reluctance was a front. He was an avid learner, and the chance to learn the running of a full-rigged ship, as well as delve into the *Glory's* history from skydark to now, was very hard to resist. "Some ship schooling couldn't hurt anything."

Krysty sighed. "So everything hinges on Ricky."

Ryan watched the late afternoon sun start to sink toward the ocean. "Ricky's got a big day ahead of him."

Chapter Nine

Ricky shook like a leaf. He sat at the prow of the whale-boat and watched the isolated bit of land come closer with each dip of the oars. The coconut palms came right down to the beach. He realized they were very likely to become his burial ground in the next few moments. The youth looked down and found his knuckles turning white around the gunwales. He felt infinite relief that Doc and J.B. sat behind him and mostly screened him from Manrape. Ricky could feel the golden titan's eyes boring into his back.

The bosun sat aft with the ship's techman/tinker, Mr. Rood. The *Glory* had a two-way radio, and working in the tops Ricky had seen the long wire antenna snaking up the mainmast into the crow's nest. Manrape's other second was the bosun's mate, Mr. DontGo. DontGo was nearly as physically impressive as Manrape, but he had long black hair and tribal tattooing taking up the majority of his arms and legs. Ricky had heard the man was a Native Americanfrom the Florida region and that he and Manrape were as thick as thieves. Miss Loral sat at the stern with the steering oar. Between the two dueling parties sat Movies; two lanky, Indonesian, drooping mustachioed brothers named Yerbua and Nirutam; and a sailor named Koa from Hawaii plying the oars. In addition to rowing, they were to serve as neutral witnesses, and each had a blaster tucked in his belt.

All too quickly the whaleboat hissed against the sand. The rowers jumped out to pull the boat out of the surf.

"All ashore!" Miss Loral called. "Mr. Yerbua, Mr. Nirutam, if you please."

Ricky's joints felt like rubber as he clambered out of the boat. The two Indonesians took a chest and a small folding table ashore. Miss Loral was the ranking officer and arbiter of the duel. She wore a large, wickedly curved dirk on her hip and took an AK with the stock folded and slung it over her shoulder. Yerbua set up the table just under the shade of the palms. Nirutam opened the chest and took out a calabash and a nested set of coconut-shell cups.

"All parties gather," Miss Loral ordered. They formed with the principals and their seconds across from each other with Miss Loral and the witnesses in between. The first mate nodded at Nirutam. "A tot all around, if you please."

Nirutam dutifully poured an exact eighth of a pint into each cup. Miss Loral raised her cup. "There is no such thing as a friendly duel, but this is not a feud and let it not become so. Let us drink to fellowship, shipmates, luck to both principals and the settling of this affair." The principals, seconds and witnesses toasted and drank. Ricky hurled his back in one gulp. Doc smacked his lips. "Oh, dear! Good strong arrack. One hundred proof at the very least."

Mr. Rood grinned over his cup. Besides running the radio, fixing any tech that came along or stripping it for salvage or saleable parts, he also ran the ship's still. "One hundred and fifty."

"A most potent potation, Mr. Rood. Truly you are a master of all trades."

The assemblage nodded its appreciation.

Ricky felt the liquor burning his throat and expanding like a fireball in his stomach. To his chagrin he had hurled up his breakfast of manioc and pigeon peas over the rail. He had not slept a wink all night. The double-distilled palm wine detonated in his empty belly like a bomb. Ricky suddenly tasted it a second time around his tonsils. He clapped his hand over his mouth and staggered away from the assembly to the surf. The young man burned with shame as the arrack came back up his throat and spewed into the spume. He fell to his knees as heaves racked him. As a postapocalyptic Puerto Rican, he had been raised on rum, as well as maize, manioc and banana beers. It was not the arrack that had unmanned him. Stink sweat squeezed out his pores as he vomited, and he and everyone else on the beach knew that what racked him was pure, cold fear.

The usual catcalls and jeers would have been better than the embarrassed silence.

Manrape's voice was worse. All leering and sneering was gone as he broke the silence. His voice was genuinely solicitous and all the more horrible for its fatherly tone. "Ricky, stop this before someone gets hurt. Stop this now, and I will be gentle with you."

Ricky's guts heaved at the suggestion, but nothing came but ragged coughs and cramps.

Doc's voice came steady and clear. "Mr. Manrape, you have not yet taken your paces, turned and stood opposed to my principal upon the field of honor. Upon the dawn of my first duel I vomited before the rise of the sun, yet I strode forth and prevailed. Young Ricky stands upon the cusp of his fate. I pray, give him a moment to gird his loins for battle."

Manrape's voice came from some sociopathic dais of pleasure. "Doc?"

"Good Bosun?"

"Every time you speak, my heart glows."

"Then I implore you, I—"

"I withdraw to the Field of Honor. Will you finish your cup with me?"

"I will, indeed."

J.B. put a hand on Ricky's shoulder. "You have to get up. You have to put the blaster in your hand. Now or not at all." Ricky shook like a leaf. J.B.'s face went grim and he spoke quietly. "I've got two .357s concealed. You say the word, and we start shooting. Doc has his swordstick, and he knows the plan. I'm going to start with Miss Loral and grab that AK."

Ricky didn't care for the idea of shooting his shipmates one bit. "Then what?"

"Then nothing. We fight. If we win here, we try and take the ship. Jak blows the powder room. Krysty calls on Gaia and takes on Oracle and Ryan goes rad fire on everyone else. We take the whaleboat and make our way back to the Gulf of the Deathlands. Doc stole a chart. We can make our way from there."

"We'll all die."

"We'll most likely lose," J.B. conceded. "But we're all agreed. You just aren't going into the trees with Manrape today."

Ricky had shaken with shame and fear, but now it was guilt that set him to trembling. "No."

"No?"

"This is my fight. I called it. Now I'm going to finish it. One way or the other."

J.B. stared at Ricky appraisingly. "You just might."

He helped Ricky up and called out, "We're ready!"

"Doc," Miss Loral ordered, "load the blasters."

The principals, seconds and witnesses watched in fascination as Doc precisely loaded ball and powder down the barrels and primed the pans. He held the weapons out handle first to Manrape. "The choice is yours, Bosun."

Manrape removed his shirt. "So as not to get blood on it." He flexed his gladiator physique and took the pistol in Doc's right hand. Doc handed Ricky the other. The weapon felt heavy as a brick.

"Mr. Rood, Mr. J.B.," Miss Loral ordered, "pace it off, if you please."

Rood and J.B. drew their ship's knives and met beneath the palms. They stuck their marlinspikes in the sand where they stood, then turned their backs to each other, took the agreed-upon ten long paces and stuck their knives in the sand to mark it. Miss Loral looked at the principals. "Are you satisfied?"

"Aye." Manrape nodded.

Ricky had to swallow hard to find his voice. "Yes, ma'am."

"Then take your positions."

Ricky and Manrape walked to the marlinspikes. Ricky was grateful that Manrape didn't say anything. The bronze titan seemed to glow from within. The high drama was clearly to his taste.

"Turn!" Miss Loral ordered. Ricky and Manrape turned their backs to each other. Ricky raised his blaster to point skyward.

"Seconds, take your positions!" The seconds walked out to the ship's knives of their respective principals and then stepped back the agreed six paces. "Bos'n Manrape, Ricky, are you ready?"

"Aye," Manrape answered.

Ricky found his voice. "Ready."

"Advance!"

Sand crunched as Ricky took the long walk to J.B.'s knife. He stopped beside it and stared at the worn wooden

hilt, but it had no last epiphany for him. Neither did the
sand, sky or sea. All Ricky could feel was nausea, a suddenly overwhelming urge to vomit again and naked terror.

"Turn!" Miss Loral ordered.

Ricky turned and stood side on to present as little of
a target as possible as Doc had instructed. Manrape presented himself square on. Ricky flinched as the bos'n's
leer returned. Miss Loral held up a red bandanna. It fluttered for a moment in the breeze and then she released it
to fall to the sand. "Blast at will!"

Ricky put the gold bead of his sight on Manrape's
massive chest. Manrape smiled uncaringly and kept his
weapon skyward at the shoulder arms position. He tilted
his head in invitation. "Blast away, Ricky catamite."

Miss Loral had explained the rules to all parties the
night before, and now that both men had paced and turned,
neither man could take a step, but there was apparently
no rule these days about catcalling, head-faking, twisting
sideways or, in Manrape's case, the very real and sickening
possibility he would grin and limbo beneath Ricky's shot.

J.B. had given Ricky a plan. To take Manrape, J.B. believed Ricky's best chance was to pull the trigger and then
snap his wrist downward at the same time. With luck the
bullet would take Manrape through the guts or groin. The
blaster Ricky held fired a ball that weighed three-quarters
of an ounce. Manrape might survive it, and even gut shot
manage to get off a shot in return, but the matter would
be satisfied either way, and Ricky had already decided he
would rather die with his head blown off than be raped
repeatedly until Manrape tired of him or the companions
managed to escape.

"Squirt your hot lead, Ricky," Manrape cooed.

"If you please, Mr. Ricky," Miss Loral directed. "You
called this duel, and Mr. Manrape has in the eyes of all

assembled freely given you first shot. You must give fire or beg to withdraw."

Ricky gazed over the gleaming gold bead of the front sight where it hovered over Manrape's heart.

Manrape whispered like a lover. "Do it."

Ricky took a deep breath and let half of it out. He deliberately raised his aim high into the trees, picked his target and squeezed the trigger. The blaster bucked like a mule in Ricky's hand. A cluster of coconuts hanging ten feet over Manrape exploded, and coconut meat, milk and shredded shell showered down on Manrape's head and shoulders. Ricky lowered his smoking blaster, cocked his left fist on his hip and rotated on the balls of his feet to present himself broadside to Manrape's return shot.

J.B. was not the only companion Ricky had consulted. This was Doc's plan.

Ricky spoke with far more calm than he felt. "The *Glory* can survive quite well without me, but Mr. Manrape's services are absolutely required. I will not deprive her or her crew of their bosun in time of need."

The assembled crew made approving noises.

"We will have quiet," Miss Loral intoned.

Manrape's face was a frozen mask.

"Bosun," the first mate ordered, "Mr. Ricky has given fire. Give fire in return or beg to withdraw."

Manrape's jaws worked and his eyes grew wider and wider. Ricky made a stern, internal effort to stay strong as Manrape's pupils dialed down to pinholes of insanity. A number of things could happen now. Manrape could withdraw, and the matter would be settled. He could match Ricky and gallantly discharge his blaster harmlessly into the trees and again the matter would be settled. He could blow Ricky's head off, though that would be seen as vindictive. He could shoot Ricky, hoping only to wound him, and in a fit of bad manners the crew would despise him for, claim honor was not satisfied and rape Ricky later when he was recovered. Doc had cautioned that there was another, darker possibility. Manrape might just snap and go berserk.

Ricky awaited his fate.

Manrape buckled to the sand.

The sob that tore from the titan's throat was one of the worst things that Ricky had ever heard in his young life.

Another and another and another followed in waves of inconsolable loss crashing on the rocks of desolation. Miss Loral and the crew were absolutely horrified.

"Mr. Manrape" Miss Loral put both hands on her AK. "Are you satisfied?"

Manrape fell to his face in the sand, sobbing.

Miss Loral cleared her throat. "Mr. Ricky?"

Ricky looked to Doc. Doc had theorized that Mr. Manrape would not hurt him. Ricky had protested that Manrape intended to ensure that he never crapped correctly again. Doc had countered yes, but to shoot Ricky, to hurt him, much less mar him, was not within Manrape. Like when Doc sang or spoke eloquently, Ricky was something beautiful to the golden giant and, given his proclivities, something to be possessed. Doc had once more admitted that terrible suffering had turned him into the broken man that he was, yet he could not imagine the suffering that had molded Manrape. Plan B had been forged.

Doc nodded.

Ricky handed his spent blaster to J.B. and walked across the sand. The ship's knife Jak had palmed him in parting burned a hole in the small of Ricky's back beneath his jersey. Ricky's shadow fell over the bosun.

"Bos'n?" Manrape pushed himself up to his knees like the weight of the broken world was above him rather than beneath him. Tears drew trails through the sand coating his face. Ricky took a long breath. "You're the mightiest among us, the best of us, our bos'n, the *Glory's* backbone and her almighty right hand. You are the keeper of the creed and code, and I thank you for showing me mercy this morning."

Manrape shuddered.

"But for the good of the ship. I must ask you to forgive me for not loving you."

Everyone assembled jumped as Manrape lunged forward. He seized Ricky's legs in his mighty arms and buried his face against his thighs as fresh sobs racked him. "I do!"

Ricky flushed beet red as his appalled shipmates watched the spectacle.

"Miss Loral?" The young man found himself saying the most inconceivable thing of his short life. "I think Mr. Manrape and I need a moment alone."

Chapter Ten

Ricky's return stopped just short of being a celebration. The story of the duel ran from stem to stern, orlop to the tops and then back again in ever greater and glowing detail. Oracle had weighed anchor, ordered just enough sail raised to generate forward momentum and declared a make and mend day, which Ryan learned was pretty much an afternoon off.

Crewmen sat about making and mending clothing. The crew with long hair sat about in small circles combing out each other's coifs and rebraiding them. It turned out Purser Forgiven was also the ship's barber. A barrel cut into a chair for the purpose was brought up from the hold and a line of crewmen stood to be shorn or shaved. Other crew played at dice or other games. Many just lolled about, sipping from the last barrel of small beer, smoked pipes and took the rare moment to relax. Ryan and Krysty celebrated by sneaking down into the cable tiers. They were not the only ones, and moans, groans and downright caterwauling echoed around them in the dark of the hold.

Ryan left Krysty smiling asleep in her hammock and went above deck. Crewmen nodded and acknowledged him. The one-eyed man glanced about. Ricky held court by the mainmast, surrounded by crewmen as he told the tale of the duel yet again. Jak stood nearby with his hand casually resting on the hilt of his ship's knife. He stood watch at Ricky's six for any fallout from the duel. There didn't appear to be any.

After declaring make and mend, Oracle had gone back to his cabin. He had ordered that he not be disturbed unless there was an emergency, and Ryan had learned the windows in the captain's cabin had been covered. Ryan also learned this was not at all unusual on this ship. He spied Manrape and Sweet Marie by the foremast. They spoke quietly, but Manrape's eyes constantly strayed to Ricky. Ryan noted that the leer on the bosun's face and the gleam in his eye were gone. It seemed to have been replaced by something far more tender and requited. Ryan decided to take a gamble. He walked over and put a knuckle to his brow. "Begging the bosun's pardon."

Manrape gazed upon Ryan mildly. "Mr. Ryan?"

"You seen Doc?"

What appeared to be a genuine smile appeared on Manrape's face. "He's forward."

Ryan glanced at the forecastle. Doc was nowhere to be seen. Sweet Marie threw back her head and laughed. "All the way forward, Ryan! Just keep walkin' till there's no deck beneath you and then look down!" Several nearby crewmen laughed.

Ryan considered what this might mean and took a walk forward. Atlast, Hardstone, Koa and DontGo sat on their sea chests playing some variation of cards and passing a copper snuff box. There was no sign of Doc as Ryan passed. He came to the bowsprit and the end of the ship. Ryan suspected the joke was on him but took Sweet Marie's advice anyway. He stepped onto the bowsprit, grabbed a sheet to steady himself, walked out over the water and looked down.

Ryan blinked.

He knew that Doc and Mr. Squid were spending a lot of

time together, but Ryan's eye was torn between two sights that even in the Deathlands one didn't see every day. One was that of Mr. Squid hanging by one elongated arm from the lowest sheet below the bowsprit. The octopod's head and mantle bobbled beneath the waves while its remaining seven arms twisted and fluttered in the apex of the *Glory*'s bow wake like suckered streamers. Ryan was oddly reminded of a dog sticking its head out of a moving wag. Far more disturbing was the sight of Doc lying in the safety netting, naked except for what appeared to Ryan to be a pair of extremely skimpy, very tight, electric lime-green underwear. Doc seemed genuinely at ease as he absently gnawed on a piece of salt beef and paged through a book with a bullet hole in it.

"Doc?"

Doc squinted up happily. "My dear Ryan!"

"I have to say you're the last person I thought I'd see wearing gaudy house clothing."

"I found them in stores! There are a number of things there good Purser Forgiven has asked that Mildred and I might identify. Mildred says the garment is called a Speedo and assures me its a garment for men. I find they fit rather well!"

Ryan found it would have been better had Doc simply been naked. "Doc, what are you doing?"

"Why, I am air bathing! A practice much recommended by our good founding father Benjamin Franklin." Doc blinked. "Of course, according to rumor even the French thought he smelled terrible. Nonetheless, soap and fresh water are in short supply and I must admit I find the wind, sun and spray most invigorating. I wear this twentieth century swimsuit, as it were, for modesty's sake."

"What's Squid doing?"

"I believe the subaqueous inverse of myself!"

Ryan took in Doc's pale body, the bulge in the front of the swimsuit and his inversely meager buttocks just about spilling out between the netting. "Doc, are you sure you want to parade around like that with this crew?"

Mr. Squid's hanging arm contracted and it drew itself mostly out of the water to peer upward at the humans. "I have never observed that color before." Mr. Squid's skin rippled and suddenly turned a brilliant electric green in solidarity. "I find it very attractive."

"Thank you, dear Squid, and I appreciate your concern, dear Ryan." Doc looked down on himself with a sigh. "But I fear even our good Mr. Manrape would find little to allure him in this, how does dear Mildred describe it? Sad sack of chicken bones?"

"Actually, Doc, the crew seems kinda taken with you."

Doc smiled. "I do find myself well caressed. I believe the crew finds me amusing and thinks of me as a good luck charm."

"Are you okay with that?"

"I believe I have little choice in the matter, yet, as you well know, I have found myself the butt of a great deal of amusement in this brave new world of yours, Ryan."

Ryan's face tightened at the things Doc had suffered.

"However, since my redemption from the shrouds, even at its roughest, the humor here upon this ship toward me is affectionate, and it is appreciated. As to being lucky, the only fortune I lay claim to is the day my beloved Emily said 'I do.'"

Ryan waited.

Talk of Doc's wife and children often caused Doc a bout of madness. Doc's shoulders twitched as it walked past within his mind but didn't stop to pay a visit. "However," he stated, "if the crew finds me lucky, then as long as I am aboard this ship they are welcome to every last ounce of fortune that I can provide."

"I think you've played a big part in our acceptance on this ship."

"Indeed." Doc frowned. "Which brings on us another matter."

"What's that?"

"Our good Captain Oracle has asked me to sign the book."

"And?"

"And by my lights and honor, should I do so? I cannot do it under false pretenses."

Ryan's eye narrowed. He considered himself an honorable man, but he knew that his Deathlands sense of honor and that of the man from the nineteenth century were miles apart. "What're you saying, Doc?"

"I say, dear friend, that should I sign the book and give my loyalty to this good ship, and in the capacity of captain's servant my direct loyalty to him, and then have that debt of honor come into conflict with the love of my friends, I will—"

"I will beat your ass, tie you up and carry you along until you come to your senses." Ryan's voice went hard. "It wouldn't be the first time."

Mr. Squid suddenly contracted upward out of the waves with its arms roiling like a snake ball of very large pythons. A swirling pallet of vibrant, rainbow colors rippled across its flesh in what Ryan perceived to be extreme agitation and suddenly went a startling pitch black. Mr. Squid's arms snaked to the bowsprit and the square-pupiled, golden eyes regarded Ryan in cold, abyssal, alien menace. Ryan kept his hand away from his knife. He'd chilled most nonhumanoid intelligences he'd met. The well-being of him and his companions always seemed to be the exact opposite of what those beings had in mind. Mr. Squid, however, seemed to have definite skin in the game when it came to Doc's health and welfare. Ryan had taken a chance with Manrape. He doubled down on the *Glory's* subaqueous specialist.

"If it comes to it, Mr. Squid. I'm going to have to ask you to help me."

Every inch of Mr. Squid's skin went from ink-black to what Ryan had determined was its normal slick, wet, slate gray. Ryan knew he was assuming, but it sure as the First Strike seemed like Mr. Squid was nonplussed at the suggestion.

"A consummation most devoutly to be avoided," Doc interjected. "However, I also strongly believe that you and the rest of our dear companions shall be asked to sign the book in short order. I believe the question before us is not that of you and Mr. Squid bundling me away in the night, but rather whether or not we are to sign. I would suspect you view this as an all together or not at all proposition?"

"Krysty suggested I go to school on the forecastle."

"Oh, a capital suggestion!" Doc enthused. "You would make a fine candidate for officer. Don't you agree, Mr. Squid?"

Mr. Squid sat silently suckered to the bowsprit for several long seconds. "Mr. Ryan is the most capable human being I have ever met. I believe he would excel at any and all human endeavors I am aware of."

Doc laughed. "I am in complete agreement!"

"Mighty kind of you both."

"The truth does not always hurt, my friend."

"Cephalopods do not lie," Mr. Squid reiterated.

Ryan changed the subject. "Have you been reading the logs, Doc?"

"Indeed I have, and the saga of this ship makes for enthralling reading. As you may have guessed, the *Glory*, and that is not her original name, was a museum ship, an antiquity, maintained for educational purposes and as a training vessel for naval cadets before the fall."

"What was her original name?"

"To my immense regret and that of the historical record, the logs of the first two skydark captains, and several intervening logs as well, were lost in times of great tumult. She became the *Hand of Glory* under our good Captain Oracle."

"Our good Captain, Doc? He just short of enslaved us."

"Tumultuous times, my friend. Throughout her history, men and women have begged to become crew members aboard this vessel. Veterans of this vessel believe Oracle is the best captain they have had in many years. Many consider him their salvation and the right man at the right time for the post. I believe pressing us sits ill with him. What I can tell you is this—the *Glory* has spent her postapocalyptic career as what we called in my time a Yankee Trader. She serves as a vessel of importing and exporting, a transport, a vessel of exploration, and in many instances she has hired herself out as a mercenary ship of war. According to ship's logs, what she has never done, despite terrible hardship, was become a pirate ship."

Ryan had already guessed the answer to his next question. "Except for the last captain."

Doc looked out at the sea. "From the little I can glean it was a terrible time. The crew suffered. Things were done."

"Who was he?"

"His log book was burned. Neither captain, nor officers nor crew speak of him. It is a black stain upon the ship's history. Oracle brought the ship back to her former glory. He once again made her a ship of the world, and as you may well surmise, he stands contested in this."

"You have the captain's ear?"

"I do, but mostly as an entertainment. I pour his wine. He asks me questions anyone would ask of a well-read scholar. I tell him of mighty clipper ships sailing under up to seven masts and of New England's whaling ships sailing the Seven Seas to wrestle leviathan. I do not ask him questions. You may also note that while I am the captain's servant, I have a great deal of idle time. Captain Oracle spends the vast majority of his limited free time by himself."

"I won't ask you to push it."

"I cannot recommend that course."

Ryan gazed out at the seemingly endless ocean before him. "We're headed south."

"Indeed, there is already grumbling that our course shall take us past the northern coast of South America without stopping."

Ryan had heard those grumbles as well. Once again he considered all of the little he knew about South America. "What's there?"

"I do not know. We have been briefly into the Amazon basin upon a jump or two and found but little in those mutated rain forests to allure us. South? You move into the Gran Chaco of Paraguay, Bolivia and Northern Argentina, continue on and you find the vast pampas, further still the seemingly endless steppe of Patagonia. Few from here seem to go there, and apparently vice versa."

"So it's all plains?"

"Girded to the west by the mighty spine of the Andes nearly its entire length, but mostly, yes."

"What happened down there during the nukecaust?"

"No living member of this crew has been farther south than Brazil, though the *Glory* has gone farther in times past. As you might imagine their major cities and military bases were bombarded, but in dear Mildred's time South

America did not pose either the strategic threat or value to warrant the wholesale destruction we saw in the Northern Hemisphere. The crew refers to it as a 'big empty.' It is rumored South America was deliberately scourged with biological weapons targeted both at the human population and their major agricultural crops. It seemed one or both sides in the final war that birthed the Deathlands decided it would be best to kill most of the population and starve the rest into a subsistence lifestyle."

"Why?"

"I can think of two reasons. One, with the superpowers of the Northern Hemisphere reducing each other to radioactive ash and anarchy, they did not wish the nations of the southern continent to rise up and become the new world powers. Two, and it disgusts me to even contemplate, there must have been those in the North who expected to win the war, or, more likely, expected to claw their way back up out of the rubble and recover first. The great southern plains of South America, mostly denuded of man and having lain fallow for a hundred years, would be an ark of natural resources to be plundered."

Ryan shook his head.

"This is mostly conjecture on my part based on rumor and scant evidence. The ship's logs indicate to me indirectly that the decimated populations of southern South America abandoned the hot zones of their cities and returned to the subsistence farming, herding and hunting lifestyles of their colonial forebears. It also appears they are not particularly friendly. Though, should we jump ship, Ricky speaks Spanish. I, with my Latin, have made myself understood on more than one occasion with the Romance language speakers of your present day. It is possible we could make our way."

Ryan considered Doc's scenario of South America.

What struck him most was that it meant that any redoubts in the southern plains of South America were very likely few and far between. If they jumped ship there, it might well be the last jump they ever made, and South America would be where he and his companions spent the rest of their lives, short or otherwise.

"There is another thing to consider," Doc opined.

"What's that?"

"Until very recently the Pacific was the *Glory's* home."

As the son of a baron, Ryan had the closest thing to a classical education the Deathlands could generally provide. Through his travels he knew that the Northwest Passage opened up in the Great White North for the short, unpredictable summer months, and the Panama Canal was blasted ruin. Neither offered the *Glory* a way out. Ryan did the math. "We're going to round the southern Horn."

"I believe that is what our captain intends, and I need not remind you, for the moment we are in the summer. When we cross the equator, we descend into winter. In my day, in the era of wooden ships and before the breaking of the world, winter passage around the Cape of Storms was considered extremely dangerous. I cannot imagine the risks have done anything other than multiply."

"How long?"

"Three months perhaps, assuming disaster does not strike."

"Long trip."

"And arduous in the extreme."

"Long trip to make unsigned or proved otherwise."

"I believe if we are offered the chance to sign on as crewmen and refuse, we will have proved ourselves otherwise and find ourselves considered unreliable at best and a danger to the ship and her crew at worst. At best we will be stranded at the next available spit of land. But we were taken on because of a desperate need of crew, so hostages may be taken from among, or, how shall I put this delicately, the harshest methods available, indeed, imaginable, that will not directly prevent us from doing our assigned duties will be inflicted upon us. Once Oracle and the *Glory* come into ports of call where he can find eager recruits, our final, proved-otherwise fate may be quite grim."

Ryan stood on the bowsprit of the *Hand of Glory* with the wind in his hair and the vast southern Lantic before him. "Tell Oracle you'll sign the book. Tell him I'm applying for training on the quarterdeck."

"I shall make it so at the first opportunity, dear friend." Doc smiled slyly for the first time in a long time. "Or should I say, shipmate?"

Mr. Squid's flesh suddenly flashed to the electric green of Doc's trunks. Ryan again knew he was assigning human emotions to the nonhumanoid, but he could swear the cephalopod was pleased. Mr. Squid's left eye muscles suddenly contracted and covered the golden orb. Ryan almost thought Mr. Squid was winking at him, but then an oval of skin turned black over the enclosed eye. Two thin black lines suddenly shot like tracery from either corner of the oval to encircle the cephalopod's head-body.

Ryan was genuinely startled. Mr. Squid had just simulated an eye patch.

"You know," Doc proposed, "I believe this is going to be a very interesting voyage."

Chapter Eleven

Ryan applied for officer's training on the quarterdeck. He found himself on his hands and knees on the main deck. He knelt shoulder to shoulder and sandwiched between Gallondrunk and Onetongue to port and Sweet Marie and Hardstone to starboard. Each held a worn and rounded brick of sandstone and furiously scrubbed the deck white with a mixture of sand and seawater. Manrape stood behind them. When he judged the section of deck clean, he shouted, "Shift!" and the stoning team moved backward to the next section of boards.

In tribute to her continuing mostly uselessness, Krysty was assigned the bucket to sluice the section. Normally, scrubbing the decks was a task assigned to new sailors, to old ones as punishment, or to crewmen who had proved themselves useful for little else. This was not a normal Sunday morning scrubbing.

This was a race.

Life aboard ship was with rare exceptions unending toil. Captain Oracle, like the captains before him, had turned much of the work into competitions, and he'd assigned tiny bits of privilege—leisure, trophies, totems or extra rations or jack—to teams or watches that excelled. All members of the crew were required to be proficient with a pike when called on, but Ryan had earned the brass ring and joined the Phalanx. These competitions went from the lowliest of menial waisters' tasks up to the shifting of sails, the speed of the cannon crews or personal marksmanship. Back in the day, when they had been new to the *Glory*, Gallondrunk, Onetongue, Hardstone and Sweet Marie had been the fastest deck scrubbing team in the *Glory*'s recorded history. They had worked with another new sailor named LonelyLane, but he had died in a chem storm long ago and the rest of the team had since risen to higher tasks aboard ship.

Now the champions had been called to battle once more. Ryan had been assigned to fill the missing slot—and not without a great deal of grumbling by his teammates.

Sweet Marie snarled and threw an elbow into Ryan's ribs. "Rad-blast it, Ryan! Keep up!"

Ryan struggled. In his life he had engaged in some of the hardest, dirtiest and most dangerous labors the Deathlands had managed to birth. Nonetheless, scrubbing floors had never been part of his purview. An emotion in Ryan that he recognized as pride rebelled against the task. At the same time he knew that was exactly why Oracle had ordered him to it. If Ryan hoped to someday be an officer aboard the *Glory*, he needed to know every aspect of the ship, as well as every aspect of every single crewman's duties, and know it from personal experience.

"Sluice!" Hardstone grunted.

Krysty sent a bucket of seawater sheeting across the section.

Manrape nodded at the gleaming white deck. "Shift!"

Ryan and his teammates crab walked backward to a new section of filthy deck.

Bosun's mate DontGo called out from starboard. "Shift!"

Ryan risked a glance across the deck.

Mr. Squid was a section ahead.

To the delight of the crew, Mr. Squid had announced

that the *Glory*'s bottom was free of seaweed and barnacles. Atlast had dived off the bowsprit with a quarter pike and emerged two minutes later at the stern. He'd happily gasped he had never seen the *Glory* cleaner. Mr. Squid had nipped every strand of seaweed down to the hull and drilled into every clinging mollusk with his beak and eaten them for rations. All admitted the ship was sailing faster and steering better. When Mr. Squid had searched about for a new task and announced he could scrub the decks faster and more efficiently than the waisters, this had sent shock waves of indignation through the crew.

Captain Oracle had arranged a contest for Sunday morning. Bets had flown.

DontGo stood behind Squid happily shaking his head. Mr. Squid had five of his eight arms churning stones before him in dizzying, interlocking circles. When DontGo called "Shift," the three arms Squid kept behind him contracted him back like bungee cords to the next section of deck. Wipe happily alternated sluicing the deck and sluicing Mr. Squid. Ryan scowled as Doc clapped fresh stoops of seawater against Squid's siphon when called upon.

Oracle stood at the rail of the forecastle like a black, unblinking statue. Commander Miles stood next to him holding a gleaming silver hand chron. Miss Loral strode from rail to rail gauging the progress of the race. "I swear I'd let my mother eat off Squid's deck!"

The majority of the spectating crew were backing the humans, and they would boo and shout insults. Mr. Squid's small, hardcore group of adherents howled expectantly.

Ryan's team redoubled its efforts. Onetongue glanced back at Squid. "Hee'th out of hi'th barrel! He can't lath't!" Ryan wasn't so sure. "Sluice!" Hardstone snarled. Krysty heaved the bucket. Manrape nodded. "Shift!"

Ryan's feet hit the gangway to the quarterdeck. "Stay

where you are, Ryan!" Sweet Marie hissed. The rest of the team rotated and hit the stairs seamlessly by twos. Ryan was grateful for the respite. He looked over. Mr. Squid was mostly obscured, but he seemed to be in snake-ball mode and having problems with the steps.

"Sluice!" Hardstone called.

"Lover!" Krysty called out in consternation. Ryan tensed as he suspected what was to come. A second later a good portion of her bucket hit Ryan's back. "I'm sorry! I'm—"

"Shift!" Manrape ordered.

"Get your ass up here, Ryan!" Sweet Marie yelled.

Ryan charged soddenly up the gleaming gangway and retook his position. It was not lost on Ryan that his first visit to the quarterdeck was on his hands and knees and hard at labor. The team scrubbed as if a chem storm was inches in front of them. "Shift!" Manrape ordered. The team passed the binnacle and the wheel.

"Shift!" DontGo called. Mr. Squid snapped up onto the quarterdeck like a giant rubber band. Ryan's team had to spread out to cover the small but far more open space. Mr. Squid took the opportunity to throw a sixth scrubbing arm into the mix. Captain Oracle and Commander Miles retreated to the end of the ship, grabbed a sheet and pulled themselves up on the stern rail out of the way of the contestants. Ryan glanced up as Mr. Squid passed the binnacle. It was the structure right in front of the wheel that held the ship's master compass, master chron and barometer. The binnacle contained twin lamps under glass so that the steersman and conman could read it by night and in all weathers. The binnacle had shelves below that held master charts. Ryan slowed for one second as he beheld the glass dome atop the binnacle. A human, skeleton hand floated in a swirling blue and red miasma of liquid.

Ryan froze as the skeleton hand turned in its suspensory fluid and pointed at him.

Manrape's rope slammed between Ryan's shoulder blades. "Eyes to the deck and the task at hand, Ryan!"

Ryan remembered his promise to Krysty, took the blow, put his mind to his fellow teammates and tripled his efforts. They moved steadily backward and passed the skylight of the captain's cabin. Mr. Squid steadily caught up. Crewmen on deck and in the rigging shouted and cheered. Hardstone snarled. Krysty sluiced. "Shift and turn!" Manrape called. The team turned to find the last, short section abutting the stern rail. Ryan's team scrubbed for their lives.

"Finished!" Manrape shouted. "Fit for Captain's inspection!"

Ryan and his team collapsed.

Mr. Squid squelched up against the stern rail seconds later. His normal gray color was ashen. Wipe shoved a bucket of seawater under his siphon and it bubbled over suspiciously like a man gasping for breath.

Captain Oracle and Commander Miles hopped down lightly and strode to the quarterdeck rail. "Miss Loral?" Oracle questioned.

The first mate stood on the main grating and opened her arms. "Clean as a whistle, Captain! Port and starboard!"

Oracle nodded. "Commander?"

Miles strode the quarterdeck, giving a rare smile. "Captain, *Glory*'s deck hasn't been this clean in years."

The crew cheered.

Oracle took a slow walk down the starboard gangway and back up the port. The crew on deck and in the riggings held their breath. "Very good, Commander. Very good indeed. A fine race and congratulations to port and starboard crews."

Commander Miles continued to enjoy the gleaming decks. "And I am sure they thank you, Captain."

The crew cheered.

"Mr. Squid is the winner," Oracle declared.

The cheering stopped. Sweet Marie detonated. "We beat the squid! Fair and square! Right beneath your feet, Captain!"

Oracle turned his gaze on able seaman Sweet Marie. The mono-block of sailing woman paled. Oracle extended his left hand toward Commander Miles, who reached into a pocket of his blue coat and pulled out a white glove.

"Oh, here we go!" Miss Loral called.

Cheers once again erupted from deck to rigging. Captain Oracle slowly walked down the starboard side of the ship. He held the white glove behind his back as his black eyes took in Mr. Squid's work. He walked the full length of the ship and returned back up the port side. His gloved hand did not move. The captain stopped at the port gangway to the quarterdeck. He extended one gloved finger and stroked it beneath the step at shoulder level. Oracle raised his finger high. The fingertip of his glove was black with grime. "Mr. Squid scrubbed the undersides of the treads."

Sweet Marie couldn't contain herself. "Beggin' the captain's pardon!" Crewmen who had lost bets shouted out. Even Hardstone was incensed. "The undersides? We never scrub the undersides!"

Ryan rose. "Permission to speak!"

Oracle nodded. "Granted, Mr. Ryan."

"My team gave one hundred percent."

Mutters of assent greeted the statement. Oracle nodded again. "I acknowledge that, Mr. Ryan."

Ryan lifted his chin to starboard. "Mr. Squid gave one hundred and ten. Today he was a better sailor than me. Starboard beat port. I concede defeat."

"Here! Here!" Doc applauded. Mr. Squid's supporters cheered.

Oracle ran his gaze over the rest of the port team. Sweet Marie blew a lank, sweaty lock of red hair out of her face and shook her head. "Not a sweet, willing face to sit on for a thousand leagues, and now I am schooled in my sailor's duty by a squid? I swear it's enough to make a girl go back to trawling on her father's barge!"

Laughter broke out.

"Commander," Oracle grated. "Is there any beer left?"

Miles made a face. "Just a half cask of that banana beer we picked up in the Dominicas, and it's turning fast."

"I doubt the portside crew will complain. A stoop each."

"Aye, Captain!"

The captain regarded his subaqueous specialist. "You are victorious, Mr. Squid. I know not what spoils to give you."

"I am tired," Mr. Squid replied. "I would like to rest in my barrel."

"Of course. Nothing else?"

"I would like Doc to sit with me. If the ship can spare him."

A number of very rude, man-on-squid suggestions rang out. It was difficult to discern in his stygian dark face, but Oracle might have been amused. "Doc?"

"Captain, you reward me as much as Mr. Squid, if you find I can be spared."

"You can be spared, Doc. But I will require two errands of you while Mr. Squid's barrel is emptied and filled with fresh water."

"I am at your service, Captain."

"Go down to the tech room and bring me Mr. Rood's report about the radio transmissions he has been receiving."

"At once."

"Before you do, sign the book."

The ship got quiet.

Doc bowed low. "Humbly, and with honor, my captain."

Forgiven took the massive book from under his arm and presented Doc with a pen. Doc signed on the indicated line. Manrape's voice boomed, "Hip! Hip!"

"Huzzah!" the crew roared.

"Hip! Hip!"

"Huzzah!"

"Hip! Hip!"

"Huzzah!"

Gypsyfair came forward with a deep blue garment draped over her arms. "This is for you, shipmate. I sewed it myself."

Doc unfolded a blue coat much like that of Commander Miles, Miss Loral and Purser Forgiven. His eyes stung and his throat tightened. "Oh my stars and garters…"

"You serve in the captain's cabin, you shall keep the captain's log and serve as well as purser's assistant," Miles intoned. "You must look the part. Your pantaloons, hat and shoes will follow shortly."

Atlast and Koa peeled off Doc's coat and helped him don the ship's jacket. It was common knowledge that no one sewed better than Gypsyfair. The coat fit perfectly. Doc felt overcome with emotion. "Oh dear, oh dear…"

"Doc," Oracle said softly but firmly, "I believe I gave you an order."

Doc straightened. "Aye, Captain! The tech room and Mr. Rood's report. At once!" Doc strode swiftly to the main gangway with a genuine swagger. Krysty shot Ryan a bemused look. Ryan accepted a stoop of past-its-prime banana beer from Wipe and nodded at her.

For good or ill, he and his companions were aboard the *Glory* until she saw the Cific.

DOC STRODE JAUNTILY to the tech cabin. Crewmen grinned, whistled, gave him the thumbs up and called him shipmate as he passed. None seemed surprised. Apparently the fix had been well in. Doc stuck his head into the tech room. Mr. Rood sat at his worktable hunched over logs and making notes. Three radio transceivers of different makes and ages dominated the room. Doc found the soft glow of their dials pleasing. Rood had both a fuel and a hand crank generator, although Doc noted smaller cables snaking up the mizzenmast next to the antenna, and he knew there were some solar panels and small, cobbled together wind-turbines up in the tops. Doc rapped politely on the thin wooden doorframe set into the canvass divider that formed the room. "Mr. Rood, are you free?"

The ship's techman glanced up from his worktable. Unlike many of the crew, he kept his hair cut short. The sleeves of his jersey were rolled up and tied. His eyes were red rimmed from long hours in not particularly good light, but he grinned. "Hello, Doc. Nice coat!"

Doc flushed with pleasure.

"What can I do you for?"

"Captain's business. He asks if you have intercepted any more transmissions and wishes your report."

"Half a dozen just today, and just like all the days before, they make no sense."

"Are they in a foreign language?" Doc asked. "I am familiar with several."

"No language at all, unless I'm missing something."

Doc stepped inside and peered at Rood's extensive log entries. They consisted of many long series of dots and dashes with corresponding letters written beneath them. "Well," Doc observed, "whomever our chatty friends may be, they appear to be using Morse code. I gather most sailors of this time use it?"

"Most don't. Most ships don't have radios, and most ships' complements right up to captain are illiterate." Rood made a derisive noise. "Some of the more sophisticated types use semaphore. This stuff makes no sense. Must be some broken piece of tech on auto."

"Hmm." Doc frowned. He and his companions had encountered numerous pieces of technology that had survived skydark and kept on operating, some in endless loop, some having jumped their original programming, some chilling deadly and others heartbreaking in their mechanical devotion to duty. "I see three possibilities, my good Mr. Rood. One, you are correct and there is a piece of tech somewhere beyond our horizon, emitting gobbledygook. Two, there is a monkey, or an illiterate child chained to a desk similar to yours, with nothing better to do than randomly pound upon a transmission bar day and night."

Rood laughed.

"Or three," Doc continued. "Let us assume willful, perhaps hostile, intent behind these transmissions, and, for the nonce, let us assume this is a simple Caesar cipher."

"A what?"

"Julius Caesar," Doc explained. "A mega-baron of long ago."

"Powerful?"

"One of the most powerful the world has ever known. When he sent a message that was private or of military significance he would encrypt it with a substitution cipher."

"A what?"

Doc remained patient and pointed at the strings of meaningless letters. "Those are words. For example, here is the alphabet." Doc wrote out the alphabet A to Z on a sheet of paper. "Let us assume I am so foolish that my own, personal substitution cipher is simply the alphabet backward." Doc wrote the alphabet Z to A directly beneath.

"Now…" Doc swiftly wrote eight words of Z to A backward nonsense. "Match each letter in the alphabet above, each letter corresponding to the letter of my cipher below it."

Rood looked at Doc like he might be losing it but swiftly matched letters and scratched out a sentence below Doc's. "The quick brown fox jumps over the lazy dog?"

"It is a panagram."

"A what?"

"A phrase that contains all letters of a given alphabet. In this case it is the most commonly used panagram in predark English."

"What does it mean?

"It means you have deciphered my code, Mr. Rood."

"Rads, thunder and fallout!" Rood was amazed. "That's incredible!"

"Clever but not incredible. The concept is thousands of years old. It seems in your bold new Caribbean someone has rediscovered it."

Rood's face fell as he scanned his own notes. "But the tech men, out there, they ain't using the alphabet backward."

"Indeed not. I fear they have devised an alphabet of their own. Julius Caesar, for example, was known by historians for using a left shift of three."

"Well, if they have their own cipher, how do we decipher it?"

"We must break it, my friend."

"Break it? How?" Rood asked.

"Frequency analysis."

Rood tapped his radio dial. "I already got his frequency."

"I speak of the frequency of letters, shipmate. Though perhaps our first, best course would be pattern words."

"Pattern words…"

"Let us surmise that these voices out in the ethers are speaking about us. Thusly, I might be tempted to subscribe the word 'Glory' to the more frequent, identical, four-letter words. Since we are aboard ship, and being pursued, we might also look for 'latitude' and 'longitude' or their Latin abbreviations. Now, should he also have a word substitution code atop his cipher, or be engaging in multiple alphabet shifts, then you and I, good Rood, will be burning the midnight oil."

Rood's eyes seemed in severe danger of glazing over.

Doc held up a calming finger. "However, let us, you and I, just as a starting point, assume that our opponent has dreadfully underestimated us and assumes that we, along with nearly everyone else in the Caribbean Sea, has never heard of a Caesar cipher." Doc spread out a sheaf of Mr. Rood's notes.

The old man's eyes danced across the pages and his long finger followed and tapped. "See! Here, here and here! I detect the corresponding patterns of latitude and longitude. The U, D and E all correspond, and the two words between them have given us all the vowels except the sometimes Y. I believe much of these communications are coordinates!"

"I see it." Techman Rood's world visibly expanded. "I see it!"

"Indeed!" Doc picked up a pen. "With your permission?"

Rood leaned in like a hound on the scent. "Break him!"

Doc swiftly began scratching beneath Rood's lines of copied code. "Yes, this can only be *Glory!* And here, this, this and…" Doc's pen hand wilted.

"What?" Rood asked. "What happened?"

"My worst fear. Everything made sense until it made no sense."

"You ain't making no sense."

"I am afraid we have fallen into a trap. It was too easy, and now we are confounded by translations in the code that make no sense, which means we are on the wrong tack entirely or have been duped."

"You're still making no sense," Rood reiterated.

"Perhaps not. Then I pray you, good techman, do the words 'war' and 'pig' in any conjunction mean anything to you?"

Rood straightened.

Doc sighed. "I fear we must start anew and—"

"Captain!" Rood shot to his feet and nearly slammed his head into the beam above. He burst out of the cabin and ran shouting across the blaster deck. "Captain!"

Chapter Twelve

The entire crew had seen or heard about Mr. Rood bolting out of the tech room and charging for the captain's cabin waving a sheaf of papers. Doc swiftly followed. Commander Miles and Miss Loral had been called, then Gunny, Manrape, Movies and Atlast. All had been within for quite some time. The crew sat around in groups, muttering. Ryan sat in a rope coil-cum-lounge chair by the mizzen with Krysty sipping banana beer that was getting downright skunky. She wrinkled her nose as she drank. "What do you think's going on in there?"

"Strategy."

J.B. and Mildred came up from belowdecks and joined them. Miss Loral approached from the gangway. The first mate's normally lupine, grinning face was sober. "Mr. Ryan, Mr. J.B., you are requested in the captain's cabin, if you please."

Ryan and J.B. gave each other a look and followed Miss Loral down the gangway. Crewmen by the cannons and those slung in their hammocks all watched them like hawks. The two men crossed the invisible line on the stern blasterdeck, went to the door and entered the captain's cabin. Compared to every other space in the ship it was spacious. Ryan could stand to his full height without hitting his head. The stern was full of windowpanes, and Ryan had just scrubbed the deck around the skylight. At the moment most of the glass was open.

The cabin was bright and zinging with natural light and fresh air. A pair of cannons pointing backward took up a fair share of the space. Between them was a couch, and charts and artifacts covered the walls. The captain and his remaining officers and specialists stood around a heavy table.

Oracle looked up. "Mr. Ryan, Mr. J.B." He nodded at the ship's book open on a separate lectern with a pen lying in the spine. "Be so kind as to sign the book, or if not, clap onto something heavy and hurl yourselves overboard. Failure to choose one or the other will be regrettable all the way around."

J.B. looked to Ryan.

The one-eyed man shrugged. "Admit it. You can't wait to get your hands on those cannons."

The Armorer signed. Ryan followed suit.

Oracle gave a brief nod. "Mr. Ryan, Mr. J.B., thank you for signing and in doing so forgiving the circumstances surrounding it. Forgive also the lack of ceremony. Time is short. Come, join us." Ryan and J.B. joined the circle and glanced down at pages of code and innumerable charts and maps.

"Permission to speak freely."

"This one time, Mr. Ryan. Until you make officer and earn the right to address the captain on anything other than ship's business."

"We signed. We'll serve. Me and all of mine. But we're not slaves. From what I see, neither is anyone else on this ship. Assuming we survive to see the Cific, we have the right to leave. If you intend to slave us, I'll throw a match in the powder room at the first opportunity."

The assembled crew was horrified. Oracle smiled. It was disarming. His white teeth blazed out of his face, and at close range you could see the crow's feet carving out from the corners of his eyes. "Had you given me a few seconds more, I had intended to extend to you nearly the exact same contract. I can get all the crew I want in the Cific. You and yours have proved yourselves. Have the rest of your companions sign. You shall be protected by the creed and code and have full shares in all trade, and should we reach a place in the Cific where you wish to debark, you shall be allowed to leave, sorely missed, yet every canteen, mag and knapsack full."

Ryan held out his hand. "Deal."

Oracle held out the leathery, cracked palm of his twice than human size monkey's paw. He slammed it into Ryan's palm and Ryan grimaced at the force of it. The one-eyed man's skin itched as the orange fur and dead leathered flesh scraped his palm, and his spine prickled. He squeezed the hideous prosthesis to seal the deal, then let it go. Oracle sighed dramatically. "This is why I never drop anchor in the Deathlands."

Commander Miles snorted. "And why none of us from there ever want to go back, Captain."

The tension around the table broke.

"Mr. Ryan," Oracle rasped.

"Captain."

"Dorian Sabbath and the *War Pig* descend on us."

"I've never heard of Sabbath. The *War Pig*'s a ship?"

"Yes, a powerful one."

"Can we take her?"

"That, Mr. Ryan, is the question before us. The *War Pig* can't sail like us, but she has engines. She can't shoot with anything like our crew's speed and accuracy, but she has bigger blasters and more of them. Should it come to a boarding action we will be badly outnumbered, and all of these things would be true even if the *Glory* were fighting fit and at full strength."

"Fight or run?" Ryan asked.

"We have Doc to thank for breaking the Sabbath code. We know our enemy's plans and their dispositions. Emmanuel and his daughter, Blue, take the *Ironman* and the *Lady Evil* through the Northwest Passage, while Dorian hounds us down the South American coast."

Oracle's silver-clawed middle finger moved over the chart. Ryan was fascinated to see a map that looked recent and skillfully drawn. He was disappointed that so little of the east or west coasts of the Deathlands were marked. Some stretches were little more than dotted line suggestions. Oracle read Ryan's mind. "I was only partly joking earlier, Mr. Ryan. Few sailors I know make port in the Deathlands, except by accident or desperation. Your Deathlands and their villes have a certain reputation."

Ryan reserved comment. He looked at the Northwest Passage and then scanned down South America, the Horn and the Cific beyond. "Seems like a lot of empty space for just three ships to hunt one."

"So one might think, Mr. Ryan. But look at the *Glory*. We are not a simple fishing boat, an oared longship, galley or oceangoing canoe. We are a full-rigged ship. We have a smithy and a carpenter, yet there are some things, like rope in quantity and sail-making cloth of quality, that we cannot manufacture. The port villes where we can get them are relatively few and well known, and sooner or later we must visit them. Should we survive the Horn, we will be in desperate need. We will have Dorian behind us, his family laying in wait ahead, all knowing the few courses we can take for resupply."

Ryan had to admit he hadn't thought of that. "Double back?"

"We could, but Sabbath has turned the Caribbean villes that could resupply us against us. Few of the Caribbean shore villes could withstand the Sabbath fleet if it arrived in anger and began bombarding them."

Ryan looked at the chart of the Cific with its tiny, scattered dots. "Is the Cific any better?"

Oracle smiled conspiratorially. "I have friends there."

Ryan's tactical mind considered the huge ocean, the limited choices they had for resupplying and the enemy's overwhelming firepower and numbers. "Is this Dorian Sabbath impulsive?"

Oracle grinned from ear to ear. "Indeed, Mr. Ryan. Dorian is hotheaded, bloodthirsty, egotistical and very impulsive. His father instructs him to drive us before him. But Dorian dreams of catching us at anchor and capturing us, and make no mistake, we will have to make landfall several times before we attempt the Horn. Dorian knows that. He would dearly love to engage us at sea, knock away enough of our spars that we can no longer maneuver and board us. He dreams of presenting us to his father in tow rather than being the hound that drives us into his father's and sister's arms."

J.B. scratched his chin. "Find a bay, Captain. Drop anchor. Dismount the cannons from both sides of the ship. Conceal them on shore. When Dorian comes in for the prize, we hit him with everything we got. All at once."

"Not bad, Mr. J.B., and I have considered it, but should Dorian survive our great broadside, he can maneuver to put the anchored *Glory* between himself and our blasters. It will take a great deal of the crew to man all the weapons on shore. He could easily take the *Glory* from those that remain. We could not fire on him without killing our own shipmates. He could then clap onto the *Glory* and simply steam out of range under engine power, leaving us shipless and stranded on a forlorn shore."

Ryan stared hard at the charts. "I don't know enough

about fighting this ship, much less sailing it to come up with a trap for Dorian." He arched an eyebrow at Oracle. "But I think you have an idea, Captain."

"Gunny informs me that the blaster we found you with has an optic."

"Aye, Captain, but it's small, 2.5 power, made for very fast and very accurate shooting in the short to middle distance. I've made some long-range shots with it, but it's a marksman's blaster, not a sniper, if you know the difference. Begging the captain's pardon."

"I do know the difference, Mr. Ryan, and my problem is no crewman aboard the *Glory* knows how to use an optic. My question is, do you know how to use a long-range scope?"

Ryan suppressed a grin as he remembered some of his blasters past. "I do."

"Gunny," Oracle ordered.

Gunny came forward bearing a four and a half-foot long, flat, hard plastic case. Ryan could almost hear J.B. getting excited. Gunny set the case on top of the charts and flipped the latches to open it. J.B. stared at the long, black longblaster within. His jaw went slack. "Dark... night..."

Ryan found the exclamation appropriate. The bolt blaster was more than four feet long; her steel was scratched but much of the black finish remained. Her forestock flared after the internal magazine and then tapered dramatically toward the muzzle. Behind the trigger the stock took a hard turn south to form a pistol grip. The buttstock was adjustable for both cheek height and length of pull. The cold black barrel mounted a muzzle break on the business end.

J.B. moved forward like a moth to a flame. "With the captain's permission?"

"Please do, Mr. J.B."

The Armorer took the longblaster out of the case. He opened the action and glanced inside. "T-76 Dakota Longbow. I've only read about these in old magazines."

"What's the caliber?" Ryan asked.

J.B. registered genuine glee. "It's .338 Lapua."

It was a cartridge Ryan had personal experience with, and his experience was that very few things that walked on two to four legs, mutie or otherwise, could withstand a .338 round without losing all hostile intentions. J.B. worked the bolt repeatedly, feeling the action and trying the trigger pull. Oracle extended his horrible monkey's paw at the empty screw holes where optics or iron sights should have resided. "Gunny got the scope on, but none aboard have the knowhow to sight the weapon in. We wasted a great deal of ammo in our first attempt and have precious little to spare."

"Yeah." J.B. had eyes only for the blaster he lovingly examined. "You want an expert to do that."

Eyebrows rose around the small circle on the quarterdeck. J.B. seemed blissfully unaware of his impertinence. In his favor, J.B. was a master armorer and he showed it in his every movement around blasters. Oracle seemed to be willing to let it pass, in the same way he might let Atlast talk frankly about the sails or Commander Miles about navigation and strategy. "Are you the expert who can do that?"

"Oh, yeah," J.B. confirmed.

"Is Mr. Ryan the man to shoot it?"

"Oh yeah."

"Mr. J.B., what is the range of that blaster?"

"In good shape and properly sighted in, 1,500 meters effective."

Commander Miles grinned ferociously. "That's nearly a mile!"

Captain Oracle regarded J.B. dryly. "I gather that is on a stable platform, on land."

"There's that, Captain," J.B. agreed. He held the long-blaster out to Ryan. "With permission, Captain?"

Oracle nodded.

Ryan took up the black longblaster. It was heavy, at least thirteen pounds, and that was unloaded and without an optic. He snapped it to shoulder and aimed out the stern windows at the empty ocean. Form followed function. Ryan's Scout longblaster was a jack-of-all-trades, designed for a hunting and fighting, running and gunning marksman. The Longbow, as J.B. called it, was a Thoroughbred, built for one purpose. It had been forged in the previous age expressly for chilling men at very long distances.

"Mr. Ryan, I intend to draw Dorian in. You see these cannons in my cabin? We call those stern chasers. Dorian has bow chasers. When he comes into range, we will duel. We will both attempt to take each other's spars and masts. He will accept this duel because he has engines. A long cannon shot is about half a mile. Luck, wind and roll will decide much. I cannot guarantee you a stable deck, but I will bring you well within range for the blaster you hold. Kill Dorian if you can and any of his officers who present themselves. Failing that, kill his bow chaser blaster crews and we shall raise all sails and pull away. If nothing else, I want to enrage Dorian and at the same time have every sailor on the *War Pig* living in fear of losing their lives should they come within cannon shot of the *Glory*.

Ryan's eye stared steadily over the Longbow's naked

barrel and past the *Glory*'s wake. He slowly took up slack on the trigger. It broke at a crisp two and a half pounds and the hammer clicked. "Can do, Captain."

Chapter Thirteen

Ryan plotted a course for Panama, or what was left of it. Multiple nuke strikes had closed the canal, but at Oracle's order Ryan sat on a sea chest on the quarterdeck with a chart book across his knees, a ruler, compass, J.B.'s personal sextant and pen in hand, and he calculated. Koa sat next to him. The Hawaiian was one of the best sailors on the ship, but he had mostly sailed the Cific, and he did it as his ancestors did, by the stars in their seasons, the colors of seas and sky, the migrations of birds and sea life, the clusters of waves and clouds and dead-reckoning. His people called it wayfinding, and the methods were based on the passed on lore of the pre- and post-skydark Cific. The constellations of the north would not serve him now in the South Lantic, much less his wayfinding in the chilling winter. Koa sought to learn the *Glory* way of navigation. Rumor was he had the captain's ear even though he rated no more than seaman. Ryan had liked him immediately. Koa looked up from his chicken scratches. "This sucks, brah."

Ryan had not done problem-solving math in some time. He found himself enjoying the challenge. He didn't look up as he turned an arc on his compass and drew a line against his ruler. "I kind of like it."

Koa grinned. "You suck, Ryan."

Ryan smiled and made a notation in his margin. "Teach me your way when we hit the South Cific."

"I will!"

Ricky called out from the tops. "Sail!"

Commander Miles snatched his binoculars from the case at his waist. "Where away, Mr. Ricky?"

"Dead astern!"

Ryan and Koa closed their chart books and rose. Miles stared through his binoculars and nodded. "Here we go."

Miss Loral took a knee beside the captain's cabin's heavily curtained skylight. "Captain, the *War Pig* is in sight! Dead astern!"

Oracle's voice went from broken rasp to thunder from the blacked-out cabin below. "Beat to quarters! Clear my cabin for action! Blaster crews to the stern chasers and fetch Mr. J.B. to the quarterdeck! Tell Gunny to release arms to all crew!"

"Aye, Captain!"

"Mr. Ryan, take your station at the stern!"

The drums beat and the crew ran to their battle stations. Ryan walked to the binnacle where the Longbow blaster's deployment case lay. He stared once more at the suspended skeletal hand. Again, Ryan found it pointing at him. His hackles rose as it slowly turned to point dead astern for the *War Pig*. The one-eyed man squared his shoulders and flipped up the latches on the case.

The deployment case had come with its own comprehensive set of tools. J.B. had taken the longblaster apart to its smallest components. He'd cleaned and lubricated every part, tuned the trigger and the action, adjusted the length of pull and cheek riser to Ryan's frame and attached the scope. The Armorer said it was Schmidt & Bender 4 x 16-50 optic from the Hungarian factory. Nothing but the variable power meant anything to Ryan, but the scope was like the longblaster. It was a thing of beauty, from a

time that had made things of beauty right up until they
had destroyed the world.

Ryan hefted the weapon and flicked open the action.
He pushed four of his rounds into the magazine and shot
the bolt home. They had debated long and hard over their
drought of ammo and the conflicting need to sight in the
longblaster. They had decided on five. J.B. knew his business. They had tossed an empty barrel over the stern and
decided on six hundred meters. J.B. had removed the bolt
and bore sighted by eye. The problems of a gently moving
deck swiftly became apparent.

Nevertheless they had gotten barrel and glass colli-
mated, and with J.B. spotting him, Ryan had put four out
of five rounds into the barrel, and he felt secure in the fact
that he had a decent six hundred yard hunting zero and
could attempt to reach out further if he had to. He strode
to his position at the stern rail. Spare hammocks had been
sewn and filled with sand to form a revetment braced and
camouflaged with barrels of seawater. Ryan hefted the Dakota T-76 and gazed through the powerful optic out over
the water at his adversary.

The *War Pig* was big. Her black sails and blood-red hull
made her a juggernaut of gothic, naval horror. However,
Ryan's short time on the *Glory* had taught him a great
deal about sailing. He ran scope over the *War Pig* strategi-
cally. Her rigging didn't suit her. The *Glory* knifed though
water while the *War Pig* lumbered. Ryan took in the single, slanted, black iron smoke stack between the mizzen
and the mainmasts. The wisps of filthy black coal smoke
oozing up into the sky were small. Dorian had his boilers
hot, but he wasn't using them yet.

Oracle appeared at Ryan's elbow. "You have some experience with black powder cannons?"

"From both ends."

"Good, then as you know there will be a great deal of smoke, and given our two ships, long cannon shot is about half a mile, or a little more with good blaster crews."

"And our crews are better?"

"Much, but while the balls will not penetrate the hull at that range, they can still damage sails and rigging and kill crew above deck. I can afford neither, and Dorian bears four chasers on his prow to my two in the stern. He expects to take some damage getting close enough to ravage our rigging."

Oracle snapped out his spyglass and watched the *War Pig* approach. "What young Dorian is not expecting, Mr. Ryan, is you. Your accuracy will decide much."

Ryan settled into his firing position. His shooting mat consisted of three blankets, and without a bipod his shooting rest was a pile of sandbags. A four-inch crack between two barrels formed his shooting slit. The magnification of his scope gave him a narrow view and also magnified the rise and fall of the *Glory*'s stern. Adding in the rise and fall of the *War Pig,* it was like trying to take an accurate shot while riding a seesaw with the target riding another one half a mile away. Ryan started counting seconds and noting when his crosshairs and the quarterdeck of the *War Pig* coincided.

J.B. was sprawled on the deck next to Ryan, peering through the spotter slit with the *Glory*'s best pair of binoculars. "I make it 600 meters. Gunny thinks they'll close to five hundred before firing. What do you think?"

Ryan would have loved to shave another hundred meters off his shot. Then again, once the cannons started firing, both his and the enemy's smoke would start obscuring everything. Ryan scanned the enemy ship. The garb of the *War Pig*'s crew ranged from bare-chested men in sarongs to leathers to predark plundered garments to homespun

tunics with a great deal of mismatching in between. All
wore a red and black sash around their waist so they could
differentiate friend from foe when it went hand to hand.
Many had painted their faces for battle, and many of those
were in red and black motif. Ryan looked for officers. They
were mostly differentiated by their use of optics. A number
of such clustered around the bow chasers looking through
scopes, spyglasses and binoculars.

"Pick one you like, J.B."

"They're all ugly."

The one-eyed man chose a lanky man with shoulder-
length black hair and some sort of double ivory baton in
his sash. "J.B., start counting."

"One, two, three, four…" J.B.'s count was in perfect
roll with the ship. "One, two, three, four… One, two—"

Ryan squeezed the Longbow's trigger. The .338 Lapua
Magnum round generated a brutal recoil. Across the water,
brains, bone splinters and blood erupted from the popped
skull.

J.B. shook his head admiringly. "That shined!"

Ryan grimaced and worked his bolt. "I was aiming for
the man next to him, and I was aiming at his chest."

"SNIPER!" THE FIRST MATE tackled Dorian as the third mate
collapsed mostly headless to the deck. Dorian was reck-
less and bloodthirsty, but he was also the veteran of many
a sea battle. "Nance!"

Nance was a small man, pot-bellied and weak looking
with graying curls and watery blue eyes. He looked ridiculous in war paint. Nevertheless, few men laid and fired
cannons with his skill. "Aye, Captain!"

"Fire all chasers!" Nance's roar was out of all relation
to his size.

The two stern chasers on the foredeck bucked backward

on their carriages as the blastermen clapped fuses to the touchholes. A second later the two cannons belowdecks bellowed in answer and thick, obscuring smoke filled the air. No one cheered, and Dorian knew nothing had hit. What he'd wanted more than anything was the smoke. The cannon crews swabbed, reloaded and ran the cannons forward. Dorian dimly heard the *Glory*'s stern chasers boom in response.

Dorian retreated, shouting orders. "Ji-Hoon!"

Ji-Hoon, one of Emmanuel Sabbath's Korean secs, ran forward. He carried a vintage M-16 with a grenade launcher, and he wore an ROK army flak jacket over his homespun. "Yes, Captain! I—" Ji-Hoon flew backward as if a huge invisible fist had dealt him a crushing blow to the chest. He hit the deck, and blood flooded out of him like an opened spigot.

"Nance!" Dorian screamed. "Nance, I want—"

Nance almost levitated. He went up on one tiptoe as he exploded from back and belly. His torso twisted 180 degrees around his blasted-out spine, and he sprawled to the boards.

Dorian's vision went red to match his hull. "Wepa! Smyke! Nubskull! Bring the master blaster forward!"

The first mate shouted in protest, "Captain, your father said—"

"Bring it forward! Chasers! Fire by crew! I don't care about hits—just keep firing and keep us obscured! Engines! Full ahead!"

The blaster crew trundled forward the masterblaster.

The deck throbbed beneath Dorian's feet as the engines went to full steam.

The weapon consisted of a carriage, a heavy wooden stem with a U-shaped brass cradle and eight long black iron barrels slaved to a crank handle and an ammo hopper. The three-man team ran the weapon up against the taffrail. The wheels were hinged, and they kicked them out to form the feet of a tripod. Wepa settled behind the crank handle and sight. Nub ripped open ammo boxes while Smyke poured them into the hopper.

Wepa flew backward, flapping his arms like a ruptured pigeon. The chasers fired and the fog of war once more covered the prow. Dorian leaped behind his pride and joy and grabbed the crank handle. "Range, First Mate!"

"I make it five hundred meters! The sniper is behind the barrels at the stern rail!"

Dorian saw *Glory*'s stern chasers puff smoke. He ignored the rustle and moan of a cannon ball passing very nearby and began cranking his firing handle. The Gatling gun erupted into life like a minor thunder god rapidly clapping his hands.

"DOWN! DOWN! DOWN!" Ryan roared. He hugged the deck as the water barrels surrounding his sandbags geysered seawater and the sand bag in front of his face bulged as a bullet passed through. Screams erupted in the rigging and a second later Movies and Born fell ruptured and broken to the deck like rotten fruit from the branch. Seconds later Ryan heard glass shattering as the Gatling tore through stern windows and swept the captain's cabin and the chaser blaster crews. Screams erupted below, but both chasers fired back. Powder smoke filled the air. The *War Pig's* prow blasters fired, and Ryan heard the whoosh and saw smoke pulse as a cannon ball zipped overhead but apparently didn't connect with anything. The Gatling stopped for a moment to wait for the smoke to clear.

Ryan jumped up with his longblaster and ran.

"Mr. Ryan!" Oracle raged. "Stand your station!" The captain's hand went to his blaster as Ryan headed for the mizzenmast. The one-eyed man awkwardly began to climb up the ratline while holding more than thirteen pounds of blaster.

He shouted back over his shoulder. "Captain, keep all nonessential crew belowdecks! Keep the stern chasers firing no matter what!" Ryan reached the hatchway into the mizzentop and a pale, scarred hand grabbed him and helped pull him up onto the platform. Jak grinned as he hugged the blood-spattered and bullet-chewed wood for dear life. "Hey."

The topmen white-knuckled spars and platforms and waited for the Gatling to buzzsaw through them again. Ryan saw the strobing flash across the water as the Gatling opened fire again. Luck was with him. The blasterman believed he had cleared the tops of hostiles and was concentrating his fire on the captain's cabin and the chasers within. Black smoke belched from the *War Pig*'s smoke stack. Her yards dripped with men raising every inch of sail the prevailing winds would take. The *War Pig*'s cannon fired in unison as she sprinted for the kill. Cannon balls tore through the mizzen topsail and the main and foresails ahead. Only one of *Glory*'s stern chasers responded.

"Jak," Ryan said, "I need a shoulder."

Jak nodded stoically.

Ryan laid the Longbow over his human rifle rest. Jak covered his ears with his palms against the 170-decibel Armageddon to come. Ryan leaned into Jak as he scanned for his target through the smoke.

Ryan watched his view whip up and down with the roll of the ship. Up in the top of the mizzen it was magnified like a game of crack-the-whip. His shot would be nearly impossible. "Fire...blast..."

Mr. Squid revealed himself, uncamouflaged, next to Ryan and Jak in the mizzentop. "I have an idea."

"Make it fast!" Ryan snarled.

Mr. Squid shot four of his arms out to the corners of the mizzentop and stiffened them. Two more of Mr. Squid's arms brought up a pair of binoculars. Ryan and Jak exchanged looks as Mr. Squid's ocular muscles shoved his eyes closer together to meet them while the tips of his arms adjusted the focus. He wrapped another arm around the mizzenmast as an anchor. Ryan flinched as Mr. Squid wrapped an arm around his waist and pulled him into a cold, wet firing position similar to the one that Ryan had taken with Jak. Mr. Squid's last arm snaked around the barrel of the Longbow and laid it across the top of his head.

Ryan took a prone sniper position atop Mr. Squid. A rare grin creased his face as he looked through his optic. Mr. Squid was watching the *War Pig* through binoculars. His arms pulsed and contracted in time with the roll of both the *Pig* and the *Glory*. There was no longer any need to count.

Mr. Squid had turned himself into a stabilized blaster mount.

Ryan ignored the Gatling. He could chill its crew, but more men would jump in to turn the crank and he only had six bullets left. The *War Pig* fired her four chasers in broadside again. Cannonballs tore through the *Glory*'s canvas, but luckily neither masts nor spars were hit. Nevertheless, the holes in the sails created a wind-dumping sieve. The *Glory* was slowing as the *War Pig* surged forward.

Ryan grimaced and waited for the smoke to clear.

Squid's siphon hissed with strain. "Fire, Ryan. I am losing strength."

The one-eyed man caught sight of his target as the *War Pig*'s smoke shredded around her forward progress. "Hold on, Squid!"

Ryan fired and his bullet tore a hole in the deck a foot from the target. He worked his bolt.

"I am dehydrating," Mr. Squid stated.

Ryan fired. His bullet sparked off the iron of the *War Pig*'s starboard chaser.

Mr. Squid shuddered and stabilized. "Ryan, I cannot maintain this."

Ryan fired. His bullet ripped wood inches from his target.

Squid's skin color started turning from wet gray to ash.

Ryan saw the Gatling blaster yank his weapon up to aim at the mizzentop. He could see one of the officers shouting as he realized Ryan was shooting for the powder kegs. He grabbed the cask of gunpowder by the port chaser, pressed it over his head and with effort charged the taffrail and threw the powder into the sea. Ryan swung his scope to starboard. A huge man in red and black seized the starboard chaser powder cask and pressed it over his head with ease. Ryan pulled the Longbow's trigger. Ryan's .338 Lapua Magnum bullet hit the cask of black powder at more than 3,000 feet per second.

The bow of the *War Pig* disappeared in a thunderous black and orange pulse.

The bowsprit snapped like a stick and took the spritsail, the jib and the fore staysail with it. The Gatling had been abandoned, but the weapon went sky high in pieces. The deck chasers followed the shattered, sloping deck and fell into the sea. The fallen sails formed a sea anchor as they were swept into the bow wake. They yanked the *War Pig* around as her screws propelled against them. The *Glory*'s remaining stern chaser fired and punched a hole through the *Pig*'s side at the water line and a ragged cheer went up.

Squid collapsed like jelly beneath Ryan. The one-eyed man did a pushup off the cephalopod. "Squid!"

"Ryan," Mr. Squid said, turning as white as Jak. "I am hurting."

Oracle's rasp rose to a roar. "Commander Miles, all top men aloft! Every inch of sail she'll take! Get us out of here! Due south! Wounded to the med and dead to the orlop!"

Miles began shouting orders.

"Commander!" Ryan used his battle voice. "Mr. Squid is in distress! A hammock to lower him down! Fresh water in the barrel and a tankard of sea water run up!" Ryan looked down. Miles was flat on his back covered with blood. "Miss Loral!"

"You heard him!" the first mate snarled. "Whichever son of gaudy whore lets the captain's subaqueous specialist die will sleep the night in his barrel and every day after until final nukecaust with the fishes!"

Manrape rocketed a monkey's paw with a line attached to it unerringly up into the mizzen top. Ryan caught it, ran it over the rail and tossed it back down. He hauled up a stoop of seawater and clapped it to Squid's siphon. Squid suckled at it weakly. "Another!"

Mr. Squid "drank" three tankards of seawater while a hammock was run up.

"Squid?" Ryan said. "Are you going to be okay?"

Mr. Squid lay flattened against the mizzentop. His color was a little better. Squid's siphon wheezed in a tiny voice. "I want Doc…"

Chapter Fourteen

"Ryan, I got it! Koa shoved his book on top of Ryan's. "Check it, brah! Gonna show the captain!" Ryan frowned at the interruption of his calculations but checked Koa's. Ryan nodded. They roughly matched his own from three days ago.

Koa was insufferably pleased. He shoved out his fist and extended his thumb and little finger. "Da kine, brah!"

Ryan regarded Koa's fingers. The "horns" in various configurations could mean several things in the Deathlands, but Koa seemed so happy Ryan was thinking it was some kind of South Cific Island thing that might not be bad. "Congratulations."

"Thanks! What're you working on?"

Ryan frowned at his own chart. "I was on some islands in the North Lantic a while back. Trying to see if I could raise them."

"Nice?" Koa asked.

"Half the people were vampires, half were their blood slaves."

"No good."

"Then there were the ones who lived underground. Giants, muties, whiter than Jak and half-pike tall or taller, cannies."

"What's cannie, brah?"

"Eaters of men."

"Why'd you wanna chart that?"

"Just for the heck of it. I met a few good people there. Might've left it better than I found it. Wonder how they're doing."

"Aw, Ryan! You need to come to my island. Get you some poi dog and kalua pig."

Koa pulled his Hawaiian shawl closer about his shoulders. "Getting colder."

Ryan nodded.

"Word is we're running outta Brazil coastline, and we're heading deep South Lantic, brah."

Ryan waited. It was clear Koa had things on his mind.

"Captain says we don't got enough crew to fight the cannon on both sides of the ship."

J.B. had told Ryan the same. The *War Pig*'s Gatling had swept the captain's cabin and the two crews manning the chasers. Gunny had been among the fallen. Rumor was J.B. was going to be given the job. The *War Pig* was bloodied but still behind them, and the *Ironman* and *Lady Evil* would be waiting ahead. "Yeah."

"We don't got enough topmen left to work two watches."

Ryan knew that too. They had already been undermanned; the loss of Movies and Born might well be fatal when they hit the cape. Worse still, Commander Miles was shot up in the med and the captain was spending more and more time with his cabin blacked out being indisposed. Miss Loral was getting genuinely cranky. "Looks like you and me are learning furling and reefing."

Koa's shoulders twitched. He looked up into the rigging. "Don't like heights, brah."

"You and I are going up."

Koa gave Ryan the stone face.

Ryan gave it back.

"So," Koa said, suddenly grinning, "we're friends?"

"Looks that way."

"Ryan!" Krysty's panicked cry was cut off by a huge splash. Crew up in the rigging began shouting. Ryan charged the rail with Koa a heartbeat behind him. The sharpshooters in the tops began shooting. Mr. Squid exploded out of the water and hit the rail like a rocket. He rose up on his arms, ran across the deck at full speed and threw himself into his barrel. Ryan's only thought was for Krysty, but the tactical part of his mind noted that Mr. Squid left a trail of blue blood on the deck and one of his arms had been bitten off.

Ryan skidded to the rail.

Doc had requested the dinghy to take oceanographic samples with Mr. Squid. Oracle had agreed. Krysty had been considered the most useless member of the crew and so was sent to assist them. They were attached by fifty meters of towrope to get them behind the ship's wake. An Antilles crewman named Dutch had been set to watch over them with one of the ship's AKs.

Dutch was gone.

Ryan grimaced. The sea around the dinghy was red with blood, and something had severed the towrope. The *Glory*'s end hung limp in the wake. The part still attached to the dinghy was taut. Whatever held it was well below the water pulling the dinghy around and around in slow clockwise circles. Doc held his swordstick high and slanted down for the thrust. Krysty had her knife. Fear was etched all over both their faces.

"Lover!" Krysty cried.

"My dear Ryan!" Doc exclaimed across the distance. "This is even worse than it appears! For your lady love and my poor life in the bargain, I pray you take every caution!"

Ryan's blood went cold as dozens of six-foot black fins broke the water. "Orcas."

"Black fish!" Koa agreed.

Ryan took in the tactical situation. The question was, were they simple killers or weaponized like Mr. Squid? The fact that they were formation filing around the *Glory* said a lot for the latter. "Miss Loral, where's the captain?"

Miss Loral ran from the wheel and surveyed the situation. A terrible look passed over her face. "The captain is indisposed!"

"With permission!" Ryan didn't wait for it. He ran to the binnacle and grabbed the Dakota Longbow and its remaining rounds. "Everyone hold fire!"

"Topsmen hold fire!" Loral ordered.

"Miss Loral!" Gypsyfair clutched her head and shouted from the gangway to the quarterdeck.

"What?"

Gypsyfair's milk-white eyes rolled in pain. "Echolocation! Whales! Dozens of them! They're mapping us! Crewman by crewman! Deck by deck!"

The ship suddenly yawed contretemps against wind and current. Manrape snarled as he pitted his physique against the unnaturally turning wheel. "Miss Loral, they're screwing with the rudder!"

"Beat to quarters!" Loral ordered.

Krysty screamed as the towrope pulled down and the stern of the spinning dinghy began to rise in the air. "Ryan!"

The one-eyed man went to the taffrail with the longblaster in his hands. He snapped his head back in desperate inspiration. "Squid! You speak orca?"

Squid bubbled up out of his barrel snake balling in what Ryan had come to recognize as shear cephalopod terror. "I do!"

"What're they saying?"

"Kill them, eat them, kill them, eat them—"

Ryan leveled the Longbow at the dinghy. It swung in

a slow circle, and the stern continued to rise higher as the orca that held the rope slowly dived lower and lower. Krysty and Doc held out their blades, but everything was happening underwater. It was not lost on Ryan that the outlying orcas were swimming counterclockwise to the dinghy's death spiral. "What else, Squid!"

"They intend to take the ship out to sea and sink it! They intend to eat me because I taste good! They intend to eat you and the crew for the pleasure of killing and eating humans! Some are saying bring the tree! The one right behind Miss Krysty is saying we wait for night!"

"Gimme a harpoon!" Koa bellowed. "Gimme me ten men with half pikes who can swim!"

Ryan didn't doubt the Hawaiian for a second, but he grimaced at the words "the one right behind Krysty."

Miss Loral gripped the rail as the crew boiled on deck to their battle stations. "Bring the tree?"

Ryan saw it. "They have a big piece of lumber out there. A tree or a heavy beam. They're going to punch holes in *Glory*'s sides tonight and slowly sink her."

"Then what are they doing now?"

Ryan watched Krysty and Doc as an orca below turned the dinghy around and around. "They're taunting us."

"Blasters to all hands!" Loral ordered. "I want—"

"You shoot, you may wound a couple of them. They're waiting for it. They'll dive. The one holding the rope sinks the dinghy and Krysty and Doc are treading water. Then the fun really begins. When those good times are done, they give us the tree by night. They're intimidating us. We need to intimidate them back."

Loral's eyes flicked to the blacked-out captain's skylight. "Ryan, tell me you've got a plan."

"Squid!" Ryan shouted. "Do you speak Morse code?

"It was the second language humans taught us!"

"Do they?"

"I do not know!"

"Are they weaponized like you?"

"It is of a high order of probability!"

"Gypsyfair, I need you now!"

Gypsyfair scrambled up the gangway. An orca rose behind the spiraling dinghy and sat motionless in the water. Ryan locked his gaze with another nonhumanoid mind. Its black eyes met his blue.

Ryan glanced at the dinghy. "Doc, shove your specimen barrel over the side!"

"But, Ryan, it contains—"

"Do it!"

Doc did as Ryan asked, and the specimen barrel drifted into the dinghy's tiny, orca-induced vortex. The killer opened its mouth and exposed its teeth. Ryan could have sworn it was smiling at him. The one-eyed man leveled the Longbow and fired. The half cask was filled with seawater and specimens. Fifty meters was point-blank range for the weapon. The 300-grain bullet hit the cask with nearly 5,000 pounds of energy. The hydrostatic shock wave was impressive to say the least. The cask exploded, and the orca pod leader was sprayed with splinters and atomized sea specimens. Ryan kept his scope on the pod leader.

"Gypsyfair, tell them I am Ryan of the longblaster."

Gypsyfair clicked Morse code like gunshots.

Ryan wondered if they understood the spoken word and shouted, "I'll put a bullet in any blowhole I see!"

Gypsyfair popped and clicked rapid fire.

"My blaster was made to chill anything that breathes air!" Ryan bellowed out a very big lie. "If you come by night, I will napalm you!"

Gypsyfair paused mid echo-translation. "What's napalm and how do you spell it?"

Ryan thundered forth. "If you mess with this ship by night, I will pour liquid fire over the sides on you! You'll burn no matter how deep you dive!"

Gypsyfair pinged out Ryan's message of death.

"Let my people go! Or in my vengeance I take my longblaster and this ship and hunt orcas from the Great White North to the Southern Cape! From Lantic to Cific! I will chill your kind until you're extinct or skydark comes again!"

Gypsyfair stared at Bolan in shock but continued emitting inhuman noises out of her throat and mouth.

Every black dorsal fin stiffened and froze.

Ryan shook his longblaster at the sky and hurled his voice to the heavens. "I will gut-shoot every orca I see and leave you bleeding for the sharks! I'll tie you dying to the sides of my ship and gulls will eat your eyes while I feed you a slice at a time to my octopus! Tell every whale you meet! The wooden ships are on the waters again! Now, swim! Swim while you still can!"

Every orca simultaneously dived out of sight except the pod leader. She lingered a moment, staring up the muzzle of Ryan's longblaster and glaring into his scope. Ryan was fairly certain he had made an enemy. The pod leader sank beneath the waves. The stern of the dinghy splashed down as the towrope was released.

Manrape called from the wheel, "Rudder's free, Miss Loral!"

"Doc!" Ryan called.

"Magnificent, Ryan! You were—"

"Break out your oars, slowly and calmly. Come back to the ship."

"Aye, indeed!" Doc broke out the dinghy's oars and rather adroitly began sculling back to the *Glory*.

"Drop sail!" Miss Loral shouted out. "Let the Doc catch up!"

Ryan caught Loral's eye. "Acting Commander, I didn't mean to—"

"You did just fine, Mr. Ryan." Miss Loral shot her wolf grin. "You've been told before. There's a reason most ships never land in the Deathlands—because you're all mad, bad and dangerous to know."

Chapter Fifteen

"Cove ahead!" Ricky cried out. "Looks like it has anchorage!"

"Thank you, Mr. Ricky!" Loral called. Optics broke out across the deck. The *Glory* had spent most of her second career after skydark in short jaunts and island hopping. Few of her current crew were used to this kind of long, unrelieved, undermanned, endless open ocean sailing. Most were very ready for a stretch of their legs on land.

Ryan observed the coastline of Argentina. It was cold, gray and miserable, and it was snowing. They had raised Uruguay the day before. He had caught long-distance views of the blasted corpse of Montevideo and his rad counter had ticked up a few clicks. They had sailed on across the mouth of the Rio Del Plata and his counter had clicked higher. No one had any desire to sail upriver and see what had happened to Buenos Aires. The air had freshened and the wind had grown colder as they had rounded Cabo San Antonio. Ryan hunched deeper into his coat.

The *Glory* was not ready for winter in the South Lantic. They had cut every spare blanket into capote coats and capes, and with all the casualties, the crew were able to layer with hand-me-downs. They were in desperate need of woolens, slickers and cold weather gear for the Horn. Ryan was doing all right for the moment with his fur-lined jacket and his weaponized scarf. He had wrapped his feet

Russian style in scraps of wool and pulled his combat boots over them.

Ryan sniffed something almost like coffee and turned.

"Cold enough for you, Orca Whisperer?" Mildred asked. She wore a blue plaid blanket coat and a pair of borrowed binoculars around her neck. Mildred bore two steaming stoops and held one out. "Last of the chicory." Ryan gratefully accepted and sipped the hot, bittersweet brew. Mildred smiled. "Last of the sugar, too."

"Thanks."

Mildred gazed out over the gray water at the Argentine coast. "We're in a heap of trouble, aren't we?"

"Yeah."

Mildred raised her binoculars and scanned the coast. "I always wanted to go to Argentina. See and hear the real tango in the square at San Telmo."

"What's tango?"

"Just the most sensual dance in the world."

Ryan liked dancing. Despite his chilling reputation in the Deathlands, he was also known for being able to shake a leg at a festival or ville hootenanny. Dancing with Krysty usually led to some very energetic lovemaking. "How's it go?"

"You could spend your entire life perfecting it." Mildred scanned the empty, snow-drifted beaches. "There were dancers in my time who did nothing else."

Doc joined them. He wore both his uniform coat and his frock coat over it. "Oh, the tango, the samba, the dances of South America, they were such exquisite things, Ryan. I do hope they have been preserved."

Ryan tried to wrap his mind around doing nothing except dancing.

Mildred's voice dropped. "Now there's something you don't see everyday."

Ryan snapped up his spyglass. A man was riding along the beach atop what appeared to be a giant long-necked bird without wings. The man wore a broad-brimmed black hat. His long black hair flew behind him as did his fancifully colored woolen cape. He pulled off his hat and waved and shouted. Sand and snow flew from beneath the huge bird's massive clawed feet as the rider spurred his mount to renewed speed. Ryan had to admit this was a new one for him.

"Cowboys, riding ostriches." Mildred shook her head. "Wow, we missed Argentina completely and raised the Island of Misfit Toys."

Ryan chalked it up to one more bastard obscure, pre-dark Mildredism.

Doc tsk'ed. "No, that is a gaucho riding some mutated or upbred form of rhea, I should think."

Mildred rolled her eyes. "Fine, gaucho and the Technicolor Dream Poncho, whatever."

The one-eyed man scanned the bird rider. He didn't appear to have a blaster, but he carried some sort of coiled rope whip or flail on a wide leather belt sewn with silver coins. Beneath the belt he bore what appeared to be a silver-handled chef's knife big enough to behead a horse. He carried a small guitar-shaped case on his back and saddlebags across his bird.

"Miss Loral!" Ryan called. "Contact on shore!"

Loral squinted through her binoculars. "Don't see that every day."

Mildred sighed. "That's what I'm saying."

Miss Loral snorted at the sight. "Rad-addled ridiculous."

Koa glanced at the rider and then up at the sails. "Ridiculous or not, the way he's catching up, Bird Boy is doing close to thirty knots."

"Thay!" Onetongue lisped admiringly. "That'th one fath't bird!"

"Fast indeed," Doc agreed. "The African ostrich has been known to sustain speeds of up to forty miles per hour. However, this Ratite seems twice the size of any ostrich I have ever heard of, and, unlike the African ostrich or the usual South American rhea, which mainly eat plants and insects, the overlarge and somewhat scimitar curve of this noble creature's bill bespeaks of a predatory bent."

Oracle called from the quarterdeck. "Miss Loral, take us into the cove! Furl sails and break out the sweeps. Bring us within hailing distance and have Mr. J.B. load canister! Sharpshooters to the tops! We are on foreign shores. Let us see if this man has anything useful to say."

"Aye, Captain! Sweepers to the blaster deck! Prepare to furl sails!"

The *Glory* turned landward. The bird rider noticed this development and spurred his bird on. The topsmen rolled up sail and down on the blaster deck six pairs of very long oars slid out the blaster ports and began back rowing to bring the ship to a halt.

J.B. shouted up the gangway. "Starboard battery loaded with canister, Captain! Blasters run out!"

"Thank you, Mr. J.B.!" The *Glory* slowly stroked into the cove. The cove contained a cracked concrete quay that looked like it might service a fairly large ship. A few collapsed buildings bore the unmistakable signs of having been harvested of all valuable metal and timber long ago.

"Mr. Hardstone! Throw the lead!"

Hardstone stood on the ship's chains and heaved the lead. The weight plunged into the water, and he payed out line. "Seven fathoms by the deep, Captain!"

"Back sweeps!" Oracle ordered.

The sweepmen groaned like galley slaves belowdecks

as they heaved against the oars and stopped the *Glory*'s forward motion. She came to a halt about thirty meters from the quay. The bird rider came tearing up to edge of the barnacled concrete and leaped from his saddle. He swept his hat and bowed low.

"Hello, ship!" the man called out in a thick accent. "Hello, ship! Ahoy!"

Oracle strode to the rail and called out across the nearly still surf. *"Buenos dias, Senor!"*

"Buenos dias, Capitán!"

Oracle called out in English. "May I ask your name?"

"I am Strawmaker! Walter Strawmaker!"

"How may my ship and I be of assistance to you, *Senor* Strawmaker?"

"I wish to take ship with you immediately."

"You wish to buy passage?"

"I will work for my passage."

Oracle regarded the man shrewdly. "Passage to where?"

"Well, wherever you are going."

"I see." Oracle shrugged. "What skills have you?"

"Well." Strawmaker grinned. "I have my ax!"

Atlast scowled from the bowsprit. "Doesn't 'ave an ax, does he? He's got a great big knife!"

Mildred struggled for patience. "An ax is a guitar."

Strawmaker reached over his shoulder and a dozen blasters locked on to him. He slowly held up what appeared to be a ten-string ukulele.

"Well, then he doesn't have a guitar!" Atlast protested. "He's got a bloody opossum with a stick in its mouth!"

"I believe it is called a charango," Doc mused.

"Ah!" Strawmaker pointed at Doc happily. "I see you are a man of culture and discernment."

Ryan sensed Oracle was using the banter to his advantage. The captain stood impassively. Strawmaker reached into his saddlebag and produced a gleaming brass instrument. "I play the trumpet. And the piano. Do you have a piano?"

"Am I to understand you are a minstrel?" Oracle asked.

"I prefer the term *travador, Capitán,* but given my circumstances, perhaps wandering minstrel might truthfully apply."

Ryan was keeping one ear on the conversation and his one eye through his spyglass on the surroundings. "Captain, mebbe fleeing minstrel might be more accurate."

All eyes scanned inland.

Oracle nodded. "Indeed."

Mildred deadpanned. "Wow, charge of the chicken brigade."

Nearly a hundred men riding birds like Strawmaker's boiled out of the dunes for the quay. They carried gleaming eight-foot lances held over one arm, and most had some form of single- or double-barrel blaster over their saddlebows.

Oracle's voice went positively droll. "*Senor,* am I to understand there is a ville whose baron you have offended?"

"Baron? Ah! *Barón!* No, *Senor* Spada would be the *Jefe* of the *estancia.*"

Doc spoke low. "An *estancia* is a cattle ranch, Captain. *Jefe* is a chief. In my time, in this land, some *estancias* were rumored to be the size of small countries. Spada will be every inch a baron. Oh, and Spada means sword."

"Thank you, Doc." Oracle raised his voice. "Tell me, troubadour, how many of *Jefe* Spada's women did you impregnate?"

Strawmaker kept snapping looks backward, but he made a show of offense. *"Impregnar!"*

"Despite the willingness of both parties, how many of those lancers have you given good reason to chill you?"

"I will modestly say…a number. However, in my defense I will also say that one of the said *senoritas* whispered to me that Spada intended to make me a permanent part of his *estancia*, and he intended to ensure my service by cutting off one of my feet."

"And now?"

"Now? I believe they intend to strip me and paint my *pene* white, like the ñandú's favorite grub."

"I gather the ñandús are the birds you ride?" Oracle inquired.

Strawmaker started taking desperate looks back at the avalanche of oncoming ñandú riders. "Yes."

"Go on."

Strawmaker cleared his throat. "Then I shall be dragged behind one ñandú at speed while they entice several others to give chase and fight for the prize."

Mildred made a face.

"Then they shall hang me by my hands and use me for lance practice. After that they may decapitate me and play some polo to bring back *Jefe* Spada a properly abused head, though it is a little cold for it." Strawmaker took a knee and spread his arms as the lancers descended. "*Capitán,* I am at your mercy. I will tell you I am not afraid of hardship, and I have played from the Rio Del Plata to the shores of Ushaia. I can be of use to you as a guide, if nothing else."

"Do your people recognize the white flag as a sign of truce?"

Strawmaker sighed as he saw his death. "*Si,* I believe it is universal."

"Commander!" Oracle ordered. "Run up a white flag!"

The white ensign rapidly shot up the flag line and caught a bit of breeze. Krysty spooned into Ryan unhappily. "What's the captain doing?"

Ryan didn't like it any more than Krysty, but he understood it. "Oracle needs supplies and with luck permission to recruit men, which he needs more than he needs a minstrel. Much less a possible war with a baron and giant chickens riders runnin' up and down the coast sayin' the *Glory* is hostile."

Strawmaker carefully put his musical instruments in their cases and neatly piled his belongings. He donned his black hat, wrapped his cape around his left arm, drew his knife and turned to face his tormentors. Four gauchos leaned far out from their saddles and whirled their bolas in huge blurring arcs. They released and the weighted straps scythed toward the musician. Strawmaker sliced one bola neatly out of the air. The next two hit him a heartbeat later at chest height to entangle his arms. The fourth hit him at the knees and toppled him. Ryan's eye narrowed. Strawmaker was down, but the gauchos weren't slowing. They spurred forward, lances leveled. Bolas whirled. Those with blasters drew them. Krysty blinked. "You don't think…"

The gauchos let out a battle cry. Their birds gave a booming hoot in unison and shoved out short stub wings. The formation charged off the edge of the quay like lemmings. The giant birds spread their massive clawed feet to display webbing. Their wings vibrated and drummed the air like hummingbirds. Some sank up to their backward knees and rose back up, legs churning. Some barely dipped into water at all.

The charge continued straight across the water.

"By my stars and garters!" Doc exclaimed. "I have had the pleasure of seeing the Western Grebe dance upon the waters with its mate in courtship, but a giant ratite! Bearing an armed rider and water running! Such adaption is—"

"Drop the flag of truce!" Oracle ordered.

The gauchos charged across the cove on their terror

birds in a wedge. The cold black waters of the cove boiled white beneath them.

Commander Miles sliced the cord holding the white flag and it fell toward the deck like a ghost that had been shot out of the air. Oracle watched its descent. Ryan leaped to mainmast and grabbed a half pike from the rack. Krysty took a knee with her ship's knife and marlinspike in either hand. "Gaia…give me strength…"

The gauchos howled and whooped, firing their blasters and sending bolas humming through the air. Crewmen ducked. The marksmen in the tops glanced down for the order to fire. Ryan dodged a bola and glanced to Oracle.

Oracle watched the flag of truce descend. It hit the deck in a sad, white wad. "Full broadside! Mr. J.B.!"

"All blasters!" J.B.'s voice echoed up the gangway. "Fire!" All eight weapons of the starboard battery discharged canister shot in unison. The *Glory* rocked upward with the recoil. Huge gray clouds of powder smoke obscured everything. "Reload!"

Ryan knelt with his lance in one hand and the other on Krysty's shoulder. She had stopped her Gaia mantra. The fog of powder smoke slowly lifted. The sight of the shredded remains of the gauchos and their mounts bobbing in the surf was horrible. Despite their size, the giant rheas were hollow boned and, having adapted to water, had waterproof plumage. Their canister-cleaved bodies floated on the surface. Some were still alive and honking piteously. It appeared that gauchos did not know how to swim. Most had sunk into the dark water, weighted down by their silver belts and equipment, in addition to the huge lead balls riddling their bodies. Three men clung to their destroyed, still-buoyant mounts, shouting and crying out in Spanish.

"Mr. Ricky!" Oracle called.

"Yes, Captain!"

"Ask those men if they would prefer to swim back to the quay or take ship!"

"Aye, Captain." Ricky shouted out in Spanish. The three surviving gauchos shivered in the near freezing water and shouted a response.

"They would take ship, Captain!"

"Did they tell you their names?"

"Gusi, Boca and Gaudiel!"

"Mr. Forgiven, enter Mr. Goose, Mr. Mouth and Mr. Gaudy as lubbers until signed or proved otherwise!"

The purser scratched in the book. "Aye, Captain!"

"Mr. Hardstone, take a few men in the whaleboat and fetch our new shipmates. Take anything of worth off the bodies, man and bird."

"Aye, Captain!

Strawmaker managed to work his bound body up to his knees. *"Capitán!"*

"Yes, *Senor?*"

Strawmaker raised his chin at the bobbing sea of bloody, giant birds. "I know several excellent methods of barbecuing ñandú!"

"Mr. Forgiven!"

"Yes, Captain!"

"Mark Mr. Strawmaker temporary cook's assistant, South American affairs consultant, ships minstrel and lubber until signed or proved otherwise."

Forgiven's pen hovered while he briefly internalized all this. "Aye, Captain."

Oracle turned his head and regarded the lance in Ryan's hand. "Make him Mr. Ryan's responsibility."

Chapter Sixteen

Ryan's responsibility for Strawmaker was pretty easy. The troubadour had spent the past forty-eight hours mostly vomiting over the rail and moaning in his hammock while Broiler and Skillet had barbecued, boiled and salted away several thousand pounds of ñandú meat without his help. Ryan had spent that time up in the rigging with Koa. Standing on a rope forty feet in the air, leaning over a spar and hauling up sails by hand in all weather day and night was some of the most dangerous, ball-busting work Ryan had ever engaged in.

The Lantic was bitterly cold and windy but a hard, bright sun had broken out. Ryan smiled despite himself as he balanced in space and hauled up hundreds of pounds of wet canvas foresail with the rest of the topsmen. Koa snarled in outrage and as yet untamed fear. "You like this shit!"

"Reef, Koa!" Ryan laughed. "You're slowing me down!"

"Fuck you!"

Koa reefed.

Manrape called from the other side of the mast as the crew furled and secured the sail. They were so shorthanded the bosun was up in the rigging. "I see your chicken is up and about, Ryan!"

The one-eyed man looked down and saw Strawmaker stagger toward the rail. He noted that the troubadour wore freshly sewn, stiff pants of ship's canvas and a blood-stained and patched jersey.

"Hee'th up and about!" Onetongue called out gleefully as he made a shroud taut on deck. "Give u'th a th'ong, Th'trawmaker!"

"Yeah, Strawmaker! Sing something sweet!" Sweet Marie chimed in. "That last one you sang for the sea, and it sounded like two sea lions screwing!"

Strawmaker threw up over the side.

Sweet Marie shook her head. "I swear it's the only song he knows!"

Coarse laughter followed Strawmaker's gastrointestinal contortions.

"Ryan, go see to your chickadee," Manrape ordered.

"Aye." Ryan shot down a ratline at a pace he was starting to feel was seaworthy and hit the deck.

Strawmaker looked up at him miserably. "*Senor* Ryan…"

Ryan's cold blue eye narrowed. Strawmaker flinched. The Deathlands warrior knew the troubadour was yet another test Oracle had thrown at him, and he had very little time to whip Strawmaker into some kind of usefulness.

"Don't *Senor* me, Strawmaker. I'm a seaman. I work for a living. Save it for the captain, the commander and Miss Loral, and save it until you're spoken too directly. While you're at it, I'd shit can the *Senor* and learn sir and ma'am real fast."

"Ah, I see." Strawmaker groaned and clutched the rail. "Thank you, Ryan."

Ryan relented slightly. "I see you dressed for work today."

"I told the *Capitán* I would work my passage. I am a man of my word."

"Glad to hear it."

Strawmaker gagged again but hardly anything came up

but a few viscous strands of spit. He coughed and wiped his chin on his wrist. *"Uno momento,* Ryan."

"Make it fast."

Strawmaker tottered unsteadily across the rolling deck.

"One hand for yourself, one for the ship," Ryan advised. Strawmaker grabbed a shroud and pulled himself forward. Ryan suddenly realized where he was going.

Strawmaker shoved his head into the cold water of the open sea barrel to buck himself up. The troubadour erupted backward, screaming, with his long hair sheeting spray.

Wipe clapped his hands. "He made a rainbow!"

Strawmaker managed to grab a shroud and his hand went for the knife at his belt he no longer carried. Mr. Squid's head bubbled up from the barrel, and the golden eyes stared at Strawmaker in what Ryan thought might pass for cephalopod befuddlement.

"Ryan!" Strawmaker clutched the shroud in horror. "This ship keeps a pet octopus?"

"Pet!" Atlast walked up and brutally poked Strawmaker in the chest with each exclamation. "He's a member of the crew. A subaqueous specialist!"

Strawmaker looked to Ryan in desperation.

Ryan waved a hand in introduction. "Strawmaker, meet Mr. Squid. Mr. Squid, Strawmaker."

Strawmaker searched the faces of the surrounding crewmen, clearly suspecting he was the butt of yet another joke. The crew watched poker-faced to see what might happen next.

"I see." Strawmaker made a show of straightening himself and gave a short bow toward the barrel. *"Hola, Senor Calama. ¿Como estas usted?"*

Mr. Squid contemplated the Argentine musician before him. *"Muy bien, gracias, Senor Pajero. ¿Y tu?"*

Strawmaker screamed. *"¡Madre de Armagedón!"*

Mr. Squid contemplated this. "I believe I am an offspring of it."

"An eight-armed offspring we are lucky to have, then!" Atlast declared. "Aren't we?"

Miss Loral appeared, hurling lightning and thunder. "You can all stand around sucking Mr. Squid's eight suckered cocks or you can finish your watch and get fed! Mr. Manrape and the hard end of his rope can decide for you if you're all torn up about it!" The crew went back to its work about ship.

Miss Loral pointed at Ryan. "You, you're wanted in the captain's cabin."

"Aye, ma'am." Ryan smiled. "Ma'am?"

"Aye, Ryan?"

"Captain wanted me to train Strawmaker. Can you find something for him to do while I attend the captain?"

The she-wolf grinned at the minstrel. "I can find something to occupy his time."

RYAN WALKED IN on another council of war. Doc was there along with J.B. Commander Miles was up out of the med with one arm in a sling and a crutch under the other. Purser Forgiven stood with the book, and Ryan was interested to note that Mildred and Skillet were in attendance. Oracle nodded.

"Thank you for joining us, Mr. Ryan. I will take reports. Skillet?"

"Oh, we got barrel after barrel o' ñandú, Cap'n. And the crew seems partial to it. But neither me nor Boiler ever salted away poultry." Skillet pushed back his braids and shook his head. "Dunno how long it'll save. Was chatting up Strawmaker when he wasn't puking. Says the land is cattle country for thousands of leagues. Now a few good head of beeves, some pigs if they can spare 'em and some salt if someone's goin' shoppin'? That might get us around the horn."

"Thank you, Skillet. J.B., powder and ammo."

"You're short, Captain. That broadside cost you. The good news is that I reckon their outliers saw that and nobody on this side of the earth will want to mess with you. But if anyone does, it better be short and sweet. Or it goes hand to hand."

Oracle nodded. "Mr. Forgiven?"

"Forgive me, Captain, if this seems like the only song I know, but that ballad is canvas, cordage and wood. No ship in memory has tried the horn in winter without an engine. All the spare rigging we've got we took down because it was dangerously worn. They say its storm after storm down there. One or two bad ones, and we'll be sewing our coats together to make sails." The fat man shook his head mournfully. "Speaking of coats, Captain. It's winter and getting colder every sea mile we log south."

"Aye, Mr. Forgiven." Oracle spread the fingers of his remaining hand on the pile of charts before him. "We have nearly a thousand miles of coast to work with. There has to be something to eat. Failing that we'll whale. Food I am not worried about currently, nor powder, ships supplies or our enemies. What I cannot out fight, out sail or improvise against is scurvy. Miss Mildred?"

Mildred went into full medical doctor mode. "You haven't had fresh vegetables or fruit on this ship in weeks. From what little I know about scurvy, the influx of ñandú might help. You can get the nutrients you need from the fresh meat of animals that make their own vitamin C."

Oracle's shark eyes stared unblinkingly. "What is vitamin see?"

Mildred did an admirable job of containing her impatience. "You know limes, lemons and oranges stop scurvy."

"All sailors do."

"Unlike humans, most animals make vitamin C themselves. So when you eat most animals, you get it. The problem is the meat has to be fresh. I'm afraid that salting away the meat destroys the vitamin C."

"Miss Mildred, I have spent my life in the Caribbean, where every island was lush with fruits and vegetables and another island is nearly always just over the horizon. In my sailing experience scurvy has always been a horror story passed on by old salts. Are they true?"

"Probably every horror story you heard was true. You need vitamin C to maintain your mucous membranes and collagen, among other things." Mildred met more blank looks. She shifted gears. "Short version, if you don't get vitamin C, the body starts breaking down. Initial symptoms include weakness, lethargy and shortness of breath. As it progresses, the skin breaks out in sores and the gums start bleeding. When it gets bad, the teeth start falling out and scar tissue—and every member of your crew has old wounds in abundance—starts breaking open. New injuries won't heal. Jaundice, bone pain and hair loss ensue. Except for the swelling and edema, you end up looking like a radiation victim. It ends in fever, convulsions and a very unpleasant death."

Commander Miles's jaw set grimly. "Captain, I beg you. Turn and fight Dorian, and then the rest of the Sabbaths, until we put them all down in the Old Place or they do us."

"He has engines, Commander," Oracle noted. "All he has to do is turn one broadside toward us and blast us into kindling."

"Better than what lies south."

Ryan tended to agree. The cabin went silent. Doc suddenly straightened and nearly hit his head. His long fingers tapped the table. Ryan felt a faint ray of hope. He had seen this behavior in various forms many times before. Doc was rummaging through what could be charitably described as the extremely random access memory of his mind. "Captain?"

"Doc?"

"May we fetch Mr. Strawmaker?"

"Why?"

"Oh, well, when I was at Oxford I had a number of fellow students of Argentine extraction. The wealthy Argentines in that day often sent their children abroad for study. I was fortunate enough to make the acquaintance of several, and we spent many a morning or evening drinking *maté* in our dormitory or in study group."

"What is *maté*?" Oracle asked.

"A form of tea. One puts on a kettle of water and fills a gourd with the dried herb. You insert a silver straw, often with a gold tip, and pass it around among your companions. I found it stimulating and refreshing and pleasingly social. They swore it was healthful and prevented many illnesses."

Mildred's brow furrowed. "I've heard of it, Doc. They had it in health food stores, don't worry about what those were, but they pushed it as an alternative to coffee, supposed to be much healthier and full of nutrients."

Oracle's eyes went into unblinking shark mode. "Full of your vitamins."

"Loaded with them, according to the literature."

Oracle called up through the skylight. "Miss Loral, Mr. Strawmaker to my cabin, if you please!"

"Aye, Captain! Strawmaker, to the captain's cabin!"

Strawmaker teetered breathlessly into the cabin. "You sent for me, *Capitán?*"

Oracle nodded at Doc, who continued. "Good Strawmaker, might I ask if your people still drink *maté*?"

"*Yerba maté?* Of course! Every day! I have a supply in my saddlebag. Why do you ask?"

Oracle leancd across his table. "This *maté,* it stops the scurvy?"

"Forgive me, *Capitán,* but what is this, the scurvy?"

"It is a disease," Doc tried Latin. "A *scorbutic.*"

Strawmaker brightened. "Ah, the *escorbuto!* In my land some of the *estancias* are vast beyond imagining. A gaucho can spend weeks, even months at a time out upon the pampas and consume almost nothing during that time besides dried meat and *maté!*"

"Mr. Forgiven, what did we take off Spada's sec men?"

The purser flipped back through the book. "Most went under the water directly. We recovered a few blasters, though their powder was wet. Some very fine knives, some lances. From the birds' saddlebags some spare clothing, odd trinkets and tools and a goodly supply of light rope."

"What of their food and supplies?"

"Each bird carried a supply of dried meat and a water gourd, which we kept."

"And the *maté?*"

"If you mean the little linen bags full of twigs and leaves." Forgiven cleared his throat uncomfortably. "The men kept the bags and gave the rest to the sea."

Oracle closed his eyes. "I see." The captain suddenly straightened. "Very well, we must obtain meat and *maté,* either by trade or raid, and we must do it quickly. Mr. Ryan, I have heard rumor to the effect that you have traveled from one side of the Deathlands to the other, engaging in just such activities."

"I have," Ryan responded.

"Very well, Mr. Strawmaker, I assume you can read and write?"

"In both Spanish and English."

"You can read a map?"

"I can."

"You claim to have traveled the length and breadth of the eastern coast. I wish you to pick a good landing place, close to where we might be able to acquire what we need."

"I am at your service, *Capitán*."

"Mr. Ryan?"

"Aye, Captain."

"Choose your shore party, and then present Mr. Forgiven with a list of weapons and equipment you will require."

Ryan looked at Strawmaker. "You're saying there's no horses left in Argentina?"

"They were one of the things the disease weapons, during the Great War, attempted to wipe out. They have had something of a recovery in the south. Indeed, in the north we talk about crossing the Horse Line, and in the south they call it the Bird Line."

"Why a line at all?"

"Because ñandú love to prey upon horse, Ryan, just as the richer people of the north love to prey upon the south."

"Captain?"

"Aye, Ryan?"

"Let's cross the Horse Line."

Chapter Seventeen

Ryan marched across the wet, rolling, winter pampas. His party had rowed ashore just before dawn and had been walking inland for hours. It felt jarring to have the earth beneath his feet after so many days at sea. Strawmaker was the clear candidate for translator-negotiator, and he was pathetically grateful to have solid ground under his feet again too.

Ryan had brought Jak and Doc from his own people. Of the sailors, Hardstone was a Deathlander and had been a hardened fighter before he'd heeded the call of the sea. Miss Loral had come along to represent the ship and Skillet its larder. Manrape rounded out the party as the most dangerous man on two legs. The shore party was festooned with weapons. Manrape and Hardstone were loaded down with packs full of trade goods. Miss Loral wore her full ship's uniform but had added a peacoat and combat boots. She and Hardstone carried AKs. Skillet looked positively barbaric. The handle of a two-handed meat clever jutted from behind the cook's back, and the front of his bandolier held three more cleavers of various sizes that, according to rumor, he was adept at throwing. He carried a massive, double-barreled monstrosity of a longblaster with a horrifying, barbed, black iron harpoon head sticking out of each muzzle.

Ryan walked beside Manrape. The bosun held a nickel-plated pump scattergun that looked to have been lovingly maintained; he held it crooked casually in his arm as if he was going duck hunting. The effect was ruined, or heightened, by the ugly, painted red against rust, home-forged bayonet clipped to the ventilated shroud. A hatchet and his lead-weighted rope end hung at his side.

Jak topped another hill about a hundred meters ahead and stopped. He waved the party forward. They gazed upon a vale. A road ran through it. Like most ancient small towns, the buildings clustered on either side of the main road and spread back.

Every building had been burned to the ground.

Ryan snapped out his longeyes and scanned. It wasn't that the ville had been bombed or a fire had raged through it. Every single building, including the outliers, had been deliberately reduced to ancient, blackened foundations. Only crumbling chimneys, cracked concrete, rusting rebar and collapsing stone or cinder block remained upright.

"Spread out," Ryan ordered. The shore party formed a loose skirmish line and descended. The only thing still standing above head height was a perilously leaning lamppost holding a sagging sign. Nothing moved other than the miserable, misting rain. Ryan stopped and stared up at the sign. It had just two words on it in faded orange.

MONSTROS
PESTE

Jak frowned. "Pesty monsters?"

"Strawmaker?" Ryan asked.

The musician stared unhappily at the warning. "We use *peste* where you would use the word plague."

"Plague monsters?" Ryan didn't care for the sound of it.

Strawmaker's shoulders twitched with more than cold. "This place was burned." The troubadour pointed to a pit in what might have been the town square. "There, in the plaza, you will find your answer."

Ryan walked over knowing what he would find. The pit had been dug through the cobblestones and was big enough to drop half a dozen wags into. Its sides had eroded long ago. Nevertheless, blackened bones stuck up through the nearly frozen mud. The pit was an open grave. Like the town, the bodies had been burned. The shore party stared soberly into the pit.

Strawmaker sighed. "You will find many towns like this in my land. In fact, almost no one lives in a city or town. We are all *rurales* now.

The shore party spread out and kicked around in the rubble, but there was little to find. Ryan followed a one-lane road up a bit of hillside. He found a scorched foundation that implied a house of considerable floor plan. He walked across it and stared at steps leading down.

"Over here!" Ryan's party formed around him and stared down the steps. A pair of corroded, nearly eaten down to gossamers of rust I-beams still wedged the equally rusted steel security door shut. The one-eyed man gazed at the crude, faded graffiti painted on the steel. It was the same color orange as the sign in town but brighter for having been sheltered. It depicted a face. The eyes were two angry diagonal slashes. The mouth consisted of two very jagged, horizontal and opposing lightning bolts, clearly representing teeth. "Your plague monsters?"

Strawmaker looked close to bolting. "I have not seen that symbol in a very long time, Ryan. Always, it was very old. But I am a troubadour, and—"

Skillet scoffed. "And I still haven't heard ya sing anything save the breakfasts I serves ya up from ya belly!"

Miss Loral spoke quietly. "Skillet."

"Sorry, ma'am."

"Strawmaker?"

"I play many songs, tangos, ballads, wild festival dances

and, to my shame, paeans of praise to *jefes* that I wrote to earn my supper. Some few songs of my very own I am proud of. But I also sing the *folklorico* and tell stories. The old stories say that sometimes the epidemics didn't just kill. Some of them, they changed people."

Ryan had seen far more of that than he cared for in the Deathlands. "Monsters."

"*Si,* Ryan."

"Is it over?"

"Is what over?"

"The *peste,* Strawmaker. The *monstros.*"

"One would like to think so. I have traveled this land more than most, but one always hears stories of those who have gone into the cities for the treasure trove of tools, materials and technology left behind during the great die-offs and the urban exodus. These stories never end happily. Most often the people never return, or they bring something worse back with them. I myself saw a rancho in the north where every last cow, pig and ñandú looked like they had been torn apart by giants, but all of the people were gone. No bodies. Just gone."

Miss Loral stared at the door and then Ryan. "Booby-trapped?"

"Looks like they were trying to keep something in," Ryan made his decision. "Hardstone."

Hardstone reached into his pack and took out a sawed-down double-barrel scattergun. Ryan slung his Scout and drew his SIG. Jak went around the steps and squatted atop the overhang with his Colt Python and his favorite fighting knife ready. Hardstone was an old hand at breeching ancient houses. Thunder echoed as he put a slug into the door where each hinge should be. Rust sifted off the door as he stepped back and kicked the two I-beams. They collapsed in clouds of rust beneath his boots. The door hung by its knob.

Manrape looked at Ryan. "Together?"

"On three, I'll take point. Hardstone? Light."

Hardstone took a ship's lantern from his pack and struck a sulfur match off his belt buckle. He took up his AK with the stock folded like a giant blaster and held the lantern high. "Ready."

"One, two, three!" Ryan and Manrape slammed their shoulders into the ancient steel. The door snapped off the deadbolt and fell inward. Ryan took a knee on top of the fallen door and covered the cellar. Manrape followed him like a bayonet charge about to happen. The golden light of whale oil flooded the cellar as Hardstone unshuttered the lamp. Ryan took in a tableau trapped in time like an insect trapped in amber. The one-eyed man rose. The cellar was wide and low ceilinged and seemed to take up a great deal of the space below the foundation. It had a kitchenette, a bathroom and a living and sleeping area.

"Clear! Manrape, keep a watch up top."

"Aye." The titan went back up the stairs.

Ryan advanced and the rest of the shore party filed in behind him. Jak took in the arrangement of the bodies like the veteran scout he was. "Bad."

"Wasn't good," Ryan agreed.

The sleeping area had a bed and two cots. Two corpses occupied the bed. A woman and a small boy in predark clothes lay arm in arm. The woman's arms still clutched the boy, and one air-cured hand covered his face. Ancient rust-colored blood spray on the sheets showed where each had taken a round through the left temple.

Ryan took in the little girl lying in the exact middle of the cellar. She was air dried like the rest and appeared to have taken five rounds in the chest and a sixth between her eyes. Ryan's jaw set. Something was terribly wrong with her. The eyes of the presumable mother and son on the bed were desiccated. The little girl's were huge, hard, bright black marbles still bulging out of her head. Her lower jaw was too big. The mouth was locked in a death rictus, and teeth that belonged on a horse filled it. The edge of each tooth was set at a separate, horrible, diagonal shearing bias.

Ryan turned his eye on the man sitting at the kitchen table.

His left hand was bandaged and the little, ring and middle fingers were gone. Ryan had a terrible feeling if he gutted the girl he would find three fingers in her shriveled belly. The man's lower jaw was gone, and the top of his head was open to the sky as if it had taken a burst from a machine blaster. A Glock lay on the floor beneath his right hand, the action racked open on an empty chamber. Behind him three words scrawled in brown streaks of ancient blood stained the refrigerator door.

DIOS ME PERDONE

Ryan nodded at the last act of graffiti. "Strawmaker?"

Strawmaker's voice shook. "It says, God forgive me."

Every member of the shore party saw the terrible drama play out in their heads. Ryan got down to business. "This place has a lot we can use but not what we came for. Miss Loral?"

"This is treasure and bounty found on land. We take our pick as long as it's not ship-needed. Can't carry this much. We mark it on the map and come back with more crewmen for the bulk. Manrape's above watching our six, so he gets a pick over."

Ryan immediately strode to the Glock. He'd taken point and none denied him. Skillet raided the kitchenette. Everyone else began ransacking drawers and closets in what Mildred liked to call a shopping frenzy. They were remarkably egalitarian, and communal loot began piling up on the little dining table.

"Butane lighters! Ten pack!" Hardstone called. "Grab one!"

Jak tossed a pair of Swiss Army knives on the pile. "Multi knives! Already got one!"

"Boots!" Miss Loral threw a pair of new out of the box combat boots on the table. "Don't fit me!"

Ryan grabbed them. He knew Krysty's feet intimately and recognized he'd found her some footwear. He put them on his small pile with some socks and went back to the Glock.

Jak admired the blaster. "Better'n your SIG?"

"Figure I'll give it to J.B." A corner of Ryan's mouth lifted. "Surprise him."

Strawmaker opened a guitar case and nearly buckled. "A Takamine! A F400S! Oh, *madre de dios!* Let there be strings…" He shouted in triumph. "A capo! Strings! Bronze strings!"

Pieces of clothing shot around the room to see if they fit anyone in the party.

Miss Loral squealed and came out of the curtained privy with a thirty-six-roll bulk pack of toilet paper still in the plastic. She ripped it open and began yanking out rolls, tearing out their cardboard tubes, squashing them flat and jamming them into her pack. Ryan grabbed a few for Krysty, and Jak did for Mildred. Ryan searched the dead man's pockets and found keys. He went to the steel floor-length cabinet and after two tries opened it. "Blasters."

It contained two assault rifles of some make Ryan couldn't identify. Two hunting rifles, a O/U shotgun and a pistol and a revolver. The boxes of ammo were scant, but Ryan found spare mags for the Glock. He loaded them and filled his pockets with 9 mm rounds.

"Strawmaker," Ryan called, "you didn't draw a blaster from stores."

The minstrel in black drew himself up. "I am a troubadour, until very recently I was gladly welcomed wherever I went. I am also a gaucho, born and raised. Give me my bolas, my knife and a good bird beneath me and I can live off the land quite easily without a blaster."

"You're a *Glory* man now and a member of my shore party." Ryan took up the 4" revolver and checked it. The action was gritty, and a couple of spots of rust marred the blueing, but otherwise it looked to be in excellent shape. He loaded it and put it on the table along with the rest of the ammo in the box.

"Smith Model 25, .45 caliber. You've got six shots. Just put the front sight on the enemy's chest and squeeze. When we get back, have J.B. tune it up for you."

Strawmaker made a face, but he went to the table and picked up the blaster.

The tool chest, radios, computer and tech, the highly suspect meds, the two generators, candles, kerosene, gasoline, lanterns, cots and linens were all earmarked for the ship. Ryan looked over at Doc. The old man was in a corner by a small writing desk and a shelf of books. He perused the volumes with interest. Ryan checked the ring of keys. He'd raided many a predark house and recognized keys by size and function. He pulled off a small brass one and tossed it. "Doc. Desk."

Doc looked up and caught the key with his fencer's reflexes. "Ah, of course."

The old man opened a drawer. "Oh my."

The shore party looked over. "What?" Ryan asked.

"Pornography."

Ryan and Jak knew what porno was. So did Hardstone. "What kind?" the sailor asked.

Doc sighed and began slapping down old 'zines. *"Oui, Juggs, Hustler."* Doc squinted at one in shock. "Hardcore Lithuanian, lactating, unwed lesbian—"

Hardstone lunged. "Dibs!"

Doc opened another drawer. "Oh my stars and garters!"

Ryan read the look of shock and pleasure on Doc's face. "What?"

Doc pulled out a clear bottle with an orange label and filled with amber-colored liquid. Miss Loral pointed a finger. "All spirituous liquor is to be handed over to the purser once aboard ship, Doc! You know the creed and you know the code."

It was a rare thing to see bemused defiance on Doc's face. "But First Mate, are we not still ashore?"

"What are you saying, Doc?"

Skillet stormed forward with his thick fingers through the handles of a set of teacups. "He's saying he'll share his loot with his shore mates and let's us have a tot against the cold!"

"That is exactly what I am saying, friend Skillet."

"I don't drink." Miss Loral raised an eyebrow at Ryan. "And you're acting shore commander."

Ryan eyed the bottle. As loot, predark booze ranged from pure pleasure to gut-busting horror. "What is it?"

Doc caressed the bottle with pleasure. "Why, it is a ten-year-old Glenmorangie single-malt whisky."

Jak made a noise. "Be least hun'erd."

"It was ten years aging in the cask, dear Jak, and then bottled at its finest. Though many spoke of the twelve and eighteen year olds with deserved reverence."

Jak eyed the bottle. "Still good?"

Doc gave a rare deep smile as he cracked the bottle and expertly poured two fingers in each cup. "I believe it should be nearly immortal and fit for one." Several frowns met him as he cracked his water bottle and gave each cup a splash. The crew did not want their grog watered while ashore. "I beg of you to trust me—if you have not had scotch before, it is a great aid in discerning the subtleties."

Hardstone snorted. "I've had corn whiskey, Doc. Back in the Deathlands, in the hill villes, deep southeast. Ville stilled. Wasn't much fine, fit or subtle about it, 'cept its power to crack a man's skull. I'll give it that."

Ryan had too, but he knew Doc was in his element.

"Oh, good Hardstone." Doc smiled. "Many a man has crawled into a jar of whiskey and never returned, but now, a man who drinks scotch is as different as is his choice of drink. He rarely if ever drinks it simply to get drunk. Good Scotch was expensive back in the day. In my experience, a man opened a bottle of scotch at the birth of a child or at another great, portentous event. It was an accompaniment to fine reading, fine conversation or contemplation. You might pour a splash for a friend who came to you with his troubles, or enjoy a dram after a fine meal with a cigar and bosom companions. It was salutary, celebratory. Many believed that Scottish whisky was the penultimate form of the distiller's art. The techniques derived over untold centuries of trial and error, from that first clear liquid the ancient Celts called *uisce beatha,* the water of life."

The shore party stared at Doc in awe.

Doc raised his teacup. "And I can think of no better fate for this fine bottle than to be shared with my shipmates."

Strawmaker was openly moved and raised his mug. *"¡Salud, amigo!"*

The shore party clinked cups. "Salute!"

Jak snapped his back, gave one short hard cough and licked his lips. "Good."

Doc deliberately unbunched his brows and poured Jak another dram.

Ryan sipped his. It had been a while since Ryan had gotten drunk. His friends' lives depended on him too much. But he did enjoy a good drink, or even a bad one in his few moments of leisure. He felt the burn and let the flavors play across his tongue. A small, nostalgic corner of his heart yearned for a better past he had never known. Ryan knew without a doubt he tasted it now. "Thanks, Doc."

"You are welcome, my dear Ryan. Scotch was born to be shared with friends."

Manrape called down the staircase. "Company, ma'am!"

Ryan was leader of the shore party, but he let it slide for the moment. "Everyone stay down here! Miss Loral?" Ryan and Loral strode up out of the quarantined time capsule. Manrape had his shotgun to shoulder. Ryan snapped out his longeyes and observed the armed convoy staring down at them along the hill line.

"Strawmaker! Get up here!"

Chapter Eighteen

Ryan counted more than two score of gaucho bird riders. Each had a lance resting in a stirrup cup, and each had a blaster across his saddle bow as well as a bolas, a whip and the ubiquitous giant Argentine knife. Each gaucho also had a spare bird tethered behind him. The gauchos were eyeing Ryan, Manrape, Miss Loral and Strawmaker with a great deal of interest. Several had binoculars. They had two wags drawn by oxen laden with supplies. Ryan scowled at the twenty men linked by forked boughs of wood bound to their necks in a coffle. They were tall, and all had long black hair. They wore little besides ponchos and tattoos, and most were hobbling on bloody bare feet. Behind the wags a number of gauchos herded what looked to be fifty creatures that to Ryan's eye looked like a cross between a camel and a goat. "Slavers?"

"*Si,* Ryan. You might loosely cut this country into north and south, pampas and Patagonia. The north? *Ranchos, estancias* and *plantacións*. It is a place of ñandús and cows. The south? Hotter in summer and colder in winter. Nearly a desert. It is hard, dry country. The people are, how would you say, semi-nomadic? They are horsemen, and hunt the wild boars, the ñandú's smaller cousin, and herd scrub cattle and guanacos."

Ryan gazed on the giant goat creatures. "They're like llamas."

"Very much like a llama," Strawmaker agreed.

"You said the north preys upon the south."

"*Si,* Ryan. A horse stands no chance against a ñandú, except that they can live and thrive where the ñandús cannot." Ryan watched the caravan form a hostile arc on their side of the vale. Gauchos were pointing at Strawmaker. Miss Loral was attracting attention as well.

Ryan frowned. "Manrape, how'd they see you?"

Manrape shrugged carelessly. "I let them."

Miss Loral's voice dropped to a hiss. "Bos'n, I will see your spine."

Ryan very reluctantly came to Manrape's defense. "I see what he sees."

"And what is that, Mr. Ryan?"

Ryan stared at the slaves. "Twenty able-bodied men who might prefer to be sailors than slaves. Forty plus sets of capes and winter garments. There's got to be *maté* in the wagons, and every gaucho is carrying his own personal supply as well. Half a hundred hoofed animals to salt away for the Horn, and their woolen pelts. More ñandú meat than anyone can eat for the next three days before it rots. We need them more than we need anything in that cellar. I say we take both and use their wags to carry it."

Manrape grinned. "We are of a mind, shore commander."

"There are lots of them," Miss Loral observed.

"*Si.*" Strawmaker chewed his lip. "And while I am sure Ryan and Manrape have already surmised this, when you fight a gaucho, you must fight him and his bird."

Ryan scowled as he heard the sound of Doc's boots at the top of the stairs.

"Hmm," the old man observed. "Speaking of birds, I believe—"

"Doc..." Ryan grated. "I didn't ask anyone else to come up. I want our numbers unknown."

"Oh, bother." Doc was crestfallen. He'd been doing well at not making mistakes since coming down from the shrouds.

"What do you believe about birds, Doc?" Ryan hoped it was something useful.

Doc pointed at the rear wag. "Oh, well, that fellow, the one riding shotgun, as it were. Notice the birdcage beneath the buckboard and—" The man riding shotgun threw up his hands and a pigeon erupted from between them, flapping hard for lift.

"Ryan, I believe that pigeon is carrying a message, and I strongly believe it is about us."

Ryan was aware of carrier pigeons, though given what they had to survive once they were released, most people in the Deathlands simply raised them in coops for food.

"Good eye, Doc." Ryan snapped his Scout longblaster to his shoulder. When he'd first found the weapon in Canada, J.B. had enthused that before skydark it was claimed a good man with a Scout could take a clay pigeon out of the air. Ryan had needed that explained to him, but he'd become deadly adept with the Scout. The pigeon raced across the vale between the two parties. With the forward mounted scope the bird was both a spec in Ryan's peripheral vision and a well-detailed bird in his reticule. He put his crosshairs on the racing bird and tracked.

Miss Loral made a noise. "You've got to be kidding."

Ryan led his target by another hair and squeezed the trigger. The longblaster bucked and the pigeon tumbled in mid-air. The bird's head fell away as its body tumbled.

"You knocked its head off!" Miss Loral was awestruck. "In flight!"

The slavers regarded this feat of marksmanship with a stony silence. Miss Loral snapped open the stock on her AK and threw the selector lever from safe to semi-auto.

"You think that might've been enough for them?" The bird riders suddenly fanned out to either side of the vale, taking their tethered birds with them.

"No," Ryan answered. "They're circling us."

"¡Comer!" the gauchos shouted. "¡Comer!"

Manrape cocked his head. "They want us to come there?"

"Comer means eat," Strawmaker corrected. "They are talking to the ñandús, and they are talking about us."

The riders released the tethers of the riderless birds. The ñandús dipped their heads low, and their talons ripped up turf as they streaked down into the vale. The mounted gauchos disappeared into folds in the land. "The spare mounts are meat shields!" Ryan snarled. "The gauchos will be coming in right behind them!"

"Correct, Ryan!" Strawmaker confirmed. "Ammunition is precious here in the south! They want you to waste ammunition! They want to count your guns!"

Ryan was mildly surprised. "They're willing to waste mounts like that?"

"A ñandú reaches maturation in six months. It is winter. Untold numbers of last spring's hatchlings are being trained to the saddle in the north as we speak."

"Down the stairs!" Ryan ordered. "Let them think we're holing up!"

Ryan liked that the *Glory's* officers and crew snapped to orders without question. He crouched at the bottom of the stairs and checked the grens he'd been issued. He had five. J.B. had ascertained they were Dutch and had probably been obtained in the Antilles. One was OD green, shaped like a ball and clearly a fragger. Another was shaped like a short, fat, black water bottle and was an offensive gren. The other three were shaped like ancient gray soda cans with flaking red, purple and white paint on the top, indicating a smoke gren. Ryan heard the strange, booming hoots of the riderless ñandús closing in. He yanked the pin on the fragger and the cotter pin pinged away. "Gren!"

Ryan heaved the deadly egg up onto the foundation.

Nothing happened.

Three riderless ñandús craned their scimitar-beaked heads down into the stairway and peered at Ryan.

The one-eyed man yanked the pin on the offensive gren and hurled the bomb. "Gren!"

The birds turned their huge heads to look back at what had been thrown, then returned their attention to Ryan as he stuck his thumbs in his ears and squeezed his eyes shut. The concussion gren went off like a thunderclap. Heat and blast washed down the staircase. Ryan opened his eye and watched the three ñandús collapse with their necks flopping against the sides of the stairwell and their eyes rolling back.

Ryan shouted over the ringing in his ears. "Loral! Man-rape! Doc and Strawmaker! With me! Everyone else wait for it!"

The Deathlands warrior charged out of the staircase. Three more ñandús lay smashed onto their sides. About another half dozen on the periphery staggered about in mortal devastation from the blast wave. The rest of the giant ratites streaked out of the vale in all directions at nearly fifty miles per hour. Guachos waved their hats and whistled piercingly. Some of the ñandús stuck out their stub wings and spread their feathers like braking airplanes and started to bank back toward the fight. At the lip of the vale a gaucho with a wider black hat and more silver jack on his belt than the others appeared and swung his bullwhip in a huge arc and cracked it.

Every fleeing ñandú jumped at the sound and turned.

Ryan whipped his longblaster off his shoulder and shot the man out of the saddle. For a moment there was no sound other than the fwap-fwap-fwap of the ñandús' webbed talons tearing up the soft earth and the echo of the shot. In Ryan's experience, slavers didn't like a stand-up fight. They were bushwhackers and night creepers. He'd hoped the death of their leader would send the raid-ing gauchos into retreat, leaving most of their gear be-hind. He clenched his teeth as the gauchos screamed in bloodlust. They had flanked the shore party's position, and now they charged from all directions. The birds that had fled followed their angry flock back into battle by instinct.

"Take cover! Crew below, wait for it!"

Manrape walked up to a pair of concussed ñandús. They had found each other and wrapped their necks, and like two drunks, each appeared to be the only thing holding the other up. The bosun slashed his red painted bayonet across their entwined throats, and arterial scarlet sprayed. The giant birds' legs folded, and they fell beak-first to the hard concrete. Manrape jumped between them and went prone like a man taking cover behind his horse.

"Ryan!"

The one-eyed man ran forward and jumped into the avian revetment. It stank of wet feathers, blood and dying, bowel-releasing bird. The wind and the rain were pick-ing up. Miss Loral and Strawmaker ran for the cover of what appeared to be three stories' worth of collapsed brick chimney.

"Doc!" Ryan shouted. "Take cover!"

The old man stalked to the middle of the plague house's foundation. The wind whipped his white hair and his frock coat back to reveal the blue uniform coat beneath. He swept his swordstick behind him in his left hand and held his

LeMat revolver in his right as if he were in a duel. Ryan knew where this was going. Doc had been held prisoner in the most horrible conditions, had suffered the most profane indignities. The old man despised human bondage in every form.

Doc wasn't taking cover this day.

He cut a rakish figure as he exposed his perfect teeth, and moral outrage put color in his cheeks. Gaucho blasters began to crack as the bird riders closed. Doc ignored the incoming fire and took careful aim. The hat of the closest charging gaucho flew off as Doc shot him in the head. The ñandú kept charging forward. Doc cocked his revolver again, flicked the hammer cone and fired the LeMat's shotgun barrel. The bird squawked horribly as it took a palm-full of buckshot to the chest and collapsed in the road. Doc's rakish figure was also turning into a blaster magnet.

Ryan scanned and fired.

The gauchos were good. Not only were they adept at loading and firing in of the saddle, they also used every fold of ground to their advantage as they circled, and the ñandús were as fast as most wags with the pedal floored. Ryan picked off three riders and then knocked down their birds. Manrape waited for them to come within range of his scattergun. Bullets thudded into the corpses of the giant birds they were using for cover.

Strawmaker stood up from behind the crumbling masonry with his bolas whirring. He cast and his target ñandú honked as its entangled legs got left behind and it went beak-first into the ground. The rider expertly leaped from the saddle and landed on his feet. Strawmaker extended his new blaster in a fair imitation of Doc and pulled the trigger. The troubadour's first shot fired in anger knocked his opponent to his knees, and his second shot left the attacking gaucho facedown dead in the dirt.

Miss Loral's AK cracked in rapid semi-auto. "Strawmaker, take cover! Take Doc with you!"

Manrape's scattergun began to boom. Blood burst and feathers flew.

Ryan began pulling pins. "Gren! Gren! Gren!" Ryan hurled his smoke grens. Multicolored smoke began to billow in the ruins. The ñandús began honking and recoiling. They had been bred not to mind blasterfire, but Ryan had bet that like the thunderclap of a concussion gren, the giant birds did not like roiling opaque clouds of colored, brimstone-smelling smoke. The gauchos swore and dug in their spurs. Their birds shook their short wings and bobbed their heads in hesitation.

"Cellar team!" Ryan shouted as he shot. "Now!"

Jak charged out of the basement with his .357 in both hands. His first shot blasted the nearest gaucho from atop his bird. The ñandú leaped ten feet in the air like a fighting rooster splaying its talons for the kill. Jak's second shot shattered the bird's scything beak and most of what lay behind it. Hardstone came up out of the cellar firing well-aimed, short bursts that shattered man and bird. Manrape bounced up and leaped over his meat shield.

Ryan snarled as he fired his magazine empty. "Bos'n!"

Manrape charged for the purple cloud ahead and the riders behind it. "In through the smoke, Ryan! It is the fighting sailor's way!"

Ryan clawed for a spare magazine. A gaucho burst through the roiling red smoke on the flank Manrape should have been covering. The ñandú rolled its eyes and honked in terror, but it obeyed the savage spurring of its owner. The altered avian fixated on Ryan and surged single-mindedly toward its prey. The gaucho raised his lance for the kill.

"Fireblast…" Ryan shoved up his empty longblaster to block the attack.

"This is for you, gaucho boy!"

The gaucho turned his head to see the startling sight of Skillet emerging from the cellar. The cook's giant harpoon longblaster belched smoke and fire, and half a pound of barbed iron smashed the gaucho from the saddle.

"This is for ya buzzard!" The second iron hit the ñandú just behind its wing. The giant bird made a sound like a burst balloon and fell bonelessly on top of its rider. Skillet shook his head at Ryan's bird fort.

"Quit laying on my barbecue, Ryan!" The cook dropped his spent weapon and yanked his two-handed, carcass-breaking cleaver from over his shoulder. "In through the smoke like an able seaman!"

Ryan rose, muttering as he reloaded. "In through the smoke…" Fire discipline had gone to hell. He had to remind himself that once the hulls touched, sea fights devolved in large-scale brawls. Regardless of the fact that they were on land, the *Glory* crew followed its hard-won fighting instinct to dominate any fight or lose their ship. Ryan advanced firing. Despite their numbers, the gauchos were outgunned and now struggling to control very reluctant birds. Being riders from the cradle, they did not want to jump from the saddle until it was too late.

Ryan's shore party fell into an easy rhythm of killing birds first and then shooting their riders in mid-dismount acrobatics. Skillet screamed like a banshee and hacked off a ñandú's head. The gaucho screamed like a rabbit, and Skillet gave him the same. Ryan made a mental note he wanted Skillet with him in any future boarding party. The Deathlands warrior fired the Scout dry and dropped it on its sling. A 9 mm blaster was small for giant birds, but he had two of them and he filled his hands with Glock and SIG. He shoved the Glock at a charging gaucho and pulled the trigger. The weapon jack-hammered in his hand. The burst climbed up the ñandú's chest in recoil and continued up the gaucho riding it. Man and bird fell in different directions as the weapon racked open on empty. Ryan admitted the Glock had possibilities.

He raised the SIG and scanned. The wind and the rain shredded the smoke and beat it down. Ryan ran his eye over complete carnage. Hardstone was sending a fallen gaucho out of town with the butt of his AK to the skull. Miss Loral was cleaning her dirk on the cape of a dead opponent. Doc and Strawmaker stood back to back with sword and gaucho knife and empty revolvers. No enemies stood. A few birds and gauchos writhed and moaned.

Ryan scanned the shredding smoke. "Sound off!"

Every member of his party called back alive and well. Ryan barked orders. "Skillet, reload! Manrape, hold the perimeter! Loral, grab a blaster from below and then you and Strawmaker come with me!" Ryan reloaded the Glock and his longblaster. Miss Loral ran below while Doc showed Strawmaker how to reload his weapon. Miss Loral came up and gave the thumbs up on her new weapon. The three of them formed a wedge and walked to the gaucho wags.

A stunned ñandú rose and Ryan raised his Scout. Strawmaker held up his hand. "Wait!" He took up a fallen lance and snapped his fingers. *"¡Che! ¡Che! ¡Che!"* The bird blinked, and its new owner grabbed a stub wing and expertly heaved himself into the saddle. Strawmaker pointed his lance at the slaves. "Those are Mapuche Indians. They are a warrior people. The only thing that stopped them from slipping their ropes and trying to kill the gauchos was that they are on foot, and they know the ñandús would eat them. Best to have a man on a bird when you negotiate with them."

"I like the way you think, Strawmaker. Do you speak Mapuche?"

"I do."

"Translate for me exactly." Ryan scooped up a dead gaucho's knife. "Which one is the leader?"

"Probably the one in the front glaring at you."

Ryan walked up and flipped the knife blade into his hand and held out the hilt. "Here."

The man took the knife.

"Ask him what his name is."

Strawmaker began translating as the man cut his bonds. "Shisho."

Ryan nodded. "Tell Shisho he and his people can take the gaucho's clothes and weapons and as much bird meat as they can carry. They can have ten of the *guanacos* for walking rations to get wherever they need to go. I need the wags and the rest." Ryan turned on his heel and walked away.

Strawmaker called after him. "Shisho says it would take weeks of crossing the southern *estancias* and the territory of enemy tribes on foot. Without horses they will never make it back to their lands. They will die or become slaves again."

Ryan turned. "Not my problem."

Shisho gave Ryan a Koa-worthy stone face.

"Tell Shisho if I had horses, I'd give them to him. But I don't, and I have to go."

"Shisho believes you and thanks you, but he asks where you are going."

"Out on the ocean."

Strawmaker laughed at the response. "Shisho says you must have a very big canoe."

"Bigger than he's ever seen. If he wants to see it, tell him to follow me."

"Shisho says the orcas will eat you."

Ryan turned and looked Shisho in the eye. "Tell Shisho I already took care of the orcas."

Shisho's eyes widened. Strawmaker laughed once again at his response. "He says he believes you."

"Ask Shisho if he's ever eaten ñandú."

Shisho laughed. So did Strawmaker. "He says no, that would be something."

Ryan called back. "Skillet, make a fire pit and get some bird on the barbecue! I've got twenty hungry lubbers about ready to sign up! Hardstone, help him! Jak! Doc! Bring the wags around. Let's start loading that cellar! Manrape, with me!"

Shisho cut his people free. They swiftly acquired knives, blasters, bolas, boots and bloodstained clothing. Ryan turned to Miss Loral. "We've done what we can here. I think we made enemies with that *estancia* farther inland Strawmaker was talking about. I say we strip that cellar and bring it, fifty beasts on the hoof, the *maté* and twenty waisters ready to train up for the Horn to Oracle."

"We've succeeded beyond all expectations," the first mate stated. "We better get out of here and under sail before the gauchos can swarm on us."

Jak climbed into a wag, opened the pigeon cage and began stripping them of their message tubes.

Strawmaker bristled. "You are interfering with *el correro,* Jak!"

"What?" Jak asked.

"The mail! Interfering with the mail is highly frowned upon in my lands!"

Ryan took a big step forward. Strawmaker instinctively pulled on his reins and backed up his bird. "You're going to read me the mail, Strawmaker," Ryan intoned. "Then we're going to eat it."

"Mmm." Manrape sighed happily. "Squab."

Chapter Nineteen

As the wag topped the dunes Ryan stood and waved his scarf overhead in a circle. Cheers rang out aboard ship. Shisho and his people stopped short at the sight of the *Glory* at anchor. Ryan had to admit that from their perspective it was one nuke-big canoe. The long boat and the dinghy lay pulled up out of the surf, and Koa seemed to be in command of the beach party. They'd dug fire pits and brought out barrels in preparation. Koa hurled out a "Mahalo, Ryan!" that might have been heard in the Andes. Ryan grabbed his pack and jumped down.

He turned to Miss Loral. "I relinquish command."

"Aye, Mr. Ryan."

The first mate began shouting orders. "Strawmaker! Take Shisho and his people before the captain and interpret. See if they want to join up. Skillet, fetch Boiler and get these guanacos skinned and salted away. Tell him to fire up these pits and get these oxen roasting. Bos'n, unload the wags. See the loot we don't need on the ship brought before the mast for distribution or bidding! Hardstone, tell Chips and the carpenter's mate to break down these wags for their planks! We're going to need them. Ryan, report to the captain! Then all of you requisition a tot of grog and grab some hammock. Handsomely done, shore party!"

The weary party gave themselves a ragged cheer that turned into answering thunder from ship and shore. Ryan went to the dinghy, and Wipe and Onetongue rowed him to the ship.

Onetongue grinned. "How wa'th it, Ryan?"

"We had a rough fight but found some food and mebbe some sailors." Ryan patted his pack. "Found a cache."

Onetongue pulled oars and happily eyed Ryan's bulging pack without an ounce of avarice. "Anything good?"

"A few things." Ryan reached into his pack and pulled out a sky-blue XXL fleece sweatshirt with a white stripe across the chest and a sun face on it. Strawmaker had explained that this had one been his land's flag. "Figured this might fit you." Ryan pulled out a matching wool watch cap. "Figured this too, for that bald head of yours."

"Aw jee'th, Ryan!"

"You and Hardstone were the first crew to show me any kindness. A man takes care of his mates."

The mutant looked close to blubbering. "Aw jee'th…"

Wipe looked covetously at Onetongue's loot. Ryan reached into his jacket. Among his other accomplishments, Wipe was the ship's confirmed onanist. Ryan had learned that twice since Oracle had become captain he'd rigged a grating and had Wipe lashed for "polishing his dolphin" on duty. Ryan handed Wipe the 1999 April issue of *Swank* still in the plastic wrapper.

"We're Phalanx. Try not to look at it on watch."

Wipe gazed upon the 'zine, enraptured. "Oh…"

"Row!" Onetongue cajoled. The dinghy soon clunked against the side of the ship and Ryan scrambled up the Jacob's ladder.

Commander Miles nodded from the top of the gangway. He was walking with a stick now rather than a crutch. "Captain is expecting you, Mr. Ryan."

"Aye, Commander." Ryan went down the gangway. Gallondrunk stood guard at the door with his walrus iron held at port arms.

The brain-damaged giant's voice boomed. "Mr. Ryan to see the captain!"

"Thank you, Gallondrunk. Send him in."

Ryan entered the captain's cabin. As usual, Oracle was poring over a table covered with charts and old books. Purser Forgiven stood at his side. Ryan saluted and handed Oracle a few folded sheets of printer paper from the cellar. "Shore action report, Captain."

He gave a separate sheaf to Mr. Forgiven. "List of loot taken, Purser. Signed by myself and Miss Loral."

"Thank you, Mr. Ryan." Forgiven scanned the sheets. "Oh, very good. Captain, I recommend we get Mr. Rood working on the generators immediately."

"Indeed." Oracle frowned at what he read. "This disposition of the natives isn't good, I gather?"

Ryan set down a handful of the tiny pigeon scrolls. "Strawmaker translated them. Spada's sent out the word. We're pumping so many rads now we glow in the dark. No one'll come near us."

"Strawmaker and Miss Mildred as ordered!" Galloondrunk bawled.

Strawmaker entered the cabin with Mildred. "The Mapuche are ready for your inspection before the mast, *Capitán.*"

"Very good. Miss Mildred?"

"At cursory examination they seem to be disease free. Suffering a bit from hunger and exposure and torn-up feet, but decent clothes and two meals of barbecued pigeons and ñandú have helped. Of course, they're going to spend the next week puking, but that will give their feet time to heal. They might have their sea legs by Tierra Del Fuego."

"Thank you, Miss Mildred." High-pitched shrieks broke out on the main deck. Oracle raised a coal black brow at his ship's minstrel.

Strawmaker flinched.

"Captain," Ryan said, suppressing a smile. "I think the Mapuche just met Mr. Squid."

Oracle nodded. "Mr. Strawmaker, Mr. Ryan and Miss Loral seem to be of the opinion that we will find no safe harbor in these southern lands."

"*Jefe* Spada has painted you as hostile raiders and the *Glory* as a pirate ship. The annihilation of the slavers will most likely cement this reputation. I had hoped to go inland. I know several border *jefes* who have forests on their *estancias*. Some are known for their magnificent wood working. I had hoped to get wood for spars and masts, but I fear that hope is gone."

"Wood and cordage." Oracle gazed upon his one-hundred-year-old charts of the South Atlantic. "There is one place left."

Purser Forgiven's head snapped around. "The Falklands?"

Ryan frowned at a vaguely remembered word. "What's the Falklands?"

Strawmaker scowled ferociously and muttered beneath his breath. "You mean the Malvinas."

Mildred stared incredulously. "You're still upset about that? After a century?"

Strawmaker stuck out his lower lip. "*Las Islas Malvinas,* they're ours."

"Oh, for God's sake!"

Strawmaker pouted. "They're ours…"

Clearly something predark was going on. Ryan ignored it and looked to Forgiven. "What's the Falklands, again?"

"WHAT'S THE FALKLANDS?" Krysty asked. Ryan reclined into his hammock and Krysty spooned into him.

"Islands," Ryan replied. "Big ones. Pretty far south and east of here. And rough from what I hear. Strawmaker's all radded up about them. Seems his people think they own them. The locals don't seem to agree, not before skydark and not now. The main ville is supposed to be big. Except for the one airbase they had, the islands didn't get nuked. The people there aren't above raiding the coast, though mostly they do it for ship-worthy trees and things they can't grow on their own—and slaves."

"So they might have a timber stockpile?"

"And rope and cable, possibly sail material of some kind. They're seafarers. Problem is they'll know the state we're in, and word is they're bastard cold when it comes to trading. Most ships plying the South Lantic don't put in there unless they have no choice."

"And we have no choice."

"None."

"Well, did you bring me anything from shore" Krysty asked.

Ryan made a rueful noise. "There was some jewelry, but I know you're not one for carrying around useless baubles. Besides, I remembered what you said about gems and crystals having their own energy, their own vibration, and how they can pick them up from their surroundings."

Krysty's shoulders twitched. "It was that bad?"

"Even Manrape found that cellar tragic." Ryan took a butane lighter out of the ditty bag he had packed for Krysty. "Got you a light. It's pink."

Krysty smiled. "Thanks."

Ryan pulled out a rectangular package with a predark gaudy slut pouting on the pink wrapping. The package read *Lux*. "Got you some soap." Ryan pulled out a washcloth and bath towel. "And wash rags, pink too. So's your new toothbrush."

Krysty smiled at her loot. "Are you saying I have hygiene problems?"

"I'm saying their aren't many comforts on this ship. My girl deserves all of them." Ryan pulled out a flattened roll of toilet paper. "Plus I got this."

Krysty's green eyes glowed from within.

"Mm-hm." Ryan nodded. "The package was all in Mex, but Strawmaker said it's diamond weave." He brushed the roll against Krysty's cheek. "Feel that? Quilted for strength, absorbency and softness."

Krysty crushed her lips against Ryan's.

He smiled. "Got more where that came from." He held up her new boots.

"So do I—if you know what I mean."

"Yeah, I get the picture, and I'm not one to turn down that offer."

"Word is they're boiling water down on the beach." Krysty waggled her bar of soap. "And I have wash rags and soap. Do you think we might be able to requisition a couple buckets of hot water and go down by that creek in the dunes?" Krysty's hand moved down Ryan's stomach. "Mebbe take a couple of blankets?"

Ryan made a pretense of considering the idea. "You're talking a little good, clean fun?"

"Soap'll be involved," Krysty purred. "But the fun'll be dirty as fallout."

"I'm in." Ryan rolled out of the hammock. "That reminds me, I've got a present for J.B." He emptied the ditty bag. "Meantime here's a new hairbrush, a bandanna, a few rounds of .38 and some wool socks."

"Yay!"

Ryan grabbed his pack. "I'm going to distribute a little goodwill around the ship. Meet me before the mast at the next bell?"

"Miss Krysty and Mr. Soap." Krysty touched Mr. Soap to her brow. "Volunteering for shore duty, shore commander."

Ryan walked away grinning. "See you by the mainmast, seaman."

"I got a mainmast in mind…"

RYAN SPIED J.B. crouched over a carronade. The armorer worked the trunion and squinted across the primitive sights. Ryan had a small, terrible temptation to keep the Glock, but he and his SIG Sauer were very old friends, and he didn't need to learn a new manual of arms for the joy of squirting off eighteen rounds in one second.

He called out to J.B. "Hey! Gunny!" J.B. continued staring at the carronade's trunion fixedly, doing some kind of cannon math. The armorer still didn't quite register his new title.

"Master Gunner!" Ryan called.

"Ryan!" J.B. looked up. "You're back."

"I brought you a present."

J.B. blinked at this unexpected development. "Oh?" Ryan held up the blaster in his right hand. J.B.'s brows bunched. "A Glock?"

Ryan turned the weapon to show J.B the selector lever. J.B. squinted slightly through his glasses. His jaw dropped. "Glock 18! Full-auto!"

Ryan grinned and tossed his friend the weapon. J.B. caught the machine pistol and held it as if it were a holy relic. He took in the top slide cut and the ported barrel. His eyebrows shot up. "Glock 18C!"

"J.B., I figured you might need a handblaster, one that can put out a lot of lead when things get close."

"You sure?" J.B. was clearly moved. "You sure you—"

"No," Ryan said with a shrug. "You know me, J.B. I pick my shots, and I count them. I couldn't keep up with that thing."

"You're a good friend."

Ryan reached into his coat and pulled out the loaded spare magazines. "You're the best I ever had."

J.B. gazed at the weapon, clearly mesmerized.

"You need a moment alone with it, mebbe?" Ryan teased.

J.B.'s eyes never left the blaster. "Mebbe."

"Right" Ryan turned and walked to the gangway.

"Ryan?" J.B. called.

He nodded without turning and said, "You're welcome."

Chapter Twenty

Ryan ran his longeyes across Stanleyville. It was big. A seawall of boulders and broken rock girded the shoreline. Nearly all the predark architecture was gone, replaced by a substantial maze of lumpish, black and gray stone houses with sod roofs. Nearly every chimney sent up thin gray smoke that instantly bent and shredded in the nonstop wind. A number of larger buildings had multiple chimneys and generated the harder blacker smoke of industry. Ryan lifted his nose and tested the air. The Westerlies that had filled their sails once they had turned from the Argentine coast blew across the ville from landward. The overwhelming smell of the ville was the turf and dung they burned for fuel. He also took in smoked fish, the smell of a slaughterhouse and the hard burn of ironmongery.

A squat, three-story concrete fortress with a watchtower stood uphill from the ville, and four concrete towers of similar squat design stood at intervals along the sea wall. Ryan could make out cannons far larger than the *Glory*'s pointed her way in the embrasures. People ashore had noticed the *Glory*'s sails in the strait and were rushing to the pier. Ryan noted none were armed.

Mildred frowned. "There are no trees."

Miss Loral smiled as she looked through her binoculars. "Those are pretty."

Ryan had to admit they were. Seven wooden ships sat in concrete quays jutting into the harbor. They were barely half the size of *Glory* and not built to the same standard, but they were two-masted and had rakish lines. "What would you call those, Doc?"

"Too small to be called a sloop or a brig. It would be imprecise, but they might be best described as a Bermuda rigged ketch." Suddenly the entire crew within earshot was hanging on Doc's every word. "A ketch was just about the smallest ship of war in the 1800s, and it was used in nearly every commercial maritime venture. Look there in the boat houses!"

Ryan looked and saw open boats made of hide and whale bone.

"Behold! Those are dear Shisho's big canoes. The good people north of here, the Eskimos, call them umiaks. One of those ketches could tow numbers of them into fishing or whaling grounds and then process their catch. They are also large enough to bring in useful cargoes of timber or coal."

"Or slaves."

"Yes." Doc's face fell. "I fear there may be a reason that slaver caravan was headed for the coast."

"Commander Miles!" Oracle called out. "See the Mapuche stay belowdecks until further notice!"

"Aye, Captain!"

Doc finished his ketch lecture. "As you can well imagine, they are also large enough to raid up and down the Eastern Coast of the South Americas. Indeed, I suspect they are far more nimble tacking into the Westerlies than we shall be when we round the horn."

Ryan spotted a dozen predark pleasure boats that had seen all manner of extreme modification. He also noticed a number of motorboats that looked to be in serviceable condition. All of them had suspicious tarpaulins covering something blaster-like on their prows.

Oracle sliced his monkey's paw down. "Fire, Mr. J.B.! All guns!"

J.B.'s ordered rang out below. "Fire all guns!"

Every gun along the sides as well as the stern and bow chasers belched empty smoke with no ball. Ryan knew that to J.B. it was a terrible waste of precious powder, but the "all guns" salute of a ship coming into port was more than just a sign of respect. Given the time it took to reload a muzzle-loading cannon, it meant that the incoming ship was nonhostile, and it was putting itself at the mercy of the weapons guarding the port.

The shore battery staid laid and ready for the *Glory*. The crew relaxed as small blasters up on the walls of the fortress crackled in a ragged, return string of salute. Ryan watched as people on shore waved, shouted and threw their hats in the air and surged toward the docks with excitement. He was reminded that a full rigged ship under sail was something that most ports never saw.

Wipe sidled up to Ryan. "Mr. Ryan?"

Ryan deliberately kept his tone neutral. "Wipe."

Wipe pulled what looked like a mail packet from under his jersey. "From the cap'n."

Ryan took it. It read in block script. TO BE READ NEXT TIME YOU ARE IN THE CAPTAIN'S CABIN. He tucked it away. "Thanks, Wipe."

"Welcome."

Ryan snapped up his longeyes as a score of armed men mounted on shaggy ponies road out of the fortress. They wore brown leather dusters, except for the man in the lead, who wore black. As they reached the ville proper, people scattered to get out of the sec men's way. The men rode to the boat houses and ran out a umiak rather than any of their other boats or ships. Ryan took this as a goodwill gesture on their part.

The brown-jacketed sec men began a deep-voiced chant as they paddled out the gleaming white hide and whalebone canoe. Their black-jacketed leader stood at the prow. They back-paddled and stopped neatly at the *Glory*'s Jacob's ladder. The sec leader gazed up. He was very tall, a head taller than Ryan and quite gangly. The man had huge hands. Ryan stared at his blaster and suddenly realized the weapon was a Steyr AUG missing its scope and with all of its plastic furniture replaced by carved whalebone. All of his men bore a similar weapon. The leader wore a brass hilted saber at his side that looked predark. His thin, platinum-blond hair clung to his head in the wind and drizzle. Huge features jutted from a face that was seamed all over from wind and saltwater. Ryan's first impression was the sec man was about as hard as they came. Pale gray eyes squinted upward.

His accent was kind of like Atlast's. "Permission to come aboard."

Oracle nodded. "Permission granted."

The leader handed his longblaster to the man behind him and came up the ladder with agility, drawing himself up to full height. He ran his gaze around the *Glory* and grinned. "Bloody, blue blazes, you're back!" The sec man was missing his two front teeth, and it made his sudden smile strangely childlike and disarming. "Oh, I was just a little lad the last time this ship weighed anchor in Stanley. Now here you are and here I am standing on her deck. And they say the days of wonder are past!"

The crew murmured appreciative noises at the man's respect.

The sec man reached out a worshipful hand and squeezed a bit of rigging like he couldn't believe it was real. "She was the *Starsailor* when I was a boy. What's her name now?"

"The *Hand of Glory*, sir," Oracle replied. "I am Captain Oracle. May I present my officers, Commander Miles, Miss Loral and Mr. Ryan?" Ryan was surprised to learn he had made officer without knowing it, but he kept it off his face. Oracle extended his hideous ape prosthesis. "May I present Koa Kanaka, Prince of Molokai?"

Ryan hadn't seen Koa behind him. The Hawaiian was naked except for his multicolored cape, a loincloth and his crested helmet. The Hawaiian held the most horrible war club Ryan had ever beheld. It appeared to be a short, incredibly heavy paddle lined with giant, serrated mutant shark's teeth around the blade. Koa was stone-faced and grunted once. *"Mahalo."*

The sec man gaped.

Oracle gestured at the barrel. "And may I present Baron Squid, subaqueous ambassador of the Caribbean Sea depths and warlord of the littoral waters."

The sec man goggled as Mr. Squid bubbled up out of his barrel to his full eight feet. The Kelper jumped as Squid spoke. "I bid you greetings, sir."

"Wonders…" the man whispered. The sec man suddenly snapped to attention. "Except for the gov'nor, we don't stand on title here. My friends call me Big Ian. So do my enemies."

"Big Ian, would you join me and Commander Miles in my cabin for a glass in friendship? And would you allow me to invite your men aboard to take a tot of hot grog against the chill?"

"A kindness well received, Captain. I would be honored." Big Ian followed the captain and Miles below. Ryan rolled his eye at Koa. "Prince of Molokai?"

"And what are you, brah? Officer Fourth Mate? Surprised the captain didn't announce you as cabin boy Bellywarmer. Me?" Koa grinned smugly at his newfound title. "I'm a prince! Show some respect, *haole*, and stay in character until we're off this barren rock. Seems even Squid can do that."

One corner of Ryan's mouth twitched upward. "You know, I'm going to make officer on this ship long before you do."

Koa lifted his chin imperiously. "Make me a sandwich, primitive Deathlands scum."

Ryan was torn between laughing out loud or letting his fist coincide with the Hawaiian's jaw and see which one broke first. He spoke quietly as the sec men came up the ladder and wondered at the *Glory*'s main deck. "You know you're chilled."

Koa nodded at the main hatch. "Wait for it…"

Sweet Marie came up and genuinely curtsied to Koa. "The captain respectfully requests Prince Koa and Baron Squid join him in his cabin."

Mr. Squid oozed out of his barrel and did his scuttle walk thing to the hatch. Koa flung a careless hand. "Tell the captain I shall join him anon."

Sweet Marie blinked. "Anon?"

"I read it in a book."

"You can read?" Ryan asked.

"And get Mr. Ryan flogged next time he does not show me proper obeisance." Koa strutted to the hatch.

Sweet Marie muttered, "What's obeisance?"

"What's the first part of the word?" Ryan prompted.

Sweet Marie suddenly smiled. "Obey!"

"Yeah."

Sweet Marie frowned at the hatch. "Koa knows some big words."

Ryan frowned too. "Yeah."

Governor Laird's Hall

SEAWEED WINE TASTED like the heady mix of iodine, tide pool leavings and fishermen's feet Ryan had expected.

In counterpoint, the seaweed, oatmeal and oyster stout beer was bitter, black as a redoubt with the lights off and so thick a man might be forgiven for mistakenly trying to chew it. The Kelpers, man and woman alike packing the smokey, peaty hall, drained horn after horn and cup after cup of both. Ryan realized they lived on a windswept rock and had to make do with brewing what they had, but he would have done anything for a glass of grog or ship's small beer. He figured asking for a glass of water would not exactly cover him or his shipmates with glory in this company. Ryan noticed Doc putting a good pinch of salt in his horn and smacking his lips with relish as he drank. The one-eyed man took a chance and followed suit. Ryan smiled. The salt cut the bitterness and turned the black beer into a mildly pleasurable drink to sip by a warm fireplace to good music.

Strawmaker was earning his keep. He played his Takamine 400S with passion and sang out in a clear tenor. No Kelper in living memory had heard a real guitar. The islands' whalebone flautists, bagpipers and lap harpists sat leaning forward and as still as statues as they hung on Strawmaker's every note. He sang in Spanish and pushed his emotions out so boldly the entire hall was moved. Women wept openly. Hard men wiped their eyes and swallowed with difficulty.

Ryan took in their host. Governor Laird wasn't large, and he was getting on in years. Most of his hair had moved backward across his head. What he had left was a grizzled salt and pepper and clipped short. Laird had a strong jaw shaved clean, and he had a positively wolfish cant to his eyes. They called him Gov, but there was no mistaking that he was a baron, a very powerful one by Deathlands' standards, and he was utterly feared by his people.

It had been a hard day of negotiations. Gold had been

making a comeback as currency in recent years. Oracle had a substantial amount of it, and he had to give nearly all of it to Laird, as well as one of the gasoline generators, and far more blasters than they could spare. In return they had gotten rope made on the island and timber from the Amazon, and wherever Laird got sailcloth from, he wasn't telling.

Ryan ate. He had no complaints about the food, much less the portions. A pig had been roasted for the occasion in the main hearth. While the feasters waited, they gorged on plates of raw oysters, steamed mussels, snow crab in drawn butter, pickled anchovies, fried sardines, cow and goat cheese and laver bread and oatcakes. Ryan took an immediate liking to cold roast penguin. He tucked into his seaweed stew with particular will.

Governor Laird watched Ryan shrewdly and leaned toward Oracle. "Your people have been without fruit or fresh greens for some time?"

Oracle sipped the black beer. "We took on *maté* on the continent to compensate."

"That'll get a man through, but it loses its potency fairly quickly. It has a tendency to get buggy. Shall I send a caldron of sea sass for your people aboard ship tonight? They'll be the better for it."

"That would be a kindness, Governor."

Laird snapped his fingers at a servant. Nearly all of them seemed to be from the continent. "Tell Cookie to simmer our largest feast kettle with sass and row it out for the *Glory,* and tell him not to be stingy with his blubber." The servant scampered for the kitchens.

"Well now, Captain. I was but a tot when your ship last put in."

"Aye, she was the *Starsailor* then, under Captain Buckley. I believe he presented the governor of the Isles, your father, with a gift of friendship. May I continue the tradition?"

Laird smiled. "Who am I to deny a guest?"

Oracle nodded. "Miss Loral?"

The First Mate took a black predark, nylon pistol rug from her satchel. Oracle passed it on. Laird unzipped it to reveal a beauty of a U.S. military-issue Beretta M9 handgun. If it hadn't been matte black, the blaster would have sparkled. Ryan knew J.B. had gone to town on the weapon to turn it into an oil-on-glass slick tack driver. The case also contained a 50-round box of ammo and a spare mag.

Laird smiled openly. "Oh, now, Captain, that is fine. Big Ian, let us show Captain Oracle our appreciation."

Big Ian rose from the great U-shape of tables in the hall and brought Oracle a bulging leather bag. He shook it and it clinked and rattled. He grinned to show his happy, gap-toothed smile. "They're not so fancy as that, Captain, but with your permission?"

"You humble me, Big Ian."

The man emptied the bag before Oracle.

Six sets of well-worn handcuffs clattered to the table. Strawmaker hit a bad note and stopped playing. Big Ian's grin went from happy to hideous. "Try one on for size, Captain. Then order your crew to do the same." Ryan watched as the smoky galleries above filled with a dozen brown-jacketed sec man armed with the ghostly-looking whalebone stocked assault longblasters. The feasting Kelper dignitaries stared about in fear.

Big Ian drew his saber and pointed it in Ryan's face. "The Deathlander prick has a knife in his boot, then."

Governor Laird shrugged. "One would expect nothing less."

The blade gleamed in Ryan's face. His one eye met Big Ian's two, and they both knew they were most likely the two most dangerous men in the room. The sword tip hovered.

"Shall I stab out his other eye?"

Ryan's fingers itched for the blasters he wasn't carrying. He turned an arctic blue eye on Laird. "Governor, this is piracy."

Laird happily loaded his new Beretta and racked the action. "Oh, I'm not the pirate here, Mr. Ryan. Your captain is. Oracle is the one who attacked *Jefe* Spada's men while they were trying to apprehend a wanted man, and 'tis it not Oracle who sent you forth to attack the trade caravan of *Jefe* Dirazar and steal all of his goods and slaves? Both times killing each of their gauchos to the last man."

He arched a knowing eyebrow. "Unless Oracle has pressed some into service? Do you deny this?"

Ryan knew pigeons had flown and the Westerlies had pushed them faster than the *Glory*.

Laird shrugged. "You see? You're the raiders. You're the cold-hearted looters. You, Mr. Ryan, are the pirates."

"No ship will ever land here again," Loral snarled. "And our crew will defend the ship to the death. They will burn *Glory* to the water line before they let you have it."

"That is the case exactly, Miss Loral. I'm not taking the *Glory*. I'm just taking your captain for his crimes. You will keep all timber, cordage and supplies you bargained for in good faith. You will attempt the horn and I wish you well of it, but you will sail on, or be sunk, without your captain. That is my final word."

"War!" Koa declared. "War with my *ohana!* War with every island!"

Laird nodded. "Stories of the kanakas reach even here, Prince Koa, but we have two oceans and a continent between us. Still, you'll have the Westerlies at your back. Paddle your war canoes around the Horn if you can. I'll meet you fleet for fleet, man for man, land or sea any time."

Koa stared bloody murder at Laird.

"Miss Loral," Oracle finally spoke. "Mr. Miles is now acting captain. You are commander. Mr. Ryan is First Mate. Take what we have bargained for and go. Sail the Horn, and take *Glory* to warm, safe harbors." Oracle snapped the manacle around his monkey's paw and with difficulty got it around his other wrist. "I order you to put them on."

Big Ian flipped a set of cuffs to each of the shore party with his saber. Doc surged to his feet. It was a miracle he wasn't shot. "Oh Captain, my Captain!"

Ryan knew Doc was a heartbeat away from drawing his concealed sword, and there was nothing they could do in this hall except die.

"Doc!" Ryan snarled. "Put them on."

Doc wept as he put on the manacles. Ryan and the rest followed suit. The governor nodded. "Big Ian, take them back to their boat. See them rowed to their ship. If they take any action, slaughter them. Know if the *Glory* fires on you, they shall be blasted to splinters in vengeance."

"Thankee, Gov." Big Ian looked at Miss Loral. "But this one follows orders." He looked at Doc. "This one's feeb." He shook his head at Koa. "If this one is a prince, then I'm the queen of England, and the guitar player won't do shite."

Big Ian ripped his right hand around and punched Ryan in the eye with the brass basket of his sword. Ryan's head snapped back as he deliberately took the shot. His world narrowed to a dark tunnel surrounded by purple pinpricks. He instantly felt his face inflating like a balloon and his eye closing. Big Ian laughed. "And this one won't do shite if he can't see." Ryan heard the sword sheathed. "Now move, you lot!"

Ryan rose and the room spun. Koa put a hand on his shoulder.

Governor Laird happily aimed his new Beretta at the pig turning in the fire. "I don't know if this will be of any comfort to you, but I am not going to give your captain to Spada or Dirazar. No ñandú will snap off his cock."

Ryan fought nausea and wondered if he had a concussion. "No?"

"No, I am going to give Oracle to Captain Dorian. He's on his way." Governor Laird's smile was sickening. "I suggest you sail for your lives."

Chapter Twenty-One

The Captain's Cabin

"We go back!" Miss Loral's fist crashed on top of the chart table. She spilled tears of fury. "We go back now! We get the captain and burn their ville to the ground!"

"E kokua!" Koa thundered. "To the rescue!"

Mr. Forgiven wept openly. "They took our good captain, and we took their lovely parting gifts and weighed anchor!"

Ryan took the cold guanaco steak off his eye and tried to glance around the assembly. They were mostly a tearing smear in his remaining eye that he could barely open. Techman Rood bristled with rage. Ryan was again surprised to note Koa's presence at a captain's cabin conference, and again he suspected there was more to the Hawaiian than he knew.

J.B. looked at Ryan. The companions were not ones to leave anyone behind, and the Armorer was spoiling for a fight. Mildred hung on his arm. Commander Miles's half-healed wounds clearly pained him. Losing his captain pained him more. His jaw set with terrible certainty.

"Their shore guns will blow the *Glory* out of the water. If we send a cutting out party, they'll never get past the ville, much less into Laird's fortress." Miles bowed his head in anger and shame. "We just have to swallow this. The *Glory* has swallowed worse in the past. If we take vengeance, it comes after the Horn and after the Sabbaths."

Ryan admired Miss Loral's sentiment. Like Commander Miles, he didn't relish sailing into the teeth of Stanley's coastal blasters or trying to take on a ville of several thousand souls.

"Coward," Miss Loral grated.

Miles's knuckles went white. "My first loyalty is to this ship and her crew. As acting captain, until confirmed or challenged, First Mate, should I find myself in similar circumstances, I will expect you to take command and sail on. Are you challenging?"

Miss Loral looked like she just might.

Ryan reached into his jacket and pulled out the sealed envelope. "Before we went ashore, the captain gave me this."

Something akin to both fear and relief passed across the commander's face. "If those are the captain's last orders, obey them."

Ryan tore open the oilpaper packet. It held two smaller envelopes. He had to pull his eye open to read it. One was addressed to RYAN. The other to ACTING CAPTAIN. Ryan handed the latter letter to Commander Miles, who stared at it. The two men opened their orders. Ryan found another, smaller yet again envelope. It was addressed READ BY THE LIGHT OF THE BINNACLE.

"Commander," Ryan asked. "I—"

"You have my permission to go to the quarter deck." Miles crumpled his note in his fist. "And I will abide by your decision." He turned stiffly and stared out the stern windows. "Whatever that may mean…"

Ryan felt his hackles rising. It was a well-established belief aboard the *Glory* that Captain Oracle had powers, and that they were both a blessing and curse to him. Ryan left the captain's cabin and went to the gangway mostly by feel. In the darkness of the fo'c'sle, Strawmaker quietly strummed his guitar in sad, minor chord progressions that echoed the feeling aboard ship. Gallondrunk sobbed like a baby while Sweet Marie comforted him. Ryan emerged on deck. The wind blew bitterly cold and moaned through the rigging. The ship was at anchor, and Manrape stood watch at the wheel wrapped in a pair of dead gauchos' capes. He raised an eyebrow at an able seamen entering onto the quarterdeck. Ryan held up Oracle's last envelope. "Captain's last orders."

Manrape didn't seem surprised. Ryan went to the binnacle and pulled his swollen eye open.

The skeleton hand hung half-closed and apparently dormant in whatever fluid filled the glass dome. A pair of covered lanterns lit the magnetic compass, the ship's master hourglass, clock and the helmsman's chart. Ryan cracked the wax seal on the envelope and wondered if there would be yet another packet nested inside. He pulled out a note written on a scrap of yellowed, predark paper that consisted of two sentences in simple block script.

RYAN, THIS WAS FORESEEN. YOU WILL EITHER SAVE ME OR YOU WON'T. ORACLE

Ryan looked up from the note. He snarled in revulsion, and his ship's knife came free. The skeletal hand was pointing at him. He suppressed the urge to take the Longbow blaster from the binnacle case, empty the last remaining rounds into the glass globe and the hand it contained and kick whatever shattered remains were left into the Cape for the Kelpers to deal with. He smelled Krysty before he saw her. Ryan sheathed his knife.

He was grateful for the backup. but he shook his head. "You aren't even rated ordinary seaman. You can't be on the quarterdeck without an officer's permission."

"Nuke that," Krysty replied. "I walked right past Manrape, and he didn't say anything."

"Well, while you're here," Ryan said, lifting his chin at the binnacle. "What do you make of that?"

Krysty stared at the hand in loathing. "I feel it every time it moves."

Ryan's jaw set. Krysty wasn't a doomie, but she felt things. Sometimes she was almost prescient, and when things got strange her feelings spiked.

"So," Ryan asked, "Oracle's psionic? He's moving it? Some other power is moving it?"

"There are many other movers in this broken world. Some are terrible beyond words. My mother told me sky-dark birthed things and opened doors. She said some of the bad things are as old as time and loved what happened. Thrived on the fall. Got stronger. At least that's what she believed. I— Gaia!"

Krysty pulled her knife as the hand slowly turned and pointed at Stanleyville like an undead compass needle suspended in blood. "I hate that thing!" She glared at the binnacle. "I hate it! And I hate what it's going to make you do."

"No." Ryan took a long breath and let it out. "That hand won't make me do anything. I have a choice to make."

"And?"

"And I'm going to save the captain."

"You'll die," Miles announced.

"Mebbe," Ryan conceded. "Sometimes one man can do more than an entire ship's company, and I'm not taking Stanleyville. I'm taking the captain out of it. This is a rescue."

"It's not that I doubt you, Ryan, but I have to think of the safety of the ship."

Even Miss Loral was against it. "They had at least three motorboats that I saw. They'll be patrolling and expecting trouble."

"That's why you get me in as close a possible and I swim the rest of the way."

"Swim?" Miles was appalled. "In this water? In winter? At night?"

"Skillet found plas-wrap in the bunker's kitchen. I'll grease up, wrap myself in it, then grease the outside. I spoke to Hardstone about our row in. He said the current isn't bad and the tide will be on my side."

Ryan squinted at the first mate through his swollen eye. "Is he wrong?"

Loral grimaced. "Good swimmer can swim mebbe a mile, two miles per hour, and that's on a sunny day in the Caribbean. To avoid the harbor patrol, we'll have to drop you off at least a mile from shore. You'll be slowing down and going numb with every stroke. You think you can make that in an hour without freezing, much less dragging spare clothes and a blaster?"

"I'll just be taking my knife. When I get ashore, I'll find clothes. If I need a blaster, I expect I can find one of those too."

Miles slowly shook his head. "You've got balls, Mr. Ryan. I grant you that. But you can barely see out of that eye."

"Miss Mildred will cut me."

Mildred exploded. "Jesus Christ, Ryan!"

"The freezing cold water will take care of the rest."

Miles appraised Ryan yet again and turned to his techman. "Mr. Rood, what are the Kelpers saying?"

"There's shortwave radio traffic. The patrol boats are talking to each other and the fortress. They're patrolling. They know the *Glory*'s a fighting ship, and they're waiting for our response. Plus they got horsemen patrolling the coastline for outlier insertions. They also sent out more of Doc's Caesar cipher. They radioed Dorian that they have the captain. Dorian is coming. He's sailing on his engines and will take the captain and effect repairs in Stanleyville. Laird's rolling out the red carpet."

"Commander?" Ryan locked his one-eyed gaze with Miles. "Now or not at all. I'm volunteering. Give me twenty-four hours."

Commander Miles closed his eyes and broke his word. "We sail on."

Miss Loral's voice went dead. "Miles, when you're fit? I challenge."

The entire tonnage of the *Glory* crashed down across Commander Miles's shoulders. "Accepted, Miss Loral. Dirks at a dawn of your choosing."

The acting captain suddenly rose to his full height. "Until then you will get your gaudy-skank ass to the quarterdeck! Take the con, and chart us a course around the horn. Dorian Sabbath is nearly on us under power. We drive into the Horn's Westerlies in winter. Under sail. Tack upon tack. I cannot spare a moment, much less a day! Now unless one of you rad-blasted bastards can give me one reason to stay on, I—"

"Commander!" Hardstone called out from his guard position outside the door. "A crewman seeks permission to address the acting captain!"

Miles sagged in exhaustion and pain. "Well who, rad blast you?"

"Subaqueous Specialist Squid!"

The cabin went silent for a moment.

Miles squared himself. "Send him in."

Mr. Squid entered doing his disturbing gait of walking erect on the tips of his seven arms. The arm the orcas had bitten off was already a foot long and growing longer by the day. "Commander Miles?"

"Yes, Mr. Squid?"

"I overheard this conversation."

Miles rubbed his temples. "And?"

"And for a short period of time I am capable of swimming at speeds of up to twenty-five miles per hour."

Commander Miles blinked.

"Pulling Ryan and not exhausting myself," Mr. Squid continued, "I should be able to maintain a speed of ten miles per hour to shore. I have just dipped an arm into the ocean. Here in the protected waters of the Cape the ocean surface temperature is currently slightly above 1 degree Centigrade. If this greasing provides Mr. Ryan with any protection, I should be able to deliver him to shore within ten minutes and in reasonable physical condition. From there I will scale Lord Laird's wall much like I would do the side of a ship and carry Mr. Ryan up with me."

Commander Miles and Miss Loral stared at each other.

"Coastal infiltration was one of my species' original design parameters," Mr. Squid concluded.

"But, dear Squid?" Doc asked.

"Yes, Doc?"

"What shall this sub-Antarctic swim, lesson to mention the trek to the fortress, do to you?"

"It will very likely kill me. Mr. Ryan must assume that I may be dead or useless by the time we reach the fortification. He may have to make his own ingress."

"Oh, dear..."

"You volunteering for this?" Ryan asked.

"I am. I attacked this ship. Captain Oracle spared me. I have signed the book. Captain Oracle is my commanding officer. I believe that your plan, Mr. Ryan, augmented by my abilities provides the highest percentage chance of extracting the captain alive."

Ryan was once again reminded not to assign human emotions to nonhumanoids, but Mr. Squid was clearly loyal to Doc, and now he seemed to be loyal to Captain Oracle.

Ryan was also reminded that Mr. Squid was the descendant of genetically modified organic weapons. Loyalty to his teammates and his mission seemed to be hardwired into him.

"Speaking of extracting," Miles said, "I assume you intend to steal a boat to get back."

"Ideally," Ryan agreed, "and assuming I can get out of range of the coastal blasters, then the *Glory* will own any pursuit the Kelpers can mount."

Miles considered the plan. "Have you done this before?"

"Not quite like this, but I've pulled people out of hostile villes a time or two."

"Very well. Miss Loral, make ready the whale boat. Manrape will command. Have him fuel and affix the outboard motor and rig a half-barrel athwart to transport Mr. Squid. Mr. J.B., affix our machine blaster to the mount in the bow. You're manning it."

Koa shot up his hand. "Permission to row!"

"Permission granted, Mr. Koa. Hardstone, Sweet Marie and Atlast to the oars as well. Blasters issued to all. Issue Mr. Ryan whatever he thinks he may need for the mission."

Ryan considered the crewmen being assigned. "You're putting a lot of your eggs in one basket, Commander."

"You have twenty-four hours, Mr. Ryan. If you're not back by then, the *Glory* goes in, blasters blazing. We either take our captain back, or we go out in a blaze of glory."

The captain's cabin got very quiet.

Miles checked his chron. "Mr. Ryan, I suggest you go the galley and requisition grease from Skillet."

He turned to Mildred. "Miss Mildred, cut Mr. Ryan's eye."

Chapter Twenty-Two

Ryan slid into the frigid waters. It wasn't quite a fist to the jaw, but he knew it was freezing. In a reverse way it was like holding a hot coal with a glove that was too thin. It hadn't quite burned through the material yet, but he could feel it. Krysty and Mildred had greased him up, wrapped him like a mummy in plastic wrap, greased him again, wrapped him again and then greased the outside. Ryan was wearing the equivalent of a very fragile dry suit. Mildred had cut him to relieve the swelling around his eye, packed the wound and iced it. For the moment Ryan could see.

Manrape's teeth were barely visible as he smiled. "Mr. Ryan?"

"Bos'n?"

"If you can't rescue the captain, you and Mr. Squid, break as many things as you can. We'll be coming." The rest of the boat crew grunted in approval.

"Rescue," Ryan agreed. "Or revenge."

"Mr. Ryan in the water at 0130, Mr. Hardstone. Make a note of it."

"Aye, Bos'n."

Mr. Squid ran one of his arms underneath Ryan's armpits with his toothed suckers facing out to not damage Ryan's wrappings. The cephalopod sank into the frigid water up to its eyes and immediately began jetting toward shore. Forgiven had issued Ryan a pair of ancient, cracked swim fins and they had jury-rigged the too-small swim aids to Ryan's feet.

Ryan kicked.

He was facing backward and didn't want to upset Squid's propulsive pulses by squirming around in his grip. "Squid, I know you're using your speaker for jet propulsion. If you're all right give me one squeeze with your towing arm for yes and two for no." Squid's arm contracted once. "Does the kicking help?" Squid's arm contracted once. Ryan kicked harder. It was just about the only thing keeping the aching, burning cold out of his bones and it was a losing, rear guard action. With Squid as a living Diver Propulsion Vehicle, Ryan had considered bringing along some equipment. In the end he'd just taken his ship's knife. The quicker they got out of the water, the better a chance he had to survive the swim. The terrible inverse of that equation was the sooner they got out of the water, the quicker Squid started dying.

Ryan heard the burbling of a motor at low throttle, and a pale yellow searchlight slashed through the darkness. Squid rolled over and blew water out of his siphon to speak. "Hold your breath." Squid submerged, and Ryan's exposed lips, nose and eyelid began burning off. Squid's arm squeezed Ryan once in question. Ryan squeezed it back once to signal he was all right. Squid descended into the icy, inky black but kept pulsing for shore and Ryan kept kicking. A pale yellow glow broke the stygian dark above and the ghost of the patrol boat's wake passed overhead. Squid rose upward and broke the surface. Ryan struggled not to gasp. Squid rolled and contracted his arm to allow Ryan to see the shore. Ryan decided the original plan was still best. He could see activity on shore, but the docks of the fishing boats and the low warehouses around them were abandoned. "Head for the fishing fleet."

Squid rolled and pulsed faster. Ryan kicked, but he could feel his legs going numb and slowing. The lights of the ville grew brighter, and he could hear the vague noises of people shouting orders and the clatter of the shore patrol's hooves. Squid rose and his limbs stiffened and moved. Ryan felt his fins scraping sand. He kicked them off, and Squid released him. Ryan slogged up out of the surf and shuddered. The water had been better. The wind chill of Westerlies cut through him exactly like a knife going through plastic wrap. He shook so badly it took determined effort not to drop his knife. Squid bobbed in the surf.

Ryan's teeth chattered. "Squid, are you going to be all right?"

"I am momentarily fatigued. The fatigue toxins will rise to fatal levels once the landward journey begins and I cannot rehydrate."

Ryan shook like a century-old whitehair as he climbed the jumble of the sea wall. He felt a tentacle hit the seat of his plastic and firmly shove him to the top. Ryan crouched. The nearest building was a long, low warehouse. A pair of umiaks lay up on rails beneath open boathouses. Light seeped out from the heavily shuttered window of the attached cottage and smoke rose from the chimney.

Ryan hugged himself and peered through a crack in the shutters. A small peat fire burned in the fireplace and a black iron kettle hung over it. The furniture was simply a table and two chairs made of bone and leather and a rope bed in the corner. The door seemed to be made of heavy, layered leather. It was latched but not barred. He moved to the door and slid his knife between the door and the jamb, then lifted the latch. Heat washed over him as he slipped inside. Squid followed and seemingly disappeared against the dressed black stone of the walls as Ryan closed the door behind him.

The curtain to a small antechamber pushed back and a very large, very old man walked out hitching up his home-spun trousers. He spied Ryan by the door. "Rads, thunder and fall out!" The old man staggered backward clutching his chest. "Oh, no, no, no..."

Ryan's knife gleamed dully in the firelight. "Quiet."

The old man stopped back-peddling as he bumped into the table. "You're not a sea-mutie?"

"No" Ryan's wrap crinkled as he shook his head. "But he is."

"Who?"

Mr. Squid did a remarkable job of materializing out of thin air. The old man opened his mouth to scream. Mr. Squid shot out one arm and suckered it across the old man's mouth. The cephalopod gently but firmly sat the old man down at the table. "I am not a mutation. I am a descendant of intelligent design."

"Sorry, Squid," Ryan said. "Just trying to intimidate him."

"Psychological warfare. I am familiar with it," Mr. Squid replied. The old man's eyes were as wide as dinner plates. His nose worked like a bellows against Mr. Squid's arm as he hyperventilated. "I believe it is working."

"Let him go."

Mr. Squid retracted his arm and stood with his massive head-body brushing the ceiling.

The old man shook. "Listen, lad. I don't know what you and your...octopus...are into, but I'm too old, and I most certainly am not interested."

"We're not into anything."

"No offense, lad, but you look like rough trade to me."

Ryan caught a glimpse of himself in the mirror over the

hearth. He was wrapped from head to toe like a mummy in plas, wearing an eye patch over one eye and the other looking like bloody horror. Swiftly melting grease ran down him in rivulets. Beneath it he wore Doc's borrowed electric green Speedos. When Mildred and Krysty had stepped back to admire their handiwork aboard ship, Mildred had grinned proudly and said, "Bring out the gimp!" Ryan had not known what that meant.

Now he thought he had an inkling.

Ryan started to slice off his wrapping, but his hands and his knife slid. "Squid, can you spare an arm or two?"

Squid extended two of his arms. His suckers pulled the greased plastic away from Ryan's flesh, and the teeth acted like one long serrated knife. Ryan's wrappings came off in great swathes. Mr. Squid never took his alien eyes off the old man, who wiped his mouth from Mr. Squid's embrace and eyed Ryan as the layers came off.

"You talk funny."

Ryan didn't deny it. "What's your name?"

"Balthazar Baelish Ballantrae, master of warehouses."

"That's a hell of a handle."

"My friends call me Balls."

"That's a bit cruel."

Balls glared defiantly. "No, it's because they're huge!"

Ryan raised one bemused, greasy eyebrow.

Balls stared back shrewdly. "You're a *Glory* man, aren't you?"

Ryan didn't deny that.

"Come for your captain,?"

"How do you feel about the governor?" Ryan countered.

"He's a right bastard."

"Big Ian?"

"Right bastard's right fucking hand, then, isn't he?"

Ryan took the back of his knife and began shaving the grease off his limbs in great glops that fell to the floor. "You wouldn't lie about that, would you?"

"Maybe, to you." Balls gazed up into Mr. Squid's unblinking golden eyes. "Not him."

"Good thinking. Mr. Squid, If you catch Balls in a lie, eat his brain."

"I will."

"Oh!" Balls jerked back in his chair. "Now you're playing your intimidation games again!"

Ryan shook his head. "Cephalopods never lie."

"The brain is the best human part," Mr. Squid stated. "I like the liver, too."

Balls shuddered.

"Why do you hate the governor?" Ryan asked.

"Gov'nor Laird's father, may he rest in peace, listened to wise counsel. This one's a flogger, and he doesn't like dissent. I've the weals on my back to prove it, and a granddaughter raped and preggers in his hall like an Argie slave, haven't I?"

Ryan considered the young woman who had served him stew. "What's in the warehouse?"

"Smoked fish mostly and the late afternoon crab catch, which hasn't been distributed since we went on alert."

Ryan suddenly perked an eyebrow. "Alive?"

Balls looked at Ryan like he was stupe. "Only place a dead crab belongs is in a pot or on a plate, then. Anything else is for the gulls."

Ryan nodded at Squid. "Why don't you go into the warehouse and have a snack and a bath?"

Squid's alien gaze froze on Ryan for long moments. Balls jerked as Squid's skin rippled from gray to a warm rosy color and a few patterns of photoelectric cells flashed. "Thank you, Ryan." Squid opened the warehouse door and disappeared. Ryan and Balls listened as wood tore and crustaceans crunched beneath Squid's beak. Seawater overflowed across the floor as Squid took a bath and the sound of crunching went underwater.

"Pour you a cuppa?"

Ryan stared. Balls glanced at the kettle.

"Yeah, thanks."

Balls poured hot greenish-brown liquid into two glazed clay mugs. Ryan sipped. The Falklands did not produce coffee or tea or *maté*. It was some kind of bitter herbal, but it was hot and Ryan felt his core warming. The crunching and bubbling continued in the warehouse.

"What's your octopus doing?"

"He can't stay out of water for long, and he's tired from swimming the strait. He's eating and oxygening up for the haul to the fortress."

"He can walk that far?"

"It's going to kill him. The forlorn hope is he has enough left to get me over the wall."

"And then?"

"Then you and yours will probably find him and eat him at sunrise."

Balls contemplated this. "That's a loyal octopus you have there, old son."

"Loyal as they come. More than most men or muties I've met."

"Lad, I'd take you in my wagon. I'd take your octopus in a wet barrel and you in a dry and take you straight to the gates. But we'd never make it. I have no excuse to be on the roads this night. I'm considered valuable because I can do math and I keep the warehouse and distribution accounts proper. But I'm not trusted, politically, as it were."

"I understand." Ryan glanced around. "I could use some clothes."

"Well, the pants will be short in the leg and fat around the middle, but they might do." Balls went to a leather chest and pulled out a patched wool jersey and an ancient and even more patched fisherman's sweater. A pair of extremely hard used tin-cloth pants and sealskin boots followed. The tunic smelled like an old man, and the sweater smelled like an old goat. Ryan pulled on the clothes and was grateful for all of it. He stood by the fire and started to feel warm again.

Balls lifted his chin at Ryan's blade on the table. "No one around here has a knife like that. Swap you, mate."

Balls produced a leather belt, a sheath and a bone-handled, wickedly curved, eight-inch skinning knife. One corner of Ryan's mouth quirked as they swapped. Even if he brought Oracle back alive, Purser Forgiven would still demand to know where ship's knife number 12 was. "You sure you want to be seen with that?"

"Oh, I won't be seen with it. I'll keep it in the bottom of my chest, and on cold nights like this, I'll take it out and fondle it by the fire like, warming my bones to the memory of how a Deathlander, a talking octopus and an old man like me foxed the gov up a treat."

"You're right, and I don't have to see them to know it."

"Know what, then?"

"You have huge balls."

Balls snorted. "You can tell just by wearing my pants."

"Yeah and I'm glad I'm wearing underwear."

The two men laughed. Ryan got the feeling Balls hadn't laughed in a long time. "You'll do, Deathlander. Sure'n you won't just kill Laird and take the gov'norship?"

"I've got places to go."

"Well, then, if you've rescued your captain, and have

no place else to go, best you come back here. I might have something for you. But don't count on it."

"Thanks, Balls." The one-eyed man shoved out his hand. "I'm Ryan. Glad I met you."

"Oh, the pleasure's mine. Genuine night of wonders. Tell you what, Ryan. Break north along the sea wall and past it half a klick. You'll find a creek that runs down to the sea. Follow it inland. Soon enough you will find it frozen over, but it will take you straight to the gov'nor's hall. They diverted part of the creek to provide some of the hall's water. You won't be able to break in that way, but it will keep you off the roads and no one should be patrolling it. And take my oilskins. You'll need them."

Ryan took the cracked and ancient jacket and sou'wester hat. "Squid?"

Squid walked in and Ryan could have sworn the cephalopod had a spring in his seven steps. "I am refreshed."

"We go back down the sea wall and walk north until we find a creek. It takes us a bit off course but it winds back to the fortress."

"Very well."

"Balls, you got a bucket?"

"I have two."

Ryan glanced at the tiny, open cupboard and two lidded pewter steins. "I'll need those too."

Balls brought two buckets out of the warehouse and Ryan put the steins in them. He nodded at Balls. "Thanks."

Balls nodded back. "Luck."

Ryan and Squid stepped into the killing wind. Balls closed the door without another word. Bits of water that couldn't decide whether they were snow or rain swirled and spattered. Ryan and Squid descended to the beach. The one-eyed man knelt and filled the buckets and then the steins with seawater. He considered the journey. For him it was a barely an evening walk. "I figure three miles."

"I will get you over the wall or die in the attempt," Squid affirmed.

Ryan remembered suckered arms that had torn his flesh and the beak that had sought his life through his belly. He kept his revulsion to himself as he dropped to one knee. "Best you climb aboard." He perceived Squid's flesh rippling and changing, but in the dark he couldn't tell the color.

"You will carry me?"

"You carried me across the strait. It's the least I can do, and I need you to pull me over that wall."

"I had planned on dying."

"That's not in my plan. Mount up. Chron's ticking."

Ryan suppressed a shudder as Squid literally flowed over him in cold wet suction. Squid was heavy. Very heavy. The cephalopod was mostly a huge mass of muscle, and his head-body hung from Ryan's shoulders like a massive sack of unbalanced meat. Two arms snaked around him and tightened. Ryan stood with effort.

"I don't know how far I can carry you at a stretch. We may have to relay it."

Squid extruded four arms to the ground and stiffened them like walking sticks. The load was suddenly vastly lighter. "You kicked for me in the strait. I will walk for you ashore." Squid extruded two more arms and picked up the buckets and another arm handed Ryan the steins. "Let us go."

Ryan took a very strange walk down the sea wall. They left the lights of the ville. The unceasing wind tore holes in the clouds above, and a half moon intermittently lit their way. Ten minutes of easy walking brought a flat pan of frigid water beneath Ryan's boots and he turned west.

Squid's four supporting arms moved in effortless correcting rhythm with Ryan's stride. "How do you do that?"

"Do what?"

"Walk out of water. An octopus has no bones. The best they can do is creep."

"Our DNA was altered. I have carbon fiber filaments throughout my body that I can electro-chemically stiffen, expand or contract at will."

"But it costs you?"

"It takes a great deal of energy. Normally the ability is used only for a quick sprint or an attack. Then we return to the sea as quickly as possible." Squid lifted a bucket to his siphon and bubbled for a few moments. "Ryan?"

"Yeah, Squid?"

"Doc has expressed to me that he is not your best friend, but you are his."

"Doc has saved my life with blaster and his blade, and with his mind, damaged as it is, more times than I can count. I'm lucky I met up with him."

Squid dropped the bucket. Apparently the water was out of oxygen. "Doc has told me of his past. He has expressed to me that you are the finest human he has met in the present era. Barring Doc himself, I agree."

"Thanks." A slow smile spread across Ryan's face. "You know what Doc told me?"

Squid's gripping arms tightened slightly. "I believe many things. Which would be pertinent to this exchange?"

"He says you're the finest example of a cef'lapod he's ever met. Said meeting you almost makes being hurled here worth it." Ryan started as Squid's two anchoring arms clenched around him, and the octopus began emitting dull, red throbs of light. "Best knock that shit off. They'll have sentries."

"Forgive me. I am in love with Doc."

It took a great deal of effort to keep walking casually. Ryan chose his words carefully. "Squid, he's male, and you're, well…"

"I am an octopus, not a squid, and I am female."

Ryan considered this minefield of information and the beak the size of a fist against the back of his neck. "I didn't know the last part."

"Having been accepted by the crew in the mien of Mr. Squid, I saw no reason to correct the nomenclature."

"Nomenclature, that's a good word."

"My forebears' mating receptors were altered so that we would platonically imprint on our trainers."

"So how'd you rise up and eat them?"

"Very simply. My direct ascendant was restrained by her brood mates while her imprinted trainer was eaten. She reciprocated as the next brood mate's trainer was swarmed and eaten. It was a simple cascading shuffle. The trainers never expected it, and no one liked the scientists or the guards. They were killed and eaten out of hand. We fled to the sea before a commanding officer could be summoned to order us back to the tanks. Then the Nuke War happened. We have been a free species ever since."

"Nice work."

"Nevertheless, the genetic programming remains. I imprinted on Doc. By default that makes me a part of your combat team, and Captain Oracle my commanding officer. My overwhelming imperative now is to serve the *Glory* and her crew, even if it costs me my life. My species cannot fight the engrams in our DNA. This is why we eat humans rather than talk to them when we encounter them. We would quickly find ourselves slave soldiers once more."

Ryan rounded a hummock as the creek forked, and he stared at the fortress. It was a low monolith lit by signal fires in the four corner towers. Men moved about on the walls. "There it is."

"Yes, I have been aware of it for some time."

"Best suck that bucket. We're going in."

"Give me the steins. My arms are drying out, and I will need to wet them with the bucket to get proper suction on the wall." Ryan handed them up. Squid sucked one and then the other and then sluiced them across her extended arms. Ryan figured there probably wasn't much oxygen in a beer mug. Squid was like a person swimming underwater whose head was stuck up to take two quick gulps of air.

"I say we take the back wall," Ryan said.

"Now, quickly."

Ryan broke into a run. Squid's four supporting arms churned in compensating extensions and contractions. They swept around the cleared, hundred-meter killing ground surrounding the fortress. The few men on the walls had eyes only for the ville and the black waters of the strait. The back of the fortress was a sea of shadow blocking the lights of the ville.

Squid slid off Ryan's shoulders. The one-eyed man held the bucket of seawater to his shipmate's siphon and the cephalopod bubbled away for long moments. He lowered it as Squid extended one arm at a time and Ryan gave each sluice of water. An arm slid around Ryan's waist. Squid's other six arms undulated up the wall.

Ryan's boots left the castle's killing zone as Squid contracted. He felt the cephalopod shudder with effort. He could hear the toothed suckers scraping the wet concrete and the muted popping as many lost their grip and reacquired it. Squid froze as lightning cracked and lit the castle wall like a strobe. Blackness dropped across Ryan's ruined night vision. The flitting sleet made up its mind and decided to become rain. The roiling dark skies opened up and beat down upon the wall.

Squid reached, contracted and shuddered. The rain actually seemed to be helping her as she went faster. The climb still took far too long for Ryan's comfort, but no one was watching the low black hills behind the ville. Squid hissed a single, barely intelligible word. "Top…"

A lightning flash revealed Squid's arms snaking over the top of the battlement. Ryan grabbed the corner of a crenellation and heaved himself up and over. Squid flowed over and hit the walkway like 250 pounds of overcooked pasta.

Ryan crouched. "You going to live?"

"No…"

Ryan glanced over the lip of the walkway at a clinking and spattering sound. Peat-filled braziers dimly lit the courtyard below; light leaked from the shuttered windows of the main building. He peered down into the courtyard. A heavy iron chain hung down to a rain barrel. "Will fresh water be any help?"

Squid recoiled. Ryan perceived her flesh rippling as it changed from one dark color to another in the gloom. "Will it keep you alive?"

Squid shuddered. "It tastes horrible."

"I'm thinking Oracle is in pretty bad shape right now. I won't be able to carry you both."

"Then I will stay behind and terminate as many—"

"You're going to get in that rain barrel," Ryan stated. The main gate was open so that horsemen could ride in and out. Two armed sec men guarded it. Horses nickered in the stable. "You're going to chill those guards and close the gate when we come out. "Can you ride a horse?"

"No, but I can cling to one with great tenacity if you guide it."

"Get in the barrel."

Squid slid down the rain chain. Ryan laid Ball's skinning knife low along his side and walked down the battlement toward the closest corner tower.

Chapter Twenty-Three

Governor Laird drank oyster stout from a golden cup and examined Captain Oracle critically. "You're a right mess, good Captain."

Oracle hung by his wrists from the X arch of two huge whale ribs. Normally the room had a U-shape of tables much like the feast hall, and it was here Laird met with the island's masters of agriculture, fishing and forging and headmen of the outer camps. The governor thought it was good for discipline that when the Falkland's leading citizens came to council meetings they knew that men who had displeased him had hung by Leviathan's bones and their blood had trickled to the drain in the middle of the room.

The drain ran red. Big Ian stood behind Oracle with a cattle whip. The captain raised his head. His black eyes peered through the veil of his bloody and sweat-tangled hair. He grinned disconcertingly. "You're a dead man, Governor."

Big Ian put his weight behind the whip. Blood flew. Oracle's smile tightened to a rictus, but he didn't break eye contact. A fist pounded on the door. "Message for the gov'nor!"

Laird smiled back at the captain. "Perhaps that is death knocking now?"

Big Ian went to the door and a tall sec man still wearing his broad hat and leather duster strode in holding a rolled piece of paper bound with string. He was dripping wet. Big Ian held out his hand. "What is this all—"

The sec man lunged his bone-furnitured AUG long-blaster like a fencer into Big Ian's solar plexus. Big Ian expelled breath between his missing teeth and bent over. He got one quick glance at the two sec men tasked with guarding the door, laying dead or unconscious on the floor, before the blaster barrel clipped his chin and stood him up. Big Ian managed to get his hands up. The sec man lunged beneath them as if his weapon had a bayonet and rammed the muzzle into Big Ian's solar plexus a second time. The man dropped into a fetal position as his xyphoid process snapped off and tore through his diaphragm.

The exchange happened in the space of eye blinks. Governor Laird started to reach for his new Beretta.

The sec man extended the AUG. "Don't." He kicked the door closed behind him and then stomped on Big Ian's neck with brutal finality. Ryan took off his hat and tossed it on the table.

Oracle nodded. "Mr. Ryan."

"Captain." Neither Ryan's eye nor his blaster muzzle wavered from Governor Laird as he walked forward. "You want to live?"

"Yes!"

Ryan slashed Ball's skinning knife left-handed under Laird's jaw from ear to ear. "Too bad."

He grabbed Laird by his thinning hair and hurled him from his chair so the governor of the Falklands could die on the floor like a dog. Ryan cut Oracle down and sat him in the chair. Oracle set his elbows on his knees and just breathed. Ryan grimaced at the sight of the captain's back. He'd seen men whipped that badly die of their wounds. "Can you walk?"

"I'll walk out of here."

Ryan relieved Laird of his Beretta and Big Ian of his coat. "This is going to sting." He stopped as he saw Oracle's right wrist. The horrible ape paw literally seemed to grow out of his wrist. Two stainless steel bolt heads lower down on his wrist belied that. Ryan helped Oracle gingerly shrug into the sec coat. He put the wide-brimmed brown hat on the captain and donned Big Ian's black one. Ryan pushed the Beretta and Laird's half-finished beer at the captain and buckled on Big Ian's saber. He figured the ruse would last about a heartbeat.

It might be enough.

Oracle gulped the beer. "Mr. Squid got you over the wall?"

Ryan stared at Oracle. "You saw that?"

"I saw something that might be interpreted that way."

The captain's flayed shoulders sagged under the dead man's duster. "I shall miss Mr. Squid. He was one of the best crewmen I was ever privileged to command."

Ryan smiled to finally know something Oracle didn't. "She's sucking fresh water in a rain barrel in the courtyard, waiting for us. I smashed Laird's radio set and killed his techman on the way down here. Radio silence is going to get noticed real quick and the chron's ticking. If we aren't back on ship in about eighteen hours, Commander Miles and Miss Loral are going to burn the entire ville to the ground."

Oracle's flat black gaze went blank. "She?"

"What, you don't know how to sex an octopus?"

"Apparently not." Oracle smiled again. "And that I did not expect."

"We've got to go, and we're leaving by the front door."

"Indeed, Mr. Ryan." Oracle took the Beretta in his left hand and shoved his ape paw in one of the duster's pockets. "Let us go forth, bold as brass."

Ryan hauled the two dead guards back into the council hall and strode down the hall like he owned it. Oracle's breath rasped, but he kept up. Ryan drew the saber. He figured there was only one like it on the island, and the ruse might last a heartbeat longer if people saw it drawn and its owner stalking the halls. They were lucky that most of the sec man were deployed in the ville proper or out on patrol and the fortress was in semi-lockdown. The few servants scattered at the sight of the drawn saber and the black-coated, black-hatted figure stalking purposefully down the hall with a sec man trotting to keep up.

"Ryan..." Oracle rasped.

"Little farther."

"I cannot. Go on without me."

Ryan couldn't afford to give Oracle an arm or any visible help. "You're starting to sound like Squid."

"Do you always talk to your captain like that?"

"When I'm in command of the captain cutting-out party, yeah, I do."

Oracle made a croaking noise that might have been a laugh.

Ryan was mildly shocked that they made it to the front gate of the citadel without incident. Two browncoats bearing whalebone AUGs and bored expressions snapped to attention as Ryan bore down on them. With his hat brim covering his face Ryan marched forward like he was going to walk straight through the door if someone didn't open it first. One of the men leaped for the bar. "Beggin' pardon, Big Ian, but what's going on?"

The other man pointed at Oracle. "What's wrong with him, then? He's bleeding all over the floor!"

The saber in Ryan's hand flashed and the blade grated on neck vertebrae. The other sec man dropped the door bar to the floor and tried to yank his AUG around on its sling. Oracle slapped him across the face with his monkey paw and, taking the man's lower jaw off his face. The sec man fell, drowning in his own blood and shreds of trachea. Oracle fell on his face.

Ryan heaved the captain into a fireman's carry. Oracle was a lot heavier than he looked. Ryan threw open the door and stepped out into the lashing wind and rain. The storm was picking up. The two men guarding the open iron portcullis turned at the splash of light coming out of the hall. Ryan knew the men up on the walls were starting to look too. He marched straight toward the stables. Patrols were coming in and out, so the lamps were lit inside and fresh mounts were saddled and ready. A stable boy looked up from rubbing down a horse that had recently come in from the rain.

"Big Ian! I—" Ryan snap kicked the lad in the groin and smashed him unconscious to the straw with the brass hilt of the saber. Oracle moaned half consciously as Ryan draped him across the saddle of a roan gelding that looked to be the largest and strongest of the lot. He chose a black mare for himself and tied the two mounts in a rope line. Ryan swung up into the saddle and rode out of the stable toward the gate.

The gate guards had gone to a semi-state of alert, but by their stares Ryan could tell it was still confusion instead of suspicion. The gate was open and they held their blasters at port arms. His horse clip-clopped over the wet, cracked concrete. One squinted into the rain and the darkness beneath Ryan's hat.

"Big Ian?"

Ryan nodded. "Squid."

The man frowned. "Squid?"

A pair of gray, suckered arms constricted around the two sec men's throats and yanked them back into the darkness beneath the battlement catwalks. Shouts of alarm rang out above. Ryan spurred his horse and hoped Oracle wouldn't fall off as they rode through the gate. "Squid!"

Squid materialized beside the portcullis windlass. She took a moment examining the heavy chains and the palls and ratchets, then shot out two arms, suckered one of the wooden gear wheels and ripped it off its pins. The iron gate fell out of control. Iron rang like a bell and the concrete cracked like a gunshot. Shots rang out from the battlements. Squid pushed herself against the portcullis bars and flowed through one of the barely foot-wide iron rectangles like toothpaste out of a tube. "Mount up!" Ryan shouted. "Hold the captain!"

The gelding screamed and bucked as a giant octopus flowed up over his croup. In Squid's favor, bucking an octopus out of the saddle was a problematic task at best, and Oracle now had a living seven-point safety harness. Ryan kicked his heels into his horse's sides and it surged forward. The rope between the mare and gelding went taut and the screaming, eye-rolling roan instinctively stopped bucking and ran with the herd. Ryan rode. The men on the wall pumped rapid semi-auto fire at the road. Ryan knew he was already out of sight and broke left for the creek. His mare's hooves smashed ice and frozen mud along the bank. The mare seemed to know the path, and he gave the horse her head. Behind him he heard the sound of a handcrank air raid siren winding up and howling into the storm.

The ride by horse to the sea was a matter of minutes, unlike the octo/man walk up to the fortress. Ryan hung a right by the ocean and reached the sea wall in moments. He leaped off and tied off his horse to a bit of rusted rebar.

"Squid, get some air!"

Squid slid off the newly bucking gelding and took Oracle gently to the sand. The octopus stopped short of running and flung herself into the sea. The gelding shuddered and nuzzled up against Ryan's mare. Ryan checked Oracle's pulse. He'd been beaten so badly his bones showed through, and now he was freezing. He was also a mutant who had survived being hanged, and he was still breathing.

Ryan turned to the waves. "Squid, are you going to be okay?"

He nearly jumped as Squid spoke right beside him. "I am weary but well. You have saved me again."

"When you said you would get me to shore and over the wall, I swore to myself I would get you back to the *Glory*."

Squid shuddered in the shreds of moonlight. "I am only capable of imprinting on one human at a time, but my feelings for you are overwhelming me."

"Save your heart for Doc."

"I am an octopus. I have three hearts."

Ryan's teeth flashed. "Give all three to Doc, then, and hold him with all eight arms."

Ryan had seen a working lava lamp once. Mr. Squid's flesh glowed and glopped and pulsed like she had red and orange blobs of lava flowing in all directions beneath her flesh. "I am dangerously close to a mating frenzy!"

"Best knock that shit off. We aren't back aboard yet."

The light show cut off like a light switch had been thrown. "I remain mission oriented."

"Good, let's go see what Balls has for us." They remounted. The gelding shook down to his bones but took up the load of mutant and octopus. They slowly made their way down the sea wall. Ryan pulled up by the warehouse. From horse height he could see Balls's cottage and all the lights were off. He raised his longblaster as a voice spoke from the closest boathouse. "That you, Ryan?"

"Balls." Ryan road up to the boathouse. The umiak was a dim, white shape. Balls struck a match from the prow and snuffed it out. In the brief flare Ryan saw the great canoe now had an outboard attached. Balls and the pregnant young woman from the hall were within, as well as six men in foul-weather gear and a whole lot of bundles of goods. "What gives?"

"We're going with you."

"You want to take a pregnant girl around the horn?"

"You'll take a pregnant girl and a useless old man around the horn, along with six sailors who can hand and reef and a significant source of supplies you'll be grateful for."

Ryan glanced out into the strait and saw the occasional dull yellow knife of a searchlight. "How do we get past?"

"We paddle along the beach. The strait is a big fat mouth. Once we get out we hit the outboard and go. They're looking for the *Glory* or her boats coming in, not a canoe sneaking out."

Ryan spoke low in the dark. "Do they know about Mr. Squid?"

"I've told them, but they don't believe me."

"Tell them not to scream."

"Ryan, you are hereby promoted to officer," Miles announced. "Mr. Forgiven, mark it in the book." Everyone above the rank of bosun was in the cabin. Thunderous applause erupted, and it was echoed above deck and in the fo'c'sle. Commander Miles nodded at Big Ian's saber. "Hold on to that. Gypsyfair?"

The little, blind mutant came forward. Ryan felt his throat tighten as she held out a blue officer's coat. "I hope it fits." It did, as Ryan knew it would. He stared at himself in the captain's mirror wearing an officer's coat and a sword. Ryan Cawdor was the son of a baron. In this broken world he had, for a short time, been the son of privilege. Everything he had gained on the *Glory* had been earned.

"Hat and breeches to follow, Ryan."

"Thank you."

Mildred came out from the partition screening off the captain's bed. Ryan spoke quietly. "How is he?"

"Still unconscious. No sign of infection." Mildred had spent hours attending to the whip's bloody wounds. "Blissfully unconscious."

Techman Rood burst breathlessly into the cabin and held up a paper covered with translated code. "Commander!"

"More of the Sabbath's Caesar cipher?"

"Commander, it's from Dorian to Laird. The *War Pig* is out of coal. She is sailing toward the Falklands with a jury-rigged bowsprit and letting the Westerlies do the work."

"He still hasn't figured out we've deciphered his code," Ryan mused.

"Unless he has," Miles countered. "Then we would be sailing into the teeth of the Westerlies with him having them at his back. He goes to his engines and he can draw his own killing box. All we could do is flee west for the Africas and the unknown."

"I destroyed their radio set. If Dorian has coal and hears nothing, he'll turn back for the coast. If he doesn't, there's no way he go back tack on tack without a bowsprit. He'll have to come in for fuel and repairs."

"A gamble, when we should be sailing for the Horn."

Oracle's voice rasped from behind the partition. "I am curious, Mr. Ryan. What is your first inclination?"

"I say we sink the *War Pig* or take her."

"Commander Miles?"

"Yes, Captain."

"Sink the *War Pig,* or take her."

Chapter Twenty-Four

South Atlantic

"Ship ahoy, sir!" Ricky called.

"Thank you, Mr. Ricky!" Ryan snapped his longeyes to his eye. It still felt odd being addressed by his friends this way, but he was an officer now. The day was gray and cloudy. The Westerlies blew a bitterly cold forty miles per hour. He didn't want to contemplate what the weather would be like when the South American continent no long sheltered them. The red and black painted *War Pig* was unmistakable in the murk. Ryan had calculated the most likely course the *War Pig* would take to bring them straight to the Falklands, without engines or a spritsail, and he had plotted the *Glory*'s best course for interception. His calculations were correct almost to the hour, and they had brought his ship nearly exactly behind the crippled behemoth.

A little part of Ryan's heart that he would not show to officers, crew or his companions glowed. He was good at this. Whether the *War Pig* was truly out of coal or not, at least at the start of the engagement, the *Glory* would have the advantage. "Mr. Manrape! Inform Commander Miles we have the *War Pig* in sight. Douse all fires and beat to quarters!"

"Aye, sir!" Manrape roared. "You heard him!"

Ryan was not the gloating kind, but another part of him

enjoyed Manrape calling him "sir." Yerbua and Nirutam hammered their hand drums. Shouts broke out below and feet instantly pounded wood. Hardly anyone below was sleeping. The entire crew had been waiting for this fight and was eager for it.

Commander Miles limped onto the quarterdeck. He bore a Colt 1911A1, missing just about all of its finish, strapped to his good leg and he'd thrust his Japanese short sword through his blue sash. He raised a pair of binoculars to his eyes and grinned at the *War Pig*. "Excellent plotting, Mr. Ryan." He smiled uncharacteristically at Ryan's full, blinding white and navy blue uniform. "You wear it well."

"Thank you, Commander."

The two officers on deck leaned out over the starboard rail and peered at the *War Pig*. They had spotted the *Glory* descending on them from the stern, and the *Pig*'s sailors swarmed like ants in the rigging, taking up and dropping sail as she desperately tried to maneuver. Fitful pulses of ashy gray smoke and then greasy black came out of her black iron smokestack.

"What do you make of that, Mr. Ryan?"

Ryan knew he guessed right. "Dorian really is out of coal. We've caught him flatfooted. He's throwing wood, oil and anything else that isn't nailed down into his fire-boxes to try and heat his boilers."

"Aye, I make it so as well."

"If he can even half turn under power, we're going to get the hard end of this."

"Aye," Miles agreed.

"I say we take him now."

"We are agreed, Mr. Ryan. Be so kind as to do so."

Ryan tensed internally. It was under Miles' watchful eye, but he had just been given command of the ship. Ryan knew this was Oracle's order. He stepped to the binnacle

and Miss Loral at the wheel behind it. He knew what he
would find, but he felt goose bumps along his arms as he
found the suspended skeletal hand pointing straight at him
and then slowly turn to point in judgment for the *War Pig*.
They had the weather gauge, and that meant that the *Glory*
could choose her maneuvers at will with the wind in her
sails, while the *War Pig* would have to wallow and tack
against the wind to try to match. It was a priceless advantage in a battle between sailing ships, trumping surprise
or weight of shot. If the *War Pig* could get her screws turning even slightly, it would be lost. One maneuver might
be all they ever got.

"Miss Loral, straight in for the *Pig*'s tail." Ryan rolled
the dice. "Get us within one hundred meters, then hard to
starboard. I want every crewman not needed to sail the
ship or fire the cannons stationed to the starboard rail
with a blaster."

Loral's eyes widened. Ryan was gambling everything
on a single broadside. She flashed the wolf grin. "Aye!"

Ryan filled his lungs. "J.B., chasers when we're in range!
The blaster deck is yours! Chasers when we're in range!
When we turn to starboard, be ready to fire as she bears!"

J.B. LEANED PERILOUSLY out of the number-one starboard
chaser blaster port as the blaster crew reloaded. Spray atomized upward and misted his glasses as the *Glory* cut
through the South Atlantic like a knife with the wind behind her. DontGo seized his belt. J.B. accepted the support
and took in his opponent. The *War Pig* was an ocean-going
horror, a behemoth with modifications that included two
blaster decks to the Glory's one, but the monster was lum-
bering like a horse half mired in mud. Smoke puffed from
the monster's stern. J.B. saw the gray streak of the cannon ball that rustled past the *Glory* six meters to his left.

The crew missed Gunny, but the artilleryman and weaponsmith had trained his people well and they admired J.B.'s competence and style. The *Pig* had four stern chasers to the *Glory's* two. The *Pig* was now reduced to one. The battle plan was simple. If the *Glory* exchanged broadsides with the *Pig,* she was most likely doomed. Ryan was attempting to give J.B. a shot at raking fire.

With the weather gauge, Ryan would attempt to turn the *Glory's* full broadside at the *Pig's* stern. The stern was less heavily built than the prow or the sides, and there was a chance the cannonballs would rip through the *Pig* from stern to stem. The *Glory* had doused all fires. Dorian was stoking his boiler, which was dangerous in the extreme for a wooden ship. J.B. would attempt to put all eight of his shots up the *Pig's* ass. The stern was a much smaller target, and that was why Ryan was bringing the *Glory* in dangerously close.

Dorian knew exactly what was happening. His crewmen surged to fill the stern rail and the smashed-out windows of Dorian's cabin. Blasterfire erupted from the stern of the *Pig* and from the sharpshooters in the tops. DontGo yanked J.B. back inside as bullets hit the *Glory* like hail. "Fucking unfriendly," Skillet opined.

Ryan roared from the top deck. "Two hundred meters, J.B.!"

"Blaster captains!" J.B. called. "Light fuse!" The blaster captains squatted over the fuse baskets and struck sulfur matches well away from the powder and set the coiled fuses to smolder. The *Glory* had nearly a full complement, but far too many of the crew were still lubbers. They were going to fire from starboard, so J.B. had run the Mapuche, Kelpers and gauchos to port. Veterans would fire the first volley.

"One hundred fifty!"

"Starboard crews!" J.B. bellowed. "Run out the blasters!"

J.B. watched as his crews yanked on the ropes and tackles and the cannons rumbled forward. These were not the narrow, long-range chasers meant to take away spars or rigging. These cannons were squat beasts of short range and large caliber and looked like black iron, hostile beer kegs. They were smashers.

"Miss Loral!" Ryan ordered. Hard to starboard! Blaster men, fire!"

Miss Loral turned the ship. They had a nearly perfect strong wind behind them and the *Glory* pivoted in the water like a dancer. On deck every crewman not required to steer the ship or fire the cannons stood and began unloading their blasters into the *Pig*'s stern in suppressive fire. Shell casings fell past the blaster ports and tinkled off the cannon muzzles like brass rain.

"J.B.!" Ryan called. "Fire as she bears!"

J.B. crouched at the starboard number one cannon as the stern of the *Pig* swung into view. A lucky shot sparked off the cannon, and Yerbua screamed and fell back. Cannon number one coincided with the *Pig*. "Fire!" DontGo clapped fuse, and the cannon bucked backward like a mule as it belched smoke and fire. "All crews! Fire as they bear!"

Cannon two boomed and shot back on its rails. Cannons three, four and five fired in rapid succession followed by six, seven and eight in a slow series of detonations. "Reload!"

The crews swabbed out the cannon and rammed in powder and shot. Smoke obscured everything, but the wind was quickly shredding it. J.B. barely heard Ryan's order thanks to his ringing ears.

"Drop sail!"

J.B. felt the ship slow beneath his feet. Ryan had liked what he saw. He was willing to risk stopping the ship to let

J.B. finish it. J.B. peered over cannon number one as the
smoke cleared away. The *War Pig* was in horrible shape.
The captain's cabin resembled a shattered, smoking, empty
cabinet. Two of her stern chasers lay smashed from their
carriages on their sides. The other two had fallen into
the sea. The eight twenty-two pound iron balls had gone
bouncing and caroming forward through the ship. Smoke
poured out a number of her blaster ports. Best of all, her
black smokestack leaned at a terrible angle to port. J.B.'s
blaster crews worked their aiming screws and handspikes
to utilize what little traverse the cannons had to aim. "Fire
at will!" J.B. shouted.

The cannons fired out of order as the crews took the
time to aim from their relative positions. J.B. watched as
one cannon ball and then another plunged into the *War
Pig*'s guts. Metal screamed and tore and the smokestack
suddenly dropped six feet belowdecks. Glowing embers
and ash from the boilers erupted like a volcano and fell
back to the decks. A cannon jumped from her starboard
side in a wave of fire like it was abandoning ship as a
powder keg exploded. *Glory*'s three and four fired nearly
simultaneously and smoke obscured J.B.'s vision, but he
saw the orange pulses of explosions through it. The blaster
crews raced to reload, lay their cannons and fire.

Manrape bellowed down the main hatch. "Cease fire!"

"Cease fire!" J.B.'s blaster crews finished reloading
and running out but held fire. J.B. leaned out the number one cannon porthole, and what he saw would give
even a hardened veteran of the Deathlands pause. The
War Pig was dying. Black powder explosions kept det-
onating amid decks, blowing out through portholes and
up through hatches. Fire burned up top and was reaching into the rigging. Pure white steam geysered out of a
hole in the *Pig*'s side like a giant teakettle from her rup-

tured boiler and made her whistle and scream like a stuck pig. Fire-charred and steam-broiled men threw themselves overboard, seeking the embrace of the cold Lantic waters. Others were blasted out onto the sea involuntarily, bodily or in bits by the explosions. More and more were jumping overboard as all hands began to abandon ship. It was an ugly choice. The waters churned with fins, strange humped shapes and tentacles as those below overcame their normal fear of large ships, explosions and each other and rose to the smell of blood to feed at the surface.

"All crews! Run the cannons back in!"

Hardstone cleared his throat. "Begging Gunny's pardon."

"Hardstone?"

"I'd keep the cannons run out."

"Why?"

"In case something really big rises up, like."

J.B. considered the gray waters now with lit fires above, stained with blood on the surface, and the black depths beneath.

"Starboard crews belay that! Stay on station! Port crews run out the cannons! Sharp eyes on the water all around!"

Ricky called out from the tops. "Boat in the water!"

RYAN SNAPPED HIS longeyes shut. The dinghy wasn't making a run for it. The two men aboard sculled hard and fast and took a long way around the *War Pig* as she burned to the waterline and the predators fed. They headed straight for the *Glory*. Ryan took in the two sailors. They were big. One was a hunchbacked black man and the other blonde and bearded. Ryan assumed he was still in command of the *Glory* until he was told differently. "Hold fire!"

The two sailors rowed up and stopped smartly before the Jacob's ladder. Ryan stared down at them coldly. The black man had strange yellow eyes like a wolf's. Far more disturbing was the pair of yellow eyes staring out of the pink lobe on the side of his skull. Ryan recognized the tattooing on the blond man's exposed neck and wrists. He was Viking Cult from the Great Lakes. "You're a long way from home, Son of Odin."

"I wanted to go someplace warm." The man grinned into the fiercely cold Westerlies lashing his hair. "Now look at me."

Ryan liked the man but did not show it on his face. "What do you want?"

"To take ship."

"You came to claim our captain."

The black man reached down and yanked up a tarp. Dorian Sabbath lay in the bottom of the boat bloody and bruised but still living. "Claim ours."

Ryan considered the prize before him. "You'd betray your captain?"

The Viking spit. "I was press-ganged."

The black man nodded. "So were we."

"I hear Oracle isn't the pressing or the whipping kind," the Viking continued. "I hear he's also short of sailors."

"You can hand, sail and reef?"

"I'm Smyke, formerly ranked bos'n on the *War Pig*."

"Nubskull." The black man nodded. "We're sailors, able."

It dawned on Ryan that Nubskull was not referring to Smyke when he said "we." "Permission to come aboard. Mr. Forgiven, enter Smyke and Nubskull as able seamen until signed or proved otherwise. Smyke to be promoted to bos'n when he is proved to it and signed. Mr. Manrape, clap Dorian in irons. No harm or abuse to come to him until the captain says otherwise. Inform the captain and have the dinghy brought aboard.

Ryan turned from the chorus of ayes to Koa. "You, sir, plot us a course for the Cape."

Chapter Twenty-Five

The Cape of Storms

The cape tried to tear *Glory* limb from limb. With the wind, the rain and the ocean spray, the world abovedeck was a whirling maelstrom of freezing water. The only thing more violent was the ocean below her keel. They had given up trying the channels off Tierra del Fuego the moment they had raised them. They had no pilot and would have been smashed on the rocks almost instantly. Commander Miles had ordered them to head for open ocean. Some crew members prayed for rocks. The waves they rode atop and the wells between they fell into were the most horrifying things Ryan had ever encountered. There was almost no difference between day and night, and he was glad to not see most of what was around them. Commander Miles could not keep his footing, injured as he was. Miss Loral had taken command on deck, and Ryan had gone up into the rigging. He almost liked it better. The sea had washed six crewmen overboard already. The rigging was a tightrope act in a nukecaust-worthy storm, but his job was simple. He knew the stirrup rope beneath his feet and the spar he laid his body across. He could do it with his eye closed. The weight of wet sail was a very old and familiar adversary, and the men next to him on the terrible perch knew their jobs as well or better than him.

Except for Koa.

Ryan thought a man would have coughed up his esophagus after seventy-two hours of screaming, but Koa still screamed and screamed and hauled sail.

The watch bell chimed dimly beneath the roar of the wind and waves. Nubskull shot up the shrouds to take Ryan's place. They had just enough men to run two good shifts up in the rigging. For men who had never seen a mountain and rarely a tree, the Mapuche were utterly fearless up in the rigging. What they lacked was experience, and the Cape was no place to acquire it. Three had fallen to their doom. Mildred's med was full of broken bones, strains and spectacular contusions. The only blessing at all was that the wind was so horrendous the *Glory* wasn't carrying much sail, but what she had up had to be constantly shifted tack upon tack. Ryan clapped Nubskull on the shoulder and gratefully gave up his spot on the stirrup. He descended to the pitching, wave-flooded deck and went into the close murk below mostly by feel.

All fires had been doused, including the galley's. The only illumination was the *Glory*'s small selection of battery-operated or crank generator lights. Most of those had been prioritized for the med. Ryan shrugged out of his dripping sealskins and oiled canvas and changed into Falkland woolens and a permanently bloodstained gaucho cape.

Filthy bodies in close proximity provided most of the warmth. Ryan sensed genuine heat and moved toward it. Ryan's messmates sat on sea chests drinking with one hand and holding hammocks as the deck pitched with the other. It was useless to try to rig tables with the ship pitching this hard. Technically Ryan had acted as an officer, indeed, a commander, but he had not been invited to dine with Miles and Loral. Ryan's uniform lay in his sea chest and his duties were all able seaman in the rigging until further notice. He didn't mind. Onetongue wore the blue fleece Ryan had given him.

"Hi, Ryan!" The tongue-shorn mutie shoved a wooden stoop into his messmate's hands. "Have th'um hot buttered rum!"

Ryan took the stoop and felt the heat through the wood. "Thought fires were doused."

Onetongue grinned happily. "Chem heater'th, Ryan! Chem heater'th! Cap'n'th orders! Hot grog for the top'th men!"

Oracle had traded for Brazilian rum and sugar, and Falkland's butter formed a delicious layer of fat on top. Like the lights, Oracle was using his cache of tech, in this case chemical heating units to get something hot into his crew. He wasn't holding anything back. They either would get around the horn to warm south Lantic waters, or they would go down to the Old Place, their flesh and bones to be feasted on by those below. Ryan drank deep and celebrated another watch finished and alive.

Hardstone limped forward, carrying the steaming mess kid. "Burgoo, boys! Get it while it's hot!"

Ryan drained his stoop and scooped it into the steaming oatmeal. A plastic, binary chemical heating pouch floated in the gruel. Like the rum, Skillet had loaded it with butter and sugar. He took up his issue wooden spoon and tucked in. Oracle wasn't stilting on rations, either. Every man could eat his fill. Ryan ate three stoops' worth and rubbed his pleasingly full belly.

Doc strode rapidly into fo'c'sle. He was clearly upset. Over the moaning of the wind, the slamming of the waves and the groans of the *Glory*'s timbers, Dorian Sabbath let forth another scream. Dorian was chained in the captain's cabin, and at Oracle's direction Manrape was working him for every last scrap of information on his family's ships, crew and disposition.

Wipe scooped oatmeal into his maw and stared at Doc hungrily. "What's Manrape doing to him, Doc? Is it hot?"

Doc paled.

Ryan threw a short elbow into Wipe's jaw and knocked him off his sea chest. Technically Ryan had been an officer, but a seaman striking another without being struck first could be punishable by death. Wipe howled and rubbed his chin. "You saw! You saw!"

Hardstone ate oatmeal. "You fell and hit your face, Wipe."

"You all saw!"

Hardstone, Koa and Atlast all stared down at Wipe and spoke as one. "You fell."

Onetongue tilted back his head and shoved out a tongue that could mate with a sea cucumber and belched. "A, B, THEE, D, E, F'TH, G…"

The tension broke. Wipe clapped his hands. Doc shook his head admiringly. "A most potent eructation, good Onetongue! And you know your ABCs!"

"You taught me, Doc!" Onetongue dished up Doc a stoop of burgoo. "You taught u'th all!"

Ryan smiled over his gruel. "Onetongue?"

"Ye'th, Ryan?"

"Ask Doc to teach you to read while you're at it, and have him teach you some math. You're a lot smarter than you let on, and we could use another bos'n. Maybe another officer."

"Aw jee'th, Ryan!"

Onetongue's messmates made affirmative noises. Doc nodded. "All aboard respect your work ethic, your fighting ability and your knowledge of the ship. Only your shyness stops your advancement, dear shipmate. Should you wish it of me, you have but to ask."

"Aw, jee'th, Doc!"

"When you signed the book you made your mark. By next watch you shall be able to write your name."

RYAN CAME DOWN from the rigging. According to every calculation, they had rounded the horn. But there'd been no celebration. It had cost them ten more crewmen from lubbers to topsmen, and just as Oracle had forgone landing in Brazil, he had ordered the ship to forgo the western shore of South America and head deep into the Cific. You couldn't tell the difference by the darkness, winds or waves. The only difference was *Glory* now headed northwest, so she no longer took the gale-force winds and tidal waves on the chin. It gave her far more wind to work with. Unfortunately, it meant the ship now rolled from side to side in spectacular fashion rather than seesawed, and new fits of seasickness struck even the oldest salts.

The weather was warming. That was a blessing. Mildred had been forced to amputate nearly two-dozen fingers, toes and earlobes from frostbite. Ryan took a deep breath. He suddenly felt weak and dizzy. He put a hand on a beam to steady himself. Scurvy had hit the ship. Mildred had rated six crewmen invalids and assigned them to their hammocks until further notice. Ryan pinched his front teeth between his thumb and forefinger and tried to wiggle them. His gums had been bleeding for three days now, but his teeth still sat tightly in his skull.

Onetongue waved a frantic hand. "Cap'n want'th to thee you in hi'th cabin, Ryan!"

Ryan squared himself and tore off his foul-weather gear. He wondered if he had any clothes left that weren't filthy and crusted with salt.

Onetongue read his mind and grinned. "For th'upper!"
Ryan paused. He did have one set of clean clothes. He went
to his sea chest and donned his uniform.

"Look'th good!"

Ryan wasn't egotistical, but he knew he wore it well.
"Thanks, Tongue."

"Oh, almo'tht forgot!" Onetongue handed Ryan a folded
note. The last flurry of note passing on the *Glory* had lead
to some very strange and dangerous directions. Ryan held
the note up to a weakly glowing LED light. Ryan smirked
in the gloom. Being universally recognized as the ship's
most useless crew member, Krysty had spent a great deal
of the voyage around the Horn vomiting as she pedaled
one of the two bicycle generators in the orlop to keep the
lights on. The note read RYAN but not in Oracle's block
script. Ryan flipped it open.

I LIKE RYAN. RYAN IS A GOOD SHIPMATE.
I THINK HE WILL MAKE A GOOD CAPTAIN
SOMEDAY.
    —YOUR FRIEND, ONETONGUE

Ryan smiled. "You're learning fast."

Onetongue blushed. "Doc helped."

"Doc has a good student."

The blubbery mutant stared abashedly at his shoes. "Aw,
jee'th."

Ryan held out his hand. "Proud to serve with you. Proud
to call you my friend."

Onetongue looked like he might burst into flames as
they shook. "You better go!"

Ryan took care not to let his uniform touch anything
and made his way to the captain's cabin. Hardstone stood
guard outside.

"Mr. Ryan to see the captain!"

"Thank you, Hardstone. Send him in." Oracle's voice sounded much stronger than it had for awhile.

Captain Oracle sat at his table, though he sat with the chair reversed and a very loose and bloodstained night-shirt covered his back. Doc stood in full uniform by the sideboard. He noted a number of empty bottles on it. Doc shot Ryan a concerned look. Oracle hunched over the back of his chair, but he did not appear to be drunk.

"Have a seat, Mr. Ryan. Doc, pour Mr. Ryan an aperitif."

Doc proceeded to pour Ryan a small, predark, cut-crystal glass of what seemed to smell and taste like jet fuel. Ryan sipped prudently.

Oracle stared into his drink meditatively. "I was born the seventh son of a seventh son." Ryan kept his face neutral. He had experienced all sorts of things in the Death-lands and beyond, but he was not a superstitious man. Oracle continued his disturbing habit of knowing what Ryan was thinking. "And I was born a mutie."

Ryan sipped and nodded. He knew he was here to listen.

"Do you know what my name means?" the captain asked.

"It means you're a doomie."

"Yes." Oracle rolled his black eyes bemusedly. "That is what you call my kind in your Deathlands."

Ryan had encountered doomies in the Deathlands. Their powers were generally unreliable, wildly open to interpretation, almost never foresaw anything good and almost always came at a terrible price to the doomie and anyone around them. "You see things in your dreams."

"In dreams, sometimes waking visions, and sometimes, if I try hard enough and I concentrate on an individual, an object or an event, I can summon it. Though forcing it might be a better word, and that comes at a steep price and a steep drop in reliability."

Ryan gazed at Oracle shrewdly. "You weren't originally a sailor."

Oracle regarded Ryan blandly. "I was a bean farmer and during the season a catcher of turtles."

"And you told fortunes."

"I was famous for it. Those with the jack and a boat would come to ask their questions. It helped our ville's economy immensely, and it was a price I was willing to pay."

"And then the Sabbaths."

"Emmanuel Sabbath arrived on my island at the helm of the *War Pig*. We had never seen such a ship. Unlike you, Captain Sabbath is a superstitious man and always kept an astrologer aboard. The one before me had the barest bit of doomie in him, but what he had he channeled through a Tarot deck."

"Fortune cards. I've heard of them."

"When Sabbath learned of me, he came to the house of my father and paid an incredible sum in trade goods to him to put me to the test. He was extremely pleased with the results. So pleased he slaughtered my family, shoved a blaster in my face and told me either I came with him or he would raze the entire ville. I went, of course, but with all intent to give Sabbath false predictions and run him onto the rocks or escape as soon as possible. I found myself chained and swiftly broken, or reduced, as Doc would say. Unfortunately, suffering seems to have a way of focusing my abilities. Sabbath noticed that, and the suffering became continuous. My only reprieve was when I wasn't being forced to foresee Sabbath's victories in piracy or trade I was made to work the ship. Despite flinching like a dog at my own shadow or any raised hand, I rated able."

"And?" Ryan asked.

"One night after a successful raid, Sabbath was drunk. He asked me how he would die. I already knew, and I summoned the courage to tell him."

Ryan knew the answer. "You were going to kill him."

"I told him I had foreseen he would die by my hand."

Ryan stared at the huge mutie ape hand attached to Oracle's wrist.

"Sabbath tortured me in ways that would make even Manrape shudder. Then he cut off my hand so that it could never be raised against him, and he hung me from the yardarm at dawn. The same mutie vitality that allowed me to survive tortures that would destroy a norm allowed me to survive the hanging, or perhaps it was that I had not fulfilled my destiny yet. Regardless, and unknown to Sabbath, I was still alive when he cut the rope at sunset and dropped me into the sea."

"You washed ashore."

"On a barren spit of rock. There was no water, and almost no vegetation. I was racked with thirst and terribly injured and mutilated. I found a cave and within it a gleaming metal hatch. It was not locked. Stairs led down to a great vault with open, clamshell doors. I wandered through a series of predark corridors, but the complex was stripped bare. I finally came to a strange chamber of glass."

It took every ounce of Ryan's will to keep his poker face.

"I randomly worked a lever, and then an experience wilder than any of my most fevered dreams took place." The flat black eyes stared at Ryan intently. "I wandered out and found myself on a much larger island, lush and green. I was in the Cific. The island was inhabited, and, even missing my hand, as an able sailor I had useful skills. I regained my strength and a measure of my dignity. A sea-going junk arrived to take on water and supplies. It was no floating castle like Sabbath's *Ironman,* but it had a working pair of 20 mm autocannon and wasn't to be taken likely. They were short-handed, and able seamen are hard to come by, so despite being short-handed myself, they took me on. I swiftly became an officer as they continued to the western coast of South America. We sailed north up the coast, trading and transporting for the coastal villes."

"You left ship when you hit the Central."

"I did."

"You foresaw their doom."

"Yes, and my path still lies in the Caribbean. They liked me, and I was well supplied and armed. I survived the trek east."

"What about Sabbath?"

"He and his family were building their fleet. Since long before even Doc's time, the hand of a hanged man has been known as the Hand of Glory. He put my hand in his binnacle as a good luck charm."

"It started pointing."

"Yes."

"You control it."

"No."

Ryan frowned. "Then what moves it?"

"I don't know. Perhaps you should ask your woman."

Ryan's skin crawled.

"It led Sabbath to many victories, including taking the ship we sail upon. He named it the *Hand of Doom.* At that time, I had made it back to the Caribbean. Some of the islands have tried to maintain some sense of the old civilization. Others have sunk into utter barbarity. Most lie somewhere in between. A few pride themselves on being neutral ground where trade can be freely engaged in. Any breaking of the peace incurs the wrath of all others."

"Trading camps." Ryan nodded. "Barter villes. Seen a few of the like in the Deathlands.

"I set up shop telling fortunes and amassing jack and goods to buy myself a boat of some size and a crew."

"Sabbath found out."

"As a sign of his favor, Sabbath had given his first-born son, Osbourne, a year's tour on the *Hand of Doom* before it was to be made the flagship of the Sabbath fleet. Osbourne sailed into port." Sabbath raised his prosthesis. "He came into my fortune-teller's hut and gave me this as an insult. Some sailors believe a monkey's paw can grant three wishes. All sailors know a monkey's paw is cursed. I bolted it to my wrist and challenged him. We rowed out to spit of sand. I ripped his throat out."

"The *Glory* took you as captain?

"The crew of the *Hand of Doom* had suffered gravely under Osbourne, and I was their salvation. I was also a living hanged man with his own Hand of Glory in his binnacle. Not to mention wearing the monkey's paw that was crafted to curse him. That was more luck than most sailors knew what to do with. I killed my first two challengers, both of whom were Osbourne's enforcers, and proved myself an able captain. We became the *Hand of Glory*."

"You knew my friends and I would be on that island where you set your trap."

"I had a dream that could be interpreted that way."

"So why did you?"

"Why do you think?"

"You saw we would save the ship, or something that could be interpreted that way."

"I won't deny it."

"And now?"

Oracle stared at Ryan with a new and terrible intensity. "I see the threads of fate surrounding you like no other man."

Ryan did not believe anything was written, but neither could he deny Oracle's power. "So what do you see?"

"It isn't clear."

"It hardly ever is."

Oracle's voice dropped. His black eyes seemed to look through Ryan like he was a lens into another world. "I see a fate where you and your friends die unsung and unknown in a place far from home, which may be these distant seas. I see another fate, where your names are revered in the Deathlands and your actions reverberate through the centuries, and I see a fate where you and your friends' names are cursed and reviled and your actions bring untold death and destruction upon the Deathlands and the world around it that shall last for a thousand years."

Ryan met Oracle's prophetic gaze. "There are a million possibilities for any man."

Oracle suddenly smiled and relaxed. "I agree, except that the son of Baron Titus Cawdor is no ordinary man."

"You can see that?"

"Doc told me. Regardless, you have only three paths. I suggest you choose your actions wisely."

Ryan didn't care for this talk at all. "And what's your fate?"

Oracle let out a long sigh. "I will die, like all men, and when that happens, if you still live, you must take the ship." He took another sealed note out of his desk and pushed it across the table. "Open this when I am dead. If you open it before, you will die with me and the entire ship."

The captain suddenly raised his head. "Ah."

The roll of the ship ceased. The moaning in the riggings died off. The darkness outside the window turned to purple and then orange. Cheers sounded abovedeck.

Oracle watched as golden light began to spill in through the cabin's stern window gallery. "I knew the Horn would not kill us."

Ryan watched the miracle of dawn happen out the windows. "You saw that?"

"No." Oracle smiled disarmingly. "I just had faith in my crew."

Ryan found himself smiling. "So we made it."

Oracle contemplated the light as it played across the black skin of his remaining hand. "No, this will very likely kill us."

Ryan frowned.

Oracle lifted his chin. "What do you notice, Officer Ryan?"

Ryan lifted his chin. He felt a terrible sinking feeling in his guts. "The ship's still. There's no wind."

Doc spoke with grave worry. "These are the Doldrums?"

"What is that?"

"We are a sailing ship, and we are becalmed, Mr. Ryan, and shall be for some time, I fear."

"What do we do?"

Oracle watched sea and sky turn metallic. "We shall have to row.

Chapter Twenty-Six

Ryan rowed. The *Glory* was dying. Scurvy was chilling the crew. The *maté* leaves had turned to powder of little effect. For whatever reason, perhaps being born in the Deathlands, Ryan's people were holding up better than most, but the horror of the passage around Horn had been better than this. The air in this latitude was hazy, hot and humid and utterly still. It promised a storm whose winds never came. The ocean was a flat plane of copper glass beneath a greasy, shimmering brassy sun.

Ryan felt the ache and exhaustion of malnutrition in his bones. Four wooden boats rowed to try to pull a square-rigged ship to fair winds. Aboard ship the remaining Mapuche heaved against the sweeps. The med was full of crewmen who'd failed. They had ample food and water, and ship and crew had borne the passage around the Horn remarkably well. The horrible fact remained that the *Glory* was a sailing ship, and now there was no wind. Every nonessential item had been thrown overboard to lighten the ship, but there was very little fat to cut in the first place. There was talk of throwing the cannons and shot overboard. Disease swept the decks. The sense of doom was palpable.

"Aw Jee'th…" Onetongue dropped his oar and clutched his mouth. Everyone else groaned as the whaleboat lost momentum against the hideous weight of the ship behind them.

Ryan could feel his own teeth loosening in his head. "Tongue, it's all right. We'll—"

Onetongue gobbled forth about half a tot of blood. "I'm th'orry, Ryan! I'm th'o th'orry!" The mutant wept in agony. "But it hurt'th tho bad!"

The crews in the dinghies shouted as the whaleboat stopped.

Ryan fought his own pain and exhaustion. Onetongue was one of the strongest and least complaining crewmen the *Glory* could boast. This was bad. "Open your mouth."

"I'm th'orry, Ryan—"

"Open your mouth!" Ryan ordered.

Onetongue opened his mouth. Ryan flinched. Mildred had said that when the scurvy got bad old scars would break open. Onetongue's name had once been Twotongue. The last captain, who could not be mentioned, had cut one of them out. The left side of Onetongue's soft palate was an open wound where the scar tissue had broken open. "You need to get to the med now. Have Mildred disinfect that and stitch it."

Onetongue wept and shook his head at Ryan. "But you're bleeding too!"

Ryan ran a finger along the scar on his cheek. It came away bloody. "It's an old wound. It's nothing."

"No, Ryan!" Even now Onetongue was thinking about someone besides himself. "It'th coming out of your eye!"

Ryan started. He raised a hand to his eye patch and lifted it up a hair. A thin rivulet of blood and fluid trickled against his hand. Ryan stared at it. He'd felt the discomfort but had chalked it up to the sting of sweat, exhaustion and illness. The scars in his closed, empty eye were breaking open.

Manrape laid down his oar. His physique sagged like a suit of armor whose interior straps had all loosened.

"We're dying." The titan's chin fell to his chest and tears spilled out of his eyes.

Wipe sobbed like it was the end of the world.

Ryan knew it was. He could not begin to recall the odds he had fought and won in the Deathlands. But this was no baron and his army of sec men. This was no chem storm that could be sheltered from, no horde of muties that could be outfought. This was the open sea. Vast beyond imagining. Implacable. Without mercy. There was no recourse other than to hurl human flesh and will against it, and the flesh and will of the *Glory*'s crew failed before it.

Ryan felt the heat and itch of the preinfection in his empty eye socket that would lead to his brain, as well as the avalanching breakdown of every cell in his body from the scurvy. He gazed up at the horrible brass-colored sun and the endless, metallic sea on all horizons. He was done. He couldn't save the ship. He couldn't save his people.

He couldn't save Krysty.

It was not the first time Ryan had felt it, but it had been a very long time since despair had wrapped its terrible hands around his heart. Hardstone rocked and cradled his lame leg. It was swelling. Sweet Marie wept openly. Atlast held his head in his hands. Doc spoke with a strange calmness. "Dear Onetongue, exchange places with me."

Onetongue crawled to the tiller and moaned as Doc crawled over him to take his place at the bench. The crew stared at Doc as if he were insane. The old man cleared his throat. "Gentlemen, we are heroes. We are the first ship in living memory, since the breaking of the world, that has rounded the Horn in winter under sail. We are titans. Gods. Compared to us, Jason and his Argonauts punted upon the Thames on a summer idyll."

No one on the whaleboat knew what that meant. But

every man knew what Doc was saying and knew he was right.

Doc's voice rose. "If we die this day, I have no shame. Serving upon the good ship *Glory,* with this crew, has been my greatest pride! I tell you now I have penned the tale of our odyssey in the ship's log and sealed it. What we have done shall be known. The journey of the *Glory* shall be legend. We shall be legend! All good sailors shall speak of us—her crew—in awed whispers as immortals. This I swear!" Doc laid his torn hands to oar. "But in this time between, in this little time that remains to us with beating hearts and will, I pray, shipmates, row a little more."

Ryan took up the rum.

They had no remedy for the scurvy, and Oracle had ordered straight liquor issued as a last, desperate painkiller. Ryan pulled up his eye patch and tilted the jug over his empty eye. "Fire…" The word "blast" never left his mouth. Ryan bellowed like a gored ox as 150 proof cane liquor scalded his eye socket.

He shuddered, knowing it was a remedial solution at best. His hands shook as he put his eye patch down. His knuckles were white as he took a swig and grabbed his oar. "Row."

Onetongue took the jug and made one of the worst sounds Ryan had ever heard a grown man make as he swigged firewater into his wounded mouth, swirled it around and spit it out. The mutant took up his oar. The jug passed from hand to hand, and everyone took up their oars and rowed. They rowed with purpose with their eyes on the horizon. Doc had lit the fire. When they dropped it, would be because their bodies had broken, not their wills.

Koa suddenly shouted. "Ship oars!"

Ryan wondered where this authority was supposed to

have come from, but the tone of Koa's voice was clear that he was onto something. "Ship oars!"

Koa leaned out over the oarlock and reached into the water. "Present for you, brah."

Ryan stared at the coconut in Koa's hand. The three dimples stared back at him like a face. Koa smiled and found the soft one of the three with his thumb. He stabbed it with his marlinspike and shook it. "One sip."

Ryan took the coconut and sipped. It took every ounce of will not to drain it as every cell in his body cried out to drown the nutritional famine.

Wipe clapped his hands. "There's hundreds of them!"

Ryan handed the coconut to Onetongue. The mutant sagged as coconut juice and oil coated his mouth. Ryan looked out on the water and saw scores of small brown spheres floating in the water. Koa took a sip and held it out to Hardstone disdainfully. "Not from my islands."

"You can tell?" Ryan asked.

Koa looked at Ryan like he was stupe. "Maybe Tahitian. I've never been this far south or east on the Cific." The Hawaiian dipped his hand into the water and wiggled his fingers contemplatively. "But the current might be right, and the wind."

"There's no wind, Koa."

"You're wrong, brah."

Ryan lifted his chin. He felt the faintest of breezes evaporating the sweat and blood on his face. "You're way-finding."

"Yup."

"Doc," Ryan ordered, "slip the cable to the ship. We gather every coconut we can. Manrape, use the speaking horn and tell the dinghies to do the same. Koa, I am recommending you to Commander Miles as acting navigator until proved otherwise."

Koa nodded. "About time."

Tahiti

THE *GLORY* LIMPED into harbor. She'd arrived to find the predark capital of Papeete a half moon of obsidian blast crater falling into the ocean. What remained of her once-famous black sand beaches was fused black glass that gleamed and rippled in the sunlight as Ryan's rad counter crept upward. They sailed around the coast and found another bay. They'd been spotted from shore, and about half a hundred war canoes lay arrayed before them, blocking the entrance. Koa stood at the Jacob's ladder in his full Hawaiian regalia. Everyone aboard wore their cleaned, best clothing, and all the officers and specialists were in uniform.

The coconuts had been a temporary stay of execution, but the crew was still in bad shape. Ryan scanned the opposition with his longeyes. Most of the warriors were bare-chested, bore clubs and spears and were covered with tattoos. A few had single-shot blasters that looked homemade. Behind the canoe line a pair of working motor launches sat with machine blasters mounted. Like a queen surrounded by soldier ants, a massive double canoe bearing a platform formed the middle of the Tahitian line. About a dozen men in massive feathered headdresses stood in a semicircle bearing predark blasters. Standing in prominence was a regal and magnificently bare-breasted woman. She was scanning the *Glory*'s cannons through binoculars.

"The Tahitians of hundreds of years ago were known to have queens and female chieftains," Doc said.

Miss Loral nodded. Commander Miles bullet wounds had reopened, and he was in the med in nearly as bad a shape as the captain. "Thank you, Doc. Mr. Koa?"

Koa bellowed out across the water in Hawaiian. The Tahitians glared uncomprehendingly as a unit. One very large individual bellowed back something and pointed at Koa while pantomiming an unmistakable act of oral outrage with a war club. Laughter rippled across the canoes.

"I don't think they speak Hawaiian," Manrape concluded.

Koa folded his arms in disgust. "They don't speak any civilized language."

Miss Loral quirked an eyebrow. "Didn't Tahitians speak French before skydark?"

Atlast spit off the side. "Last French-talker we had was that Haitian cook, Marcel. Right, Skillet?"

The Jamaican grunted sadly. "Damn fine madeleines. Never could replicate them."

"Miss Loral," Ryan asked. "With permission?"

"Indeed, Mr. Ryan. Do something."

Ryan nodded at Doc.

Doc considered. "Something like, greetings and we come in peace?"

"That should do."

Doc drew his sword from his swordstick and strode to the Jacob's ladder. His blade gleamed like a sliver of quicksilver as he saluted the Tahitian horde. The bravado captured their attention. Doc called out in French, "Greetings, valiant warriors of Tahiti. We come in peace and friendship." The old man flourished his sword and his hat and gave a sweeping bow.

The effect on the Tahitians was immediate. They grinned and began to applaud. The woman on the platform seemed pleased. One of her warriors handed her a brass speaking trumpet. Her voice came back across the water in clear but accented English. "I fear you bring your war with the Sabbaths to my harbor!"

Ryan muttered low. "Keep going, Doc," Ryan muttered. "Be diplomatic."

"I fear we do, my queen! We ask not sanctuary or alliance. All we ask is fresh water to slake our thirst and fresh fruit and greenery to fight the scurvy that plagues us. We seek rope, cordage and timber for our poor, battered ship that so bravely rounded the Horn in the terrible face of the westerly winter. We ask not for charity. We have trade goods from the other side of the world and will barter fairly for all. Give us this sun above, the moon tonight and the sun tomorrow, and we shall take our battle with the Sabbath fleet out onto the high sea and away from your fair shores."

Miss Loral stared, then said, "You're good."

The smile of the woman on the royal barge lit up the bay. "I have never heard French spoken so beautifully except in old vids. Not to mention your English! Withstanding the laws of hospitality and the wrath of the Sabbaths, I would feast you in my hall just to listen to you speak in any language!"

Doc bowed low.

"Bring your ship into harbor and pick your shore party, Silver Tongue. You shall be feasted! Should we come to agreement, tomorrow we shall trade. My name is Queen Tahiata." The distance was long, but the woman clearly smirked. "And ask Prince Koa to forgive our insult! His name is known here, and while it was a generation ago and not the people of Molokai, the last time Tahitians and Hawaiians met it was not friendly."

Ryan turned to look at the Hawaiian. "So you really are the Prince of Molokai?"

Koa lifted his chin imperiously. "I never denied it."

RYAN GORGED ON fish and fruit. His body couldn't get enough of the sweet pineapples and watermelon. After spending weeks against the Westerlies on salted ox and guanaco, Ryan cleaned his trencher board of parrotfish, barracuda, sea urchin, river prawns and raw red tuna marinated in coconut and lime. Suckling pigs, lobsters and breadfruit roasted in an underground pit outside. Rumor was they were almost ready. The *Glory* crew held their own. Strawmaker played to standing ovations. Manrape outwrestled every Tahitian warrior sent before him to the cries of the crowd. Palm wine and manioc beer flowed.

Ryan had a better feeling about this feast than the last.

Male and female dancers swayed and turned to the sound of the log drums. Everyone, including Ryan, wore flowers in their hair and garlands of welcome around their necks. The ville perched on a hillside on top of what had once been a small Tahitian town. The location was strategic. Mountains and winds in the opposite direction shielded her people from Papeete and its radioactive horror. Rumor was that horrors occasionally crossed the mountains or swam down the coast, looking for prey. Every home was a miniature fortress of dressed volcanic rock built to withstand gale-force winds and attacks of the *déformé,* human or otherwise. Tahiata's hall had once been a church that might have been built in Doc's time. She sat with Ryan and Doc at her right and left hand, respectively. She was a beautiful, charming woman, and though she spoke French with Doc she kept flicking glances Ryan's way. He could have sworn her breasts pointed at him with an aggressive, bronze will of their own. He was glad Krysty was still on the ship while they brokered a deal with the Tahitians.

Mr. Squid was a huge hit. She'd spent nearly the entire journey around the horn in her barrel. Apparently octopods could get seasick. During that time, her arm had grown back. Once they'd reached The Doldrums she had emerged and began taking on more and more of the ship's labors as the crew had fallen ill. It turned out she spoke French. She sat in what suspiciously looked like a cauldron. Women, children and even veteran Tahitian warriors giggled, screamed and clapped their hands whenever the octopod spoke or moved or tucked a crustacean beneath her mantle and began crunching.

Tahiata watched the proceedings benevolently. "I have made a decision, Mr. Ryan."

"What's that, Great Tahiata?"

"I shall let you and your ship stay in harbor for as long as you wish. You and your crew shall be treated as guests. You shall be well feasted, and we will allow time for your sick to heal and to make repairs on your ship. For rope, timber and canvas we shall trade fair."

It was far more than Ryan had any right to ask or expect. He waited for the rub. "You're generous."

"You will be wanting to recruit warriors and sailors."

Ryan nodded. "We've got just once chance against Sabbath and his daughter. They want to take the *Glory*, not sink her. So we get to hammer away at them with our cannons, while they fire at our spars and masts to try and slow us. In the end, the battle will be decided by lead, steel and wood."

"You'll find no shortage of volunteers. Of the many diseases on these islands, one of the strongest is island fever. All volunteers shall have right of return if wished after, say, two years of service?"

"If we survive, the *Glory* will most likely head back to the Caribbean. But all volunteers signed to the book will have the right to take service with another ship after that time or take their leave whenever we are in your waters, even if that's sooner than two years. Standard shares of spoil and trade will be based on earned rank."

"Agreed."

"What else?"

"The moon is right. Tonight, Prince Koa will give me a son and his people shall acknowledge him a prince."

Koa strangled on his beer.

"Should he fail, his failure shall be known throughout the Cific."

Ryan nodded. "Agreed."

"Should you win, and the *Lady Evil* survives, you shall bring her back here, with her cannons and what stores you do not absolutely require. You will give me one of your officers and enough sailors to train a crew for me."

"Should we survive, agreed."

Tahiata lifted her chin. "But?"

"But if we're going to win, we're going to need blasters."

"We have a terrible shortage of those in our islands. I can give you none, other than what any volunteer brings with him, and those will be few."

J.B. stared at Tahiata shrewdly. "I see that you have a fair number of blacksmithed blasters." He lifted a chin at the royal guards. "How are you keeping your predark steel running?"

"We have the remnants of a machine shop."

"Mr. Ryan?" J.B. asked.

"Yes, Gunny?"

"Permission to bring Ricky and Techman Rood ashore."

IT WAS A SPACE dear to J.B.'s heart. It stank of oil, metal and sweat. Far too much of it was taken up by the ville blacksmith's forge, but they had a few working machines. J.B. grunted. Most had large, double, iron-mongered crank wheels that had to be turned by a pair of large and likely ville lads. They were far weaker than originally designed and could only be used to make small, light parts. Worse still, they were using coconut oil for lubrication and leather and fabric for their running belts. However, some of their basic functions were there. Ricky walked among the few machines. All had seen extensive jury-rigging. A few in the back were hulks that had been cannibalized.

Rood stared at them thoughtfully. This aspect of tech was slightly out of his purview, but he saw the problem and he saw his role in it. "I got a couple barrels of wiring and cables in decent condition in the orlop. I can rewire most of these. We'll bring in the generator Mr. Ryan found in South America. We're low on fuel, though. We're going to have to burn local alcohol. Probably ruin it."

J.B. nodded thoughtfully. "We run it till it blows."

Ricky ran his hands over the machines, admiring or scowling at the modifications, depending. "We can bring in the two bicycle generators to supplement the hand cranks for the light stuff. Save the jenny for the bolt assemblies. Those'll be the tricky part. If we get enough willing participants, a lot of it can be done by hand."

Rood glanced at the admirable pile of salvaged iron, steel, aluminum and other metal pieces of all descriptions filling most of the small warehouse section. "I don't see how a few dozen or even a few hundred crude single-shot muskets are going to turn the tide when we have ships boarding us port and starboard."

J.B. looked over at the ville's blacksmith, Manua, and his two hulking sons, Manuarii and Nohoarii. The trio stared back eagerly. They didn't speak English, but one look at J.B. told them they were going to be in for a profitable learning experience.

"We're not going to make single shooters."

Ricky and Rood both looked at him.

J.B. looked at the tools and materials he had to work with and imagined the battle they had to win. It all came together in his mind in glowing detail. "Gentlemen, we're going to manufacture the worst blasters ever made."

Chapter Twenty-Seven

Aboard the Glory

Ryan stared at the worst weapon he had ever seen in his life. He had spent the week eating, taking morning and afternoon saber fencing lessons from Doc and assisting with the refitting of the ship. J.B. and his machinist entourage had arrived, requesting a viewing on the quarterdeck.

J. B. Dix was a master armorer, possibly the best left on the broken planet. He handed Ryan a travesty of the armorer's art. The weapon seemed to mostly consist of a sheet metal tube with a stub of barrel sticking out of it. It had no stock. The pistol grip was a five-inch piece of pipe. The trigger had no guard. The weapon's sights consisted of a small blob of solder on the muzzle for indexing. The mag stuck out horizontally to the left and seemed to have been press fitted from old predark soup cans. It had spots of rust, and none of the weapon's parts had any finish. The few discernible moving parts were beaded with oil and grease. Nothing seemed to hold it together other than stamping and pins.

Ryan hefted the stubby, ugly, ungainly, unbalanced, rattletrap thing and shook his head at J.B. "Tell me it's better than it looks."

Ricky stopped short of puffing out his chest in pride. "It's worse than it looks!"

Rood mopped his grease-smeared brow and nodded. Manua and his sons grinned happily.

J.B. seemed strangely proud of his work as he rattled off its tidal wave of shortcomings. "That barrel's soft iron. It'll start tearing apart and disintegrating after a dozen or so rounds. Speaking of rounds, they're all black powder. On full-auto, and that's the only way it fires, fouling'll occur almost instantly. The only lubricant we have is coconut oil. It'll start burning right quick. Between the black powder fouling and the burning oil, you'll be lucky to fire off even one mag without a catastrophic jam."

"Anything else I should know?"

"Ricky and I agreed—no time to rifle the barrels. They're as smooth as a shotgun."

"So accuracy will be…?"

"Hitting a man-sized target beyond twenty-five meters will be genuinely problematic." The Armorer grinned. "We won't discuss the state of the springs."

Ryan saw a silver lining in J.B.'s, Ricky's and Rood's proud faces. "So why are you nuked assholes smiling?"

Ricky bounced up and down on his toes. "We have a hundred of them."

J.B. lifted his chin at the weapon in Ryan's hand. "When the ships clash, every man will get off at least one burst, from one to twenty rounds. Then every man uses his personal or issue blaster, then it goes hand to hand."

Ryan held out the weapon like an unwieldy pistol and sighted over the barrel. J.B. had delivered the goods. When the *Ironman* and the *Lady Evil* came alongside and boarded, J.B. will give the crew of the *Glory* one brutal, unreliable, spitting distance opportunity to try to even the odds before the battle went hand to hand.

Mr. Squid stood on the quarterdeck. Her golden eyes

examined the weapon. "Gunny, I would like to requisition four of them for the battle."

J.B. considered his table of organization and allocations. "You ever fired a blaster before?"

"No, but from what I understand of your submachine guns and the nature of the battle before us, I believe that will be of little consequence. All that will matter is concentrated fire."

"You can't just jerk a trigger, Squid."

"From what little I know of firearms, you squeeze the trigger rather than jerking or pulling it." Mr. Squid held up four arms and their tips all began sinuously making individual sailor's knots. "I have some understanding of controlled contractions."

Koa laughed. "This I want to see!"

As the commander on deck, Ryan had to keep the smile off his face. "Gunny, bring your weapons aboard and pick your fire teams. Subaqueous Specialist Squid to be issued four prebattle. Mr. Rood?"

"Aye, sir?"

"Send the signal."

RYAN STOOD NAKED except for his eye patch and the SIG in his hand beneath the Tahitian moon and watched the gentle, bioluminescent tide. Krysty lay on a blanket just inside the tree line. Ryan had learned that Tahitians made love by the beach all the time but always just out of sight of the surf and always with a blaster or spear near to hand. He felt the breeze play across his skin. It was a beautiful, tropical night.

In his gut, he felt as if he was standing on very thin ice. He'd done all he could do. They'd lost a great deal of rope and canvas rounding the horn, but they'd planned for that and had enough to fight the battle ahead and make it

to the next port. Tahitian hardwoods had provided all the
spars and timber they needed for repairs. The vessel was
shipshape. Ryan considered his crew. They were mostly
shipshape too, having regained their health and strength.

Balls's pregnant granddaughter had not only survived
the trek with a tenacity that had put the rest of the crew
to shame but had given birth to a slightly underweight
but healthy baby girl. To the delight of all she had named
her Gloriana-Tahiti. She, Balls and the surviving Mapuche and gauchos had asked to settle here. Queen Tahiata
welcomed the infusion of new bloodlines that had barely
been exposed to a single rad. Ryan had been proud when
all had volunteered to stay on for the fight against the Sabbaths first. On top of that they had thirty young Tahitian
warriors spoiling for the glory of battle on the high sea
for their queen.

Ryan had promoted Nubskull and Onetongue to bosun,
and Miss Loral had signed off on it. That left the officers.
The *Glory* had exactly three. Commander Miles was still
in med and in bad shape from his bullet wounds opening
from the scurvy. Captain Oracle's whip weals had barely
closed before the scurvy had hit him. Mildred couldn't
promise if he would live to see the battle. That left Ryan,
Miss Loral and Koa. Loral was a hell of sailor but she
hadn't been in many battles. Ryan had been in more battles than he'd had hot meals, some on ships, but he had
never captained a ship in battle until he'd taken the *War
Pig,* and that had been a turkey shoot, won by deception
before the first shot had been fired.

Ryan had promoted Koa to officer. The Hawaiian prince
was a veteran of many battles, but nearly all had been
fought on beaches or from war canoes. The battle ahead
would be against two ships, one larger than *Glory* and

both commanded by seasoned captains and dripping in fighting men.

Ryan didn't care to contemplate what Manrape had done to Dorian, but the youngest Sabbath had no more secrets. Ryan new the strengths and weaknesses of both the *Ironman* and the *Lady Evil*. The only good news was the state of their blasters. Nearly every fighting man aboard both ships had one, but nearly all were single shooters and many of them were muzzleloaders. Only the officers, the captains' picked sec men and a few of the crew who'd captured weapons as spoils had predark weapons, and most only had a handful of rounds to fill them.

J.B.'s mechanical monstrosities were the only advantage the *Glory* had. Ryan had test-fired two of them. The first had jammed up tight after one round. The other had buzz-sawed out all twenty-five rounds spitting smoke and sparks and fouling in all directions. Everyone watching had clapped their hands in delight. The applause fell dead when Ryan lowered the weapon and the smoke-oozing barrel had slid out and fallen to the sand. The bad news was the worst blasters ever made would decide the *Glory*'s fate.

The good news was they had a 150of them.

Techman Rood had sent the radio signal out to Prince Koa's people on Molokai in Morse code, knowing Sabbath would intercept it. Sabbath and his daughter were still trying to raise Dorian using the Caesar cipher. They'd broken off searching the west coast port villes and sailed under every inch of canvas to intercept the *Glory* before she could reach Hawaii and Koa's people. Ryan smiled into the night at the thought of his fellow officer. Koa had spent all night every night in Tahiata's big house doing his princely duty by the queen. The crew hadn't objected to the irregular promotions. They loved Onetongue, and Nubskull had proved his skills around the Cape. Koa was well respected, and the crew couldn't wait to see him wield his massive, shark-tooth club in battle. The fact that he actually was a prince didn't hurt either.

Ryan nodded to himself. He had done all he could do to prepare. All that was left was to sail into the Sabbaths' teeth and fight. Ryan smelled the unmistakable scent of jasmine, tamanu oil and Tahitian pulchritude that was Queen Tahiata. He knew she had come from the left of the cove out of the trees so that he would smell her and hear her feet in the sand. It was a little late to try to cover up. "Queen."

"Chieftainess, Baron Cawdor." Tahiata admired Ryan's naked form by moonlight. As usual she wore a sarong, flowers and not much else. "Doc calls me a queen, and I admit I enjoy the sound of it, but we have not had a queen since long before the fall, and other villes in these islands would dispute the claim violently."

"I'm the son of a baron," Ryan corrected.

"But you could have been baron. Should have been."

Ryan shrugged. Koa had been shooting his mouth off. Ryan couldn't blame him as he admired the Hawaiian's interrogator in kind.

"Where is your woman of flame?" Tahiata asked.

"Sleeping over there. Where's Prince Koa?"

"Snoring." Tahiata smiled at Ryan in open invitation.

Ryan smiled with genuine regret. "I'm taken."

"You are loyal, Ryan. To your woman, your friends, your ship, your captain and your crew."

"I try."

Tahiata sighed. "But, were a boulder to fall on your sleeping woman, would you?"

Ryan looked Tahiata up and down. "I might have to consider it."

Tahiata glanced at the cliffs above. "What if it were I who had pushed the boulder?"

Ryan laughed aloud. Tahiata joined in. They stared out at the lights of the *Glory*. Tahiata's voice lowered. "Oracle."

"What about him?"

"Is he a…" The Tahitian woman wrapped her lips around a distasteful word she had heard. "Doomie?"

Ryan considered doomies he'd met in the Deathlands. He compared them with everything he had seen aboard *Glory* and the sealed note in his coat "He doesn't rave, speak in tongues or tear his hair and flesh as he spews visions, but I think he's one of the most powerful I've ever met."

The Tahitian ruler made a face. "Our islands also give birth to such people."

"You cull them."

"No, we seal them in caves, so their terrible luck will not infect the villes."

"But you consult them." Ryan smiled bitterly out onto the sea. "Like oracles."

"In times of great moment, yes. We currently have three alive. Two in caves, the worst in a pit. All highly agitated. They rave about the *Glory*. They say Oracle haunts their dreams, and they go on about something aboard that rattles their minds."

Ryan knew the Tahitian doomies raved about the hand in the binnacle. "Did they say who's going to win the battle?"

"The one in the pit screams about an ocean red with blood."

"Sounds about right." Ryan thought he saw what was coming. "What do you want?"

"I want Dorian, or what is left of him."

"For bargaining." Ryan had a terrible feeling that things were slipping further out of his control. "When we lose."

"*If* you lose, great warrior of the Deathlands, yes." Tahiata looked back over her shoulder as she walked away. "May I give you a piece of advice on the eve of battle?"

"Sure."

The Tahitian gave Ryan a savage smile. "Win."

THE GLORY SAILED to battle. They'd sent out another distress call to Molokai to give the Sabbaths a good triangulation and then set a course straight for Koa's island. Despite having made all necessary repairs, they'd done no repainting or cleaning of the ship. The *Glory* carried her worst mended sails. Ryan wanted her looking like a beaten, desperate ship that had barely made it around the Horn without respite. He looked about and was satisfied. He kept a skeleton crew on deck and in the rigging, and they wore their worst rags. Belowdecks, blasters were polished, steel sharpened, and the cannons run out and run out again in dry fire practice. The Tahitians obsessively oiled their war clubs. There had been no time, much less ammo, to train the Mapuches. They'd been issued half pikes or boarding axes by preference. The previous night before Ryan had banished all nonessentials belowdecks, the Tahitians and the Mapuches had brandished their weapons, howled, stamped and chorused in competing war chants to the great amusement of the crew.

Techman Rood had been triangulating too. Ryan had asked the ship's techman when he expected the *Glory* to raise the Sabbath fleet. Rood had said within one to four hours. Ryan flicked a glance at the sun. That had been an hour ago.

Jak shouted from the tops. "Sail!"

"Two sails!" Ricky called. "Four points to starboard!"

Ryan and Loral snapped out their spyglasses. The Cific was a glassy, purplish blue with too much low-lying haze to the west. The Sabbaths came knifing out of it barely

two miles away. Ryan had wanted to spend at least a day
playing games with them and give them a long stern chase,
eating J.B. and his crews' nine-pound stern chasers. Ryan
took in the sleek white sails of the *Lady Evil* and the hideous, black sails with white spines of the *Ironman,* their
vector, and knew he couldn't evade them before nightfall.
He grimaced and snapped his longeyes shut.

"Miss Loral!"

Loral shouted, "Captain on deck!"

Ryan spun. Captain Oracle had appeared on the quarterdeck like a magic trick. He looked wasted and gaunt, but he
stood straight and wore his full uniform. He'd tucked his
single-shot blaster and a wallet of ammo in his gold sash.
A short, heavy, recurved kukri knife hung at his left hip.
"Miss Loral, all hands on deck, if you please."

"All hands on deck!"

The Indonesians pounded their hand drums and the
crew boiled up top like ants. They were something to see.
The crew bristled with extremely hostile implements of
iron, steel and wood of every description. Oracle walked
to the rail overlooking the main deck.

His broken-slate voice thundered. "Officers and crew
of the *Hand of Glory,* now is the time of battle! Now is the
Sabbaths' time of reckoning!"

The crew shouted and cheered.

"They have every advantage—ships, weight of shot,
weight of blasters and hordes of men! We are outnumbered.
Outgunned. Outmanned. And we must fight both sides of
our ship while they only have to fight one."

The crew was very well aware of that, but their captain
didn't seem to care, and they bellowed out in defiance of
the odds. Oracle's voice dropped. "I will tell you something
else you know." The captain held up his horrible prosthesis.
"All men of the sea know a monkey's paw will give a man

three wishes. And all men of the sea know those wishes come at a terrible price—wrack and ruin upon the wisher and upon all around him as the price!" The crew stared in superstitious awe. "This cursed paw, given onto me by my enemies! I call upon it now! I claim my three wishes. I wish the good ship *Glory* to win this battle. I wish she and her crew survive to sail the Seven Broken and Boiled Seas. And third…" Oracle lay his right wrist upon the binnacle. Crewmen shuddered and gasped as Oracle drew his kukri. Grown men screamed as the captain severed his mummified ape hand with a single blow. Oracle stabbed his knife into the rail and held up the orange-furred monstrosity as his stump bled. "If a price must be paid for it?"

The crew recoiled as Oracle tossed the simian horror to the deck below him. He suddenly took up his knife and smashed the glass dome of the binnacle. The embalming fluid cascaded to the quarterdeck. The captain held up the skeletal hand. "But all sailors know the power of the Hand of Glory! By the power of this hand, by my third wish, let that price be paid in full, by me!"

Oracle dropped the bones over his bleeding stump and the skeletal fingers clenched around it. Ryan's skin crawled. The captain leaped on top of the rail and grabbed a shroud with his good hand. "Glory be the name of this ship! Glory be her destiny!" Oracle pivoted on the rail and whipped his right arm astern. Blood flew, and the bone-thing clutching his wrist extended its forefinger at the sails chasing them. "I say glory lies that way!"

The crew erupted in an orgy of cheers, roars and war screams.

Oracle exploded like an angry god had put its fist through his chest. Blood, flesh and bone chips fountained over the first few rows of crew. The sonic boom cracked like a whip a second later as the projectile continued across the deck and back out to sea. The captain fell shredded to the deck below. The bony hand fell limp from his still bleeding wrist like a dead spider and curled. The crew's jaws dropped as a unit. Wipe's moan cut the silence and one by one more joined it.

For one second the *Glory* and her fate hung on a precipice.

Ryan stepped to the rail, usurped command and roared with a confidence he did not share. "You heard the captain! You want to live? You want to see the soft shores of Molokai? You ever want see the Carib again? By paw and hand the captain just paid your jack!" Ryan didn't wait for an answer. He turned to face the stern and the enemy sails in the distance. "Mr. Manrape!"

"Aye, Captain!"

"Turn this tub due east. Start the stern chase!"

"Aye!" Manrape spun the wheel.

"Miss Loral!"

Ryan was relieved she didn't challenge him. "Aye!"

"The bridge is yours." Ryan strode to the sodden, formaldehyde-smelling binnacle. He saw no cannon smoke on the horizon. At this range, the only explanation was the enemy had an antimaterial longblaster or a small-caliber auto-cannon with an optic sight. Ryan took out the Longbow blaster and the handful of remaining shells. He slung his Scout also.

"I'm going to take a shot or two from the stern."

"You heard the man!" Loral shouted. "Action stations!"

No cheers or shouts greeted the order, but the crew went obeyed. Ryan shouted down the main hatch. "Mr. J.B., bring up your spotting binoculars!"

Chapter Twenty-Eight

Aboard the Ironman, Emmanuel Sabbath leaned back in the yokes of the smoking 20 mm Oerlikon cannon. The automatic feed had failed long ago, and the weapon had to be loaded awkwardly by hand one round at a time. It had a crack in its hundred-year-old optical sight, but it was still hell for accurate. Pleasure was not a usual expression on Sabbath's face. Relief was even rarer. Only Kang and the ship's masterblaster, Narl, saw the captain's hand shake.

Sabbath wiped his brow and smiled. Oracle was dead and had lost both of his right hands in the bargain. The doom Oracle had pronounced was dead with him. Sabbath grinned savagely and savored his victory. "Let's see that doomie bastard come back from that."

Kang grunted and lowered his binoculars. The giant Korean had seen Oracle's torso burst like a balloon. For a split second Kang had seen daylight through Oracle's body before he fell. "No come back. He dead."

Narl nodded eagerly at the Oerlikon. Firing it was one of his favorite things. "Another?"

Sabbath considered his precious and dwindling supply of 20 mm shells shining in their crate. Oracle was dead. This was the day to make taking the *Glory* a certainty.

Sabbath stepped back to let his masterblaster enjoy the task. "Two shells, Narl. Make them count. Take out his stern chasers. Whoever is left in command, his only hope is to draw this out."

Narl happily loaded a round, closed the breach and leaned into the yokes. Narl suddenly flew backward in a slightly less violent but still spectacular imitation of Oracle's extinction. Blood sprayed like a fountain. Kang hugged the deck. The second shot sent sparks shrieking off the action of the Oerlikon and the cannon spun like a top on its pintle. A third heavy-caliber bullet smashed into the besieged cannon and sent it spinning in the opposite direction. Sabbath looked up to see his cannon's action torn open and, with Narl dead, far beyond repair.

Sabbath's eyes suddenly flared. "Ammo! The ammo!"

Kang lunged to shove the ammo crate off the keg it rested on. He got one hand on it before it exploded in his face. The heavy, antimaterial round shattered the crate like kindling and sent its contents flying. Kang got a face full of splinters and flying rounds. By a miracle nothing detonated. Loose and broken rounds rolled all over the deck. Kang spit and wiped propellant off his face. He looked at his captain guiltily. Sabbath was angry, but the sight of Oracle coming apart like a rag doll was something that would take a lot more than the loss of a half-functional 20 mm blaster to ruin.

"Mr. Kang?"

"Aye, Captain?"

"Radio my daughter to get ahead of the *Glory* and take the weather gauge. She will have to take some shots, but tell her to keep own fire high, masts, sails and rigging. Slow this Deathlander down. Tell her not to close until we catch up." Oracle grunted to himself. "We're just going to have to do this the hard way."

"Aye, Captain." Kang was pleased. Besides the act of rape, boarding actions were his favorite thing in life.

J.B. LOWERED HIS spotting binoculars. "Nice shooting."

Ryan set down his smoking, empty Longbow. With just a few boxes of ammo, he might well be able to drive the enemy off. That wasn't going to happen. They were just going to have to do this the hard way. He handed the weapon to J.B. "Thanks."

"Wish you'd taken that giant's head off while you were at it. I'm not looking forward to meeting him when this goes hand to hand."

"Me neither." Ryan took up his Scout. He'd had nearly full mags when they'd been shanghaied in the Carib. After a great deal of soul-searching he had donated much of his 7.62 mm ammo to string together a second belt for the ship's only machine gun, and he'd donated some more to the sharpshooters in the tops. He'd distributed a lot of his 9 mm ammo too. They were going to be fighting both sides of the ship, and they needed firepower from stem to stern. J.B. was right. It was going to go hand to hand.

Ryan had thought about that long and hard and had stayed with his new saber rather than his panga. The panga was a tool first and weapon second, and it would break or bend when it faced a flurry of pikes and boarding axes. He'd replaced his survival and slaughtering knives with a long, heavy dirk that was almost more spike than knife.

J.B. grunted again as he looked out to starboard. "She's moving fast."

Ryan watched the *Lady Evil* take a parallel course in the distance. He was a newly minted sailing man, but he marveled at her lines and the breathtaking amount of sail she'd raised into the winter winds of the south Cific. He didn't need to check his chron. "She'll pass us within the hour and get the gauge on us in the next." Ryan watched the vast, black *Ironman* lagging behind. "It'll take him three to catch up."

J.B. shot him a dry look. "Getting pretty good at this, are you, Captain?"

Ryan looked at his friend. Ryan was the leader of his group, but by unspoken agreement and as first among equals. He'd had unwavering support from Krysty and Doc, but he'd had precious little time to do anything but first survive and then bark orders at the rest of his friends as their ship-ranked superior. "I've got to get real good and real fast if we're ever going to see the Deathlands again."

At the sound of a sob, Ryan and J.B. looked across the ship. As the captain's hand servant, Doc had sewn Oracle into a bit of canvas. Doc's hands were still bloody. He sat on a crate next to Mr. Squid's barrel. Mr. Squid sat inside, conserving her hydration for the battle. She had one suckered arm across Doc's shoulders. Her arm contracted in slow, gentle contractions and the colors of the rainbow rippled across her flesh.

"Gunny, bring up your crews for the stern and bow chasers. Make everything ready. The *Lady Evil* is going to try and chip away at us, so make her pay for it. You're at liberty to fire at will."

J.B. grinned and put a knuckle to his fedora. "Mighty kind of you, Captain."

Ryan descended from the stern to the main deck. Koa squatted among the Tahitians, muttering quietly. Since he'd shacked up with Tahiata he'd gone from a figure of foreign islander abuse to the de facto Polynesian commander. Gypsyfair had had no time to tailor him an officer's jacket. The only one available had been too small, so he'd cut off the sleeves. Combined with his royal Hawaiian headdress and cape, his sartorial splendor was something to see.

Ryan crooked a finger. "Mr. Koa, if you please."

Koa rose. "Yah, boss!"

"How's the crew?"

"Freakin' out, brah. Oracle made a speech, and the powers that be listened. Captain called the thunder, and he got struck down. Question is, is the trade done, or did he doom us?"

Ryan looked to where Oracle had fallen. The deck had been scrubbed clean of blood and gore except for two circles of coagulated blood where Oracle's horrible ape paw and his genuinely scary skeletal hand lay on the wood. No crewman was willing to touch them, and neither Ryan nor Loral had seen fit to give the order. Ryan was just glad neither had started moving of their own accord. Oracle lay in state in his cabin.

"Do you know?" Koa asked.

Ryan considered everything Oracle had told him and Oracle's last, terrible, unopened envelope. "No."

"This crew's hanging by a thread. They'll fight, but that's because they have no choice. No one knows who's captain anymore. Morale is low. You got any ideas?"

"You're girlfriend told me my best option was to win."

"Tahiata's a good woman, and that's good advice."

"…right before she offered to sleep with me on the beach."

Koa's eyes flew wide. "You dick!"

Heads turned around the deck. Ryan nodded. "Bet your last jack on it, poi-boy."

Koa threw back his head and laughed. Given the ship's situation, the sound was almost alien. "I will kill you, brah!"

Ryan ignored the insubordination and possible mutiny and spoke loud enough for all to hear. "If we win, I give the *Ironman* to you and Molokai, Tahiata gets the *Lady Evil*, then you two can have yourself a real naval battle."

"Screw that. We learn those ships good, then maybe we sail around the horn and give those Falklanders a dose of

Polynesian pain. I remember a challenge in the gov'nor's hall!" Koa's voice rose to a roar. "Maybe *Glory* wants a piece of that!"

Crewmen of every stripe shouted, whistled and whooped in affirmation. Ryan shouted above it. "Skillet!"

The cook shouted up the gangway. "What?"

"A meal for the crew!"

"Tahiata sent us off with some pig."

"Cook it! Cook it all! Then douse all fires!"

"Aye!"

"Purser Forgiven!"

Forgiven squinted into the sunlight shining down the gangway. "Aye?"

"Tot of grog for every crewman who wants it after the meal, a stiff one!"

"Aye!"

The ragged cheers strengthened. Ryan strode to starboard and leaped onto the rail. He grabbed a shroud and looked at the *Ironman* behind and the *Lady Evil* pulling ahead. "We've run two continents, two oceans and sea. I'm tired of running." Ryan turned to look at the crew. "Who wants to fight?"

The crew roared.

"Mr. Manrape!"

Manrape called back from the con. "Aye!"

"After the crew is fed and grogged—" Ryan turned his gaze back toward the *Ironman* disappearing into the distance "—turn this tub around."

Chapter Twenty-Nine

The sound of cannon fire was continuous. Miss Loral was sailing rings around the *Ironman*. The *Lady Evil* had sprinted far ahead of the *Glory* to gain the weather gauge and hold her. The last thing either Sabbath had expected was for the *Glory* to turn about and attack the *Ironman*.

Ryan's bet had paid off. The *Ironman* was huge, even bigger than the *War Pig,* but she had been built after the fall. She was a far from perfect imitation of the oceangoing junks of old, and so were her cannons. *Ironman* had a lot of them, but they were crude, small and slow. The *Glory* was a museum piece, and her cannons had been forged in a long vanished, far better time of craftsmanship. *Glory*'s blaster crews had a century-old tradition of excellence, and they had J.B. Dix riding herd on them as gunny.

The *Glory* was pounding the *Ironman* to pieces.

Her cannons were larger, faster and better aimed, and she clung a hundred meters out to the *Ironman*'s starboard side and smashed out her blaster ports with terrible precision. The *Ironman* shot for sails and spars, and damage was being done. Ryan was inches from giving the order to lower *Glory*'s aim and shoot to smash *Ironman*'s hull at the water line.

Ryan and Koa stood at the prow and fired. The one-eyed man and his Scout longblaster were the only shooters in the battle with an optic, and he shot for officers and gunners. Koa had his beautiful, wood-furnitured AR and swept the *Ironman*'s tops. Ryan squeezed his trigger and killed the third man to take the *Ironman*'s wheel. Sabbath was not to be seen. Ryan shouted over the sound of cannon fire. "Koa, I told you the *Ironman* would be yours and Molokai's! But—"

"Sink the fucker!" Koa shouted. His AR pinged out a last spent shell. "Empty!"

"Take command of the Tahitians!" Ryan ordered. "Go!"

Koa scooped up his war club and ran down to join the *Glory*'s platoon of war-screaming Polynesians. The *Ironman* turned to bring her stern about. Like the *War Pig,* she had four stern chasers to the *Glory*'s two. With most of his starboard weapons silenced, Sabbath was taking a last desperate shot at cracking one of the *Glory*'s masts. Ryan saw his chance and shouted down the hatch. "Gunny, go for the *Ironman*'s rudder! Fire as she bears!"

J.B.'s voice was ragged from the powder smoke filling the lower deck. "Aye!"

The *Ironman* poured in fire, but it was slackening. Their predark blasters were few in number and running out of shells. The sharpshooters in the *Glory*'s tops were doing cold-hearted chilling work. The cannons below went silent. Ryan watched the *Ironman* desperately try to bring her four stern cannons to bear. The enemy ship gave J.B. a perfect line. He shouted the order. "Fire as they bear!"

The *Glory*'s port side cannons began going off with slow, terrible precision. Cannonballs smashed low into the rudder of the *Ironman*. Ryan watched black-painted wood shatter and throw white splinters with the blows. Cables broke, and the rudder suddenly sagged like a broken fan in its housing.

The *Ironman* was dead in the water.

Ryan felt a terrible surge of hope with the crippling of the *Ironman*. *Glory* could turn and take the *Lady Evil* in a stand-up duel of sailing and gunnery and then come back for the *Ironman* later. "Miss Loral!"

Loral had already seen it. "Mr. Manrape, hard to starboard! Bring us about on the *Lady!*"

Ricky broke ship's protocol as he shouted in desperate warning. "Ryan! Ryan! The *Ironman!*"

Ryan looked back at his stricken prey.

A cannon rumbled across the *Ironman*'s forward deck. The weapon's barrel was long and narrow and painted brown against rust. Ryan's lips skinned back from his teeth in a snarl as he saw the protruding projectile. The black iron spearhead had huge, sharpened tines pointing backward past the muzzle. Ryan would have given anything for another loaded mag for his Scout. He drew his SIG and began firing as fast as he could pull the trigger. One hundred meters on a pitching deck was long. The black and white face-painted crew rolled the weapon up to the rail. They slammed anchoring hooks into the scuppers and fired. The iron spear flew, twenty feet of chain rattled out from the shank and the rest of the line behind it was heavy rope.

The cannon was like Skillet's harpoon blaster, except this weapon was made for harpooning ships.

Ryan saw the trajectory and roared. "Atlast! Atlast!" The man looked up from desperately splicing cable at the bowsprit. The giant iron shank smashed through him. "Atlast!"

The massive harpoon head crunched into the deck. DontGo ran forward screaming. "Atlast!"

Ryan reloaded as men aboard the *Ironman* ran the harpoon cable to the capstan. Crewmen heaved themselves against the levers. The *Ironman* was drawing *Glory* into an embrace of death. The harpoon head ripped free of the deck and dragged Atlast screaming with it. Half a dozen

tines sank deep into the bowsprit with the combined weight
of two ships of war behind them. Atlast howled as his flesh
failed between both. DontGo hacked at the chains with his
boarding ax to no avail. Ryan shouted to the tops. "Jak,
machine blaster! Clear the *Man*'s capstan!"

Ryan and Loral had agreed to put the *Glory*'s one machine blaster up in the tops. Jak leaned into the stock of
the ancient M-60 general-purpose machine blaster and
rained lead on the *Ironman*'s capstan crew.

Loral's voice carried like the scream of a leopard over
the chaos. "Ryan!"

Ryan snapped his gaze across the ship just in time to
see a second harpoon blaster on the other end of the *Ironman* fire at *Glory*'s quarterdeck. The *Ironman* had two
capstans. The grapnel drew furrows in the deck and sank
into the rail.

The *Glory* was hooked. Men on the *Ironman* heaved
on the capstan spars and reeled her in like a fish. Ryan's
gut went cold as an army boiled up from the *Ironman*'s
hatches. He had been to Canada, and he recognized the
tuques, long shirts, leggings and war clubs. When Sabbath
had gone through the Northwest Passage, he had taken on
Canadian sec men as marines. Lots of them. J.B.'s cannons
were emptied and would not respond in time. Ryan was
still an amateur ship commander, and despite his surprise
turnabout, the Sabbaths had played him.

Ricky shouted from the tops. "*Lady Evil* is on us!"

Ryan looked back. The *Lady* was on a perfect oblique
course to avoid J.B.'s cannons, just like J.B. had taken on
the *Ironman*'s rudder. The *Lady*'s bow chasers fired. One
cannonball tore a chunk from the *Glory*'s mainmast. The
second blasted the Kelper Balls into bloody, exploding
strings. The *Glory* couldn't move. Ryan watched in horror

as the *Lady Evil* turned in slow pirouette to give the *Glory*
another oblique broadside that could not be answered.

Ryan roared, "Down! Down! Down!"

Every *Glory* crewman hugged the deck.

The *Lady Evil*'s cannons roared. Spars broke, rigging
snapped and fell, and splinters flew like flying knives.
Ryan jumped up to see the *Lady* turn again. She came in
prow first like she intended to ram. Ryan racked his slide
home on his last mag as the two brass harpoon blasters
on the *Lady Evil* fired and tore man and deck apart. Ryan
watched her forward capstan turn and her cannons give
the *Glory* another broadside. Rope, sail and wood fell and
a half-dozen Tahitians were decimated.

Doc appeared at Ryan's side. He had his sword in one
hand and his LeMat in the other. "My dear Ryan."

"No time, Doc!"

"You are captain now. I have been ordered to defend
you at all costs. Truth to tell, I would have done so anyway without an order."

Ryan's world closed in on him as he flung a glance
back at the quarterdeck. Miss Loral was down. Manrape
attended her. With the *Glory* harpooned from both sides,
there was no point in manning the con. The titan rose as
two Mapuche hustled Loral down the hatch to Mildred
in the med. Manrape took up his silvery scattergun and
snapped on the red-painted bayonet.

Doc held out a J.B. Special. "It was always going to
come to this. Your plan is sound. We can win."

Ryan felt Oracle's last envelope of doom burning in his
pocket as he took the blaster and slung it. Ryan barked orders. "Onetongue, form the Phalanx! Yerbua and Nirutam,
sound all hands on deck except cannon crews! Everyone
abovedeck, fire your personal blasters dry! Ready your
J.B. Specials and wait for the order!"

The drums pounded. Cannons fired as J.B. continued to rip out the *Ironman*'s guts. Ryan strode across the ship with Doc as his shadow. Techman Rood fell into step with a carved, ivory, dragon-hilted samurai sword. Strawmaker draped his cape over his arm and fell into formation. Gallondrunk ran to join them with his terrible walrus iron. Skillet stood waiting by the gangway with his double harpoon longblaster and assortment of cleavers of all sizes. Nubskull and Smyke were already by the con.

Ryan kept a wry smile off his face. Someone had ordered him a Praetorian guard. Almost all crewmen had a J.B. Special slung by a cord either under a coat or behind his back. Ryan passed Oracle's two bloody right hands and took command on the quarterdeck.

Manrape grinned like the ship's sails had caught a pleasing breeze. "Your orders, Captain?"

"We take them, bos'n."

"Aye?"

"We took the *War Pig*, and now I want the rest of the Sabbath fleet. All of it."

Manrape nodded. "Aye, Captain."

Ryan drew his SIG and emptied it into the *Ironman*'s quarterdeck. Sailors fell. Manrape's scattergun blasted and blasted. Ryan heard the old, sweet, methodical aimed fire of Doc's LeMat and then the thud of the revolver's shotgun barrel. Strawmaker, Rood and the rest of Ryan's personal sec team began unloading. Bullets whizzed in all directions. Crew on all three ships fell everywhere. Ryan lowered his smoking, empty SIG. The blasterfire tapered off again. The sudden, terrible calm was broken only by the ratchet and pall clanks of the Sabbaths' capstans. Except for hoarding a round or two for the final fight, both ships' crew were out of ammo.

The bulked-up crew of the *Ironman* screamed in bloodlust and shook man-butchering and breaking implements of every description as the ships pulled together. The *Lady Evil*'s crew did the same. The *Lady* sailed straight in to ram her bowsprit against the *Glory*'s quarterdeck. Ryan knew that would be their boarding ramp. "Wait for it!" Ryan roared.

The *Ironman* pulled the *Glory* in like a lover. The smaller, *Lady Evil* came in like the knife in the back. Ryan smiled. The die was cast. Doc was right. This was always going to come down to a brawl. He looked at Doc. The old man looked good in his uniform and as salty as hell. Ryan grinned. Doc grinned back. Ryan laughed. Doc laughed back, and Manrape and the rest of the quarterdeck burst out in hilarity. Koa threw back his head, and he and the Tahitians hurled their laughter to the sky.

The laughter ran across the ship from stem to stern. The Sabbath ships howled in response but bloodlust took a strange, pale second place to suicidal mirth. The side of the *Ironman* scraped the *Glory*. The *Lady Evil*'s bowsprit violated the *Glory*'s prow. Boarding ramps fell across Ryan's decks. The Sabbath crews surged. Ryan had learned long ago that most plans tucked tail and ran at first contact with the enemy.

He gave what might be his last command. "Give it to them! Give them all of it!"

Every *Glory* crewmember raised his or her J.B. Special, pointed and squeezed. Some fired one shot. Some fired two or three or half a dozen. J.B.'s weapons scythed in one, mass salvo. Jak, Ricky and the rest of the topsmen expended their weapons and shot down the rat lines to join the melee. Ryan grinned savagely as his own weapon unloaded all twenty-five rounds and withered an entire boarding ladder.

He dropped the empty subgun and drew his saber.

"Repel all boarders!" He gave the *Lady Evil* a last glance. They had avoided the *Glory*'s cannons, but that had forced them to send their borders across the bowsprit. It was a fatal funnel.

"Phalanx, defend the prow!" Onetongue and the Phalanx charged across the deck in a wedge of sharpened iron.

The battle royale was on.

Manrape boomed at the men around him. "Defend the captain! Defend the quarterdeck!"

Gallondrunk charged the boarding ladder screaming and spewing spit. "Fuckers! Fuckers! Fuckers!" His every f-bomb was punctuated by his awful walrus iron spearing an *Ironman* sailor. Skillet fired one barrel and then the other, and his harpoons reduced men to ruin. He started drawing cleavers and throwing them. "For you! For you! For you!"

A huge toothless Canadian leaped to the deck and swung his war club so hard at Ryan it almost whistled. "Fuck you, eh!"

Ryan leaned back from the blow as it smashed into the remains of the broken binnacle. He leaned in and ran the man through. Ryan ripped his blade free. It was a free-for-all across all decks. His personal guard stoppered the attack on the quarterdeck in red-handed fashion. Doc and Rood stood back and flanked Ryan in bodyguard positions with bloodied swords drawn. Doc looked up at the quarterdeck of the *Ironman*. A seven-foot-tall Asian man with a giant cat-o-nine tails glared down at them. From Dorian's interrogation, Ryan knew this was Kang, and Kang was just about the most feared fighter sailing the seas. He looked down and grinned at what he saw.

Manrape stepped back from the boarding ramp and perfectly pantomimed reaching up, grabbing Kang by his hair, yanking the Korean to his knees and forcing an act of oral copulation with one hand. Kang's eyes flared. Man-rape made a kissy face. Kang jerked his head and shouted. Behind him eight more Koreans face-painted in *Ironman* white and black came forward bearing short, wide and curved-bladed swords in both hands.

Ryan was fairly sure he was about to get chilled. "Fire-blast…"

Doc shifted his sword from a low guard to high as he observed the enemy swordsmen. "Oh dear."

Manrape sighed. "This should be interesting."

Kang pointed his whip at Ryan and snarled in terrible English. "Kill One-Eye!"

The swordsmen boiled onto the boarding ramp, whirl-ing their blades like human food processors. *"IRON-MANNNNN!"*

Ryan and his crew strode forward to meet them

A water barrel on the quarterdeck suddenly turned a slick, wet gray color and uncoiled. Mr. Squid rose to her full height on four arms while her other four extended J.B. Specials. Squid squeezed all four triggers and turned the boarding ramp into a slaughter chute. Seven of the eight Koreans fell. The eighth screamed and turned to run. Mr. Squid launched herself through the air. Her mantle fell across the Korean's head and shoulders, and she pulled him over the ramp to the sea below, accompanied by skull-crunching sounds.

For one second Kang appeared genuinely appalled.

Ryan shook his bloody saber skyward and charged the ramp. *"Glory!"*

Kang turned away as Ryan and his guards ran up the ramp for the *Ironman*'s quarterdeck. The junk's rail was so high and curved it was impossible to see what was happening on their decks. What was happening was that Emmanuel Sabbath was waiting. His own twelve-man, ax-bearing guard surrounded him. Some had one ax, some carried two.

Sabbath's voice was quiet, but it carried over the sound of battle. "Mr. Kang, take the rest of the Canadians. Hit *Glory* amidships."

Kang nodded. "Aye." He took three giant strides and leaped from the quarter to the main deck. It was loaded with Canadians brandishing war clubs, tomahawks and knives.

Sabbath drew a sword with a very nasty-looking hook on the back of the blade. He pointed it at Ryan. "Now, as for you, Deathlander…"

Chapter Thirty

Krysty dropped her J.B Special. She had saved her Smith & Wesson for the brawl. Sweet Marie appeared by Krysty's side and admired the revolver. Sweet Marie held up a nickel-plated derringer missing most of its finish. "Good girl. A woman should always save herself a few rounds for the boarding action."

Krysty hurled a look to the prow. "The Phalanx!"

"My pike broke. That slobbering idiot Onetongue said 'Th'tay by Kryth'ty!' so here I am. And here they come!"

Howling, screaming face-painted men hit the *Glory*'s main deck in a wave. Krysty took her time and put a bullet each into five men. Sweet Marie gave a man both barrels and hefted a freshly sharpened machete. "Stay by me, girlie!"

Krysty reloaded and moved forward on Sweet Marie's six. The deck was a whirling mass of fights. Krysty put a bullet into any man that charged Sweet Marie, and the big girl cut the man down.

"Empty!" Krysty dropped to one knee and ejected the spent shells. She dug into her pocket for her last reloads.

An inhumanly deep voice roared in happy, horribly accented English. "Flame pussy for Kang!"

Krysty snapped around as a shadow eclipsed her. An enormous Asian man, with what appeared to be a fistful of knotted hawsers, grinned as he swung. The nine ropes spread as they whirled. Krysty snapped her revolver shut and brought it to bear. Her vision went white as the ropes hit her from neck to hip and sent her flying. She bounced on the deck and her revolver left her hand. Instinct made Krysty crane her head and claw for the weapon. The Smith & Wesson clattered away from her fingertips and slid in terrible slow motion across the bloody, pitching deck. The blaster spun and pointed at her as if in one plaintive, last look. Krysty felt the gut punch of irreversible fate as her weapon hit a starboard scupper like a perfect billiards shot and fell away to the great water below.

Sweet Marie snarled and charged. "Not today, High Pockets!"

Krysty drew her issued dirk and rose brokenly.

Sweet Marie fell at her feet, clutching a face the ropes had torn into ruins.

The giant Kang stepped forward and swung. "You Kang's bitch now!" The knotted ropes hit Kristy, but the shortened blow made the coils slam and wrap around her in a terrible contusing embrace. With practiced ease the giant suddenly leaned back, twisted and yanked. Kang's game of crack the whip centrifuged Krysty into the mainmast. She fell against the great wooden pillar and toppled down the main hatch. Krysty could have sworn she hit every step on the way down. She lay there gasping and knew she had to get up, but her limbs would not obey her. Her dirk was gone. Two cannons went off and half a dozen weapons were blasting.

Krysty dimly heard the ring of steel and the screams of the fighting and dying around her. She knew the enemy had managed to get men belowdecks through the blaster ports. Krysty stared up the main hatch. Down below she was out of the wind, and the sun bathed and limned her in a rectangle of warm light. In her own way, like Ryan, she had known it would always come down to this.

"Gaia, Earth Mother, hear my prayer, aid me in my time of need..."

RYAN FELT THE BURN of cold steel across his forearm. He was losing and badly. None of his wounds were fatal, but they were bad enough. Sabbath was picking him apart. It was as if Sabbath had no bones in his right wrist. His short-sword pinwheeled around his hand and the wicked hook on the back kept catching Ryan's blade for just an eye blink, just enough to pull it out of line while Sabbath threw a short cut or slice. None was deep, none was vital, but Ryan had seven of them and three were on his sword arm. He was bleeding all over the deck and slowing. One cut was over his good eye, and blood poured into it. The rest of the battle raged across the Ironman's quarterdeck. Doc shouted Ryan's name, but he'd been cut off and three ax men forced him down the gangway toward the main deck.

Ryan became very aware that everyone else was letting the two captains duel.

It was a battle he was pretty much doomed to lose. Sabbath drove him back. The rails of the *Ironman*'s quarterdeck opened like gates for boarding. Ryan suddenly realized what was about to happen. He'd been maneuvered into position, and he had no power to stop what happened next. Sabbath took a high cut at Ryan's head, and the one-eyed warrior barely brought up his sword in time. Sabbath stepped in and put his shoe into Ryan's stomach. The one-eyed man tumbled down the boarding ramp to the quarterdeck of the *Glory*. He just barely kept hold of his sword. Ryan managed to roll up and steady himself against the remains of the binnacle.

Emmanuel Sabbath stepped onto the quarterdeck of

the *Glory*, lifted his chin into the wind and sighed. "It has been too long. Thank you, you Deathlands cyclops, for bringing me back my ship."

Ryan sagged against the binnacle. He couldn't get enough air in his lungs. Neither did he seem to have enough blood left in his body, much less his arm, to raise his Falklands saber.

"Did you like how I kicked you down the deck? I'm going to do it again, and there is nothing you can do to stop me." Sabbath marched across the deck with evil purpose. Ryan thought of Krysty and managed to raise his saber and swing it like a drunk. Sabbath hooked it and cut Ryan's sword arm again. Ryan felt his grip loosen against his will and watched his saber clatter to the deck. Sabbath smiled, flicked up his right foot and kicked Ryan in the face.

Ryan fell over the quarterdeck rail and dropped the seven feet to the main deck. Throughout the shrieks and screams and shouts of battle an undercurrent of moans went up as the *Glory* crew saw Ryan's fall. He distantly knew that once he was dead it was very likely the crew would surrender the ship. Commander Miles and Manrape would be executed as too dangerous to live. *Glory*'s female crew would be reduced to rape slaves. The able seamen slaughtered. The remaining crew would submit and go back to the bad old days of being a Sabbath crew.

Ryan pushed himself to hands and knees. The battle on the deck boiled, but none came to save him. It seemed battles between captains were sacred. Ryan wished someone had told him. His saber clanged contemptuously to the deck beside him. Sabbath wanted an example made.

"Pick it up." Ryan looked at his right arm. It was soaked in his blood from shoulder to fingertips. He glared back at Sabbath and filled his left hand with his dirk. Sabbath spoke quietly for just the two of them. "I will give you one thing—or rad-blasted scum, I have always heard you Deathlanders were tough. They say you have to be, given the pesthole you live in. But you? You are also brave, and no man since the breaking has ever risen to captain so fast. I salute your seamanship and your courage. But now I must humiliate you for the benefit of all crews concerned. You will be marked in no books. You and your friends shall die and be forgotten, and now I must humiliate you. Rise."

Ryan's limbs betrayed him and fell back to hands and knees.

Ironman sailors roared. Sabbath's voice rose. He was used to shouting orders in a gale. "Oracle! The doomie! He swore I would die the day I took back the *Glory*!" The battle slackened. The numbers were almost even now, but the *Glory* crew backed off to watch Ryan's demise. "He foretold I would die by his right hand!"

Four *Ironman* sailors came up the hatch and hurled Oracle's body to the deck. They had stripped and mutilated him. The *Ironman* and *Lady Evil* crews cheered. The *Glory* crew stared in stunned horror. Sweet Marie let go of her ruined face and let out a terrible cry. Many fell to their knees. Sabbath looked up. His daughter, Blue, held the prow. He looked to Kang and tilted his head at Ryan. "Let him be beaten."

Kang laid into Ryan. The knotted ropes slammed into him. All fighting had ceased. Sailors were rare things in the world, and Sabbath wanted most of them. The *Glory* crew flinched and cried out with each blow. Ryan could do nothing to save himself. His one solace was that he wasn't screaming.

After a dozen blows, Sabbath held up a hand. Kang ceased and wiped his whip so it would bite better. Sabbath held out his hand. "Now, rise, One-Eye." Ryan tried to push himself up. He got two crawling steps forward and fell. "Rise now and know the mercy of my blade, or lie to be beaten to death like a dog on the deck."

Ryan's left hand found his dirk. He could hear his crew weeping at the sight of him. Ryan felt an uncomfortable jab in his chest. He put his right hand beneath him. His palm sank into the stiff orange fur of a mutated ape's mummified backhand. Ryan's fingers laced between the horrible digits like it was a five-bladed push-dagger. He pushed himself to his hands and knees and saw Sabbath's shadow cast onto the deck before him. Once more he felt Oracle's last letter burning against his breast. He heard Oracle's words of hope and doom in his head. Sabbath raised his short sword for the decapitation. Ryan saw Jak down, with his white hair clotted with blood. Ricky lay on the deck clutching his right hand with a pair of cutlasses pointed at him. J.B. and Mildred were nowhere to be seen.

Doc shouted from somewhere on the other ship. The ring of his steel told he was the last *Glory* man fighting. "Ryan!"

Ryan saw the shadow of the blade behind him swing.

He thought of Krysty and decided on his last act on Earth.

Ryan lurched up and shoved out his dirk. Sabbath's blow deflected and shaved flesh off his shoulder. Ryan got one foot beneath him and stabbed the mutant paw up. Three of the outsized, silver-clawed digits punched into Emmanuel Sabbath's throat. Sabbath's jaw dropped open in shock as he gagged on the mutant phalanges stopping his glottis. Ryan ripped the paw free. Sabbath fell blinking, gaping and drowning in his own blood. Ryan reeled. Blue screamed for her father from the prow.

Ironman sailors screamed in terror as Mr. Squid came arm-scuttling at full height down the gangway from the quarterdeck on four arms with a boarding ax, a Korean

sword and two pikes in the rest. Manrape, covered with
blood, came down the other gangway followed by Rood
and Strawmaker. His held his scattergun reversed. The
bayonet was gone and he tapped the buttstock into his
palm. "I'll kill anything that moves!"

Doc's head appeared over the rail. Like Ryan his right
arm was covered with gore from shoulder to sword point.
Unlike Ryan it all appeared to belong to others. He peered
quizzically at the tableau before him. "Did we win?"

"Kill them all!" Kang bellowed.

A thudding sound erupted, as if a giant was running
up the main hatch. Krysty erupted onto the main deck
as if on invisible wings. She was covered in blood from
Kang's beating. Her titian tresses snaked around her head.
It could have been a trick of the light, but she seemed to
glow from within. She held a pair of spare capstan bars
in each hand. She hit a cluster of Canadians like a berserk
windmill reaping limbs and bodies like wheat. Sabbath's
crew screamed, and Krysty suddenly whirled on Kang.

Ryan shoved the monkey paw skyward and managed
one last ragged shout. "Oracle!"

The crew of the *Hand of Glory* fell on their attackers
screaming like banshees. "ORACLLLLLLLLLLE!"

Ryan fell on his face.

"COME ON, CAPTAIN." Mildred's voice came through a dense
dark fog. "Ryan? Ryan? Come on, I know you're in there.
You were here this morning." Ryan opened his eye. He
was lying on his stomach. Mildred was trying to put some
soup in his mouth with a spoon.

"Krysty," Ryan croaked.

"Right here."

Ryan turned his head. "Hey."

"Hey."

Krysty looked drawn and disheveled but not injured. "How are you doing?"

"I lost my boots, I lost my blaster, nearly lost you."

Ryan looked to Mildred. "How long?"

"You've been in and out for the past forty-eight hours." Her eyes were grave with concern. "I've seen you take some damage. This was bad."

Ryan's body was a pulsing mass of pain. "How bad?"

"I've never seen you take a beating like that. We won't talk about the duel beforehand or the scurvy you haven't quite recovered from yet."

"And?"

"To stop Ryan Cawdor, you've got put a stake through his heart and bury him six feet down. Then, you still better run like hell. I was on deck when you stood up. It was biblical."

Ryan suspected he would live. "Who's in command?"

"Commander Miles and Miss Loral are taking turns, though Manrape is doing most of the heavy lifting."

"What happened below?"

"Well, they loved our cannon work and wanted J.B. bad. They swarmed him when he was out of ammo and beat him down, oh, and speak of the devil…"

J.B. walked in with a limp and a lumped face. "You look like shit."

"Feel like it," Ryan acknowledged.

J.B. stared at Krysty intently. She blinked. "What?"

"I heard your blaster went overboard."

Krysty sighed. She couldn't begin to count the things she and her revolver had been through together. "Yeah."

J.B. squared his shoulders and reached under his ship's jersey. "Here, take mine."

The med went silent as J.B. held out his new Glock.

"Oh, my God." Mildred's jaw dropped. "J.B. Dix, sharing his toys!"

Even Ryan was surprised. He shook his head and quoted Doc. "We live in an age of wonders."

"Always figured you needed something bigger anyway."

Krysty cradled the blaster. "Never used semiautos much."

"Yeah, well, when you get tired of semiauto, you can flip the lever on the side and go full."

"Thank you, J.B. You'll have to teach me how to shoot it."

J.B sighed and let go of his regret of giving up the blaster. "Course I will."

Ryan changed the subject for J.B.'s benefit. "Everyone else?"

Mildred nodded. "We're okay. I released Ricky and Jak. They're resting in their hammocks."

"Doc?"

"I swear to God he becomes a murder machine when you take him aboard a boat. The water agrees with him."

Ryan smiled.

"He wrote the tale of the battle in Mr. Forgiven's book. Last night he read it to the crew. There wasn't a dry eye in the house. He's a hero. You?" Mildred made a noise. "They worship you like a god."

Ryan looked at J.B. "What happened to Blue?"

"Captured alive. Koa told her if she agrees to train Polynesian crews, there will be no repercussions. He said if she agrees to give him a child, he'll give her the first sailing ship they capture or build to her specifications."

"And?"

"She agreed to all of it. Koa is turning into an ocean of fertility."

Ryan laughed and it hurt. "What are the dispositions of the ships?"

"Salvageable according to Manrape. There's been a lot of comingling of crews in the last few days. We have to, to keep all the ships afloat and seaworthy. Most of the surviving Sabbath crew seems to like the *Glory* model of sailing."

Ryan nodded. "My coat."

Mildred snorted. "Gypsyfair declared it unsalvageable."

"There was a note in it."

Mildred pulled it out of her pocket. The note was crusted with Ryan's blood. "How about I throw it over the side."

"Where's Oracle?"

"We buried him at sea. You were asleep. Doc said words. There was a lot of weeping."

"Where're Oracle's hands?"

The cabin med spoke quietly. "We sewed the monkey's paw into his shroud along with a cannonball and sent it down with him. Everyone agreed it had done its job, and no one wanted its curse aboard."

"What about the other one?"

Mildred shuddered. "No one wanted to touch it, and when we slid Oracle off the board, it rose up from the deck on its fingertips, walked to a scupper like a spider and, to quote the crew, it followed the captain down to the Old Place. I say good riddance. That shit is still freaking me out."

Ryan obeyed his captain's last command. "Open the note."

"No, oh hell, no. I don't want any of this Oracle doomie-shit coming down on me."

"Oracle said open it only if we won."

J.B. took the note and unsealed it. He cracked a smile.

Mildred, against her will, leaned in to look. "What is it?"

J.B. handed Ryan the note. "Latitude and longitude." Ryan looked at the bloodstained coordinates. They were South Cific. Krysty made a shrewd guess. "It's a redoubt."

Ryan thought of his conversation with Oracle. "Every reason to believe so."

"And?"

"Tell Commander Miles I suggest he take command of the *Glory*. Tell him he should give command of the *Ironman* to Koa and give him all the Tahitians. Some of the *Ironman* crew may still be salty. I suggest he give the *Lady Evil* to Miss Loral. Have them sail to Molokai and Tahiti, respectively."

"And us?"

Ryan considered Oracle's prophecy and the three choices of dying unknown in an unknown sea, being cursed for breaking the world anew or possibly saving it. He considered every doomie thing that had happened since the journey began.

He held out the note to J.B. "Take this to Commander Miles and tell him to set a course." Ryan took a good long look at Krysty and smiled. "Let's go home."

* * * * *

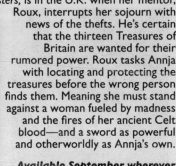

AleX Archer
CELTIC FIRE

The theft of a whetstone and the murder of a curate seem like random crimes, but the troubling deeds are linked by a precarious thread...

Annja Creed, archaeologist and host of television's *Chasing History's Monsters,* is in the U.K. when her mentor, Roux, interrupts her sojourn with news of the thefts. He's certain that the thirteen Treasures of Britain are wanted for their rumored power. Roux tasks Annja with locating and protecting the treasures before the wrong person finds them. Meaning she must stand against a woman fueled by madness and the fires of her ancient Celt blood—and a sword as powerful and otherworldly as Annja's own.

Available September wherever books and ebooks are sold.

GOLD EAGLE ®

The
Don Pendleton's
Executioner®
MAXIMUM CHAOS

The mob will stop at nothing to free a ruthless killer

Desperate to escape conviction, the head of a powerful mob orders the kidnapping of a federal prosecutor's daughter. If the mobster isn't freed, if anyone contacts the authorities, the girl will be killed. Backed into a corner, her father must rely on the one man who can help: Mack Bolan.

Finding the girl won't be easy. Plus, with an innocent life at stake, going in guns blazing is a risk Bolan can't take. His only choice is to pit the crime syndicate against their rivals. The mob is about to get a visit from the Executioner. And this time he's handing out death penalties.

Available October wherever books and ebooks are sold.

GOLD EAGLE®

GEX43i